A USER'S GUIDE TO
MAKE-BELIEVE

By Jane Alexander

A User's Guide to Make-Believe

a&b

A USER'S GUIDE TO
MAKE-BELIEVE

JANE ALEXANDER

Allison & Busby Limited
11 Wardour Mews
London W1F 8AN
allisonandbusby.com

First published in Great Britain by Allison & Busby in 2020.
This paperback edition published by Allison & Busby in 2020.

Permission to reproduce extract from 'A Note to the Difficult One'
granted by the estate of W. S. Graham

A CIP catalogue record for this book is available from
the British Library.

10 9 8 7 6 5 4 3 2 1

ISBN 978-0-7490-2434-5

Typeset in 11/16 pt Sabon LT Pro by
Allison & Busby Ltd

The paper used for this Allison & Busby publication
has been produced from trees that have been legally sourced
from well-managed and credibly certified forests.

Printed and bound by
CPI Group (UK) Ltd, Croydon, CR0 4YY

To my family

This morning I am ready if you are,
To hear you speaking in your new language.

– from 'A Note to the Difficult One'
W. S. Graham

CHAPTER ONE

Outside the Georgian townhouse where the meetings were held, Cassie hesitated. Scraped her thumbnail against a fleck of rust that had stuck to the sweat on her palm when she'd chained her bike to the railings, and tried to count the weeks since she'd been here last: ten, or twelve, or even more.

She had known it was here if she needed it.

The steps up to the open front door, their smooth-worn stone, were familiar under her feet. Inside, a handful of early arrivals was gathered by the refreshments table – placed, as always, at the point furthest from the door, so as to entice people all the way in. Once they'd made it this far, they were less likely to bolt. That was the theory, at least. She wasn't sure it had ever been tested.

The woman pouring tea was someone she should know.

'Cassie! It's a good while since we've seen you . . .'

A motherly woman, middle-aged. A face that was wide with perpetual surprise. Her name had an *ay* sound, like May, or Tuesday, but it was neither of those and in the end Cassie fudged it with a 'Hi there, nice to see you . . .'

'Tea? Milk, no sugar?'

People didn't ask, here. If someone disappeared for months at a time, you didn't ask, *Where have you been? What's been happening with you?* You waited, instead, for someone to tell; and in the meantime, there was tea.

'Biscuit?'

Cassie had done the welcomes herself, a couple of times. It was nobody's job. They took it in turns. She hadn't been much good. Remembering names and faces: a lot of them struggled with that at the group, Cassie wasn't alone. The woman on duty today was unusual; she was good, fetching up Cassie's name with barely a hesitation. But it wasn't just the memory thing. Though no one had said so, Cassie was distant, too closed, knew that about herself. She was better on washing-up. Still, she'd done her best: always pushed hard on the biscuits, like sugar and fat could make up for a basic lack of human warmth.

April. A full minute too late, the name arrived in Cassie's head. April was looking over Cassie's shoulder now, ready to greet the next body, so Cassie smiled her thanks and took her tea round the circle of chairs. She'd have gone for the seat nearest the door, but someone else had got there first. No one she recognised. She gave a brief nod, left a space empty between them. She needed company, not talk. She was here for steadiness. For a hit of routine.

She scalded her mouth with tea, then glanced round to check no one was watching her before she placed the mug by her feet. She didn't want to invite concern, the kind of conversation that could only become awkward. Surreptitiously, she reached into her pocket and drew out the memorial card.

As soon as she had torn the envelope, she'd known what it must mean. A glimpse of black border, and her vision had blurred; she had leant against the door in her flat, blinking hard, the card half-out of its envelope moulding to the damp heat of her hand. Blinked, till the name had come into focus – and relief had knocked the breath from her.

In Loving Memory
Please join us for a memorial service honouring
Valerie May Lauder

Not Alan. Only his mother. It was only his mother who'd died.

The meeting was filling up now, April remembering names like nobody's business. Late afternoon light fell from the tall windows, making slanted squares on pale walls, on the worn Persian rug with its pattern the same as always. The space was strange and familiar both at once, but most of all it felt safe.

Safe: as if the notion had summoned him, in walked Jake, folder under his arm and the old purple piggy bank clutched in his hand. He saw her and smiled, waved the pig in her direction, and she lifted her hand in return. It was Jake who'd been manning the welcome table her first time here, and it was Jake who usually led the meetings, in a calm, quiet voice. Facilitated, he preferred to say. Whatever he called it, people paid attention.

He sat, now, the chair child-sized beneath his bearlike frame. Opened the folder on his lap, and waited. Around him, seats were chosen. Conversations tailed off. There was a moment of quiet: Cassie felt a lift of anticipation, a tide of silent disappointment – a swing of feelings almost too fast to name.

Just as Jake started to speak, the door thumped open.

'Sorry I'm late,' said a young man, looking not sorry at all, looking confident and tall. He glanced round for somewhere to sit, and because the circle was full there was a pause while another chair was fetched, and then they all had to scoot backwards to open up space for this guy – Lewis – whom everyone seemed to know.

Cassie kept her irritation concealed behind a neutral face, wondered if everyone else was doing the same. As the meeting got underway with the usual reminder of confidentiality – *What we say here, stays here* – she studied the new arrival. He was wearing shorts, two pairs – Lycra under cargo shorts that looked like they'd been ironed. His naked legs intruded a mile into the circle. Until now, Cassie hadn't realised she had a prejudice against men in shorts. As Jake spoke, Lewis shifted in his seat – and something flashed, making her blink. Unbelievable: his turn-ups were specially equipped with reflective stripes. Cassie priced him in her head: a hundred quid for the shorts. Another hundred, at least, for the top of the range Dutch pannier stowed under his chair. He was one of those guys for whom cycling was a way of life, not of getting from one side of town to the other. He probably owned multiple bikes for slightly varying conditions of road and weather, and he'd never dream in a million years of using a hacksaw to liberate an abandoned frame from the stairwell of a low-rise council block.

She watched him, enjoying her dislike for him. Told herself not to judge, and carried on judging.

And then he lifted his hand, and gently touched his ear.

Cassie stared. The pad of his thumb, the side of his forefinger, rubbing the lobe and the curve of cartilage. She could see he wasn't aware of it; his attention was fixed on the woman who was talking, on the progress of speech around the circle. You might think he was checking a new piercing. But there was no ring, no stud, and that wasn't what it meant, that gesture. Still holding the memorial notice, Cassie's own hand lifted – and she pulled it down again as she realised, suddenly, that he was staring back at her.

She snatched her gaze from his face. Felt her own face hot. It took all her willpower to stop herself checking whether he was still watching – because in the fraction of a second their eyes had met, she'd felt like she could see straight through to the back of his skull, or the back of her own. Like something was aligned.

He was like her. The same as her. Maybe – probably – had to be—The proof would be if it came his turn to speak – and he chose not to. Wouldn't it? Wouldn't that be a sort of proof?

The purple pig moved round the circle, passed from hand to hand: when it reached you, that was your turn to talk. A woman with a dragged-down face said how tough it was to get a job. The fat man beside her explained how he was trying to rebuild a relationship with his sons. *It's hard*, they said, everyone said. Even the people who'd had a good week. *It's always hard, but . . . right now – today – I'm doing fine.* It was a kindness to those who were struggling, and a superstitious insurance. *This week I'm alright*, they were telling the group. *Next week, I could be you.* Cassie hurried them on in her mind. Watched as the pig came closer. Along with everyone else, she watched as Lewis took it. Shook his head. Handed it straight to his right.

His neighbour began to speak, but Cassie kept her eyes on Lewis. Was still watching when he raised his head and glanced at her.

The card forgotten in her lap, Cassie touched her hand to her ear; deliberately, slowly, holding his gaze all the while. A signal. She saw his eyes widen, then narrow – and she shouldn't be doing this, was going to end up in trouble, in a whole lot more trouble than ever. She bent her head. It felt like she'd peeled off a layer of skin. She stared at the rug, stared so hard that the pattern blurred and danced.

When the pig reached her she didn't touch it, just pushed a little further back into her seat, and waved it past. Didn't look up to see if he was watching. Knew he had to be.

Once everyone had talked, or chosen not to, the pig arrived back at its starting point. Jake stood up, thanked everyone, and gave it a shake.

'You know the score, as always, donations welcome; whatever you can manage helps keep us in biscuits.'

He set the pig down by the tea urn. People flowed round him with coins ready to slot into its back, and empty cups ready to be refilled. Cassie pushed the memorial card back into her pocket and counted out her change. 50p would mean £17 to last the rest of the week. Which was fine. Which was doable. Without looking, she knew where Lewis was in the room. She knew he'd dropped some coins into the piggy bank. Knew he was ready to go, but not going, fiddling instead with the straps on his bag, on his helmet.

By the time she reached the table, Jake was stuck in one-sided conversation with someone Cassie didn't know. She made her donation, then waited her turn, hovering till eventually Jake manoeuvred his way round the talker.

'Cassie, good to see you,' he said. 'How've you been?'

'Yeah, alright, I mean – you know.' She shrugged. 'Just, keeping on. And you?'

He pulled a face. 'You're lucky to find us here still. We lost the last of our funding a few weeks back.'

'Oh, no . . .'

'Well, we knew it was coming, but . . . We're on the lookout for a new home, and we're down to Sunday afternoons and Tuesday evenings.' He shook his head. 'It's brutal out there. But what can you do? I'm glad things are going OK for you, anyway. Will we be seeing you back next week?'

'Hopefully,' said Cassie. Without meaning to, she glanced towards Lewis, curiosity pulling her gaze like a magnet. He was waiting by the door, just as she'd guessed he would: waiting to make it seem like they both just happened to be leaving together. *Trouble*. The word sounded inside her head, and when he tried to catch her eye, she stared right through him. Looked away – and felt herself reddening under Jake's observant gaze. 'Or – soon, anyway,' she said.

Behind her, April was patiently waiting her chance for a word with Jake. Cassie stood aside, raised her hand in a farewell to the both of them.

Head down, she made for the exit. *Keep going. Don't stop. Walk away.* She could feel Lewis watching her as she passed him; it took all her willpower not to look up. When she reached the street, she realised she'd been holding her breath.

* * *

Someone had left a bike overlapping hers, on the same stretch of railings. A sparkling clean road bike, double locked; when she pushed it aside to free her rear wheel, with a sharper shove than was strictly necessary, it felt weightless despite its extra-large frame. It had to be his. She felt the ancient rubber of her handlebars sticky against her palms, heard the complaint of her rusted chain, and shoved down hard on the pedals, building speed as fast as she could – till a sudden grating sound made her glance down, just as the pedals locked.

'Shit!'

She jerked to a stop, hauled the bike back onto the pavement and crouched to examine it. The chain, stretched and stiff, had slipped off the worn-down gears, wedged itself between the crank and the frame. She grabbed hold of it and started to pull.

'Oh, come *on*, you bastard . . .' No matter how hard she yanked, it wouldn't budge. If she had a pair of pliers, maybe – but she had nothing with her. She sat back on her heels, swallowing hard. It was a long walk home.

'Need some help?'

Lewis: she looked up to find him towering over her.

'I'm fine,' she said, in a voice that didn't sound it. She gave the chain a heave. 'It's just – a bit – *stuck*.'

'Here, let me have a go.'

Defeated, she stood up, moved aside. Lewis squatted, turn-ups flashing. He wrapped one hand around the chain, and with a single sharp tug it came free. He looped it back around the gears, and stood back with a smile.

'No way. How did you do that?'

'You probably loosened it . . .' He looked at his palm, striped dark with grease, and used his clean hand to open his pannier.

'Well – thanks.'

'No problem. Want one?' He was offering her a plastic packet: the man travelled with a bumper pack of baby wipes, just in case. He probably had pliers in there as well. Spare inner tubes, plural. A multipack of Kendal mint cake. A sarcastic comment was poised on her lips – but when she looked up at him, there it was again. That dizzying sense of connection, of being aligned. Like the same thought was bouncing between them, back and forth.

She swallowed her sarcasm. Said instead, 'You didn't talk.'

He blinked. 'Nor did you.' For a moment they stared at each other, saying nothing. Then: 'Do you want to go somewhere else and . . . not talk?'

She shrugged, thinking, *Walk away*. Thinking, too, of £17 to last her the week.

'Coffee?' he said.

'You buying?'

'Sure. Yeah. Alright.'

She nodded. Made a silent apology to the card in her pocket, the presence of Valerie, as she put off a little longer the call that was waiting to be made. Reached for a wipe, and started working oil and dirt from her hands.

As they wheeled their bikes back past the meeting house Jake was outside, locking up. She saw him recognise them, saw him stand for a moment, watching. He'd be thinking all sorts, Cassie knew. Making assumptions. He'd warn them both off, if he could. Intense personal relationships, he'd be worried about – two people in recovery. And he was right about the danger, and he didn't know the half of it. Just how they were the same. Just how dangerous that might be.

FREQUENTLY ASKED QUESTIONS

Q. What is Make-Believe™?

A. You tell us! Make-Believe™ is whatever you want it to be. This is virtual reality like you've never experienced it before, all generated by your own amazing brain. No clumsy headset. No motion sickness. No screens, lenses, suits or gloves. And with nothing to come between you and your dreams, no wonder our users tell us it's better than real.

Ever wanted to fly? Visit ancient Rome, or take a tour of the solar system? Make friends with a dragon, or hang out with a film star? Become a rock legend, a martial arts master, or even a tiger hunting in the African savannah?

Whatever your fantasy, you can live it with Make-Believe™. Score the winning goal in the World Cup Final – or just tell your boss what you think of them.

Make-Believe™. It's as wild as you want it. The only limit is you.

Make-Believe™ is a trademark of Imagen Research

CHAPTER TWO

'So . . . that wasn't your first time.'

'My first time what?' Cassie sucked coffee from her spoon, relishing the bitterness. She wasn't sure what he meant. Didn't want to answer a question that wasn't being asked.

'At the group, today. You obviously know them, Jake anyway.'

'Ah, yeah. I used to come before. I stopped for a bit.'

'And now you're back.'

'Well observed.' When she held his eyes, the dizziness was gone; the coffee smell, heavy and rich, buzzed her brain with each inhalation. Keeping her straight. They were ordinary eyes, nothing astonishing about them, and certainly everything felt a bit more normal now she and Lewis were out in the everyday world. Dark eyes. Narrow. A hint of a slant, making him look amused. But his mouth was unsmiling, straight and wide; his jaw was set. She didn't have the measure of him, not yet. She held him at a distance.

'Why have you come back?' he asked.

Straight out. How could he not know? That you didn't ask? 'Seriously?' Cassie gave him the long, hard stare he deserved.

His flush was just visible. 'No, well obviously you . . . I'm not asking . . .' He gave up. Looked away. 'Never mind.'

A silence. Cassie lifted her cup, but the servings were as tiny as they were strong, and already there was nothing left but foam. He hadn't meant to pry. He was clumsy, not nosy. Dog-like. Something big and long-legged, a wolfhound or a deerhound, meaning well and causing chaos.

'When did you start?' she asked. 'The group, I mean.'

'Just a few weeks back.' He was eager, grateful for another chance. 'It's good, I like it.'

'You think it's helpful?'

'Yeah. Yeah, definitely.'

'But what, you just don't feel like sharing? D'you always pass on the pig?'

'The pig . . .' He laughed. 'I guess I'm just more of a listener. Like you.' Serious now: he held her gaze. A challenge, or maybe an invitation.

She shook her head. It was her turn to look away. If she was a listener, it was only because she had no choice.

She couldn't tell her story, talk of how she was feeling, which was why she'd stopped coming. She'd begun to worry that her presence was resented. If she could have explained herself . . . it wasn't pride that kept her private. She wasn't holding herself apart, judging the others as they revealed themselves. But since she couldn't explain, she'd skipped a week instead; then two weeks, then a month, and then it wasn't a place she went any more.

'No,' she said. 'No, I'd like to speak.'

'But you don't.' His tone was easy, but suddenly they were in a high place – near the edge – and she wasn't decided yet. Step back, be sensible; or inch on forward, lean, or tip, or leap—

Sideways seemed a good move. She tilted her head. 'The guy sitting next to us,' she murmured. 'On our left.' She'd noticed him as soon as he walked in. If she was right about Lewis, he would have noticed too.

Lewis turned to look, subtle enough. Turned back, eyes narrower than ever.

'What do you think?' said Cassie.

'About what?'

She showed him what. A gentle pinch of her ear, between thumb and knuckle: the receiver the guy was wearing. A sleek new model, titanium.

Lewis nodded. He'd known, really. Had wanted, of course, to be sure he'd guessed right. 'Ahh . . . I think he's an idiot,' he said, 'wearing that outside – and I think if he gets mugged he'll have no one to blame but himself.'

They were at the edge now, poised. 'Did you never

do that?' said Cassie, softly. 'Never wear yours outside?'

Lewis barely hesitated. 'No. I didn't.' His hand was at his ear again; she would have bet her weekly budget he had no idea he was doing it.

'No,' she said. 'Nor did I.'

It was out; they were falling, and it felt more like floating – like a long, stuttering out-breath, like noiseless laughter.

Lewis was smiling now, a small smile that slanted his eyes even higher. She leant towards him, close enough to catch a trace of his scent: clean laundry, soap, sandalwood. 'Bet I can tell you what you did,' she said. 'Your first time.' This was a kind of party piece, one she hadn't been able to use in a long time.

'We're not talking about the group now?'

She shook her head.

'OK,' he said. 'Guess.'

It was what they all chose: ninety-four per cent, if she remembered accurately. 'Flying. Right?'

He didn't have to admit it; his sheepish expression was all the confirmation she needed. She laughed. An easy guess, but she still felt pleased. She'd impressed him.

'What about you?' he said, and she laughed again, shook her head. 'Go on.'

'Guess. I'm sure you can guess.'

'What – flying too?'

'Of course.' She shrugged. 'Everyone does. Almost everyone.'

'God, that's depressing, isn't it?' he said, still smiling. 'To be so predictable.'

Cassie could feel her face mirroring his, an unfamiliar lift in her cheeks. Only at the top level, she wanted to tell him. That was predictable, yes, but when you started to drill down – the subcategories – that's where it got interesting. *[Flight >> unaided, solo; winged; altitude: high; value: tranquillity; additional elements: Invisibility] was quite different from [Flight >> unaided, group; unsupported; altitude: various; value: thrill-seeking, velocity; additional elements: Interactivity]*, and so on . . . Anything Make-Believable could be subcategorised, but the branching trees were longer than you'd ever think, and the combinations were, theoretically, infinite. She wanted to tell him this so he'd think she was interesting, and clever – but she had to watch herself. For all they seemed to have in common, she didn't know this guy. But then, he wasn't pushing anything. And speaking, actually speaking to someone: it felt like the sun coming out.

'I've never met anyone the same,' she said. 'I mean. I don't know how much the same we are. I don't know what happened with you. But you are . . . ?' She hesitated, wary of asking, of putting it into words.

Lewis helped her out. 'Terminated? Yes: I'm barred, completely.'

They were leaning close to each other now, heads together. Speaking quietly.

'I thought it was only me. That's what they told me.'

'In their interests, isn't it?' Lewis said. 'Make us feel like we're alone, like we're the problem.'

It was more than the sun coming out. It was haar lifting. A view coming clear: a landscape she hadn't guessed at. 'Yes,' she said. 'Yes: because that's what I've never got. How it's not that way for everyone. They told me it was me, like basically I was unstable and that's why I reacted how I did.'

'Which was?'

'Oh God.' She peered into her empty cup, and before she could tell him not to Lewis was on his feet, fetching refills.

She was buzzing already, not used to the caffeine. A long time since she'd sat in a coffee shop, drinking pricey espresso. She gazed around as she waited; the place was tucked away in a basement, had a hidden feeling despite the other customers. Perhaps that's why Lewis had chosen it. How did it keep going, a place like this, while the world around it fell apart? There were enough people who had kept their jobs, she supposed, who were doing alright, were happy to splash out on little luxuries. Lewis was clearly one of them.

'Thanks,' she said as he placed a fresh cup in front of her. She inhaled the spiralling steam. 'D'you know, that's one of the things I could never quite get. Coffee. Something about the smell. I used to try and Make-Believe it, but it was always a bit – off.' She shrugged. 'That and chocolate.'

'What was wrong with the chocolate?'

'The way it melts. It just – didn't.' She took a sip, and lowered her voice another notch. 'You know we can't do this. I can't anyway, I can't speak about it, they made me sign something. Did they – you too?'

He nodded.

'But you weren't an employee?'

He stared at her. 'You – work for them? For Make-Believe?'

'For Imagen, yes.' She checked over both shoulders, wanting to be quite sure no one else was listening. 'Not now, not any more. But, yes.'

He was quiet for a moment, absorbing this. Then: 'No,' he said. 'I was a beta tester. I'm a web developer, and for some reason they offered us all a free trial, the whole tech team.'

'Because you were connectors.'

'Sorry?'

'Well-positioned to influence the behaviour of potential early adopters across extensive virtual networks.' She'd impressed him again; it was slightly pathetic how pleased she felt with herself. 'Yeah,' she said, 'I wrote that marketing strategy.'

'Ah.' He considered. 'So does that make it your fault, that I'm here?'

'I suppose, technically, it does.' She was pretty sure he was joking. 'How did they make you sign? I mean, with me – they just, they had me. I was in breach of contract. I'd properly fucked up. But why did you agree to keep quiet?'

'I, uh . . . I hacked the bioware.'

His expression was one of embarrassed pride.

28

'You hacked . . . What and how, exactly?'

'Because – I was so – it was just, my perfect world.' She could see his gaze turning in. 'I wanted to be there constantly, always – and it started to feel like two hours was just nothing, and every time the sessions ended, it was like – it was painful. You know, literally. Painful. To be yanked out, thrown back into the real – the grey, cold – nothing—'

Her face had gone soft as she listened, a tide of sympathy for him, and for herself. 'Don't,' she said. 'Because, anyway, I know. I know exactly.'

'Sorry.' He closed his eyes for a few seconds. Mentally shaking himself. 'Well, so what I did was I fixed my receiver. I hacked it so the—' He paused. 'How technical d'you want me to be here?'

'I mean I know how it works, obviously I had to know all that. But I'm pretty far from a techie.'

'OK: the antenna that picks up the data transmitted by Imagen – I modified it so it blocked the disconnect signals. So I could stay as long as I wanted. I could stay for hours at a time.'

'Hey, clever!' she said, genuinely impressed.

'Not so clever, as it goes. It took them a while to notice, but when they did' – his voice had gone lower, rougher – 'they screwed me, totally. They banned me, of course. If I try to re-register, pretend to be someone else or whatever, my DNA's on a blacklist so they'll know straight away. I'd broken the terms of the service agreement, which meant they could have prosecuted. That was it, that was how they got me. I promise not to talk about it, and I don't end up with a record. It was a no-brainer. I could have lost my job, could have been sued – I could even have gone to jail, I suppose, if someone had wanted to make an example.' A pause. 'I don't know. Perhaps I could have called their bluff. They wouldn't have wanted it to go public, any of it: the fact that the whole thing is so addictive, the fact that the receivers can be hacked like that.' He lifted his coffee, but didn't drink. 'And there must be more of us, you know? Otherwise, well – too much of a coincidence, isn't it?'

'Coincidence, like how?'

'Us, meeting here, at the group. There's no way it can be just the two of us, can it?'

'No. No, I suppose not.' He was right. The thought hadn't occurred to her, though of course it should have. 'That would be a ridiculous coincidence.'

'But they've kept it pretty quiet, haven't they. You don't hear about people getting addicted. You don't read about it, people don't talk about it. And it's right what you said, how they make you think there's something wrong with you. But actually, I think it's the opposite. I think you have to be really imaginative, and really' – he stopped, searching for the word – 'committed, I suppose, to Make-Believe a world you can't bear to leave.'

She found herself nodding slowly. 'Like the theory that it's only the most determined people who become smokers? Because the first cigarette is so horrible, you have to really persist in order to develop a habit.'

'Kind of like that, yeah. Which makes us pretty special.'

Cassie shrugged, noncommittal.

'Sorry,' he said. 'Going on a bit. I must really have needed to . . . not talk about it. So what about you? Can I ask now, without massively offending you?' He was taking the piss, but that was OK. She deserved it, for being precious.

'Can't talk about it,' she said. 'Obviously. But actually, that aside, I don't know how well I can explain it.'

'Try?'

She took a breath, right down deep. How much did she really want to tell him? Her jacket was slung over the back of her chair, the memorial card still in the inside pocket. She wouldn't talk about Alan. Wouldn't talk about her family, either. Wasn't going near any of that. 'Well. The perfect world thing, and the yanking out. The painful stuff. That. All that was the same as you said.'

He nodded: understood.

'It just happened,' she said. 'That I was staying longer. It was sudden, I remember the first time—' Remembered the disorientation; the disbelief; how the world had flipped inside-out. 'I honestly didn't do anything to make it like that, I didn't hack anything or fix anything, I wouldn't know how; they said I must have altered my account privileges but I didn't. So I still don't understand, really. But fair enough – what I didn't do, and I should have done, was to tell them. It got to the stage I was spending all night in Make-Believe, and going to work and just getting through it, finding somewhere to sleep for an hour if I could get away with it, at lunch in an empty office, then the next night, the same thing again. I must have looked like the walking dead.' She laughed, though it wasn't funny. 'I could barely speak. They thought I was having a breakdown or I don't know. And then, eventually, they realised what was going on. And' – she smiled, spread her arms wide, a gesture of defeat – 'they screwed me. Totally totally.'

'And,' he said, 'is that it, is that why you're at the group?'

'Is there anything else, you mean? Yeah, well, afterwards – there was other stuff to deal with – or, not deal with.' Other stuff. Her sister Meg, the kids, and the whole sorry aftermath. She shook the thoughts away. 'So cos of that, there was a while where I was drinking too much, and other stuff, and – I didn't have any money and I was kind of, actually in a lot of trouble and – it was hard.'

Finally: here she was, telling her story – and it was just the same as all the other stories. *It was hard*. Enough. She was boring herself.

'You?' she said. 'Any other little addictions, or was it Make-Believe pure and simple?'

'Make-Believe,' he said. 'Nothing else can touch it.'

Cassie was suddenly aware of a lack of music. Tables were being wiped around them, lights flicking off. They were the last two customers.

'Suppose we'd better go,' she said. 'Let them get closed up.'

She waited as he gathered his things, his pannier and his helmet, and together they climbed the steps from basement to street level. The wide bright sky made her blink: it had felt late, tucked away down there. But then, it was late, after all. It was nearly June, and it would stay light the whole evening.

They began to walk back to the meeting house. There was more, lots more for them to not talk about. More she wanted to find out about Lewis. And there was something else she was curious about. His smell – its warmth, its spice – brought a memory, a feeling, almost within touching – and she couldn't remember if it was real or Make-Believe, and she shook it off because *he* was real. Lewis was real, and the here and now was real in a way she hadn't felt in a long time.

That layer of skin was still missing, the one she'd lost in the meeting when she'd raised her hand to give him a sign. What she needed now was another sign: something from him. Something to let her know what was happening inside his head or his body, behind his skin and the wall of his skull. She stole a glance at him, hoping for the dizziness back again, hoping to see into his thoughts. But his eyes were too dark. Too narrow. Unreadable.

They had reached the railing where their bikes were locked. She fished her key from her pocket, undid the chain. When she straightened up, she saw Lewis was smiling, like she'd done something funny.

'What?' she said.

'Just surprised you have to lock it!'

She stared at him, eyebrows raised. So her first impression of him had been right after all. She stuffed the lock into her satchel, turned away to swing into the saddle. 'Yeah, well. It gets me there.'

'No, wait: I didn't mean . . . Look, that front wheel seems a bit out of true. Does it steer OK?'

Cassie glanced back at Lewis. Shrugged.

'If you want – we could go back to mine. I could fix it for you.'

She paused, foot poised to step on the pedal. To cycle back to her crummy bedsit, where she'd be kept up half the night by the music from her neighbour's flat, by the trickle of customers chapping his door at all hours. Where she'd stare at Valerie's memorial card, and think about Alan, alone. About the memorial service in five days' time – how she couldn't bear to go, and knew all the same that she must.

Or Lewis's place. For just one night, to step out of her bleak reality, into the brief escape he seemed to be offering.

It was a risk, of course. Perhaps that was what made it irresistible. Or it was her curiosity about him; or else it was simpler than all of that. She had started to share her story with a halfway presentable man, after too long on her own, and that was all it took.

CHAPTER THREE

Lewis hadn't imagined how it would feel to have another woman in his flat. How she would change the air around her, set the molecules vibrating in each room she entered.

But once he'd made a pot of tea, and they'd started to talk again, it didn't feel too bad. It was Make-Believe they talked about, of course. Nothing personal. Nothing that mattered. She complained about what it had done to her brain, how she forgot things; he was the same, he said. She sat at the kitchen table, right-angled to him and close enough to touch, and she seemed quite comfortable – or no, that was the wrong word. There was nothing *comfortable* about her. He'd seen that as soon as he'd walked into the meeting this afternoon, how she'd held herself contained, compressed. He'd pretended not to notice her, had carefully let his gaze slide past her. But then he'd felt her watching him. And when he glanced up, he saw that she'd figured him out – though he hadn't said a word. *Because* he hadn't said a word. A sign, to show they were the same: it was as simple as that.

Outside the window, the sky turned midnight blue, then black, and then it began to rain.

'Your bike . . .' he said. 'I could bring it inside, maybe. Take a look at it in here.'

'Although . . . it's pretty late.' She paused. 'You could wait till it gets light again. Look at it in the morning.'

She did that thing, that girl thing of dipping her head and looking up at him through her eyelashes, and he felt his stomach twist. He was out of practice, but still he knew you couldn't invite a girl back to your place, couldn't spend hours together in conversation, and not expect something to happen. Part of him must have wanted this.

Only, once her tongue was in his mouth, he knew that he didn't. He didn't want it. Even if it wasn't technically cheating, it felt all wrong. Her taste was wrong, and her smell, her long trailing hair, and the whole situation – but when he pulled back, he could see her packing herself away, hear the locks turning, the bolts slamming home.

'Sorry,' he said, and that must have been the wrong thing to say because she stood up and folded her arms.

'What for?' she said. 'My mistake.' She was on her

way to the door – he'd messed up everything—

'No, wait,' he said, following her. Reached out, placed his hand on her arm, and she stared like a bird had shat on her until he let go, but at least she was standing still. Waiting to hear his excuse. 'It's my fault,' he said. 'I'm just – I'm sort of, recently out of a relationship. It's a bit complicated but . . . I'm not ready, basically.'

She shrugged, like it didn't matter, and perhaps to her it didn't. 'No law against changing your mind,' she said, reclaiming her jacket from where she'd left it hanging over her chair. But if he let her go now it would be over before it had even begun. She wouldn't want to see him again, not after he'd screwed things up like this. Once more he spoke without thinking, trying to rescue things.

'Look – you should stay.'

She pulled a face. 'Why would I stay?'

'Because it's late. Because it's chucking it down out there. I'm not going to throw you out into the rain, am I, in the dead of night?'

'How very gentlemanly.'

'And also, I'd like to carry on getting to know you. I've enjoyed tonight. Talking about stuff.' He saw her considering it. 'Please. I'll sleep on the sofa, you can have the bed.'

She sighed. 'Alright, I'll stay – just because, it does sound like it's pissing it down and it's, like, a forty-minute cycle. But I'm not stealing your bed. We can share it – if you're *ready* for that?'

37

He would have preferred the couch, but he couldn't say so. Couldn't turn her down for a second time. 'Deal,' he said.

He lent her a T-shirt, and they took turns in the bathroom; she emerged bare-legged and unselfconscious, and he wasn't sure whether or not he should avert his eyes. She was a strange mix: brittle defensiveness, with a kind of indifferent confidence that made him wonder if she did this sort of thing all the time. It made him feel less bad about the situation, the idea that she made a habit of sharing beds with strangers.

When he switched out the light, the dark came as a relief – except that every sound seemed so loud. The drag of the quilt as she turned her back on him. Her breathing, and his. He lay straight as a plank, wondering if she felt anything like as weird as he did. Expecting at any moment that she might move closer, might touch him. But it wasn't long before her breath grew slower, deeper. He stayed motionless, ignoring the urge to change position, wary of waking her. Resigned himself to a sleepless night.

It was early when he woke, his dreams still clinging, and he must have been dreaming of Cassie: a tender dream that meant she didn't feel, now, like a stranger. Her head on his pillow, her mass of hair. Blonde in the light, mouse in the dark, in-between in the half-light of dawn. It was the dream-residue that let him recognise her, reach for her. Let him pull her close, wrapping them

38

both in the leftover feeling of comfort, of consolation. He knew he shouldn't be doing this, but he breathed the warmth of her neck, the smell of her hair, and all those things about her that had been wrong the night before were somehow familiar. Were deeply, irresistibly right.

CHAPTER FOUR

Cassie waited for Nicol in their usual place, the grassy square that lay right at the heart of the university. The morning promised sun, an early haze just beginning to lift so the edges of things – of buildings and trees, of people – seemed to shimmer. The shimmering was inside her, too: an unsettled, buoyant feeling that threatened to tip her off balance.

She had gone to the meeting yesterday because she wanted stability. Familiar faces, the reassurance of ritual. And she'd come away with the opposite: with everything changed, and uncertain. But for a few hours, at least, she'd felt like she wasn't alone.

Too much of a coincidence, Lewis had said, for the two of them to meet as they had. But coincidences did happen. They had talked, remembering fragments of their previous lives – how it had felt, that first time, to hover an inch off the ground, and then lift and lift and imagine yourself free from the anchor of gravity, and by imagining to become so, wind rushing through your hair and stroking the soles of your bare feet, soft wet of clouds veiling your skin – to spin and feel your stomach lurch, see the ground pitch and tilt, and to fly so entirely that the armchair or bed where you'd left behind the drag of your body, *that* was the place that became unreal . . . They had talked, and she'd almost felt safe. Because, for all that the company had left its traces irrevocably inside her skull, how could Imagen know what she was doing? There was surely no way for their words to be overheard. With Lewis last night, she'd felt safe enough to sleep in his bed, to sleep all the way through – or nearly. Just once she'd woken from a dream of him to find his hand on her hip, and she'd shifted towards him and he'd turned to spoon her and she could feel his erection against her back. *Not so complicated now*, she'd thought as she pushed back into him so his breath came faster, but he hadn't moved his hand from the safe zone of her hip, hadn't pushed back, and eventually he'd softened and she'd fallen into another welcoming dream. And when she woke again in the morning, it was from the most comfortable sleep she'd had in a long, long time.

But feeling safe was not the same as being safe. Cassie pressed her lips together, caught the lingering, bitter taste of the espresso Lewis had made with his fancy machine. Just because she'd felt it, didn't mean that she was. Didn't mean she should see him again.

She looked up from her thoughts as a shadow slipped across her face.

'Morning, morning,' said Nicol. Without taking his hands from the pockets of his hoodie he dropped his skinny frame onto the bench beside her. Leant back, eyes narrowed against the sun. 'Nice day for it, eh?'

'Here.' Cassie delved into her satchel, handed him a package.

'What's this, then?' he said.

'Breakfast meeting. It's breakfast.' Lewis's flat had been a lost world of ordinary luxuries. Spotless kitchen. Cupboards stacked with food. Fat soft kitchen roll in a special counter-top holder. Croissants for breakfast.

Nicol took his pastry, slightly misshapen, from its buttery kitchen roll wrapper. He looked baffled but pleased: breakfast had never been part of their arrangement. 'Hey,' he said. 'Thanks, man.'

He should be able to see the difference, she thought: Cassie on Friday, and Cassie today. He should spot her shimmering edges. But he was oblivious. 'This is good,' he said, mouth full. 'I'd forgotten about croissants.'

'Funny,' she said. 'So had I.'

'Don't s'pose I can put in an order for the same again next time?'

She gave him a look. 'I wouldn't count on it.'

Nicol crammed the tail of the croissant into his mouth, swept pastry flakes from his hoodie and into the folds of his army cut-offs. Then he opened his bag and started to rummage. The backpack he carried was studded with logo pins, some of them familiar to Cassie (three downward-slanting arrows that stood for antifascism, the encircled A for anarchy) and others less so. She had asked him once to explain the more mysterious symbols: a reverse copyright symbol, a grid with five black dots. Copyleft, he'd said; means maximum freedom, free distribution, open source, all that. And the grid, that was a glider – a configuration of a particular two-dimensional cellular automata, and a means of transmitting information. Then he'd cracked a smile at her blank expression. Simpler version, he'd said: it's kind of a hacker emblem. Means sharing is good. Co-operation leads to complexity. To the unpredictable.

Now, from the depths of the bag, he retrieved his memory card. 'That's Watts, Valencia and Tan,' he said, his mouth still full. 'Deadline for the other two's Friday, right? I'll have them done midweek.'

Cassie took her screen from her satchel. She skipped past the ads – one for easy credit, another for discounted pizza – then she clicked the card in and copied the files. It was an archaic format, but more secure than wireless transfer. 'You're a star,' she said. 'Hang on and I'll pay you now.'

'And mind you still owe me for the last lot . . .'

She clapped her hand to her head, tapped out the instruction. 'There. All done.'

Nicol was her best employee, without a doubt – her best *operative*. That was how she thought of them, the PhDs and the postdocs, the unemployed graduates, the

43

odd genius dropout fuck-up, all making pocket money working for her. Operatives: it made the whole thing feel like playing at spies. She chose them carefully, recruiting on word of mouth, tested them on dummy assignments before she let them go live; but still they ranged wildly in reliability. One or two, she'd no idea how they'd ever made it through their degrees. Nicol, though, was solid. He kept her on track when her system of lists failed her, reminding her about deadlines and payments. She paid him more than any of the others, a full fifty per cent.

Nicol was almost a friend.

'There might be another coming up that's in your ballpark,' she said. 'Third year history and philosophy of science. Sound like you?'

He shrugged. 'Aye, could be.'

'Deadline would be—' She checked the message. 'Next Monday. Would that work?'

'Nae bother.' He stood up, shedding crumbs. 'Right then, duty calls. Later . . .'

She watched him amble off in the direction of the science buildings. His patch. She wasn't sure how long Nicol had been at the university; the best part of a decade, she thought. His slow progress, she suspected, had nothing to do with a lack of intelligence, was more a consequence of time he spent on other, informal, commitments – not just the work he did for her, but the various activist networks he was part of.

For all that she saw him most days of her life, more than she saw anyone else, there was a lot she didn't know about Nicol. He'd told her and she'd forgotten, or else she'd never asked. Wasn't sure what, exactly, he studied, though she knew his specialist subjects – computer science, programming, artificial intelligence – and passed on assignments accordingly. If there was a module in conspiracy theories she'd have sent it his way too.

Of course, there was just as much he didn't know about her.

In her pocket, Valerie's memorial card was no longer sharp-cornered. Cassie studied the envelope, her name and address, wondering who had written it. Someone who didn't know who she was, who had simply copied her details from Valerie's address book. Not Alan, that was all she could say for sure. It was nothing like his spiky scrawl. Which meant . . . She shook her head. It didn't have to mean the worst.

There was nothing on the card to say how or even when Valerie had died, no *suddenly*, or *after a long illness*. That was more for death notices. But it must have come unexpectedly. Otherwise, surely, she'd have been in touch. She would have asked Cassie to look out for her son, after she was gone. No matter that it was over a year since Cassie had really seen Alan; no matter how bad that looked. Valerie would have known – wouldn't she? – that Cassie would always have Alan's back.

She would go, of course, to the memorial. St Stephen's: the church round the corner from where Alan and Valerie had lived, from the house where Cassie had lived too, aged sixteen to eighteen. Where she had been

45

happy. It had been no real decision to move in with them: she'd been spending most nights there in any case, and when she did go home the house was still full of her mum's stuff, pulled out and half-sorted for hand-ons and charity; was full of a thin grey fog that chilled every room, spreading silence and the sad smell of damp, so that when her dad had told her he was leaving – a fresh start close to his sister in Melbourne – she had thought of leaving Alan behind, and known there was no contest.

She did leave, of course – later. Did travel to the other side of the world, did leave him behind, even if she hadn't meant to. But don't think of that now. Think instead of that house of Valerie's where she'd lived in all seasons, though somehow in her mind the leaves were always turning: the world turning gold, and Alan gold beside her, golden hair and freckles. Always Alan, right there at her side. The hills and woods around the house. Back seat of the school bus. Shared bed at night. There had been a conversation, very adult, around the kitchen table. Alan crucified with embarrassment, face burning, long legs kicking the table and catching her shins, *Sorry, sorry*, as he squirmed in his seat. His mum heroically rising above the awkwardness: *I'd rather you do it safely under my roof than off somewhere in the woods* . . . Hadn't stopped them doing it off in the woods. Sixteen, seventeen. The smell of it still. Damp and deep. Heightened, and blurred. Grass honeyed into hay. Clover. Clover.

* * *

She hadn't meant to close her eyes. Opened them, blinking. High above, a gull was coasting, drifting like a cursor across a screen.

She stood, pocketing the card. Routine. That was what she'd needed yesterday, and it was what she needed now. The streets around the square had filled with students and staff on their way to lectures and seminars, to the library and the labs. She fell in with the stream heading towards the library: swerved to avoid the bio-touch panels, and swiped her card instead through the visitors' gate. A 'borrowed' visitor's pass; a hefty tip at the 3D-repro shop, and she'd been able to get it duped, return the original before its owner reported it lost. All she'd needed then was for Nicol to hack the control system, altering her security clearance to allow access across the university estate and resetting the expiry date to ten years from now, and: freedom. It was as if she didn't exist.

While he was at it, Nicol had loaded her pass with limitless print credit. Now, she logged in to an idle printer and, after a quick glance to check she was unobserved, ran off two dozen flyers. She had spent a long time on the wording, making sure the target market would understand what was on offer while the university authorities would find nothing irregular in her sales pitch. *Bespoke academic editorial services*, that was all. *Support with writing essays on a wide range of subjects*. Assignments to order: it had been a lucrative sideline back when she was a student, and in the year since Imagen had sacked her she'd gone back to what she knew. *Help with meeting deadlines. Qualified experts. Improve your grades! Call now.*

With the flyers stashed in her satchel, she left the library, taking a small pleasure in navigating the lobby so she walked straight through a 3D recruitment ad: a group of graduates talking and laughing soundlessly, looking forward to a bright future with a global corporation. The ads were new since she'd been a student. So much was new. In four whole years of study, she had thought for perhaps as many hours about careers. About money. About the future. Had she been lucky? Or stupid? She was the last of something. Last to have it so good, to live fully in the present – or to fail to understand that something important had changed. As she passed through the visitors' gate she caught chatter in Korean or Mandarin, in US-accented English. The students looked like brand-new businesswomen and men: the boys in pale chinos, the girls in this year's summer dresses, shifts and A-lines in bright fruit-chew colours. Groomed and glossy, advertisement-ready. In contrast, she doubted she could pass for even a mature student: face bare, clothes pre-worn from the charity shop.

She overtook a slow-moving clutch of women in headscarves, swiped in to Philosophy and worked her way up the building, checking the noticeboards on each floor. Though her flyers promised nothing illegal, week after week they disappeared, torn by disapproving staff from scores of noticeboards. It was cheating, of course, the service she provided, but still it frustrated her that her posters were targeted while those recruiting for night-shift dancers and medical guinea pigs remained untouched, week on week. From one department to the next, she slipped unobserved up stairs and along corridors, waiting for lobbies and hallways to empty before delving into her satchel. English Lit. Languages. Sociology. She targeted her promotion according to her own resources as well as client demand, and she had a wealth of arts grads on her books with no money and no prospects. Psychology – her own field, which reminded her she had an essay to finish for a waiting client. *Environmental factors in addictive behaviours*. She was in danger of becoming her own least reliable operative. The business school: her biggest frustration. There was potential to rake in the money, but business graduates tended to have prospects so recruitment was tricky. Certain modules she could manage herself – Advertising Theory and Practice, Consumer Behaviour, Contemporary Marketing. And some she could farm out to Nicol, though he sniffed a bit at Managing Technology. But if she could just get her hands on a qualified expert, she could make a killing. In the meantime she kept on advertising, building brand awareness.

Last on her circuit, the union. By now she was out of flyers, so she unpinned an old one from the board in the cafe and put it up in the bar. Her theory: wealthy students were likely to eat in regular cafes, and instead visit the union to blow their cash on booze. More money than brains, that was her target market. Or perhaps they weren't brainless. Perhaps it was just that they saw nothing wrong with outsourcing the more tedious obligations of life. They would pay for a cleaner to mop up the mess of their New Town flats, a caterer to manage their pompous dinner parties. If you could pay someone to write your assignment, what was the difference? And that was fine – more than fine, for her own personal economy. Without the rich and the lazy, she'd have drowned by now in an ocean of debt. So she did try not to feel contemptuous towards them. Apart from anything else, if she despised her customers she'd have to despise herself too.

By the bar, three boys and a girl sat at a table loaded with drinks. All four had variations of the same haircut, styled to show off the receivers they wore as ornament: the boys cropped close on the right side of the skull, longer on top, and swept over to the left; the girl with a buzz undercut, her hair adorned with an assortment of clips that lifted it up and away from her face, her receiver full-stopping a line of earrings. Cassie shook her head at the sight. There was no rule to say you could only wear your receiver in the privacy of your own home, but it was common sense to be careful. Before you could sign up to Make-Believe, there were certain criteria you had to fulfil: income, prospects, mental health, criminal records. The technology was still aspirational, and scarcity created demand. If these kids wore their receivers beyond a small safe zone round the university hub, they were asking to get robbed.

'Yeah, and then she woke up . . .' said one of the boys, in a voice that carried – a shortcut to an in-joke – and they all brayed with laughter. Cassie felt her jaw clench. This lot, their whole lives would be made up of shortcuts and in-jokes. She was looking, in fact, at the effectiveness of her own Make-Believe marketing strategy. They'd be signed up for Basic accounts at the moment, but a year or two after graduation they'd be Platinum, guaranteed. Wealthy kids with excellent prospects, plenty of time on their hands. An instinctive acceptance of biotechnological modification. And young enough not to worry about risk – not that there was anything to worry about, the technology had been tested and tested and tested, was proven to be safe, all of that – but still, people did worry. Just, not the young. Young rich men, in particular, knew they were immortal: *I mean come on, you're telling me I'm going to fucking die one day? Dude, I don't think so.* So they wore their receivers as status displays – because of her. Inside, her own success and failure were twisted together into a tough, prickly rope.

She had trained herself not to go there in her thoughts. She noticed the receivers, of course, that couldn't be helped: the girl wearing the latest release, which no doubt boasted all kinds of new modifications; one of the lads sporting a first generation, over two years old and technologically dated, but showing what an early adopter he'd been. Cassie even allowed herself to speculate about their users, how they would translate into stats once their Make-Believe experiences

51

were categorised and sub-categorised. The way the girl had let her shoulder strap slip, leaning back in her seat with one arm raised, hand at the back of her neck. *Sex*, of course. *Exhibitionism? Multiple partners? Unknown partner/s?* Cassie broke her down into percentages. Perhaps all three of her drinking companions would feature, unknowing, when she next connected, while her real-world reputation remained spotless.

Just a guess. But then, it was never much more than a guess, even with the stats in front of you. Not that she'd ever said so, while she was at Imagen. The data was gold: to the companies that bought it, to Imagen's profitability analysis. It was hyped as the closest thing to mind-reading, but really it was more like scanning someone's music library, or their book collection – you could identify broad preferences, forms and genres; you could speculate about the personality of someone who read nothing but noir crime fiction and listened to early blues, decide he might want to buy a Cadillac. What you couldn't know was the meaning. The feeling. That the music reminded him of a lost lover: that it made him feel sad, and that he enjoyed his sadness. That, rather than wanting to be Philip Marlowe, he wanted to be the dame. Her own categories, for instance, might promise revelation. *Flight: velocity / thrill-seeking. Self-image: strength, increased; attractiveness, increased. Sex: known partner/s; consensual / unknown partner/s; thrill-seeking; consensual. Transformation: gender, f-m; animal* . . . and so on. But 'known partner/s; consensual' said nothing of Alan. Of Alan then, and now; of what had drawn her to Make-Believe, hooked her there, made it impossible to leave.

She caught herself. That was the point at which she should think about something else. The week's deadlines. What was left in her fridge. Whether she could afford to pick up milk and bread on the way home as well as meeting her next debt repayment. Today, though, was different. Today the receivers, their users, her own Make-Believe, were harder to ignore. Because of last night, with Lewis. How she'd let herself remember.

It struck her now that, all this time, she'd been staying silent from shock as much as fear: shock at everything they'd been able to do to her.

Outside, she crossed the university square to where she'd left her bike. As she passed through the shadow of the Bray Tower, her screen buzzed an alert. *Lewis*, she thought, with a bump of adrenaline – but the message was from her old colleague, Harrie: *Hey, how's things? Let's meet up soon?*

She would answer later. For now, she was eager to put some space between herself and the tower. It might have been the shade that was making her shiver – or it might have been the coincidence: because hadn't she been with Harrie, the one time they'd seen the inside of the Bray building? A departmental tour of Imagen's research and development sites. The highlight, a guided tour of the Bray Tower led by the woman behind the Make-Believe technology – Professor Morgan herself.

Cassie stared at the top floor where Morgan's office lay, till the sun climbing over the roof flared and forced her to look away. Bray Tower was the one place she never flyered. The way she'd arranged it there was no need; Nicol did the rounds every now and then. It made sense that way. He belonged there, in the domain of maths and science, could wander at will without raising suspicion. Unlike her, he wasn't risking anything when he walked through those sliding doors.

She kept her back to the tower as she unlocked her bike. Yes, it might have been shock that had silenced her till now. And perhaps that shock was wearing off. But that didn't mean she should stop being afraid.

MARKETING REVIEW: VR PROFILING DELIVERS REAL RETURNS FOR LUXURY BRANDS

When UK biotech start-up Imagen Research launched the first truly immersive, individually generated virtual reality, its world of Make-Believe promised to transform consumer profiling and data analytics. So what has been the impact of virtual reality profiling in the high net worth market?

Though Imagen was initially formed to develop the commercial potential of VR in healthcare, the company transferred its research focus at an early stage to the more immediately profitable goal of entertainment VR – and for brands that have long used neuromarketing and aspiration analysis tools to establish meaningful customer relationships, the imaginative data captured by Imagen was hailed as an industry game-changer.

'The unique thing about Make-Believe from

a marketing perspective is that it enables brands to understand consumers on a completely different level,' explains Sarah Westland, director of brand vision at Imagen. 'It allows our clients to tap in directly to the aspirations of potential customers. And since currently 60 per cent of our Basic subscribers and almost three quarters of our Platinum subscribers are classified as high net worth individuals, or potential HNW individuals, this model offers an extremely effective way to reach a cash-rich, recession-proof market.'

The precise method used by Imagen to extrapolate meaningful data from unstructured virtual experiences is a closely guarded secret: all the company will reveal is that biological data generated by individuals during their immersive experience is translated to digital data by the specially programmed biomolecules that deliver the user's VR experience. This data is picked up by the user's electronic receiver, encoded as digital packets and transmitted via the 6G network to Imagen's central servers, where it is grouped together with existing data for machine and human analysis.

According to Westland, the resultant VR profiling can supply an aspirational throughline that enables brands to target campaigns effectively across media channels and new platforms. 'Traditional methods of data gathering and analysis can lead to campaigns that are insufficiently personalised, but with VR profiling as part of the mix, brands can make individual aspirational connections and maintain those connections across the whole media spectrum. For example, a Platinum subscriber based in London might choose to unwind in Make-Believe by speeding along the West Australian coast in a luxury sports car. So the client to whom we supply this data can extrapolate that for this individual, relaxation is linked to speed, action, adrenaline and to a certain setting, and they can personalise their marketing message accordingly.'

Imagen's VR profiling has proved popular with luxury brands; Westland confirms that their clients include major suppliers in wine, art, travel, property, private aviation and high-end retail. So are these brands seeing worthwhile ROI?

Michael Roscoe, head of marketing and ecommerce at JLP Opes, is positive about the added value created by VR profiling. 'Data has become super-abundant, but insights from that data that can improve profitability are tough to generate. Integrating VR data with our existing CRM systems means we can individually target HNW consumers with relevant content that meets their needs. What we're gaining is a more rounded view of our customers that's enabling us to create intimate and memorable customer relationships and constantly reposition our brand via personalised communications. Ultimately our offering has become more direct, more agile and more responsive, and we have seen that reflected in our ROI.'

Until now Make-Believe has been available exclusively in the UK, but Imagen is poised to expand overseas. The technology has recently been licensed for use in Japan, Korea and several other south-east Asian countries, and a US licensing application is pending. The company aims to sign up international luxury brands alongside its domestic clients, and as subscriber numbers increase at home and abroad the data sets will become correspondingly wide, allowing meaningful analysis of broader aspirational trends to complement personal profiling.

And what of the rumours that Imagen is developing a social capacity for Make-Believe – enabling users to share and collaborate on their VR experiences? For marketeers, it's an exciting possibility. Westland will neither confirm nor deny that such a 'collaborative mode' is on the cards. 'We're aware it's something people would love to see – subscribers as well as clients. Make-Believe is the product of over a decade of research and development and hundreds of millions of pounds of investment, and any significant addition to functionality would be similarly resource-intensive.' For now, then, it remains a tantalising – but distant – prospect.

CHAPTER FIVE

It looked like her neighbours had thrown a party. The evidence was all over the scrubby lawn: empty Tennent's cans winked in the sun; someone had brought out a couple of dining chairs, then forgotten to take them in again. A leather jacket lay abandoned, still wet from last night's rain, and a square of flattened grass showed where a speaker must have squatted. From the looks of things, last night had been a good time to be somewhere else.

Inside, the stairwell reeked of stale beer and damp concrete. Cassie navigated the dregs that had leaked from a discarded can, stepped over a congealed chunk of pizza, a fast-food tray smeared with red sauce, a trail of cigarette ends. As she climbed the stairs to her flat, a background voice grew more distinct – a fast-talking DJ, local radio turned up loud. When she unlocked her front door and closed it behind her, the voice followed her in, seeping along with the smell of fried food through the thin skin of plaster and studwork that separated her thirteen square metres of space from her neighbour's.

With its permanent gloom, her room barely dimmed when she pulled down the blind on the single mean window. She was eager to get out of yesterday's knickers, wished now she'd showered at Lewis's place. Somehow in the morning she'd felt shy in a way she hadn't the night before, and taking a shower had seemed too intimate – but it would have been clean, and private. In her dressing gown, towel under her arm, she carried her toilet bag down the hall, bolted the door to the shared bathroom and spent a full minute skooshing stray hairs down the plug before she could force herself under the spray.

Usually she would wear whatever clothes came first to hand; now, for some reason, she found herself thinking twice about her choice, tugging tops and skirts halfway off the rail, holding them out to check for a match or a clash. In the end, annoyed at herself, she closed her eyes and grabbed something at random – black trousers, and a Thin Lizzy T-shirt that must once have been her dad's. At any rate, it wasn't one that Alan had chosen for her. Those she kept separate, folded away in a drawer of their own. Her sixteenth birthday; the first one he gave her – the classic Sonic Youth shirt. Neither she nor Alan had heard the album, but the black-and-white 60s couple was the coolest thing Cassie had ever seen: the woman with her cigarette raised to her lips, the man with his arm draped round her shoulders, both of them sealed, expressionless, behind the solid black of their shades. *I stole my sister's boyfriend*, began the hand-written text alongside the picture. *Within a week we killed my parents and hit the road.* She'd worn it to school, under her regulation shirt, and the bold black lines had ghosted through thin polyester, making her teachers frown. Against the spirit of the rules if not the letter, the deputy head had told her – but he couldn't get her for having the wrong spirit, and he knew it. Later, Alan did the same with a shirt she'd found for him on a market stall – designed and made in China. The slogan read HAPPY EVERYDAYS GREAT on the front, and SMILE & KEEEP on the back. The deputy head had pulled him aside for the same talking-to. Cheerfully, Alan had disagreed: this one broke the letter of the rules, surely? The rules of the English language. That had been his first detention.

No reason now to hide pictures and slogans beneath a bland outer layer – but she did it still. Sometimes it felt like a connection, something shared with him, though he couldn't possibly know. Sometimes it felt like a message to herself. She'd lost the Sonic Youth shirt years ago, but she still had HAPPY EVERYDAYS. The message was faded, only just legible: SMILE & KEEEP.

From the pocket of her discarded jacket, she took the dog-eared memorial card and propped it on the chest of drawers. *In loving memory of.* The thing to do now was to get in touch – to let Alan know she'd be coming to the memorial, that she was there for him. She had the number for Valerie's old landline; it was just possible she might reach him there.

But first – the plant. She should water it, before she forgot. Her concentration, these days, her memory, wasn't all it could be, and it was important to keep the plant alive. Schefflera was the name on the label, but it was an umbrella plant. At least, there had been one at home, and that's what her mum had called it, though it didn't look like an umbrella, more a profusion of drooping hands. Hers was growing well now; she'd been taking good care of it. Dust had begun to settle thinly on its dark leaves, so Cassie took her sleeve in her fist and wiped them clean, one by one, careful not to crease them.

When the leaves were shining and the soil nicely damp, Cassie settled cross-legged in the space beneath the platform bed, between the clothes rail and the chest of drawers. She held her screen, tried the phrases in her head, and then out loud. *I'm so sorry – I was so sorry to hear – I'm sorry about your mum* . . . Coughed once, to clear the gruffness from her voice, and made the call.

The ring had a scratched, echoing quality, like a sound that was distant in time as well as space. She imagined the phone where it had always lived, on the low table in the hall, ringing into an empty house. When it went to voicemail, she listened to Valerie's message all the way through before she hung up. It felt like a tiny act of respect, of remembrance, not to cut her off halfway through.

Six steps took her to the kitchenette; she made herself a mug of tea, saving the bag for a second cup later on. She rolled a skinny cigarette, and smoked it out the window while she waited for the tea to cool.

There was another number she could try. It was there in her contacts: Raphael House. And she'd call it in a heartbeat – if it meant they could talk the way they used to. If it meant she could talk to the real him.

He had always talked so easily, like it was as simple, as obvious as breathing. Had arrived oblivious or unimpressed by the school's social hierarchy. Everyone said he'd moved from the Borders, but if they'd said he came from another planet she would have believed it. She'd seen it go either way, with new students. As a body, the year would decide: in-crowd or outcast – and once you were tagged there was no shifting it. Alan was lucky. Skilled on the pitch, so boys wanted to be him. Nice enough looking for girls to fancy him. For Cassie to fancy him. He shone. Red-gold hair curling over his collar, into pale blue eyes. A mouth she wanted to press, to trace with her forefinger. He should have been a grade-A arsehole, should have strutted into the fourth year and settled right into his throne: top boy. But he fucked it for himself, not knowing, not caring. It was like he hadn't seen that there were trenches, there were sandbags and barbed wire. Hadn't realised there were folk who you spoke to, and then the rest of them. He was an idiot who hadn't known any better than to speak to Cassie. He was a perfect idiot.

Her hand, poised to press call, was stiff, like the blood in her veins had thickened and slowed. When her screen buzzed with a volley of ads, it felt like a reprieve. *Science textbooks at unbeatable prices! Impartial financial advice . . . Fresh food delivered fast . . .* She put the screen face down on the windowsill beside her, lifted her mug. Hesitated.

A speck of black, vibrating on the surface. A tea leaf, escaped from the bag. A tea leaf with legs, sculling. Cockroach. Tiny, new-hatched. Boiled, but still alive. Of course: because they didn't die. Roaches never died. She got up, arm outstretched, walked calmly over to the sink and poured the tea away – and as she turned the taps on full, she realised her mistake. She should have thrown it out the window instead – thrown it as far as she could. Now the creature was deep inside, and way beyond her reach. In the wet black, it could grow. Breed. Multiply. In a month's time it could climb back up, head of an insect army, squeezing its meaty body through the plughole.

She clenched her teeth. It wasn't the first time. Could be any one of the neighbours – leaving food out to fester, dishes piled unwashed, takeaway cartons mouldering, living happily with an infestation that spread through the walls of the whole block – and it would take weeks and endless phone calls for the landlord to do anything about it. In the meantime, from under the sink, she fetched out the sticky papers left over from the last infestation. It was the hot spots they liked. Microwave, toaster, kettle. Hence, cockroach tea.

On her screen, the ads had finished, replaced by the wallpaper pic of her nephew and niece. Next door, her neighbour had changed the radio station: back-to-back hardcore, urgent and shrill as a panic attack, 200 beats per minute hammering at a wall so shoddy that sound passed through as if through nothing at all. And yet there was space inside for life, for insect-specks to crawl, and breed, and spread.

First in her head, then out loud, she practised a new phrase.

I enjoyed last night . . . I had a nice time last night . . . I had a really nice time with you . . .

Made a new choice, an easy choice; spun the contacts in her screen, and called quick as blinking.

'Lewis?' She smiled. Heard how it warmed her voice. 'Yeah, me too . . . a really nice time.'

CHAPTER SIX

It was the thought of his flat that had drawn her – his big, clean, comfortable flat – as much as his bed, his hand on her hip, his warmth against her back. Though when he'd suggested coming to hers she'd almost agreed, just to see his face, see him bite down hard on his dismay: the bleakly functional estate, the single shop with its permanent steel shutters, the shared bathroom. But that might have made her resent him, and resentment was not what she wanted to feel.

He met her with a well-judged kiss on the cheek, halfway between friends and bedmates.

'Welcome back,' he said. 'Been a while.'

'Twelve hours, at least. Wasn't sure I'd recognise you.'

He closed the door behind her. 'So, have you eaten?'

'I could be tempted.'

'I hope so,' he said. 'But, have you eaten?'

She narrowed her eyes at him, laughing; shook her head as he led her into the kitchen. He was different today – and she liked it. More direct; less complicated. She couldn't imagine him saying a thing like *I'm not ready*.

'Glad you're amused,' he said, 'but that wasn't the reaction I was going for.'

'Laughing *with* you, Lewis. Not *at* you.'

He shrugged. 'It's OK, I'll survive. I was going to do pasta. Just linguine with blue cheese and walnuts, something like that?'

Something like that. The last meal she'd cooked had been instant noodles and a slice of toast. 'Yeah, that sounds good. Need any help?'

'Just keep me company.'

She watched him work at the counter, thinking how unexpected this all was. How quickly she'd come to feel at ease with him. On the way here, she had jolted her way over cratered tarmac, roads folded and cracked like something living was forcing its way to the surface of the city; turning onto a stretch of canal surfaced with green slime, broken only by plastic bags and shopping trolleys, she'd been greeted from every bench along the way by huddles of men drowning their dead time with party-sized bottles of cider, had passed under a bridge colonised by the local young team and taken a couple of direct hits from the stones they'd thrown before she could outdistance them. Then she had reached Lewis's flat, and entered a calmer, kinder world. Late sun warming the notched wood of the table where she sat. The roll of boiling water, the cooking pasta smell, the steam glazing the windows and diffusing the light. It was all the more comforting because it was food being made for her by someone else. She couldn't remember the last time anyone had cooked for her. Knew she shouldn't get used to it, shouldn't relax too much. But while she was here, she meant to enjoy it.

Lewis was chopping stuff, his back to her. 'So,' he said, 'how was your day at work? Where is it you work, by the way?'

'The university – boring admin stuff, I – Jesus!' Something thumped onto the table, coming from nowhere to land right beside her. Ginger fur. Fierce matching eyes.

'Oh. Yeah. This is Pita. Didn't you meet, last night?'

'We did not.' The cat settled into a crouch and a narrow glare. Uncomfortable, Cassie slid her gaze away. 'Seriously, you called your cat Peter? It's not a common feline name.'

'No, *Pee-tah*. She's a she.'

'Right. Pita . . . like the bread? Because you do know that's even weirder?'

'Yeah, spelt like the bread, but that's not why. It's an acronym. Stands for Pain In The Arse.'

'Wow, OK. Say what you feel.' Cassie lifted a tentative hand, trying for a stroke. Judged, was how she felt. With her relentless stare, Pita seemed to know all, condemn all. The cat ducked, flicked an ear, backed abruptly out of its crouch and turned – presenting Cassie

69

with a brief close-up of a puckered behind beneath a switching tail – before dropping heavily to the floor.

'She's usually friendlier,' said Lewis, shifting his attention back to the food. He put the walnuts on to toast. Drained the pasta. Threw everything in a bowl, dug it all together and brought it to the table.

'Olive oil,' he said, depositing a sleek ceramic bottle. 'Probably doesn't need salt, because of the blue cheese, but . . . in case.' A little matching bowl of flaky crystals. Two glasses of water.

'Looks great. Smells great.'

Lewis lifted his glass. 'Cheers.'

Water, because of her.

'Look, you can drink if you want,' she said. 'I mean obviously you can, but – if you normally would. If you're not, because of me.'

He shrugged. 'Sometimes I would. Not always. You don't ever, I take it?'

'Easier just to stop, completely. To be honest it's not a big thing, not like you might think.' She started to eat. 'You know, some folk at the group – their recovery is like their child. Constantly needing to be protected, needing to be fed and nurtured. They can't take their eyes off it. Whether it's drink or drugs it's no different; it's always going to be the central thing in their lives.'

'But for you it's not like that?'

'Not with drinking, not at all. That was only ever a displacement for me, I didn't ever need it in that physical way. I wanted the blackouts, the blanks, I wanted the way it cut me off from real life – but the sickness, the hangovers—' She pulled a face. Opiates had been a more satisfactory substitute for Make-Believe, but hard to come by. Alcohol, though . . . She'd never craved that first drink of the day, had to force it down like medicine, like punishment. It wasn't much of a temptation these days when she caught the smell drifting from pub doorways – though she tended still to hold her breath, and turn her face away.

'I'd feel a real fraud going along to the meetings,' she said, 'if that was all it was. Sometimes I feel like a fraud anyway – like, was it really an addiction? But then I remember. How it crept up on me. I mean, right from the start I was using it every day – but it was part of my job, you know? Research, getting to know the product, testing for glitches. Or when it was recreational, it was just like watching TV or reading a book, only better. Although, I don't know about you but sometimes I did choose TV or a book instead – if I was really tired and just wanted someone to tell me a story. I didn't want to have to make my own.' Lewis was nodding in agreement. 'Not that it was about stories, really. It's more sensations, isn't it? Or moments. Intense moments.'

'Sounds like you were just a normal user . . .'

'Although, it was amazing how quickly two hours would shoot past. But then what happened was . . . I don't know, I suddenly got better at it. At imagining. All those hours of practice, maybe. And once that happened, the whole thing was more absorbing. Harder to keep away from. It was like *The Wizard of Oz*, you know when everything's black and white and then suddenly it's in colour? That's what it felt like, real life versus Make-Believe.'

'Yes,' he said. 'That's exactly it. That's exactly what it was like.' They were quiet for a moment. Then: 'It's easier for us, in a way,' he said. 'It doesn't matter that we're tempted every day of our lives. We can't get back.'

'Yep.'

'Doesn't feel easy, though, does it.' He was lifting pasta onto his fork, letting it slide back to the plate.

'That's our own central thing, I guess. You not hungry?'

He looked up. 'I read something interesting today, about Make-Believe. Hang on. I'll show you.' He got up to fetch his screen from the counter, sat tapping with one hand, twirling linguine with the other. 'It was in my news feed . . . somewhere . . . hang on – yeah, here we go. Imagen just released their latest user numbers. What do you think they showed?'

Cassie frowned. 'Usual, I'd guess. Up twenty per cent, something like that?'

Lewis spun the screen so Cassie could see it. 'According to this, they've actually *lost* subscribers over the last quarter. They're still up on the same period last year, but compared to the previous quarter – I mean it's not drastic, it's something like half a per cent – but still . . .'

She scanned the text. There wasn't much more than what Lewis had said. The stats had been announced late in the day, and it would be hours before the web responded with the inevitable slew of argument and analysis: tech commentators claiming they'd predicted a slow down; finance journalists presenting speculation as fact; privacy campaigners denouncing the sale of neurological data; and the Campaign for Real Life spinning the drop as the beginning of the end for Make-Believe.

'Still,' she said, 'when you're expecting growth in double figures, that's pretty major.'

'See here, in the last paragraph . . .' He pointed. 'The spokesman's quoted as saying it's part of their sustained expansion plan . . . always aiming for a period of consolidation, etcetera.'

She found the text: glanced up, saw the question on his face.

'Nope. I mean unless their plans have changed completely since my time.'

'And how likely is that?'

Cassie shook her head. Returned to the report. It was accompanied by a stock shot of the chief exec, Eric; he'd been carefully positioned in front of the Make-Believe logo that illuminated the Imagen office reception. She knew he would have spent fifteen minutes adjusting the knot in his tie, and then made a show of impatience when the photographer directed him towards a flattering angle. 'They have sidelined things before,' she said, distracted. 'Areas of development, I mean. Like way back, there was a whole capacity they were developing for some kind of therapeutic use, but I think it wasn't profitable or something. Before my time, anyway.' She flipped the screen back round to Lewis. 'But I can't see why they'd deliberately cut growth like that. There was never any "period of consolidation" in the strategy, specially not consolidation that involves losing subscribers – which, cutting through the bullshit, is actually retrenchment.'

'So – what could it be?'

'Who knows? All I can tell you is that it's not my problem.' She pushed her plate away. 'I can't finish this, sorry, I wish I could cos it's really, really good.'

'Save it for breakfast?'

She gave him a raised-eyebrows look.

'But hang on,' he said, 'let's not get distracted. I mean, yes – let's – but not yet. Do you think there could be something – connected to us? To what happened to us?'

She could feel the food solid and comforting in her stomach, but her plate was still within picking distance. She reached for a crumb of walnut. 'Like how?' she asked.

'I don't know, just – I suppose I was thinking if there are more of us—'

'More addicts . . .'

'Yeah – then, could that be the reason?'

'You mean they're not losing subscribers, exactly; they're cutting them off?' Cassie stared at him. 'A half per cent drop against expected growth of twenty per cent? That's a lot of people. That's—' She shook her head. 'I

don't know how many, but for the sake of argument –
five hundred? A thousand? Is it even possible that so
many people would be able to do what you did?'

Lewis smiled. 'I am, obviously, a technical genius – but
yeah, that's just about possible. The real barrier would be
keeping ahead of the tech team at Imagen. So the hack
I built, they'll have fixed that loophole now, but that
doesn't mean there's not another way. There's bound to
be another way.'

He was leaning forward, eyes wider than she'd
thought they could go. Without meaning to, Cassie did
the opposite, leaning back in her chair.

'OK,' she said, 'so maybe that's it.'

'But that's got to be important. Don't you think?'

'How? I don't see it.'

'Because . . . it could mean it wasn't us; we weren't to
blame. If there are more of us, enough of us – it could
mean Make-Believe is inherently addictive. It's unsafe or
– or insufficiently regulated. We could sue!'

She felt herself closing up, pulling back. He must have
seen it in her face.

'What? What have I said?'

For a moment she couldn't speak. That resentment
rearing up again. What did he have to sue for? What
had he lost? He had his home, his career, his future – he
didn't understand. Because she hadn't explained. There
was stuff she couldn't, wouldn't, stuff she still nursed
deep inside, and he didn't need the details. But he needed
to know how lucky he was.

She took a drink of water.

'Listen,' she said. And she told him.

Make-Believe: the last time she'd seen that glowing logo. Moving dreamlike through the lobby, detached from everything, uncertain what was happening. They were sending her home – but she wasn't ill. Not ill, just tired. So tired. The security guards, Dave holding her left arm, Justin holding her right, marching her through the exit, round to the car park. Waiting for her to drive away, but she couldn't start the car, couldn't see straight, wasn't safe, so they called her a cab and waited right there till it came to take her away.

The buzzer waking her from a dead sleep that had lasted a day, a night, and into a second day. Three of them standing at her door: two of them company directors – Leanne, HR, and Xav, operations – and the third a lawyer. They sat down on her sofa, on her chairs, and spoke without meeting her eyes, like they'd never known her. Spoke about what would happen if she didn't sign the papers the lawyer pulled from her briefcase. *Sign here. And your name, and the date. Again: here, and here.* Still too tired, too fuzzy to understand. Her brain pulsing against her skull, and every cell crying out for the world to re-arrange itself into something soft, warm, kind.

Later – a week, two weeks – reading the papers again, and understanding this time. What they were taking from her. *It is hereby agreed as follows . . .* She would not work again in emerging technologies. She would not contact her former colleagues. She would not communicate with anyone about Make-Believe, and Imagen. *Without prejudice to any other rights or remedies that either Party may have, the Employee acknowledges and agrees that: Damages would not be an adequate remedy for a breach of any of the provisions of this agreement; Imagen Research and any other relevant subsidiary company of Imagen Research shall be entitled to the remedies of injunction, specific performance and any other equitable relief for any threatened or actual breach of the provisions of this Agreement by the Employee; No proof of special damages shall be necessary for the enforcement of this Agreement.*

Her bonuses reclaimed for the whole of the year, her last month's salary forfeited. Understanding now, and knowing – though she didn't tell him this – that she deserved it. Just like no one would feel sorry for a junkie who stole from her family, no one should feel sorry for her. Ask her sister; ask Meg. Cassie deserved it all, and more. Deserved to fall behind on her rent, to be forced to borrow at extortionate rates from any rip-off lender that would oblige, and then to lose her flat anyway. To end up in a bedsit on the edge of the city, a three-bed ex-council flat chopped into four and infested with roaches.

And none of this came close to what she'd really lost.

When she'd finished she got up, went to the sink to refill her water glass. Drained it in one.

'And you,' she said, pointing her glass at him, 'you

still have everything you ever had. So – sorry, but I don't see what the hell you have to sue for.'

For a moment he was silent. She saw him decide to say something, saw him change his mind. His face, his jaw looked tight, but when he did speak his voice was calm. 'I get that,' he said. 'You're right. On paper, you're right. But come on, Cassie. We don't live on paper. There's stuff I've lost too, not like you maybe, but – OK, here's how I think of it. It's not about money. It's not about compensation. It's about power. Right? If we had something over them, like if we knew something they'd prefer people not to know – something we could prove – then, we could negotiate.'

'Negotiate – for what?'

'What do you want? They took your future. Don't you want that back?'

She said nothing. Held tight onto her empty glass.

He glanced down. Rubbed at a smear of something on the table, kept rubbing once it had vanished. 'They'd have to let us back,' he said.

In her chest, something suddenly too big, pushing up against her breastbone, into her throat. That was it. What this was about; what he was about.

'No.' She said it fast and loud, before she could think of not saying it.

When Lewis looked up his eyes were black with longing, with the same desire that twisted inside her. 'As much as we wanted. They'd have to.'

She couldn't. She couldn't even think about it. She

said it again: *no*. Then she set her glass down on the draining board and walked out of the room.

In the bathroom she ran the taps, and stared in the mirror. She remembered how Jake had watched as she and Lewis left the meeting, the concern that had creased his forehead. Some people sabotaged themselves. And some took others down with them.

She should leave. Delete Lewis's details. Block any contact.

Her reflection clouded, steam rising from the scalding water. Clumsy dog. He knew nothing. Any minute he'd be knocking at the bathroom door, asking was she OK, had he said something wrong. But there was no sound from outside. She turned off the taps, undid the bolt. He knew nothing – but he knew when to back off.

He was still in the kitchen, sitting where she'd left him, and the first thing he said was sorry.

She stood in the doorway. 'I don't want to speak about that.'

'No. I get it. I'm sorry. I promise I'll shut up.' He pulled an imaginary zip across his mouth.

'Because they can claim damages from me, just for talking about it.'

'OK, it's OK, I won't—'

'They can prosecute me, they can take me to court, they can—'

'Cassie. Shh. I get it.' He risked a brief half-smile. Then, serious again: 'You look like you're going.'

'Thinking about it.'

'Don't.' He tilted her abandoned dinner-plate, with its cold nest of pasta. 'You'll miss out on breakfast.'

Later, in the lounge, she sat on the sofa with his arm around her. Tried not to talk about Make-Believe, and talked about it anyway.

'Do you know,' she said, 'I actually remember the day I got better at it, the day it went technicolour. At first I thought they must have upgraded it in some way. Because everything was just – it's not like there was a technical difference, not like a graphics upgrade on your PC, not that kind of thing. If anything it was – brighter, but less clear. More impressionistic, if that makes sense? Confusing, sometimes; more dreamlike. But when I say it felt more real, that's exactly what I mean: that it felt more. *I* felt more. Does that make any sense at all?' There was more to it, of course, more that had kept her coming back, and back again. There was Alan. But she didn't want to go into any of that. And Lewis seemed to know what she meant, anyway. She could feel his nod, stubble catching at her hair. 'I guess I'd broken through in some way. You know when people say you've got a good imagination like it's just something you have, like being left-handed or having red hair. But it's not passive like that – not in Make-Believe. It's all conscious, isn't it? I mean, you're consciously, constantly making decisions. Like, I'm flying: so do I make the air dry or damp, is it still or breezy? Or, I started off on a sunny day but now I want to make it night, and it's a clear night so moon and lots of stars, but summer so it's warm on my skin – all of that. Those details, those choices. To Make-Believe really well you have to put in that effort. And if you practise, keep practising, maybe you can do it so easily that it feels like instinct. It feels . . . frictionless. So that's what I think must have happened. And it was sort of an emotional difference, as much as anything else. Two hours every evening, it was the bright part of my day, and the rest of the time it was like I was on hold. Like my life was on hold. Because none of the rest of it mattered, in comparison. I even, I stopped seeing friends, so I had time for Make-Believe. But I was still managing it. Was it the same, for you?'

'Pretty much,' he said.

'It was only when the cut-off stopped working. That's when it got out of control. And that was a gradual thing. I didn't notice at first – but then I realised, that session was two hours and twenty minutes; that one was almost three hours . . . It kept building up. And I know I should have said something, I should have reported it at work, but I was scared they'd reverse it, so I never said a word.' She pulled away slightly, smiled up at him. 'Anyway. Sorry, I'm talking so much and I wasn't going to talk about it.'

'No, I remember you saying.'

'Let's talk about something else instead. Let's talk about . . .' She couldn't think.

'Music?' he offered. 'I see you're a Thin Lizzy fan.'

'Mmm, kind of.' She looked down at her shirt, stretching it straight to see the picture. 'You approve?'

'As it happens, no. I hate Thin Lizzy. Take it off?'

When you enter Make-Believe, there's a transition between the world you know is real, and the world you Make-Believe. When the information coming from your body – from your flesh and your skin, your eyes and ears, nose and mouth – is muted in your brain, fading, fading to nothing at all. A moment of nothing, in which your neurons release a wash of opioids to counter the emptiness. A moment in which you float, perfected, lifted free of yourself – before the Make-Believe kicks in, and you rebuild the world as you want it to be. An infinite moment, over in seconds: like the threshold between waking and sleeping; like the moment of forgetting when your self dissolves and there's no such thing as you or him. A moment you could chase for ever, back in the real world.

It wasn't anything like that, with Lewis. Perhaps sleeping with him was more like the very first time in Make-Believe, the calibration sequence that matched the individual patterns of your neurological activity with the appropriate sensory experience. A series of instructions for physical actions: raise your right arm, your left, stretch, crouch, turn around, *turn around, keep going, lower, no, lower, yes, on top, now* – a series of instructions for imaginative tasks: Imagine that you are thirsty. Now, you are drinking a long cool glass of water . . . Imagine that you are extremely cold. You are freezing. Now, imagine the sensation of warm sun on your skin. Now remember a time when you felt extremely happy. *But what if remembering makes me sad?* Remember a time. Imagine a time. Imagine that you are happy.

Afterwards, in her dreams, everything muddles together. The new body memory, close to the surface, of heat and solidity: a man next to her, on her, under and in her. Deeper memory: his eyes, clear, blue. There's a place at the base of his back, that smooth white dip, where his skin is so thin she can see through to a web of broken veins, a fragile tracery. Elsewhere he is gold, the public parts of his skin, from being outside all the time: pale gold and freckled from the neck up, thighs and forearms down. All of this is clear and perfect in front of her while at the same time he's behind her, looping her in his arms, pulling her close so she leans, melts backwards into him, into all the ages of him – sixteen – nineteen – twenty-two . . . There is no need to wake, not ever to wake, from this soft, destroying dream, but she wakes anyway, and finds herself alone.

No: not alone. Lewis lay next to her. She turned sideways so they were just, just touching, from shoulder down to thigh. Listened to the creak of his breathing, a not-quite snore. Unselfconscious animal. Heard her own blood, the rhythm of herself. Imagined it was his heartbeat, shared through their glancing skin.

He was not what she'd lost – but he was here, and he was comfort. He was what she could have.

CHAPTER SEVEN

Cassie had tried, often, to pinpoint it: a moment when the present becomes inevitable. The last moment she could have chosen differently, steered herself and Alan both towards an ordinary, perfect future. Her dad's suggestion of a trip to Australia: *Both of you, come and try your luck*. Ideas of family reunion, of blood thicker than oceans. Struggling from one temp job to the next, and her dad's sister pulling in favours to promise a real graduate job in Melbourne. The logic of her leaving before Alan, of saving up once she got there, sending him the money to join her. Calling home, apart for the first time in their adult lives. Telling herself he'd always been unfiltered, unconventional – that it was only absence making her feel they'd been jolted into separate worlds, talking at angles to each other. No need to speak to Valerie, to raise her concerns, to book a flight on the first plane home.

If there was a moment, it was irretrievable – but as the bus carried her through the streets where she'd grown up, and on to the neighbouring village where Valerie had lived, she felt herself close alongside it: their past, and their possible future.

At the church, she was one of the first to arrive. The organ was playing: 'O Love That Will Not Let Me Go'. She slipped into a pew near the back; from here, she'd be able to see when Alan appeared.

She kept her breathing slow, inhaling the smell of damp hymn books and dust. Pushed her clammy hands up inside her sleeves as the chill seeped into her. The chapel was filling up well – Valerie had made herself central to the life of the village: singing in the local choir, sitting on the community council – but the front pew stayed empty, until a couple in their sixties walked the length of the aisle. Cassie recognised Alan's uncle and his wife, taking their place as family. She looked back at the entrance, expecting Alan to follow, and when a young man appeared, burly and fair, for a moment she thought it was him – but no, it was no one she recognised. A nephew, perhaps. And then the door was closed, and the organist fell silent. Cassie waited for the moment when everyone rose to their feet, stood with them, and 'Excuse me,' she muttered, 'So sorry' as she squeezed her way out from the pew, the minister intoning at her back, '. . . the eternal God is a dwelling place, and underneath are the everlasting arms.' She stepped into the porch, let the door swing shut behind her.

For Alan to miss his mother's memorial. It must be very bad with him, worse than ever before. There was only one place he could be – and this time, Cassie didn't hesitate to call. She knew what the receptionist would tell her, even before she asked. Yes, Alan was still with them; visiting hour, yes, that was still the same, from two until three.

Saying his name, hearing it said in someone else's voice. What she'd been putting off for days was suddenly urgent. Before she ended the call, she was already calculating: which bus she could catch, how long it would take. Whether she'd make it in time.

CHAPTER EIGHT

Low hills, land seamed into fields: yellow-ochre, acid yellow, soft green splashed with poppy-red. Villages, every high street the same. The single pub, the shop-and-post-office, the small-windowed cottages. Cassie watched through a window sandblasted with grime, not thinking of where she was going. Thinking instead of the first time Alan spoke to her, in the dinner queue at school.

She asks for chips, and the dinner lady shovels them onto her plate.

'Is that cos you're vegetarian?'

He's in the queue, right behind. But he can't be talking to her. She ignores him, slides her tray along towards the till.

'Are you? Vegetarian?'

She glances back – hiding the gesture with a flick of her hair, so that when she sees he's with someone else she won't have embarrassed herself by imagining he might ever speak to her. But he's not with anyone else. It is: it's her he's asking.

She stares, searching for any sign that he might be taking the piss. His eyes are wide, transparent.

'No,' she says, and turns away. Her skin is thrumming.

'Oh right,' he says to her back. 'I just thought you looked quite vegetarian.'

I just thought you looked quite vegetarian. She tells him: 'I'm not.'

'So you just – like chips.'

She almost laughs, because what is she meant to say to that? Yes, she likes chips. She likes them because you can tip them into a cardboard cup, take them outside, eat on your own without needing to sit apart from everyone – and they keep you warm; or you can imagine them keeping you warm.

Cassie swayed as the driver turned left. She glanced down at her screen, checking how far they'd come. Remembered the first time she'd visited, Meg in the passenger seat for moral support, chatting through her nerves like they were on a day trip; the return journey, the two of them silent, Cassie nudging the radio up, up a bit more. By bus, it was a longer journey, a roundabout route that linked a dozen villages and towns.

At last, her screen pinged. The arrow flickered, in the centre of a pulsing bullseye. She'd reached her stop.

It took all of three minutes to walk through the village. The standard pub, shop and bus shelter was all. She kept on into the countryside, checking her map to make sure she was heading in the right direction, stepping every so often into the verge to let the cars shoot past. The road sloped up – farmland on either side, wheat fields patterned in pale strips – and she could see nothing but the brow of the hill, a line against the sky that didn't seem to be coming any closer. It took twenty minutes to reach the top. Just ahead was a turning – and now she recognised the road. This was the way she'd come before, in the car. She was almost there.

The second time he speaks to her is a few days later. It's like he's done it on purpose, slipped into the queue behind her.

'Same again?' he asks, as the chips land on her plate.

'Yep,' she agrees. Same again.

The dinner lady asks what he's wanting.

'Chips, please,' he says – and whatever he's up to, it's making her want to smile.

'Is that cos you're vegetarian?' she asks.

'I am, actually. Well, actually, I'm kind of just trying it out. There's not much, you know, if you are vegetarian.' He looks at the lasagne, the chicken curry, the fishcakes, and his face is mock-sorrowful.

'Salad?'

'Mmm.' He frowns. 'Yeah, I suppose.'

She pays, takes her tray to the drinks stand and tips

her chips into a cup. She can feel him follow her. Feel him standing right beside her.

'OK if I sit with you?'

For a moment she doesn't know what to say. Then: 'I'm going outside,' she tells him.

'Aye, I know,' he says. 'I've seen you before.'

He does just like her, pours his chips into a cup, spilling them over the edges.

'Is it OK if I come with you?'

They stare at each other.

'Yeah,' she says. 'OK.'

Later, she asks him if this is something he often does – striking up random conversations in the dinner queue.

'Aye,' he says, 'sometimes. Maybe. If it's someone I want to be friends with.' His eyes are as wide as ever, a darker shade of blue. He says, 'If it's someone I fancy.'

It was discreet, unsigned, the turning for Raphael House. It opened into a gravel drive that crunched under her feet, curving off towards a building arranged as three sides of a rectangle and set in front of a hill, a small patch of woodland. She had been pleased, the first time she came, thinking the wood and the hill might help him feel at home. The hospital, though, was nothing like a home. A low blocky building, smooth and drab in mustard render, with an ugly glass portico jutting over a sliding door.

She glanced at her screen. Somehow, despite the endless bus journey and the uphill walk, she was ten minutes early. They would let her wait inside, she was sure – but instead she turned, skirted the building, following the path that led around the back of the hospital.

She wished it could have been harder to find him. Wished it could be impossible. For her, selfishly; but more than anything, she wished it for him. Over a year since she'd seen him last, and it seemed like nothing had changed.

But it would have to change now, or so she guessed. She couldn't imagine how Valerie had been covering the fees for so long. Raphael House was a private facility, after all, part of the Chrysalis Healthcare Group. And now Valerie was gone . . . The house would be sold, perhaps; the money used to make sure Alan could stay a while longer. That was the best worst-case scenario.

She was near him now, walking down the side of the wing that housed his ward, passing right under the window she thought was his. Here, by the fire exit, there was a paved area with a bench half-hidden by a stand of bamboo. She sat, and her foot knocked against a flowerpot filled with cigarette ends. Not from patients, she guessed, but staff on their breaks.

It was overdue, this visit. To sit and listen, or try and talk: it shouldn't be too much to offer. It was how he'd saved her, kind of, by talking. Like how he'd asked straight out that time: 'Is it right that your mum died?' That's how he said it, like it was just another question. *Are you vegetarian? Is Cassie short for Cassandra? Do you not have any friends at school? Is it right that your mum died?* Like he wasn't scared of asking, or scared of Cassie, or of Cassie's dead mum.

'Cos I heard people talking, but – people say lots of stuff, eh, so I wasn't sure.'

'Yeah, well. Not to me they don't. They talk *about* me, not *to* me.'

He's holding her hand – loosely, lightly, not a loaded squeeze to accompany a difficult conversation. He just is. He just does. 'What happened?' he says. 'Was she ill for a long time or – or do you not want to talk about it. Sorry, if you don't want to.'

She does, and she doesn't, and she does. No one else asks. No one asks: *What's it like for you?* Not since Meg left for uni. Not her dad, and not any of the teachers. Not the girls who'd been her friends till life got shit and they all freaked out and scurried away. So she's forgotten how to talk. How to be herself with someone else. How to not be on her own. She keeps waiting for him to see the darkness around her, inside her, and run – fucking run, a million miles. Instead he's lit something: a match, a candle, an emergency flare. Instead, he's cracked her open, and let the light creep in.

This bench: it was where she had come on her final visit, last spring – after the orderlies had arrived to settle him down. This was where she had sat, needing an interlude before she got back in the car, before she had to drive. Here, gazing up at the hill, at birch and willow blurring as she blinked and scrubbed her eyes, while on the other side of the wall she knew Alan was fighting a forced sleep. Fighting, and losing. Where, just for a moment, she'd acknowledged the unthinkable thought: that what he was living was not a life. That she wished she could grieve for the loss of him. Where she'd fumbled in her satchel for a tissue, closed her hand instead round the smooth case of her receiver. A risk, to Make-Believe right there, outside and alone, but the real world was somewhere she hadn't been able to bear. To escape, just for a short while, to a place that wasn't cruel; to push him out of her head, that poor copy of him—

—where she'd come back to reality two hours later, receiver still in place and the bones of her arse aching, damp creeping through her jeans – the contrast making her gasp, bending her double so she cried out as her spine locked and cracked at the too-sudden movement. The last drifts of Make-Believe tailing away, leaving her bleak and real: hollow, slumped with her headache in numb hands. Knowing that something was different, that she'd never Believed like that before. That for the very first time, she'd succeeded in imagining something so technicoloured, so perfectly realised that, even as she staggered stiff and cold back to her car, anticipation stretched inside her. Counting the hours: how long, till she could try it again? How long before she could go back?

Cassie's screen read 1.59. She stood, and retraced her steps to the front of the hospital.

Reception was determinedly non-clinical. She remembered the butterfly logo, its wings outspread. The friendly yellow curve of desk in an off-white space.

Eggs, sunny side up. She gave her name, told the woman behind the glass who it was she'd come to visit, and an orderly was summoned to collect her – a man in his fifties with his hair in a sleek grey ponytail. *Paul*, said his name tag.

Paul led her in the opposite direction from the one she'd have chosen: into the block that formed the left arm of the hospital, till they reached a heavy door with a strip of meshed safety glass that chopped the corridor beyond into hundreds of tiny squares. He pressed his palm against the security panel, then pulled a card from the neck of his shirt and swiped it across. With a faint click, the door released. Cassie felt her hands sweating as she followed him through. Last time she'd visited, there had been a simple intercom system to gain access to the ward.

The door closed behind them. For a moment they were nowhere. Another door faced them, identical, as though not even air was allowed in and out. The orderly checked that the door at their backs had clicked and locked before going through the same procedure again: press the panel, swipe the card.

'He's locked in here?' she asked, and he turned, looked at her for the first time.

'You've not been to see him before?'

'Yes but – a while ago. He wasn't here, he was—' She gestured off to her right.

'Aye, well, he's been in the locked ward ever since I've been in the job.'

'He used to be able to go in and out. Go outside.'

'There's a courtyard,' said Paul. 'But Alan'll be in his room. Prefers to stay in his room. Some of them do.' He checked that the second door had locked, then he started down the corridor.

'You know it was his mother's memorial today?'

'I did hear she'd passed away,' he said. 'I was sorry to hear it. Nice lady, she was.'

'So Alan wasn't well enough to go?'

Paul shook his head. His face said *No danger*, but what he actually said was, 'Hen, you'll need to ask the doctors about that.'

Sweat dampened her underarms, the top of her lip; the heating was turned up to tropical. The walls were the same cheerful yellow as the desk at reception, with glass doors opening off to both sides. Through a series of large windows she glimpsed a bright room that looked like a coffee shop, with patients settled in armchairs and sofas; another room with long trestles – a cafeteria, perhaps, or an activity room. Further along, the doors changed from see-through to solid, each bearing a number, and a handwritten name on a cardboard slip.

As they passed number 5 the door swung open, and a man stepped out.

'Alright there, Jimmy?' said the orderly.

If Cassie was hot, Jimmy must have been melting, swaddled in layer upon layer of jumpers, sporting a blanket as a shawl. He nodded at Paul, frowned at Cassie, face settling easily into disapproving folds. She looked away, anxious that eye contact might seem like challenge, or invitation. Felt his stare on her back as they carried on down the hall.

At number 12, the orderly stopped. Knocked on the door, and pushed it open.

'Alan. I've brought you a visitor.'

Don't go, she said inside her head – *please, don't go* – but Paul stepped aside, and then she was alone.

No. Not alone.

He was sitting with his back to a small high window, a book on his lap, one finger inserted into the pages, ready to turn over. He had lifted his head at Paul's voice; now he looked back down again.

She stood in the doorway, telling herself this was him. This was Alan. If she'd seen him in the street, she doubted she would have recognised him. His hair had grown long, darkened to a dull brown threaded with grey. Last time she was here, he'd put on some weight – the drugs, the lack of activity – but now he strained the seams of an extra-large plaid shirt, bulked in a chair with his stick balanced against its arm. She glanced at his feet, encased in unlaced canvas trainers, the left one still twisted inward. Remembered that long-distance call in the middle of the night, Valerie telling her Alan was fine not fine—Valerie explaining what Alan had done: how, in the flat Cassie had shared with him till she'd left for Australia, he had balanced on the first floor sill, spread his arms, leant further and further. Thinking he'd fly. Believing he'd slip into air like water.

Now, at the entrance to his room, Cassie blinked, and for a moment saw him leaping, not from a window to the street below, but to save a goal. Monday nights, after school, she'd watch him sometimes, running forward and back in front of the net, flinging himself towards the ball, stretched out long and thin like he trusts the air to catch him. On Tuesday nights her fingers skirt round grazes and bruises, fresh pink scrapes and bluish shadows on the white of him, on the bones of his hips, his elbows and knees.

She snapped the memory shut. Wanting to keep it intact, a perfect miniature, far away from here.

'Alan.'

Slowly, he raised his head. In the beard that trailed down to the barrel of his chest, she caught the faintest glint of red. The beard blurred his mouth, concealed the whole lower half of his face; what skin was visible was puffed, pale as a corpse. When was the last time the sun had touched him? The outside air? If she could see his eyes, she might recognise him – but they were concealed by the glasses that sat on marshmallow cheeks, thick-lensed and heavy-framed. The bright overhead light flashed off the glass, hiding him behind another layer.

She couldn't just hover by the door. She took a few paces into the room. It was tidy, plain: the mirror of the ward he'd been in before. A single bed, a navy blue duvet. Wardrobe, bedside table made of veneered chipboard. The chair Alan occupied was the only one in the room. She didn't want to sit on his bed; she stayed standing, but looking down on him felt wrong, like she was threatening him, so she crouched, and then it was like talking to a child. In the end she gave up, and perched herself on the very edge of the mattress.

He hadn't said a word. Just watched, his finger still inside the book, ready to turn.

'Hi,' she said. 'Do you . . . I don't know if you recognise me?'

He moved his head, slight, definite: *No*.

'Cassie.'

Shake: *No*.

'Remember, from—' Where? From everywhere; from for ever. 'Your girlfriend Cassie.'

No.

'Come on, you must.' She was smiling, trying to make a joke of it. But there was no joke, and no must. No rule, no law, that just because something had happened, been important, been everything, it had to be remembered. Only, if it wasn't remembered, how could she be sure it had happened at all? If she had only herself to rely on, it might as well be something she'd imagined – her and Alan, all their years together.

'Listen,' she said, leaning in. 'I'm so sorry about your mum.'

His face didn't change. She wasn't sure which was more disconcerting: the way he'd been when he first came to Raphael House, talking with his ordinary, open enthusiasm about mutual friends who didn't exist, about all the conversations he'd had with people who were dead, people who were famous, people who were dead and famous. How he'd been on her last visit: incoherent and urgent, his stare intense and apparently unseeing. Or this. Silence. Absence. Nothing. Perhaps he didn't understand that Valerie was gone. Perhaps she shouldn't have mentioned it. She gazed round his room, looking for something to talk about, something that might spark some communication between them. Apart from a built-in screen there was nothing on the walls. A mug on the bedside table, and a photo of Valerie in winter hat and scarf, squinting into sun.

'The guy, Paul, he said you don't go out. In the courtyard. Don't you miss the sun?' She hated her voice. It was a public voice, a jollying voice, as if she were a nurse. 'Are you – are you even in there?'

In a film, if she was sitting at her lover's bedside, with him in a coma or whatever – basically unable to communicate for some reason more romantic than severe mental illness – in this film, she would tell him stories from their life together. She'd say, *Remember chips?* She'd tell story after story, and eventually – zoom in, close-up – it would happen: a flicker of recognition, and the audience would know the happy ending was on its way.

She leant in further, knowing she shouldn't, unable to stop herself searching. Trying to see behind his glasses. 'Are you in there?'

The book slid from his lap, flipped itself shut. *Cool Science for Kids.*

'Alan? Are you there?'

'No.'

His voice startled her. 'OK,' she said, and pulled away, palms up: *Look, I'm backing off.*

His head was angled now so she could see through the glass of his lenses, but his eyes were squeezed shut. His hands made fists in his lap. Sealed off from her and the whole of the world – just the way she used to cut off, closed eyes and fists, hunched into herself. In Alan's room, upstairs, in his mum's house. She could feel the duvet tangling round her bare feet, feel her chin pushed into her knees, fists pressed against her head. The times when missing her mum had caught her afresh in its absolute unfairness, and stirred itself up with the guilt of forgetting to be sad. When Alan had said *I'm here it's OK it's OK*, his hands on her arms, and she'd wanted to lift her head, to open her eyes, to soften her fists and say *Yes*, say *I know* say *I will be OK.*

And then she remembered the code.

They'd learnt it so they could speak in maths class. Like T-shirts under school shirts: secret messages. Sitting two desks back from him, across the aisle. *Tap tap*, her biro on the table. *Tap tap*, his dancing fingers. *Dash, dash, dash. Dash dot dash.* Morse code.

You could do it with drumming, with squeezing. You could do it by clenching and unclenching your fist. You could do it with your eyes closed and your knees folded up to your chin.

Dot dash dot dot. Dash, dash, dash. Dot dot dot dash. Dot.

And it would help: those gentle measured beats. Building them into letters, into words. Eventually she would dot dash back: O-K.

Like sin, cos and tan, it was still there, lodged deep in her brain.

She tapped it out on her knee, slow, careful, not sure if he'd hear. If he was even listening.

H
E
L
L
O

Behind the beard she could see his lips moving, straggles of hair drawing in and puffing out. Chest rising and falling. Breath coming fast. Was he trying to speak to her? His eyes stayed shut.

She reached towards him, to the wooden arm of his chair, a couple of inches from where his elbow rested.

O
K

A pause.

O
K

She could hear now: he was muttering, under his breath, like a mantra or a spell. '*No* no no no no. *No* no no no no.'

'*Yes*,' she said, and began to tap again – hand close to his arm, almost touching.

A single movement: his body jerking, his fist shooting out to punch her away – and she was on her feet, scrambling back—'*No no no no no*—' His hands were raised now, clutching his head. Scrubbing at his hair, left hand tugging and worrying. The heavy glasses jerked free, fell to the floor – and at the side of his ear she glimpsed a patch of skin, angry red. A scar, healed and re-opened – around it, hair pulled out by the roots. Fingers scrabbling, sharp-nailed. Her fists pressed to her mouth: she was backed against the door now, wanting to shout for a nurse or an orderly, wanting to escape but something making her stay where she was. Stay still, so still that the breath was trapped inside her, till he slowed the scratching, the rat-like scrabbling. Till he slowed, and stopped. Till the muttering tailed away.

She waited another minute, then a minute more. He lowered his hands, eventually. Laid them in his lap. His eyes stayed closed. Wetness shone on his puffed-up cheeks.

She should leave, now, right now.

Her satchel was lying on the floor, beside his bed.

She spoke softly: 'I'm just going to get my bag.'

He didn't respond.

She took a step towards him, then a couple more. Crouched. The lace of his shoe snaked across the carpet, grey and frayed. She looked away from the uncanny angle of his foot. Picked up the bag, and retreated once again.

When he lifted his head, his beard was stuck in damp strands round his mouth. There was no recognition in his watery stare: if she could see anything there, it was fear. With difficulty, he bent to collect his book and his glasses. Fitted the specs back onto his face and folded the book open, seemingly at random. A greasy smear obliterated his left eye; he made no attempt to wipe the lens clean.

There was nothing of Alan there. There was only a body slumped in a chair, waiting to turn the page.

CHAPTER NINE

He had thought he was on an island, awake with the book safe in his hands, but they could get in anywhere. Back again, in her disguise, making her look the way she used to, making her walk into his room in the broad daylight – wasn't that new? But they could make the daylight too, wide as the sky, a staring eye – just as they could speak in her voice. Different from all their everyday voices which were loud, or like rusting metal, or there were many of them, all at once, saying the same things or different things, or whispering, gentling, lulling until he forgot to guard against them and then – then they burst inside his brain – exploded him into nothing, into nothing but voices; but this voice, now, was hers. It was clever, yes, very clever, light and quick – the river running low at the back of the garden. *Sorry*, she said, and the word sliced through him. *You miss the sun*, she said, and her hair would be sun flowing through his fingers, or soft so soft against his face, but they could make that happen too. *But* but, however clever, they'd made a mistake – because a long time ago she had flown away to the far side of the world, and her flying had fixed her. Her pinned to a present that became the past, and him moving further and further away into the future that became the present – so that when her face on the screen said *come* it was light from a star, it was old light, so that when she said *Follow me like we agreed*, so that when she said *Please* she was talking squint, wrong-angled – light and sound fired at the place where he used to be, coming dim from the far-off past. And that was the mistake, because now – now, the full beam of her gave them away. She was too bright too close too clear. She was too blood too breath too skin. She was too much herself, and not her self at all.

Under his fingers was paper, were pages soft from turning. Under his fingers were facts, nailed to the page. Things that were fixed and couldn't be altered, like page 27 the speed of light is 299,792,458 metres per second, like page 35 humans have forty-six chromosomes, like page 52 giraffes rarely sleep and never lie down. Those were the facts and so long as he kept a hold of the book they couldn't change any of it, and that's how he hung on to what was real – by the skin of its scruff, by the teeth of its tail – that's how he hung on as they crawled inside and made him do what you did when you found you were not on an island after all.

Are you in there, they said in her voice, and grew bigger and closer and stared at him out of her eyes, and he tried to cling on but the facts slid away. He closed his eyes to keep her out but she was still there. She was breathing. They could make her breathe. They could stretch a skin of daylight across the dark, drum-tight across the squirming shuddering dark, and they drummed on it, drummed on the broad skin of the fake daylight, beat at his clenched mind, and each beat was a seed forced inside him, to crack and sprout and twist – into messages – *OK* into words – *HELLO* into lies – *OK – OK – NO*—

He flung it up, a wall of *NO!* and the lies fell back but were buried still inside him – he could feel them itching, hatching – *there*, right *there* – and he scraped and scratched at the part of his skull where the darkness bred, till the hot red pain was like the speed of light, a fact he could hang onto – you could be on an island and then not, you could never be certain, on an island and suddenly drowning – and they would come disguised, come as Paul, Mike, Ken, as men with strong arms and a needle, and after that there would be no way out – so he hung on to the sharpness in his head, and breathed, and kept his eyes. Shut. Tight.

Wait. Wait.

Open?

She was small now. Far away. Safer. She was not a fact, so he turned away from her. His book was there, on the floor. He reached for it, let the soft pages fall open. Page 14. The deepest part of the ocean is 35,797 feet. That was a fact. His left-hand nails were rimmed with red, with plasma fifty-five per cent, with erythrocytes leukocytes platelets forty-five per cent. That was another fact.

CHAPTER TEN

She made herself walk. Back along the hallway, counting down the numbered doors. When she reached the big windows into the day rooms, she stopped – looking for someone in uniform, someone with a staff tag. But the room with the long trestles was deserted, and next door, as far as she could tell, was occupied only by patients: half a dozen women and men. Though the seats had been sociably arranged round low coffee tables, each patient had dragged his or her chair away from its group, angled it alone to face the TV screen. None of them noticed her staring in through the glass – or if anyone did, they paid her no attention. The swaddled man was there, frowning up at the screen, and a dark-skinned man who seemed to be talking, to himself or to the TV. One overweight woman, one who was very thin. And a young woman in figure-hugging clothes, full make-up and a high, shiny ponytail, looking as if she was waiting for a date. She sat with one arm wrapped across her chest, and her other hand cupping her ear; her fingers burrowed into her dark hair, absently massaging her scalp, till the ponytail sat squint and began to come undone. As Cassie watched, the woman suddenly tugged her hair free, shook it out and smoothed it back and up, fastening it into a new ponytail. She sat for a moment, arms folded, before her hand slid up to her head once more, started to rub again.

Further along on the other side of the corridor, Cassie glimpsed a uniformed figure through a half-open door. A nurse, she guessed. He was standing at a high desk, she saw as she approached, head bent over a pile of papers.

'Excuse me . . .'

He raised his head. Studied her briefly. 'Can I help?'

'Yes. Please. I'm visiting Alan Lauder.'

'Oh, yes?' A curious look flitted across his face. 'If you're finished, I'll get someone to take you out—'

'I wanted to ask about something.'

The nurse stood up straight, head tilted back to look down at her; he folded his arms, and didn't say anything.

'Why is he here? I mean not in the other ward? When I came before he was in another ward – he wasn't locked in like this, he could go outside.'

A shake of the head. 'I can't give you any information

relating to Alan's specific condition, unless you're down as next of kin.'

He knew fine well she wasn't next of kin. 'No,' she said. 'But his mother, I don't know if it says in his files somewhere, she was his next of kin and she's passed away, so—'

'I can tell you that patients are admitted to this ward either because they pose a risk to themselves, or because they are a danger to others.' He gave a little shrug, as if to say: *Draw your own conclusions.*

'He's got a scar on his head,' she said. Again, there was no reply. 'Why? How did he get it?'

'As I've said, I can't give you any information of that kind. Details about the patients' treatment are confidential. I can only discuss Alan's treatment with his next of kin.'

'But who, now his mother's gone? Who's going to look after him? Who's going to pay for him to be here?'

'There's no problem with that,' said the nurse. Cassie opened her mouth, ready to press for more, but he was hailing one of the orderlies. 'Ken,' he said, 'if you wouldn't mind showing this lady out.'

Back through the airlock, back to reception with its sunny yellow desk. Her signature in a book, to prove she'd left the building. Walking, still walking, through the sliding door – out onto the gravel drive – and now she let herself speed up, jogging along the dirt track, round the back of the hospital. Past the wing she'd thought was his, back to the bamboo screen and the hidden bench where she perched, arms tight across her chest, eyes fixed blankly on the ground.

With the building at your back, you could imagine it didn't exist.

The scar. She shuddered, felt the sweat chill on her face. When her mum had got really sick, the cat had started overgrooming. He would twist round and rip the fur from his hind legs, leaving bald, reddened patches. That's what Alan had reminded her of.

You would almost think it was a rash from a receiver. She'd had them before, those times when she'd Believed for hours, after the cut-off had stopped working – head sideways on the pillow so the metal of the receiver was pushed hard up against her ear, the bony skin behind. But that was impossible. There was no way a patient at Raphael House would be allowed into Make-Believe. They could never provide the doctor's slip, the clean bill of mental health, that was a prerequisite for signing up. Alan would have liked it in Make-Believe, would probably have Believed some really wild stuff, but by the time it was launched he'd been sectioned for well over a year.

Cassie lifted her gaze from the fag-end flowerpot at her feet, as something occurred to her. That nurse. He'd tried to tell her nothing, and in doing so had told her something – something that felt significant. Because if Alan had hit his head off the wardrobe, or got in a fight with another patient, or believed again that he could fly and dived off the end of the bed – that wouldn't be confidential, would it? It wouldn't be part of his treatment.

They used to operate on people with schizophrenia. Not that long ago, either. Used to dig right into their brains, and slice the nerves apart. But lobotomies didn't happen any more, did they – and if they did, wouldn't the scars be somewhere else? Cassie touched her temples, felt the flick of her pulse against her fingertips.

In the trees, in the distance, something moved – made her jump. Just a bird, or a squirrel. She shook her head, impatient with herself. There was nothing lurking here. God, she hardly knew what she was thinking. She had to get home. She checked her screen: half an hour before the next bus was due. Started back along the path.

Before, when she'd found herself there stiff and cold and alone as the afternoon ebbed into evening, the worst thing was what she'd left behind. Or rather, that was the best thing – the best ever – and the worst was knowing it was only Make-Believe. *Better Than Real* was one of their straplines, and yeah, she'd Believed plenty of amazing stuff before, had flown and changed sex, been a basking shark, a superhero made of flame – but she'd never emerged and felt the world back-to-front like that. Like she'd spent two bright hours in her real life, then been vomited into a washed-out dream called reality. And the strangest part of it all was that she'd Make-Believed Alan before – of course she had – but she'd always got him wrong: flat, or blurred, or with bits of other people mixed in by mistake. She would re-run memories, and while parts of them would come alive, the rest lay dead around her – so she'd get the blue smell of his deodorant, but not the lightness of his voice, would Believe his sleeping face up close, but not his deep, slow breath. And always he would do and say just what she made him. He couldn't surprise her, because she couldn't surprise herself. Imagination wasn't enough.

Except for when it was.

When she'd mentioned it to the tech team the following Monday, tried to report it as a glitch, she found it hard to put into words what the difference had been. *Brighter, or something*, she'd said. *Less clear? I don't know.* The guy from tech had refrained from rolling his eyes, just. *But what was actually wrong?* he'd asked. And she'd shrugged. Because nothing was wrong, and everything was right.

If it wasn't a glitch, perhaps it was like training your body: you pushed it and pushed it and eventually you were faster or stronger than you'd ever thought possible. She had made some kind of leap, that afternoon, had unlocked an imaginative capacity she never could have guessed at. And from then on, there was no point to swimming with dolphins or interspace travel. Those were a child's games. From then, it was Alan, always Alan – the way it always had been. And from then she couldn't bring herself to return to Raphael House, to endure the terrible remnants of him. Not when she could Make him, Believe him, every night the way he ought to be.

As she left the path and rejoined the drive, her crunching steps grew steadily faster. Her whole body wanted to run, to leave this place behind. Leave *him* behind. The slumped body that was meant to be Alan.

She kept on seeing him. His hand jumping to the side of his head. And she saw Lewis too, hand lifting to his ear – and she felt that same urge to movement in herself. In her arm, to rise. In her fingers, to touch.

FREQUENTLY ASKED QUESTIONS

Q. How do I enter and leave Make-Believe™?

A. The first time you enter the world of Make-Believe™, simply use the single-dose nasal spray to introduce our specially engineered biomolecules to your brain – exactly as you might use a smart drug spray to enhance your mental performance. It's these clever biomolecules that will translate your wildest imaginings into virtual reality. Then just pop your receiver onto your ear, and you're ready to begin.

Once you've entered Make-Believe™, each session will automatically time-out when you've used your daily limit of two hours – but you can end your Make-Believe™ session at any time, just by thinking your preset exit command. Don't worry, you don't need to understand how all this works! All you need to know is that you're in control. You can enter and leave Make-Believe™ whenever you choose.

'Chips,' he said. 'You just like chips.'

There was no one else around, so he had to be talking to her.

'I've always liked that vegetarian way you look, but you could do with some blood. Some red meat. An enormous steak. Maybe just some vitamins. Leafy greens.'

'Salad?'

'Mmm. Yeah, I suppose.'

'You've never said that before; about blood.'

'When would I have said it before?'

'Other times, when we've been here.'

'But we've not been here before. Or I haven't, at least. Where is here, come to think of it?'

It comes gradually into focus. First there's the sound: a soft drumming, a forest of dot dot dots.

'It's raining on our tent. Funny. I thought the sun was out.'

But they're not in a tent. Leaves. Above them, a glossy canopy, dark green. Big tropical looking leaves, hand-sized, dinner-plate-sized.

'It's raining, but it's not cold. At least, are you cold?'

'A bit.' She's not cold, not at all.

'Here.'

His hug is meltingly warm. She can feel her limbs grow heavy, like all the energy, all the determination the hard work of standing alone, of moving alone, is ebbing away. It is such a relief.

'Oh . . .' he says, long and soft, and she knows he is feeling the same.

'What's the rain saying?' she asks. 'It's like it's saying something, but it's too fast. Is it all dots, or are there dashes?'

'I don't want to listen to that,' he says, 'there's too much of it – too many voices and all at once.'

It fades as he speaks, diminishing, almost gone, just the odd fat droplet falling from the tip of a leaf.

'I want to listen to just your voice.'

'Makes a change,' she says. 'You don't usually.'

'Hey,' he says. 'I was good at that, you always told me I was. A good listener.'

'Oh yeah. Sure: before. Not lately. You were a better talker, mind, you've always been a totally first-class talker.' She means it, and her meaning it glows from her, yellow and bright, and they're both lit up, delighted.

'Say something else nice.'

'I love you?'

'Yes.'

'Your turn: say something nice.'

'Um. You're the bonniest vegetarian I know.'

She punches him, a play punch.

'Vegetarian or not, you're the one for me. Listen, do you remember that time . . . up by the falls?'

'Summer,' she said. 'Or maybe it wasn't; just in my head it's always summer. Late summer.'

'That'll do. So long as it's warm enough still to take off our clothes.'

'Go there now?'

'Yes. Please.'

The raindrops are gone. Instead, water laughing, water falling.

'That's good. It's softer than it was.'

'I remember twigs. Scratchy. I made you go underneath.'

'I was a gentleman.'

'There you go: feather bed for the gentleman.'

'Much appreciated. I would lie on a bed of stones for you . . .'

'I can do stones. If that's what you're into.'

'No, thank you, I'll keep this, whatever it is. Bed of clouds, bed of delight . . .'

'You've been playing football?' Bruise. Bruise. She points them out: one on his bicep. One on his thigh.

'If you like. You like me damaged?'

'Not damaged. Perhaps – it makes you more real.'

Him pulling back. 'Oh, Cassie. How am I not real? Don't you believe in me? Here, you're not going to cry? Eh?'

'I'm not, if you don't want me to.'

'Not. Definitely not. Tears begone. That's better.'

He kisses her eyelids, then her lips.

'Alan. I believe in you. It's the other you I don't believe in.'

'Him – let's not talk about him. Let's not talk at all, for a bit. Mm-hm?'

'Mm-hm.'

CHAPTER ELEVEN

Lewis was calling, from up ahead. He'd reached the curve of the hill.

'The view – it's amazing!'

She had no breath to shout a reply, couldn't lift a hand to wave. The track was taking all her strength, all her focus to ride; her boneshaker would never have coped, but this mountain bike was a joy, strong and flexible, eating the hills. She hadn't asked where it came from: a small-framed Norco, shiny purple, stashed in the cupboard in his hall, needing nothing more than air in its tyres and a squirt of lube on the chain. Ex-girlfriend or ex-flatmate, it had to be one or the other, but Lewis hadn't offered and Cassie wasn't going to ask. Letting him guard his past meant she could keep on guarding hers.

She yanked up, jumped a hollow in the dirt, plunged forward, losing altitude, then threw all her weight on the pedals to climb uphill again. She was nothing but action, burning muscles and gasping lungs – no thought, just focus, just staying upright, riding the trail. It was the last day of the sunshine. The weather was poised to turn, the way it so often did at the start of July, and the forecast said rain by tomorrow. Lewis had time off owed to him, and she had no assignment deadlines. There was nothing that couldn't wait. A day out had been her suggestion; in the month since they'd met, they'd barely left his flat. *Not that I don't like your kitchen*, she'd said, *and your bedroom too, but perhaps we could spend some time together outwith these four walls.*

She'd thought he might take the chance, finally, to introduce her to some of his friends – not that she was about to arrange them a night out with Harrie, or Nicol . . . But instead he'd chosen a bike ride, just the two of them. They'd have the hills to themselves, he'd said, on a weekday – and he'd been right. A few dog-walkers, a hiking group with poles and backpacks; those were the only people they'd passed.

She pushed harder, legs burning. Powered on towards the top – and forgot the pain of the climb.

'*Wow*.' It was a gasp – all she could manage, draped forwards over her handlebars, ribcage heaving as she chased her breath. The reservoir spread itself out before them, mirror-smooth, reflecting the high blue overhead. Patient. Perfect. Sun startled off the surface, flashing white.

'Can you swim?' she asked. 'Swim here?'

Lewis gestured towards a sign: DANGER. 'You're not meant to. You can get pulled under, apparently.'

'But – it's so still . . . D'you think people do swim, ever?'

'I bet they do, yeah. Kids jumping in for a dare. People coming up here with a few beers, and suddenly it seems like a good idea. Never seen it myself, but . . . I've seen people fishing here, plenty of times.'

'There's fish?'

'The guys with the rods seem to think so. Ready for lunch?'

They dropped their bikes at the top of the slope, made their way down to the water. Their side of the reservoir was sheltered; a little further out, wind rippled pale through the grass. Cassie let herself fall back, spread out flat. The day wasn't hot, but she was burning up from an hour's hard cycling. She closed her eyes, let the breeze mop her face. Meanwhile Lewis was unpacking his pannier, laying out a picnic. Sandwiches. Apples. Chocolate. Tea.

Cassie opened one eye. 'Water?'

He handed her the canteen, and she sat up to drink. Her breath was back to normal now, more or less. She drank and drank till the canteen was half empty, then picked up a sandwich, dramatically hungry all of a sudden.

'I can't believe,' she said between mouthfuls, 'I've never been up here before.'

'Your bike would have disintegrated in five minutes flat!'

'No – but even walking . . . Have you been here a lot?'

'Do I come here often?' Lewis was smiling. 'Yeah. I used to. It's a while, though, since I came last.'

'Listen.' Cassie tilted her head, and Lewis raised his eyebrows in a question. 'Exactly,' she said. 'It's just – perfect quiet. It's like being above the whole world. It's like being in a dream. It's not, is it? We're not dreaming?' He reached out, gently pinched her waist, and she batted his hand away. 'No, can't be. You don't get ticklish in a dream.' She finished her sandwich, started on a second. 'It does seem like a dream sometimes. Us, I mean.'

'I'm your dream man? Really?'

'Not that,' she said. Though he was, in a way; because every night as she slept beside him he followed her into her unconscious, into dreams soft and sweet enough that sometimes she couldn't be sure whether something had really occurred – a touch, a look, a conversation – or had happened only in her sleep. 'No, what I mean is, it's so separate from everything else, you and me. From the rest of my life. It all feels so . . . unlikely.'

'I know what you mean. I am real, though, I promise.'

She gave his arm a mock-punch, prompting a yelp. 'Just testing. Maybe it's not like a dream up here. More like something from Make-Believe.'

'Except in Make-Believe there would be no DANGER. No currents.'

'And you'd be able to breathe underwater.'

'And I'd probably swap the ducks for mermaids.'

'Oh, you would?'

'Yeah, why not? Perched round the edges. Bobbing

up to say hello.' He waved at the water, sandwich in hand, at the ducks and gulls and moorhens sailing on the surface. 'I think they'd enrich the scene.'

'Sure. Very enriching.' She picked up an apple, polished it on the hem of her vest. She could stay here for ever, just her and the water. It was hard to believe there were fish in there, and currents that wanted to drag you down, invisible under the bright, smooth surface. It was hard to believe that the first time she'd seen Lewis, his shorts had offended her so. Now she let herself look at him, muscles and brown skin, easy and healthy and strong, propped back on his elbows, legs bent in front of him. When they were together she felt that, somehow, things were going to be OK; she liked the thought that being with her might make him feel the same.

'Do you iron them?' she asked.

'What? My shorts? Course I don't iron them. They come out of the wash like that. They're technical.'

'Ah. Technical.'

'You should get some.'

'What's wrong with my shorts?' She looked down at her legs, her denim cut-offs.

'Can't be that comfy in the saddle.'

'Yeah, but they didn't cost a hundred quid, so . . .' Immediately she wished she'd kept her mouth shut. She sounded chippy, and she hadn't meant to. He had bought the picnic; he'd been keeping her in dinner, and breakfast, and it was out of order to throw it back at him like that.

'You do look good in them, though,' she said, trying to make amends. 'So I guess they're worth it.'

'They totally are. They last for ever – and they're seam-free. No chafing.'

'Uh-huh. I'm finding them strangely less attractive now.'

'I'll just shut up, I think.'

'Good idea. Less talking. More eating.' She handed him the apple she'd been shining, chose another for herself, and began to twist the stalk. *A, B, C* – an old game, one she used to play with Meg. Each twist was a letter, and when the stalk fell off you had the first initial of the man you were going to marry. It was a loaded game, of course. You had to master a really vicious twist-and-tug to get yourself an A, and otherwise you were stuck with a Dave or an Ed, a Fraser or a Greig. *H, I, J* – the stalk came free before she reached L-for-Lewis. Kevin, Kieran, Khaled, whatever. Then for the surname you tapped the stalk against the fruit till the skin broke, but she couldn't be bothered with that. The whole game was ridiculous. She dropped the stalk, crunched into the apple. Chewed, swallowed. Turned to Lewis.

'You know what you were saying a while back. About Imagen losing subscribers.'

Lewis stared at her.

'And about, if we knew something that Imagen didn't want us to know?'

He frowned. 'I thought you didn't want to talk about that.'

'I know. It's just, you put it in my head, I suppose.' She waited for him to speak, but he stayed silent. 'Were you serious about it?'

'How do you mean?'

'Like, serious about using it, if we had something to bargain with.'

'Yeah,' he said instantly. 'Yeah. Absolutely.'

'Even knowing how much of a risk you'd be taking? You know what they did to me . . . that doesn't put you off?'

He stared out across the reservoir. Shook his head.

'And all so you can get back to Make-Believe?'

Lewis shrugged. Finished his second sandwich, and started on the apple she'd given him.

How come? That's what she wanted to ask. What could make it worth the risk – worth risking everything? Was it anything to do with the woman whose bike she was riding? But every question she asked, every answer he gave, allowed him an opening in return. So she swallowed her curiosity.

'Thing is,' she said, 'your idea about the drop in user figures? That those lost subscribers could be like us, that Imagen could be cutting them off? Well, I don't think it can be like that.'

'Why not?'

'It's the scale of it. All those hundreds of people, maybe a thousand of them. How could Imagen keep that quiet? All it would take is one single person to post something online, and it's out there.'

Lewis looked reluctant: he could see the sense in what she was saying, and she knew he didn't want to.

'I'm not saying we're the only two people who've been blacklisted,' she went on. 'Like you said, that's too much of a coincidence. I know there must be more of us. But I can't believe there's *that* many.'

'OK,' he said. 'Maybe not. But even if there's another fifty of us – even another ten – that's got to be serious, still. Otherwise why would they be so keen to make sure nobody knows?'

'Yeah. I guess so.' It was her turn to be unconvinced. 'And – if not . . . there might be something else, I suppose. Some other thing they don't want to shout about.'

'What kind of thing?'

She shook her head, gazed out at the water, at an upside-down puff of cloud drifting across the surface. 'Just thinking. Nothing particular.'

It was nothing she could explain. It was what she'd seen in Alan – that gesture – in the leap of his hand to his head. In the wound behind his ear. The girl with the ponytail, rubbing, scratching. A question, too unformed for words; a glimmer of a connection, between Alan and Make-Believe.

'You could be right, though,' Lewis was saying. 'There's loads of stuff they wouldn't want anyone looking at too closely – I'd imagine, anyway.'

'Like?'

'The kind of stuff people must get up to in Make-Believe. You know, they make such a big thing about

128

it not being moderated – the only limit is you, and all that. And the advertising's all, "Be a rock star, visit the moon", but the subtext – is that the right word?'

'Maybe. Depends what you're trying to say . . .'

'Well – they don't come out and say, "Live out your darkest, most illegal sexual fantasies", for instance, or "Murder your boss with impunity" – but that's part of it. And everyone knows it, but it's not real so it doesn't matter. But imagine if they had to release details of what everyone was getting up to.'

'I mean, the data's anonymised, so it wouldn't be like unmasking the paedophile next door, kind of thing. And there's less of the illegal stuff than you might think. Even with something so immersive, most people retain an awareness of – not of being watched, exactly, but of the possibility of being watched. But yeah, the categories we use – they use – for data mining and analysis: some of them are pretty disturbing. Wouldn't reflect well on the company. But if it's fantasy it's not illegal, is it. You could say Make-Believe provides a safe outlet for those kinds of urges. That's their argument, anyway.' Cassie took a last bite of her apple. Normally she would have eaten the lot, left only the stalk, but today the dark seeds nestling in pale flesh made her think of cockroaches breeding inside her walls. She dropped her core, and reached for the flask. 'Tea?'

'Please. So – what's the worst thing you've done?'

'Ow!' Cassie passed him a flask-lid cup, and blew on her hand where she'd splashed herself. 'In Make-Believe?'

He nodded. 'I'll share mine, if you share yours.'

She knew instantly; she just didn't know if she would confess it. The memory that still shamed her – in the visceral details of what she'd done, and in how it would be categorised (*Violence >> killing >> mammal; blood* – with no record of the remorse she'd felt). But perhaps Lewis would laugh. Perhaps the whole thing would lighten, become a silly joke.

'I killed a cat,' she said.

'A *cat*? Why would you kill a cat?'

'It was – I'd been working on data segmentation, and it's like we were saying, some of the categories . . . Rape, murder, torture. Physical violence, psychological violence. And you could see patterns: like with a small amount of people it was all the time, every day, that was just how they used Make-Believe, but others, it was more like a one-off. Just trying it out. Like someone asking themselves: *I wonder what it feels like to murder someone?*' She glanced at Lewis; he nodded slightly. She cleared her throat, and carried on. 'I wanted to see if I could understand – why you would do something like that. But not with a human, I couldn't . . . It's not in me. And now I think, thank God at least I didn't – because even though it's Make-Believe . . .' She took a sip of tea. It had a plastic taste from the thermos. 'It's like, you haven't *really* done it – but you've still done it. I'm not . . . I don't want to go into details.' (A cry like the scream of a terrified child; the sick crack, the soft give of its skull under the iron bar; the caved fur, and the blood, and the staved-in eye still staring—) 'But that's what I did, and that's why I did it. I had to force myself, and afterwards . . .' She swiped a hand through the air in front of her. 'I wiped it clean, completely clean. The mess, the . . . remains. Then I Make-Believed it alive again; but I still felt like I'd killed it.'

'You wish you hadn't done it,' said Lewis, and she nodded. 'But it's OK. I'm not judging.' Then he did exactly what she'd hoped; he made a joke. 'To be honest, I'm not much of a cat person myself.'

Her laugh was unconvincing. 'That's the stupid thing,' she said. 'I really am. That's why I chose a cat – to make it harder, more like a person. And I tell you what else: Pita knows. She can see straight into my soul – and it doesn't matter how many extra biscuits I feed her. But, so – if you're not a cat person – why do you have a cat?'

'Yeah – I kind of inherited her.' He held out his apple core. 'Do you think it's OK to chuck this in the water?'

'Probably not.'

He threw it instead into the long grass behind them. Snapped off some chocolate.

'Your turn,' she said.

'Alright, well – I didn't kill anyone. Or any *thing*. But maybe it was worse, what I did.' He looked at her, and there was a hardness in his expression. A distance she hadn't seen before. 'I hurt someone.'

'Hurt them. You mean . . . ?'

'I'm not going into details,' he echoed, 'but – badly, yes. And slowly. Intentionally. He deserved it.' He shrugged, drained his flask lid.

'And – do you wish you hadn't?'

'I don't wish anything, one way or the other. It made no difference. To anything. But I wouldn't do it again.'

For a minute they were quiet, staring at the deep glittering water. Then Cassie shook her hair back from her face. 'Worse things happen at sea,' she said. She wanted to wash it off, their whole conversation. 'I might go for a swim.'

'No, don't. Please don't.'

'Look. It's like a mirror. There's no way it's dangerous.'

'Cassie, come on. If you go in and there's a current and it drags you down, I've got to go in after you, and I really don't want to drown.'

'You wouldn't have to rescue me. On my own head be it.'

'Yeah, but I would. You can see that, right?'

Reluctantly, she supposed she could. 'Uch, really?'

'Anyway, where's your costume?'

She shot him a slow learner look.

'Oh. Well, maybe I wouldn't mind if you had just a little swim, right at the edge . . . stop it!' Cassie's apple core bounced off his chest, followed by a scrunched-up sandwich wrapper. 'Hey, listen: I'm sorry, though. All that . . . I didn't mean to bring us down. But I like that we can talk about this stuff.'

'About . . . skinny dipping? Murdering cats? Acting out scenes from *Reservoir Dogs*?' She broke him off another piece of chocolate.

'All of that. And about us, and Imagen, and Make-Believe. I suppose,' he said, mouth full, 'it's meeting you that's made me think – maybe, I can get it back. Reclaim it. You know, I can either sit here running my mouth off, or I can do something. Find something to bargain with.'

'What kind of something?'

'I guess – try to find any other users like us, anyone who's been blacklisted. That's what I need to figure out: how do I find those people.'

'You could try visiting all the support groups in the country – same way you found me.'

Lewis laughed. 'Everyone gets their one coincidence,' he said. 'Can't see that working again. But – I know it's a long shot. I'm open to any better ideas . . . ?' He paused, and when she said nothing: 'Well. I can do it on my own, if I have to.'

'More chocolate?'

'But if there was two of us . . .'

'I'll pack it away, shall I – and the flask, if you're finished?'

'Cassie.' He moved the flask out of her reach. 'Stop for a minute, and just . . . Look, do you think you'd help me?'

'How?'

'I don't know – if you had any contacts, still, at Imagen—'

She thought of Harrie – of all her former colleagues, the only one she could call a friend – and shook her head. 'I can't . . .'

'Or if you could remember anything that might help, from when you were working there, or if you had any ideas for finding people like us – or like you said just now, there might be some completely different thing they want to keep quiet – anything that could be a way in.'

'I can have a think. I don't know whether there's anything . . .'

'Even just knowing you're with me. You're on my side. So it's not just me, David up against Goliath.'

Cassie stretched for the flask. Screwed on the lid, and tugged to tighten it up. 'D'you believe in that?'

He laughed. 'No. You?'

'Nope. But belief doesn't matter.' She began fitting everything neatly back into the pannier. 'People like to support the underdog because they identify with the weaker, the smaller, the upstart. We're all acutely conscious of our vulnerability. Deep down we know we are tiny, we are nothing; we cling to anything that gives us hope that we might be more than we are. That it's possible for us to achieve beyond our ability, beyond expectations. Pass me the sandwich wrappers? So, we're all David.'

He was staring at her, mouth half-open. 'Sure you're not Goliath?'

'Ha.' She cracked a lopsided smile. 'I'm definitely David.'

'OK, David – what about you?'

'About me, what?'

'Miss U-turn. You said it was me put ideas in your head – about Imagen. So what are they getting up to in there?'

She didn't know, not really. But it seemed like both Lewis and Alan needed the same thing from her: to dig around Imagen, looking for – what? Something not quite right. It was as vague as that.

'Oh – scuttling about a bit. Finding some friends, maybe.'

He gave her a quizzical look. Reached out and, playfully, with one finger, tapped her forehead. His touch echoed through her: *dot dot dot*. A familiar chord, played just out of tune.

CHAPTER TWELVE

Even if she hadn't been breaking the rules, Cassie would have felt uneasy.

The Employee shall not contact, directly or indirectly, for any purpose, any persons employed by Imagen Research . . .

As she shut the gate behind her, walked up the path to Harrie's front door, she ducked her head under the too-big, drizzly sky. It was bungalow-land round here, dormered villas with double garages, back gardens stretching for ever. The doorbell seemed to announce her arrival to the whole cul-de-sac.

'Come in, come in – you're wet!' Harrie swung the door wide, opened her arms. 'Thanks for trekking all the way out to the suburbs.'

Over the last few days the weather had settled into

a dull, steady rain. Cassie kicked off her damp trainers before she set foot in the cream-carpeted hallway, followed Harrie into the kitchen. 'Here, I brought house-warming biscuits. Cardamom and something.'

Harrie put on a stern face. 'Hobnobs would have been fine, you know.'

'Well, you're providing the tea . . .' Harrie was right, the biscuits had been expensive – but that was OK. She still had enough cash, just about, to last her the rest of the week.

'I'll give you the guided tour in a bit, but sit down and let's have some tea first.' Harrie pulled out a chair for her at the table, set out a tea set that looked straight out of the 1960s, and sat down opposite. 'It's been ages,' she said.

'Ages,' agreed Cassie. She'd seen Harrie just once in the six months since Ayesha was born. They'd gone for coffee in town, and Harrie had insisted on paying. 'But then you've had your hands full. The kids, the move . . .'

'Just a bit! You're looking good, you know.'

'Oh. Thanks.' Cassie looked down at herself, and shrugged.

'No, but you are! Not your clothes, there's nothing wrong with your clothes but it's not them. It's your skin. It's your face.' She stopped, looked at Cassie from over her specs. 'Cassie McAllister. Have you been getting some?'

Cassie tried for an indignant look, but at the same time she was smiling. She couldn't help it.

'Oh my God, you are!' Harrie dissolved into laughter – a kind of overtired, uncontrollable giggling that set Cassie off too.

'Stop it!' The command came from the kitchen doorway, a small outraged voice. 'Mummy, stop laughing!'

Harrie pressed her lips together, turned her mouth down at the corners, but her shoulders were still shaking as she held out her arms to her daughter. 'Why, don't you like it when Mummy laughs?'

Ruby crossed her arms, stayed firmly planted in the doorway. 'No, I don't.'

'But why?'

'Because it's too loud!'

'Oh, well.' The kettle began to whistle: Harrie got up to make the tea, tousled Ruby's head on the way past. 'This is Mummy's friend Cassie, remember? And she's very funny, so we might be laughing quite a bit I'm afraid.'

Cassie smiled and waved. 'Hello, Ruby.'

'No!' Ruby spun on her heel, and stomped off down the hall.

'We'll try to keep it down . . .' Cassie called after her.

'Sorry about that. Honestly, she's turning into a little dictator. She doesn't like me talking on the phone, telling stories to her sister, leaving the house without her, ever . . .' Harrie's voice was shaky, and Cassie wasn't too sure if it was the remnants of the giggles or the onset of tired and emotional.

'How is baby Ayesha? Is she upstairs?'

'Yeah, she's sleeping, for once. I sometimes think I should keep her awake in the day, you know, jab pins in her or something, and then she might sleep at night for more than an hour at a time. And of course she wakes Ruby, and then you've got two of them to deal with . . .'

'God. I don't know how you're still upright.' She'd done it herself, of course, days without sleep – but no, you couldn't compare. Her Make-Believe with the slog, the blood and guts of motherhood. It wasn't at all the same.

Harrie hoisted the smile of someone who has no alternative. 'Hoooo . . .' she breathed out long and hard, like she was taking control again. 'I just keep reminding myself it won't last for ever – thank Christ.'

Hey, Cassie wanted to say, *remember the all-nighters we pulled in the run-up to the Make-Believe launch, when we were both still new and enthusiastic? Remember that time we slept in the office, and you ate instant coffee straight from the jar to keep you awake?* Instead, she smiled sympathy. It was like Russian dolls. On the surface, there was this image of motherhood, all calm and radiant and complete. And then inside that was the shell-shocked soldier on a forced march, staggering on with no end in sight. And inside *that* was the kernel, the unconditional bit, the jump-in-front-of-a-bullet bit. It was all different levels of real.

'Anyway,' said Harrie, 'that's not exciting – let's hear your news. You have a gentleman.'

'Well. Sort of.'

'What's "sort of"? He's a man. With whom you're having sex.'

Solemnly, Cassie agreed: 'Yes . . . yes, I am.'

'Which is a hell of a lot more than I am at the moment, so less of the "sort of" and tell me all about him . . .'

Eager to oblige, Cassie smiled and leant in. Then she hesitated. It was as if she knew the deep-down Lewis, without having to know the facts of him. She knew that he softened the hard edges of her world, that nights without him felt somehow chilled, left her huddling under the covers in her platform bed even at the height of summer. But that wasn't what Harrie was asking.

'Alright then – three questions,' Harrie said. 'Where did you meet him, what does he look like, what does his father do?'

Cassie laughed. 'In reverse order: no idea; tall, dark and' – she made a so-so gesture with her hand – 'kind of vaguely handsome; and, at the group.'

'Oh, wow. Great. So – you're back there again?'

'Yeah, but don't worry.' Cassie put on a comedy voice. 'I haven't relapsed.' Straight away, she imagined Jake listening, and felt ashamed. Why had she done that – said it like that? To make it seem less twelve-step? To show she didn't really need to be there? That she was different from the rest of them, with their ordinary, tawdry dependencies?

In any case, the group seemed to have run them into silence. Cassie reached for a biscuit, took the chance to change the subject.

'So remind me again, when are you due back at work?' She already knew the answer – but it was a safe way to nudge the conversation in the right direction. She had to be careful with this. Had to take her time.

'Not till January,' Harrie said. 'Another six months' maternity, plus some holiday. To be honest I'd go back sooner. Get my brain working again.'

'I suppose you feel a bit out of it. So much can happen in a year.'

'Although, I know once I've been back there a week it'll feel like I've never been away.'

'God, so much must have changed since my time. Even in a year.' She imagined Harrie staring at her, but she didn't look up to check. 'I don't suppose I'd know half the people there now.'

'There have been a few changes.' Harrie's voice was cautious, her words carefully empty.

'I kind of keep up, a bit, with what's going on; you know, product announcements or whatever.'

'Do you? Hasn't been much to keep up with lately, I wouldn't have thought. Just, business as usual.'

'Except there has been a bit of a blip, hasn't there.' Cassie risked a glance, to see Harrie's expression. 'It was in the news the other day, how growth was slower than they'd been planning.'

It was Harrie's turn to look away. 'I've actually, I've had my hands full here, Cassie. I haven't been following what's going on at the office.'

She was avoiding the issue, for definite. But that didn't

mean anything, not necessarily – because this, Imagen, was something they didn't talk about. The agreement was unspoken, but solid, and Cassie would never have pushed at it except for the fact that her friend was six months into her leave – the chance that maternity might have distanced her from her professional self, enough that her lips might loosen.

The flipside, of course, was that if Harrie did give in to gossip, it would be lukewarm at best.

'Yeah,' Cassie said, 'there's been lots of speculation about that, why it might be. Just from what I've seen online, you know?'

'I don't know about that.' Harrie reached for a biscuit, broke it in two, put one half back into the packet. 'I'm not really involved with that side of it.'

Cassie knew she should give it up. Change the subject, chat about light stuff, neutral stuff. Enjoy an afternoon with a friend, instead of acting the undercover agent. This wasn't like playing at spies – managing operatives, transferring secret documents. This was another kind of spying: manipulative, and grubby. She closed her eyes. Thought of Alan in a secure ward, his confidential treatment. Scrabbling at his scalp, drawing blood. His wet cheeks.

'People wondering whether it's the result of sales focusing on international launches, or maybe something more unforeseen . . .'

Harrie looked alarmed. 'Come on, Cassie – you know I can't talk about this. I understand, it must be really hard for you. You want to feel involved. I get that – you feel connected; you have to really care, to do your job well – and you always did do your job well. They want you to feel like Imagen is your family, that's how they get the best out of you. But it's not your family. It never was.' Her face was soft with sympathy. 'It was just your job. It was only your job you lost.'

Cassie swallowed. Drank some tea, forcing it down along with the sore lump in her throat. *I understand*, Harrie said; but she understood nothing, of course. How could she?

'Anyway,' Harrie was saying, 'you'd know as much as I do about international launches. There was plenty for me to focus on with the domestic market.'

Cassie would have given up, if she hadn't said that. But if Imagen was gearing up as planned for overseas expansion, Harrie would certainly have been involved before she went on leave. A tiny sliver of information – a suggestion that she could still reveal something useful. One more question, but what should she ask? Alan: the injury by his ear, scabbed over, scratched open. 'I did hear something about next generation receivers being implantable—'

Abruptly, Harrie was standing. 'That's Ayesha,' she said, and hurried from the room.

All Cassie could hear was Ruby singing somewhere down the hall.

She sat alone in the kitchen, shaking her head at her own idiocy. Harrie was too fucking loyal – to the company, as well as to her. How could she not have predicted this? Because it was Harrie's loyalty that had kept them in contact, through the whole shitstorm. It would have been the easiest thing in the world for Harrie to let Cassie disappear from her life. Like the rest of Cassie's former colleagues – the ones she'd thought of as friends, as well as the water-cooler acquaintances. But Harrie hadn't let that happen. And the only way it could work, their staying friends, was to comply with the spirit of the ban on contact even as they flouted it. They had never touched on what had happened. The fallout, yes. The darkness, yes. The consequences. But not on what Cassie had done to cause it – and not a word, a whisper, about Harrie's continuing life there.

'Where's my mummy?'

Ruby stood in the doorway, clutching a picture book.

Cassie cleared her throat. 'She's just upstairs. Baby Ayesha was crying.'

'She's always crying,' said Ruby, disgusted. 'She just cries cries cries. And she needs a new nappy all the time.'

'Did you not cry when you were a baby?'

Ruby shook her head, definitely: left – right – left. 'No, I did not cry, and anyway that was a very long time ago.'

'You never cried, not once?'

But Ruby had lost interest in that conversation. She marched over to Cassie's chair and thrust out the book she was carrying. 'Can you read this?'

'Now? You want it now? OK.' Cassie took the book: *The Owl Who Wouldn't Fly*. 'Um . . . where do you want to sit?'

Not on Cassie's lap, apparently. The little girl climbed onto her mother's seat, and Cassie angled her own so they could both see the illustrations. She turned the pages, pointing out the parts of the pictures mentioned in the text – the moon, a ladder, a baby owl – and doing funny voices for each of the characters. The voices were new to Ruby. She stared at Cassie instead of the illustrations.

'The end.' Cassie closed the book.

Ruby gazed at her with big brown eyes. 'But it's not the end if we make up a bit more story.'

'True. So what happens next, do you think?'

'The baby owl flies all the way up to the moon, and . . .' Ruby stopped, curled a lock of hair round her finger. Self-conscious, suddenly.

'And when he gets there he meets a family of space-owls,' Cassie suggested. 'And they lend him a spacesuit, and they feed him dried frozen worms . . .'

'Space-worms,' said Ruby. She screwed up her face, closed her eyes. Loving the let's pretend. Believing hard.

'Yes, space-worms. And then—'

'But he's homesick – and he flies back home and – then, he finds his mummy and the end.' Ruby's eyes snapped open again.

'That's a good story,' said Cassie. Overhead, the stairs creaked.

'Yes, and I've actually got another good story. You

can read it to me.' Ruby slid down from her chair, and trotted off to fetch another book.

Cassie flipped back through *The Owl Who Wouldn't Fly*. Ella would like it, perhaps; her niece was only a year older than Ruby, and her birthday was coming up fast. Over on the counter there was a pen, some scrap paper torn into shopping-list strips. Cassie stood up, noted the title and the author, not trusting her memory.

Harrie's voice from the hall: 'Ruby, what are you doing with that? You're not bothering Cassie, are you?' A stream of Ruby's protestations announced them both back into the kitchen, Harrie jigging Ayesha at her shoulder.

Cassie slipped the note into her pocket. 'Harrie, sorry – forget that, please. I was being an idiot.'

Harrie shook her head. 'No, sure. It's fine, don't worry. Hey, say hello to Ayesha. D'you want a hold?' She passed the baby to Cassie, who cuddled her in the crook of her arm, offered a finger for her to grab.

'Hello, beautiful . . .' Under the warmth and the weight of her, Cassie felt her chest constrict as Ayesha curled four fingers, tiny and damp, round Cassie's one. The baby blinked, tolerating her compliments. Cassie breathed her warm, powdery smell till she was half-smothered by sadness, passed her back to Harrie in an awkward almost hug. They were both pretending. If they pretended hard enough, it might be OK.

'Do you want some more tea?' But Harrie was still standing, right by the door.

'Thanks, I'd better make a move,' Cassie said. 'Let you get on. Get some rest!'

'Fat chance. Almost time for Ruby's snack. And you!' Harrie's face lit into a smile, and Ayesha copied, a bright mirror. 'Yes! Hungry too, aren't you? You'll have to see round the rest of the house, next time,' she said to Cassie, as they drifted out into the hall. 'But it's a bit chaotic upstairs, stuff still in boxes . . . Hey, how's your sister, how're the kids?'

'Oh, they're all fine, yes. Doing great. And Tim, how's he?' A trickle of small-talk carried them to the front door. A goodbye hug, like everything was fine. Cassie smiled at her friend. 'See you soon,' she said.

'Thanks for coming.' Harrie held Cassie's gaze with her punched-looking eyes. 'You take care, yeah?' she said. Then she swung the door slowly closed.

CHAPTER THIRTEEN

Cassie made an adventure track of the fucked-up roads back into town: head down, pedalling fast, shaking the rain from her eyes. A van sliced past too close – touching distance – and she whacked it with the flat of her hand, following up with a finger as it pulled off, horn blaring. She muttered the registration as she kept up behind, knowing she'd forget it the instant she couldn't read it any more, knowing even if she remembered it the last thing she would do was complain to the police. Knowing that if she did complain, her name would go on record and nothing would be done, since they barely had the manpower to chase up actual, serious crimes. But it made her feel better, a slap and a curse. She'd worked out some of her frustration by the time she reached the bookshop, sandwiched between a vacant unit and a clothes shop that shouted EVERYTHING MUST GO.

The children's section was tucked in a corner, bright with beanbags and character cut-outs: princesses and pirates, animals and aliens. Cassie headed straight for the picture books. A week today, Ella would turn five. On her fourth birthday, Cassie had given her nothing. She had barely known if it was summer or winter, was no longer fixed in real time, inside the frame of months and weeks and days that held things steady. So she'd forgotten her niece's birthday – and when weeks later she had realised, she'd told herself it didn't matter since Meg would have intercepted any gift that Cassie might have sent, taken it straight to the charity shop.

Meg would probably do the same with *The Owl Who Wouldn't Fly*, but Cassie picked it up anyway. It turned out to be one of a series; she swithered, wondering whether it mattered which story came first, but in the end she chose the same one she'd read with Ruby. She would have liked to buy a birthday card too, but once she'd paid for the book she would have £3.48 to last the next four days, and it would cost her to package and post the book too.

Just for a moment she thought of dipping into her debt clearance fund – taking a tenner, or even a fiver. But £2.99 for a birthday card was a self-indulgence. It might make her feel good, but it would do nothing to protect the kids. That was what her screen wallpaper was for: the photo a stranger had snapped, of Finn and Ella. To remind herself of the danger she'd put them in.

It was the only time she'd missed a repayment, the month she'd moved into the bedsit and closed her old bank account, thinking she might outrun the debt. The threat had been swift and efficient. Trusted Financial Solutions might not know where she lived any longer; she'd forgotten they knew where her sister lived. A picture sent to her screen, of the kids playing in the back green. Ella crouching, absorbed by something in the grass, a ladybird maybe – she loved to draw them, used to call them babybirds – Finn beside her, holding aloft a stick which was no doubt really a sword or a magic wand. It was a charming snapshot, the sort you might frame; and just for a second, Cassie had been confused. She'd thought the picture must have come from Meg. Had been swamped by a tidal wave of relief, of gratitude for her sister's forgiveness. And then she'd realised. Relief curdled to fear, gratitude to guilt. In less than a minute she had made her back payments – and made certain that each time she picked up her screen she would be confronted by that image. A constant reminder of her responsibility.

Every month since then, she'd been sure to pay on time.

She had spent so long lately at Lewis's flat, with its acres of polished floorboards, that the bedsit felt smaller, more grubby than ever. Cassie propped her rain-wet bike against the wall. Checked the sticky papers for trapped insects. There were only a couple, cockroach babies the size of pumpkin seeds. What she wanted to do was take the papers by their edges and fling them out into the rubbish chute – but that would be a waste. There was plenty of sticky surface left. She left the bodies where they lay, turned her back to the counter so she wouldn't have to see them.

She stuck a finger into the soil of her umbrella plant: not too thirsty. Needing just a drop of water. You could kill as easily with too much as with too little. She stood back, examined its leaves, pleased with their shine, with how well she was looking after it.

'You're doing fine,' she said out loud, because plants liked to be spoken to.

A few steps to her under-bed den. She sat cross-legged with *The Owl Who Wouldn't Fly* open on one knee, and unlidded her biro. Paused, sucking her pen like a rollie. Then in a rush she wrote her message.

Dear Ella, I hope you like this book. I chose it for you specially because I thought you would like the baby owl. His bright red legs remind me of you and your red woolly tights, I always remember you looking very cool with your red legs. Hopefully we will read the story together sometime. Wishing you lots of love and a VERY HAPPY BIRTHDAY! Miss you. Auntie Cassie.

xox

The book went into the padded envelope she'd bought, and the package into her satchel.

Cassie leant back against the flimsy wall, trying not to think of the insects that might be alive inside. Next door her neighbour was on the phone. *You fucking do it*, he said. *I'm not fucking doing it*. She could get out of here, go to Lewis. Find some comfort in him. He'd given her a set of keys, last time she was there; if he was out, she could let herself in, curl up in his bed and wait for him. But if she saw him tonight she knew she'd feel resentment as much as reassurance. Though it wasn't his fault she'd jeopardised her friendship with Harrie – wasn't for him she was playing detective – it was easier to blame him than to blame herself.

She let herself slide a little further down the wall. The guy next door would be able to get her something, she was sure. People came to his door at all hours, stayed only a minute or two. She had told Lewis she wasn't addicted to anything other than Make-Believe, and that was true. But when the world took on a hard shape that had no space for her – when her failures piled on top of her, so she could barely breathe for the weight on her chest – then, there were ways to take the edge off.

Her neighbour might give her a freebie. He'd welcome a new customer, particularly if she worked the next-door angle. Or if he didn't do freebies, perhaps he'd give her something on account. She got to her feet, stood and listened. He was still on the phone, still arguing. She would wait till he'd finished, then she'd go round and ask. She moved to the door and waited, her fingers poised on the snib. Listening for silence. There: it stretched for thirty seconds, for a minute. She turned the lock, opened her door – and as she did, she heard his closing. Caught a glimpse of him heading for the stairs. Heard his descending footsteps.

She shut her door again. Locked it. Stood with her head down, arms wrapped tight around herself. Then, from the chest of drawers, she pulled an old T-shirt, one of Alan's. Climbed the ladder to bed, and rolled fully dressed under the covers. Just for a few minutes. Then she'd get up, make toast and tea without milk.

She pressed the shirt against her face. HAPPY EVERYDAYS. A few minutes safe under the covers, with rain dotting the windowpane, dot-dotting like it was all OK. Like everything was OK—

OK—

OK.

CHAPTER FOURTEEN

There must be a theory that straight lines were detrimental to learning. Throughout the library, desks were kidney-shaped, benches and partitions likewise curved. But rounded lines or no, Cassie's attempts at research were leaving her uncomfortably aware of the limits of her intelligence.

She'd started with abstracts of studies from the biotech team who'd created the prototype Make-Believe, going right back to the early iterations of a technology designed to be applied in healthcare settings. But so many of the sentences left her none the wiser. She closed her eyes, leant back in her chair. Was she kidding herself to think she would have grasped this stuff, before?

'Thought we were meeting downstairs?'

Cassie snapped her eyes open, turned to see Nicol standing at her side.

'Shit, sorry.' Onscreen, the time read 10.23; they'd arranged to meet at ten. 'I got caught up with something,' she said.

'Looks fascinating, right enough.' Nicol's tone was deadpan. Cassie pulled a face, unsure if he was being sarcastic. The text she'd been wading through was tangled with abstract, unfamiliar terms. It was tying her head in knots, but perhaps it was Nicol's idea of light reading. 'What's the assignment?' he asked.

'Ah, no – this is personal interest.'

Nicol nodded. 'Cool,' he said. He dumped his backpack onto the desk, settled into the seat next to hers and slid his memory card across the table. 'Anything else come in?'

Cassie shook her head. 'Holiday slump,' she said. The library was their rainy-day meeting place, and today it was eerily quiet, the study pods empty, the stacks deserted. The students had vanished in search of what work they could find: hospitality and call centres for the fortunate; for the rest of them, cleaning, or dancing in strip clubs, perhaps labouring on a building site if they could find one that wasn't mothballed. Only the wealthiest remained, cementing their advantages by taking extra classes. 'Remember,' she said, 'it picked up a bit last year once the summer schools kicked in.' She clicked the card into her screen, transferred the docs, and made Nicol's payment.

'Guess I'll call this time off, then. You're burnt by the way, did you know that?'

'I'm . . . ?'

'You've got the sun. Should watch for that. Sign of skin damage.'

'Yeah, well luckily for my skin there's no chance of further damage for the foreseeable. But thanks for the concern.'

'No worries.' Nicol tilted his head towards the screen. 'It's outside your field, no?'

'Ha. Just slightly.' Cassie scrubbed a hand through her hair, as if she could rub right through her skull and massage her struggling brain. 'Ever feel like the thick kid at the back of the class?'

'Aye, that stuff can be pretty dense, right enough. Be the same in any field, though. Like in psychology or whatever, there'll be things you'd fly through that I'd never make sense of.'

'I doubt that. Doubt there's much you don't know.'

'There's plenty I don't know,' he said, easily. 'Plenty plenty.' He stood, hitched his pack onto his shoulder. 'It's what that Chinese dude says: know how little you know, and that's the start of wisdom.'

Cassie raised her eyebrows. 'I'm the wisest woman on earth, then.'

'But if you need anything translated, oh wise one – techspeak to plain English . . .'

'Thanks,' she said. 'Might take you up on that.'

When Nicol had gone, she closed the page she'd

been studying, switched her focus to more accessible publications: *New Scientist*, the *Financial Times*, the *Economist*, the broadsheets. She flipped past endless opinion pieces on Make-Believe and Imagen, trying to find something meaty, something containing a few facts. She skimmed through announcements of government funding, of key milestones, through a tsunami of publicity around the launch of the world's first true virtual reality. There were company profiles explaining how Imagen had been set up to monetise the university's groundbreaking research. Individual profiles of Professor Morgan, the 'mother of virtual reality'. Breathless pronouncements of world-leading technology and wide-eyed analyses of economic impact. A couple of reports trying to create controversy over the decision by the Department for Innovation to license Make-Believe as entertainment technology, despite the invasive aspects of its functionality; several attempts at exposé from privacy activists and the Campaign for Real Life. Imagen would lift the whole economy. Imagen would be the salvation of the nation. Imagen would turn us all into narcissistic zombies. It was nothing she didn't know. Nothing the world didn't know.

The problem was, she couldn't be sure what she was looking for. But research was like that sometimes, or it was for her, at least. You were blind until suddenly you saw. So she was searching, mole-like: pushing forward in all directions at once, keeping a note of everything she read to avoid going round in circles, and trusting that eventually she'd figure out what it was she was hoping to find.

Her attention snagged on a two-year-old article from the *Observer* technology supplement. VIRTUAL RETURNS ON A REAL PUBLIC INVESTMENT, ran the headline.

Imagen is emerging as the great hope of the biotechnology sector, thanks to massive government subsidies – but what sort of returns should the taxpayer expect?

In the wake of the collapse of several high-profile UK technology start-ups, it's hard to overestimate how much is riding on the success of Make-Believe, the groundbreaking new VR from Imagen Research.

This week details were announced of a further £10m government investment in extending and commercialising the company's world-leading patented technology, which industry experts predict could have applications ranging from education and healthcare to defence.

With Make-Believe already receiving rave reviews, we examine its game-changing potential in five key areas: healthcare, education, sport, defence and sex.

Healthcare
The future . . . VR technology presents huge opportunities for new treatments and services.

Patients suffering from chronic pain would be able to find relief in imagined, painless virtual experiences; VR could also ease the passage of patients receiving end-of-life care. There are suggestions that the Make-Believe model could eventually be used extensively by mental health service providers as a powerful therapeutic tool. For instance, 'guided stories' could help patients to relive traumatic incidents but experience different, more positive outcomes.

The present . . . Imagen's VR technology is already being tested for pain management, but there are ethical concerns around its use in palliative care, particularly in patients suffering from dementia: the technology would have to enable medical professionals to monitor the quality of the patient's VR experience. Similarly, the therapeutic use of guided stories would demand some way for medical professionals to connect and communicate with the patient in VR, and ultimately to control the patient's virtual experience.

Probability: 2/5
Profitability: 4/5

Education
The future . . . Educational materials could be developed that would reduce the need for costly equipment and travel, opening up access for all

to overseas field trips, remote site visits, complex scientific experiments and so on. Immersive experiential learning could unlock the potential of children with learning difficulties such as dyslexia. Perhaps the most revolutionary possibility is of assessing potential and performance in creative subjects by analysing students' neurological data – rewarding direct imaginative skill and potential, alongside more conventional creative outputs. A student of choreography could be graded on a virtual ballet featuring hundreds of dancers; an architecture student could submit a virtual building, to scale and in three dimensions.

The present . . . There is currently no way to integrate pre-conceived educational elements with individuals' VR experience, and techniques for analysing neurological data are rudimentary: there's a long way to go before we can fully appreciate, or even share, each other's imaginative experiences.

Probability: 4/5

Profitability: 3/5

Cassie blinked, and her eyes scraped in their sockets. Two years after this article had been written, education technology was still firmly located in the present. Instead of wandering virtual stacks that arranged and rearranged themselves according to her thoughts, Cassie was stuck in the library reading articles onscreen. Universities were waiting, watching: after investing millions in obsolete Second Life campuses, and millions more in the clunky headsets that had briefly promised to be the future of VR, they were wary of being burnt again.

At the edge of her vision something flickered – the screen, or the lights that buzzed overhead. When she stared directly at them they stared straight back, a constant brightness; maybe the flickering was inside her. Was her. Her, here – not here – here . . . She tugged a hand through her hair. Clipped the article she'd been reading so she could skim it later, and swiped the screen to pull up the next title in her search results.

Implications of rewiring cellular quorum sensing.

Quorum sensing: it was a term she'd registered a couple of times already that morning. She tapped the words for a definition.

A phenomenon where microorganisms communicate and coordinate their behaviour by the accumulation of signalling molecules.

The wording wasn't familiar. She raised her hand to call up more detail; let her arm fall. Her edges flickered: here, not here, here—

Not here.

She logged out, shoved back her chair, and headed for the exit.

* * *

The light outside was grey and steady. She perched on a wall, half-sheltered from the drizzle by a concrete overhang, and rolled a cigarette, a single paper with a skinny line of tobacco. Sat doing nothing but making a circle of her breath, drawing the smoke in, and round, and out . . . in, round, out . . . Doing nothing but feeling human, feeling the drizzle pepper her skin, and the breeze lift the hairs on her arms. Watching the scattering of summer students as they sat and strolled, smiled and chattered to their devices, passing blindly through space. A couple of Chinese girls were sharing an umbrella, talking face-to-face. Cassie pressed her hands into her dried-up eyes. Stupid. So stupid, to risk a friendship – her only friendship – for nothing. She should have approached it differently, thought more about Harrie, about the sort of person she was. Her values, her loyalty, her kindness. Should have asked for help, instead of trying to weasel details out of her, details that in all likelihood Harrie didn't even know. Expert saboteur; she would have to wait now, for Harrie to be in touch, wait to see whether she'd managed to burn yet another bridge. *You take care, yeah?* She blinked her eyes open. Under the umbrella, one girl leant towards her friend, their shoulders making a connection. One smile, two smiles. Laughter.

Or maybe she didn't have to wait. Maybe she should reach out, send Harrie a message. She pulled her screen from the pocket of her jeans, and a crumpled scrap of paper fell to the ground. *The Owl*

Who Wouldn't Fly. Cassie bent to pick it up. On the back was a picture – a butterfly, missing half a wing – and some torn-off text:

–THCARE
–solely for the authorised recipient and may
contain confidential or legally privileged
information. Any use without the sender's explicit
consent . . .

It was a standard email confidentiality statement. Cassie shoved the paper back in her pocket, woke her screen, skipped an ad for a singles site – *Sign up for free*, don't leave love to chance* . . . Started to write a message to Harrie.

Broke off, mid-sentence.

That butterfly. It reminded her of something. Of somewhere.

She retrieved the paper, studied the picture, the fragment of text beneath. She had seen that image recently – hadn't she? Something similar, at least. But the longer she looked, the more she felt herself drawing a blank. On her screen, she saved her message to Harrie then called up her recent clippings.

VIRTUAL RETURNS ON A REAL PUBLIC INVESTMENT
Imagen is emerging as the great hope of the
biotechnology sector . . . we examine its game-changing
potential in five key areas: education, healthcare . . .

There it was. Healthcare. She jumped to the relevant section.

> . . . the Make-Believe model could eventually be used extensively by mental health service providers . . . the therapeutic use of guided stories would demand some way for medical professionals to connect and communicate with the patient in VR, and ultimately to control the patient's virtual experience . . . Probability: 2/5

All at once she was sitting up straight, clearing her screen, starting to scribble. She didn't know yet what it meant – how it might fit together, but—

Make-Believe

—she had to catch it before she could lose it. A dashed line:

Raphael House

A butterfly, roughly sketched. The letters beneath:

Chrysalis Healthcare Group?

Another line, another scribble:

Doctors connect with patients?

A fourth line, and she added what she could recall of the definition she'd found in the library:

Microorganisms communicate . . .

Stopped. Sat gazing at the screen, worrying at the dry skin on her lips.

She knew now – what had happened, what was happening.

She added a fifth line, a final word:

Alan

Stared at what she'd mapped, simple and clear as a child's drawing of the sun.

CHAPTER FIFTEEN

Say – just say – it was true.

She was walking, because her thoughts were too frantic to sit with. Her skin felt like tiny electrical shocks were jolting across her, making her twitch.

Microorganisms communicate.

A microorganism: like a biomolecule. Like, for instance, the biomolecules that were the basis of Make-Believe.

Was it possible? To communicate within Make-Believe? In the long term, it was what Imagen were banking on: the development of a collaborative mode and two-way communication between users. But it was miles beyond anything they'd planned for when she was still an employee. It was ten years into the future at least.

Just say, though, that she'd guessed right.

Microorganisms communicate. Doctor communicates with patient. What exactly did she think was happening?

Start from what she'd seen.

Alan. In distress, in torment, in a state she'd never seen before. Digging at the root of his pain, trying to gouge it out.

The wound behind his ear, long strands of hair sticking. Between the skin and the bump of bone, that thin layer of flesh. A receiver in there; it would have to be tiny. Slender. Even elegant.

She walked, avoiding collisions by instinct, hardly noticing the wet streets, the summer-school students ducking through the drizzle. Instead, she saw mice. White mice in polycarbonate tanks, under strip lights. Shredded paper nests in individual cubes. Like the single beds in the numbered rooms at Raphael House.

Alan was an experiment.

And not only him: the woman she'd seen, in the day room, scrubbing at her skull underneath her ponytail. All of them, maybe, every patient locked in that ward.

And if they were subjects, what was the test? *Therapeutic use would demand some way for medical professionals to connect and communicate with the patient . . . ultimately to control the patient's virtual experience.* It made her think of the twelve-step programme, and the part she'd never been able to buy: the promise of rescue from the madness of addiction. Step two – *we believe that a power greater than ourselves can restore us to sanity.* A doctor inside Alan's head. A

167

psychiatrist inhabiting his madness, gazing on his skewed world. Shaping it. Straightening it. Hearing his voices – guiding his visions – working from the inside. Buried in his consciousness, like an engineer rewiring him. Severing this, and soldering that. Mending his brain. It was how Imagen had begun, after all. Where their initial funding and research had been focused: on developing therapeutic applications for VR technology.

An astonishing idea. If it could work . . . Imagine, all that madness, all that lonely suffering. The minds made well. The broken pieces fixed.

Something pressed up from inside her chest – into her throat – pushed out in a tiny, strangled sound that she did her best to swallow.

But. But. It wasn't working. Was it? Because Alan was not fixed. That body, that brain – hiding and hidden, locked behind doors behind doors behind doors. More broken than she'd ever seen him.

No: the experiment hadn't worked. Something had gone wrong.

And now it wasn't a whimper inside her, trying to escape. It was a slow, hard feeling, fierce, and building.

The thing was, it didn't matter. Something was wrong, badly wrong – and no one had to care.

It was, actually, genius.

A cohort unable to sue, if it all went down the pan. A subject unable, even, to complain; a patient whose grasp on reality was so weak that when he raved about what was happening inside his skull the doctors would

168

tilt their heads, prescribe another fist of pills, another knock-out jag. Families kept sweet by the waiving of fees, their loved ones protected from failing state care, kept in sunny-side-up luxury.

It sounded like one of the conspiracy theories Nicol was so fond of. In all her research, she'd found no mention of Imagen running medical trials. Could she really believe it, of the doctors at Raphael House? The psychiatrists whose job was to care for their patients? Perhaps, yes – if they truly believed in the project. Believed it could allow them to treat people, heal them as never before.

Her pace slowed to a halt. Without thought, she'd made a circuit of the university square, and now she found herself at the foot of the Bray Tower. It rose skyward, shining white: it promised to rejuvenate the whole area, lifting its neighbours on its coat-tails, and instead made them look every day of their forty and fifty years. The tower was part of the university – unconnected, officially, with Imagen. But it marked the birthplace of Make-Believe; after the commercial entity of Imagen had been spun out to exploit the university's research, the Bray was built on that success. This was the closest she'd dared to come, since Imagen had screwed her. She stood a single pace from the building, close enough to touch. Kept her hands punched into her pockets. If she did touch, it would be icy, frictionless; and like an iceberg it was more than you could see, stretching dark and deep beneath her feet.

It was win-win for Imagen, if she was right. If the experiments worked, they'd be followed by pilot programmes, a licence for therapeutic use, huge profits from healthcare budgets here and in the US. And if the experiments failed? Well, perhaps you couldn't call it a win, but you could say nothing was lost; nothing that mattered was lost.

What she thought, then, was: Lewis. Wasn't this exactly what he'd been searching for? If Imagen had been running clinical trials with subjects whose mental state was such that they were unable to give informed consent, and if Imagen had botched those trials – well, that was his ultimate bargaining chip. He could go to Imagen, give them a choice: let him back into Make-Believe, or he'd blow the whistle. Either way, they would stop the experiment. They'd have to. It would be too much of a risk to carry on, once they knew information had started to leak. They'd get out of Alan's head, reverse whatever they'd done – and Alan would still be lost, she knew that, still sealed in himself, in his own unreality – but the torment would be gone, whatever it was that hurt him so much he clawed his skin until he bled.

Only, she had no proof. Just a deep-down certainty that would convince no one, except perhaps Nicol and his fellow conspiracy theorists. And more than that, she found – for all Lewis's talk, for all his longing – that she didn't believe in him. This was deeper stuff by far than a lake with a DANGER sign – and if Lewis wasn't scared, it was only because he'd never seen Imagen's ruthlessness, hadn't felt it the way she had. Her career destroyed, fear of prosecution hanging always over her – and for what? She'd breached her contract, yes, and losing her job was a fair price to pay – but she'd caused them no real injury. Yet they'd done all they could to erase her.

Above her, scores of eyes slit the building's skin. A glittering illusion of openness. From ground level, she couldn't see in. But they could see out.

Everything until now had been scrabbling around the edges. Her visit to Harrie. Her library research. Her involvement with Lewis. All this, she guessed, was invisible. She was nothing to them; why would they watch her? Why would they care? She was safe in her obscurity.

But any action, now, would be stepping into the light.

The render on the Bray Tower was so smooth, so austere, your eyes could slide across with nothing to catch your focus. And there, at the top of the building, was where the secrets lived. In a glass-walled office, in the head of a woman Cassie had met just once: once, in her old life. A woman who could be watching from her window. Could be looking down at her, right now.

She dropped her gaze. Turned, and walked away.

In the nearest Superdrug, Cassie studied her cropped reflection in a cloudy strip of mirror; chose a lipstick tester, and stroked her lips a bright *Trust Me* pink. Hovered, fiddling with eyeshadows as though she were choosing between shades, till the security guard moved into the next aisle. Then she cracked the plastic seal on

171

a mascara tube that promised *XXX-tra volume*, and dabbed it furtively onto her pale lashes. It was for ever since she'd worn make-up, and now that she'd started she would have liked to paint a whole mask: foundation, eyeshadow, blusher, the lot. But the guard was still hovering, and lashes and lips would have to do.

She slotted the mascara back into its display. Fished a hairclip from the depths of her satchel and secured her hair in a twist at the back of her head. The mirror strip showed a half-reflection. She dipped to check her eyes, stood straight to check the lips. The make-up was meant as armour, as disguise; now she worried it might have the opposite effect. The half-faces that looked back at her were a glimpse back in time, of her old, professional self. But the polish gave her confidence, would smooth her way into the Bray Tower.

And there was no reason why the professor should recognise her – not from one brief meeting, three years ago. No reason she should know who Cassie was, when she walked into her office searching for answers.

CHAPTER SIXTEEN

Braced for klaxons and flashing red lights, Cassie marched into the foyer. Her fingers turned to thumbs under the stare of the security guard as she scrabbled for her visitor's pass – but the gate slid open, and the foyer accepted her just as if she belonged.

Space rose around her, open to the roof six storeys up: a huge central atrium that was the ultimate show-off. It shouted, *See how we need such a great height to accommodate all our grand ideas. See how we conceptualise your future, transform the way you will live.* Cassie imagined those concepts – abstract, embodied but invisible – hanging here in the tall space. And then she stopped gazing, and concentrated on looking like she was meant to be there.

The layout was loosely familiar from the visit she'd

made with her Imagen colleagues. She remembered how they'd crowded into the glass lift – laughing, excited to see where the magic happened. Today, she preferred not to sail up through the centre of the building in a transparent cube; made for the edge of the ground floor, and started up the stairs. Up to a gallery that snaked around the thought-space before stepping up again to snake round at second-floor level, and again and again till the roof of the building was almost touchable and Cassie stopped to catch her breath, and played a game of blocking out the people in the foyer with her thumb.

Where the magic happened. That had been a colleague's phrase: Becca, the marketing assistant. Cassie had always reckoned it went to the heart of how Becca thought about the business. Like all of them she'd mastered a simplified explanation of how it worked, could answer the frequently asked questions and give bland reassurances of safety. But Cassie had heard her giving the spiel, could tell she didn't understand a word of it. Didn't *believe* a word of it. As far as Becca was concerned, it was impossible, what they were doing. It had to be magic.

Which made Professor Morgan chief wizard. Another hat, to add to the several she wore already: professor of synthetic neurobiology at the university; chief scientific officer at Imagen; Commander of the British Empire for services to science, technology and innovation. Though she hadn't looked like a wizard, or a CBE, that time when she'd met them outside the building in a plain white shirt and creased suit-trousers. Hadn't looked important at all. You could have lost her instantly in any crowd of office workers. Cassie had stared, trying to imagine her alien brain, what went on inside it: the zillions of neural connections that must be zapping and buzzing constantly, to let her understand concepts and mechanisms and possibilities of which Cassie, at best, might glimpse an outline – an outline she could hold in her own mind for maybe a minute before it fuzzed into ungraspable complexity. And then the professor had caught her staring, and turned slightly pink, and of course she was not just an extraordinary woman but an ordinary one as well – a woman with a distracted smile, a quick handshake, and a scrap of Sellotape holding together one leg of her spectacles.

Glass doors. Glass walls. Everything was transparent – so the ideas could see each other, could join up, mate, breed new ideas that were even better and bigger and more world-changing. Cassie was fairly sure Morgan's office was on the top floor. Although on their visit they hadn't been shown round this level, she remembered how Morgan had gestured as they stood outside, to the highest point of the tower. How her lifting arm had tugged her shirt free from the waist of her trousers, so she'd had to stuff it back in while they all pretended not to notice.

Cassie walked past a series of boxy offices, sneaking

sideways looks. Some were empty but for equation-scrawled whiteboards, minimal office furniture, the occasional yellowing peace lily; some were occupied by women and men so focused on their screens that not a one glanced up as she passed. But Morgan wouldn't work in a little see-through cube, not like these underlings.

Cassie followed a right angle, found herself passing a larger office that seemed to have several doors opening off it in turn. Glimpsed a row of filing cabinets, and two large desks, one of which was occupied by a dark-haired woman in a black-and-white-striped shirt. Kept walking, till she was out of the woman's sightline. She felt grubby, suddenly, in this sparkling space. Sweat needled her armpits. She doubted the power of her lipstick, doubted her clothes: today's charity-shop T-shirt, black with a small sans serif text: *Is that your final answer?* She tugged her cardigan closed, buttoned the slogan away. She'd come this far; what was she doing here, if she wasn't going to chance it? That fierceness swelled in her chest again. Do it, or step back into the shadows. That was the choice.

The instant Cassie stepped into the office, the woman looked up from her desk.

'Can I help you?' she said.

Cassie smiled brightly. 'I'm here to see Professor Morgan – am I on the right floor?'

The woman didn't return her smile. Checked her screen. 'Did you have a meeting?'

'Yes, we'd arranged it for, um, twelve o'clock, I

think – unless . . .' Cassie gazed round, acting scatty. Clocking each door, each nameplate. *Prof Angela Khan. Dr David McLean. Prof Fiona Morgan.*

'There's nothing in the diary.' The woman gave her a hard stare, folded her arms: *You shall not pass.* 'What was your name?'

'Don't say I've got the wrong day . . .'

'If you give me your name, I'll search the diary.'

There was no way she'd get past this guardian. Cassie shook her head. 'I'm so sorry,' she said. 'I have, I've got the day wrong – I completely forgot she'd rescheduled.' She backed out, closing the door as she went. 'Honestly. Forget my own head if it wasn't screwed on . . .'

As she retreated down the corridor, she imagined the woman following her to the door. Felt her stare as a weight on her back.

Slowly she made her way down the snaking stairs, trying to figure out her next move. By the time she reached ground level she'd come up with nothing better than hanging around, and trying not to get thrown out.

Across from the exit was a coffee kiosk, with a handful of tables and high stools. Cassie strolled over, scanned the price list. Espresso was cheapest, but you couldn't nurse that for long without arousing suspicion. Instead she counted out the money for tea in a takeaway cup, and claimed the seat with the best view of the exit. The rain was off now, sun streaming through the glass atrium; with luck, the woman whose job it was to guard

Professor Morgan would feel the need for lunch, fresh air and a dose of vitamin D.

Groups of people came and went: they arrived in small flocks, perched with their screens and coffee cups crowding the tables; they talked briefly and seriously, and dispersed again. Distantly, she recognised herself. Recalled the sense of small, regular accomplishment, the satisfaction she'd felt in her own efficiency. She remembered the seductive, self-contained shape of a task, a plan, a project, of a day, a week, a year. Remembered how the scaffolding of routine had boxed her days, holding it all together. Surrounded and separate, she sipped her tea and tried to blend in, to sit like them, angled forwards, screen on the table in front of her. And this was why she had left – the first time she'd abandoned him. To be like them, to feel professionally fulfilled. This was why, at the airport, she'd held him, and left him. Each reassuring the other: *This'll be you in a couple of months. It's going to fly past. It's going to be fine. It's going to be amazing.*

It was only the laughter that made her look up. A loud gust, unexpected, resounding through the muted space – and there was the woman from upstairs. A smile had transformed her face as she shared a joke with the security guard, but the black-and-white shirt was the same. Carrying her handbag, jacket over her arm. Heading out for lunch.

The moment the woman had passed through the barrier, Cassie was on her feet. This time she took the lift, all the way to the top. She walked briskly down the corridor – but when she reached the glass-walled office, she stopped. The desk was still occupied, by a young man this time. Professor Morgan was clearly too valuable to be left unguarded. Cassie watched, swearing silently, knowing that while she could see the replacement, she herself could be clearly seen. She turned, took a few steps towards the lift. Turned back, moved forward once again. Stood there, swithering – and as she hesitated, the replacement left his seat, got down on his hands and knees, and stuck his head under the desk.

Paper jam.

Cassie didn't hesitate. She opened the door just enough to slide through, made sure it closed without a sound. As the replacement, still on his knees, began to crawl backwards, Cassie stepped lightly across the carpet, making straight for Morgan's office. Now she could see her, through the glass of the door, she could see her leaning towards her screen, her cropped head bent, her shirt creased tight across her shoulders.

'Hello? Excuse me—' The replacement had emerged from under his desk.

In a single movement, Cassie rapped her knuckles against Morgan's door, pushed it halfway open and stepped inside.

'—sorry, but do you have an appointment?'

Cassie closed the door on the voice at her back. Now, it had to look like she was expected, or security would be up here before she could ask a single question. She smiled at Morgan's startled face, stuck out her hand.

'Professor Morgan? Sorry to intrude.' The fake name she'd prepared was on her lips – and then she saw it. Recognition flickering in Morgan's eyes. More: the professor looked wary. Cassie's stomach yawned. What had Morgan heard? How much did she know about her, and what she'd done? 'You won't remember me, I'm sure . . .' Was there any way to avoid giving her real name? No time to think it through. 'Cassandra McAllister,' she said.

'No, I do, of course.' Morgan stood up, made as if to offer her hand, then seemed to change her mind, and gave a nod instead. From the furthest corner of her eye, Cassie saw the replacement return to his desk. Relief pulsed through her. Her smile became almost genuine.

'Well,' said Morgan. 'An unexpected . . .' The sentence trailed away. *Pleasure* was too blatantly false – and with her failure to utter the social nicety, Cassie's hopes rose. The woman was a bad liar.

Morgan was still standing up – so that Cassie couldn't sit down. She was a woman who wanted to be polite, who had by necessity learnt the tricks of protecting her time, her intellectual territory. Cassie kept up her smile, and under the surface she kicked and struggled, because she'd known, ten seconds ago, exactly what she'd meant to ask, how she planned to play it – and now she'd blanked. She forgot stuff, she did; she forgot a lot of stuff.

'I'm so sorry,' she said again, playing for time. 'I know I'm interrupting you.'

'I am actually due at a meeting, I'm afraid.' Morgan was palming out of her screen as she spoke. 'You might want to make an appointment with the departmental secretary? I should warn you, I am generally fairly busy.'

It was a smug understatement – and Cassie thought of Alan, and hated the professor for her self-satisfaction, for her glass office, her clear desk that held nothing more than screen, notepad and a single pen, no ordinary clutter to get in the way of pure clean concept, and somehow her hatred sparked her brain into action.

'Some time next week, perhaps,' Morgan was saying.

Cassie gave her most ingratiating smile. *Trust Me.* 'I wonder – would you mind if I walked with you, and asked just a couple of questions . . . ?'

Morgan picked up her briefcase, slung the strap over her shoulder. 'By all means,' she said. Outside her office, she locked the door and led the way straight to the lift.

'I'm not sure if you know,' Cassie said as they waited, 'I've moved on from Imagen, some time ago.'

Did Morgan's expression soften, just a little? She couldn't be sure.

'I'm actually based at the university now, and I'm involved in some psychological research.'

The glass doors opened, and Morgan ushered her in.

'We're studying some early users of the Make-Believe environment, and looking at the more subtle aspects of how their virtual experiences affect their real life perceptions.'

The atrium slid past. Each level was painted a different colour. Cerise. Sage. Blue-grey. Lilac. Orange. Yellow.

'Sounds interesting, very interesting.' Morgan spoke as if she'd been presented with a dish of slugs, politely telling the waiter how delicious it looked. 'You say, the more subtle aspects?'

'Yes – so we're not duplicating the extensive safety testing that's already, obviously, been carried out by your colleagues. Or questioning that, in any way. We're actually focusing on the potential for Make-Believe to enrich people's real lives. Unexpected benefits. Qualitative research, rather than quantitative, at this stage.'

They stepped out of the lift. 'And I might be able to help in some way?'

'It's just really . . . well, it's a bit delicate, but – one of the difficulties we're encountering is to do with the, uh, solidity of the data. The tendency of a number of participants to indulge in fantasy, and to experience difficulty in distinguishing this from reality.' She walked with Morgan across the foyer, through the exit gate. 'Some of the effects that participants are reporting are – let's say they're highly unlikely. So there's a question about the reliability of these reports. And it occurred to me that it would be helpful if we could rule out any aspects of these supposed experiences that are simply not possible. Not technologically, biologically possible.'

They were outside now. Morgan stopped walking. Turned to face her. In the daylight she looked older than she had indoors: unslept, and furrowed. 'And can you be specific about the possibilities you'd like to exclude?'

Cassie was ready with her test question, her calibration. 'OK, so one is the suggestion that users might be able to exceed their daily allocation of 120 minutes. Now I know of course there are all sorts of factors here to do with perceptions of time – it's such a fascinating area – and all I wanted to do was just rule out that possibility that a user might *actually* spend more than two hours a day, real time, in Make-Believe.' She felt herself flush as she added a tacit acknowledgement of what she herself was supposed to have done. 'That's without any kind of alteration of account privileges.'

If Morgan lied, she would know; and she'd know, then, *how* she lied – what she did with her eyes, her mouth, her hands. She wasn't expecting the truth.

Morgan answered easily. 'Ah. Now you see, we couldn't categorically rule out that possibility.'

'Oh? Really?'

'I'm going this way, do you mind if we walk?' Morgan pointed towards the Newman building and started across the square, leaving Cassie to scurry after her. 'I don't know if you're aware that there have been a very few isolated instances of bioware being modified.'

'I didn't know that.'

'As I say, a very few instances. And we've improved the safeguards against this happening, we're improving them all the time – really it's a matter for the computer science team at Imagen. An encryption issue.'

'Yes, of course. And so, this modification—'

'Would allow users to remain in Make-Believe for as long as they choose. Theoretically, an unlimited period of time. Although there are always limits. Physical limits.'

Physical limits. You needed the toilet. You realised you were hollow with hunger. You fell asleep, exhausted, crossed the border between Make-Believe and dreams and woke back in the real world cold and stiff, lying wet in the empty bathtub – the flat deserted – the front door open—'If that's everything . . . ?' Morgan was making a show of checking her watch.

'Uh, yes' – Cassie forced herself to focus – 'just one more question, if that's OK . . . One or two of the participants have reported being able to share their virtual experiences. I mean, not telling other people what they Make-Believed, after the event, but actually collaborating on an experience, in real time – like we're collaborating now, on this conversation.'

For the briefest fraction of a second, a shadow flickered across Morgan's face. Then she shook her head emphatically. 'Not possible.'

'Good. Well – good. Categorically, you're saying?'

'Yes.' They had reached the Newman building, were standing face to face; Morgan held her eyes, with a gaze so direct it felt like a challenge. 'You must know that, Cassandra. With your background. If you spoke to your former colleagues at Imagen, they would tell you the same.'

'No, of course. Just, for the study, we need to be absolutely sure that it's not possible. And so . . . a

184

participant who claims they've had an experience that was in some way controlled or – or simply shared with another party—'

'Would be delusional, I'd suggest. Of course, if the user is delusional,' she said, 'their subscription should be terminated.'

'Oh, yes. Already has been, in this case. And you're right, in fact; this participant does have a history of mental health problems, quite severe problems as I understand – I don't know how he ever passed the medical history check. But it's a ridiculous idea, of course. To think he could somehow connect to another individual, another Make-Believe user . . .' She laughed, shook her head. 'God, if that were possible I'm sure Imagen would already be making a fortune out of it!'

Once more, Morgan stared straight at her. 'It hardly sounds plausible, does it, spontaneous connections within Make-Believe. As you say, a ridiculous idea. Now, if that's all . . . ?'

Cassie blinked. Smiled. 'Thank you so much, that's been incredibly useful.'

'Glad I could help.' The professor looked looser suddenly, but still guarded. Like she'd come through a job interview with flying colours, and all that remained was to make a graceful exit.

'Sorry again for the interruption, I should have made an appointment, I know. If there's anything else that comes up – would it be OK for me to email you? Or give you a call?'

'Fine. Of course. Email is generally best.' She reached for the inside pocket of her jacket, handed over a card.

'Thanks.' Cassie patted her satchel. 'I've run out – but I'll email my details. Just in case you want to contact me. Well . . .'

'You might take a look at the new Make-Believe exhibit, if you haven't seen it?'

'The . . . ?'

'It's here, in the public access space. It's very good; there are some other exhibits, too, from various other research strands, but Make-Believe is the focus. You'll be familiar with the information, of course, but it's interestingly presented. There's a charge for entry, I believe – but if you're interested, I could have a word?'

'That's very kind. I'd love to see it.' She walked alongside Morgan to the entrance, past a group of students who were huddled together, showing off their personalised receivers. Cassie gestured towards them. 'You must feel – when you see people using your technology – it's an amazing achievement.'

'Well.' She looked surprised. 'I suppose I do.'

Cassie was improvising now, reluctant to let her go. Off the top of her head, she said, 'I mean, I'm completely out of the loop, but in terms of the original growth targets . . .'

'Not my area.' Morgan seemed to bristle, her tone suddenly clipped. 'It's the nature of unforeseen complications. They're impossible to predict.' She raised a hand to catch the attention of a uniformed man, gestured towards Cassie, then to the exhibition space. The man smiled, tilted his head in an *OK* sign. 'He'll let you straight through,' said Morgan. 'And now I must get on.'

She walked briskly through the security gates. Didn't offer a parting handshake. Didn't look back.

CHAPTER SEVENTEEN

When she'd finally managed to lose the girl, Morgan took the lift to the first floor. There, she went straight to the ladies'. Placed her briefcase by the basin. Washed her hands, the water as hot as it would go.

'Christ,' she said, staring at her reflection. 'What. What now.'

She had recognised the face – and then when the girl introduced herself the name had been familiar. But it had taken a minute for her to remember. Cassandra McAllister. She was part of the team at Imagen, a mid-level employee. And she'd been a red flag. One of the first.

Morgan rubbed her scalp, digging her fingers into her hair, trying to massage away a growing headache. Her first jolt of concern, once she'd placed Cassandra, had been for her private research. A fear that the girl had been tasked to find out about any unauthorised projects. But no one could be aware of how far that research had progressed – and indeed, Cassandra had seemed to know nothing of it. Which was not to say she knew nothing at all.

Morgan knew she shouldn't have spoken to her. Should have insisted she make an appointment, then told Lisa to put her name on the blacklist. But she'd been taken by surprise, which was presumably part of the plan. Whatever the plan might be, and to whomever it might belong.

God, she looked a fright, with her hair out in spikes like some stereotype of a mad scientist. Grimly, she persuaded it back into a more respectable arrangement. That was the real issue, wasn't it: who had the girl been talking to? Was she acting alone, or had she been sent – perhaps as some kind of test? The time outs, the collaboration, a user with mental health problems . . . she knew something alright, but her questions had been . . . odd. Not what you'd expect, if the girl had been briefed by someone with access to the facts.

Either way, she would have to report the encounter. To warn Imagen, or simply to cover her own back.

Of course, it was just about possible the girl had been telling the truth. That she really was working on a psychology project. Well, that would be easy enough to check. She'd moved on from Imagen, that was her story – but hadn't she, in fact, been sacked? For overstaying in Make-Believe, for not reporting her time out failure. Morgan shook her head. A brutal way to silence someone. But if that was so, perhaps the girl was merely investigating her own circumstance, hoping to bring a claim for unfair dismissal. In which case, it was even more essential to warn Tom and the whole of the senior management team, in order to avoid any tricky publicity.

Morgan picked up her briefcase. Walked out of the ladies', down the stairs and out of the Newman building, across the square and into the Bray Tower.

Ten minutes after she'd left it she was back at her desk, door locked, screen in hand. Readying herself to make a call.

CHAPTER EIGHTEEN

In the centre of a white room hung a head, two metres tall and made of light. Pale curves and outlines rendered the skull, the mass of brain within. The display must have worked on a motion sensor: when Cassie stepped towards the head, it glowed a fraction more brightly, and a short text appeared in front of her. *Make-Believe: how does it work?*

As the text faded, the head spun round to present her with a profile. At the bridge of the nose, colour bloomed, a pulse of turquoise that dissolved into thousands of pinpricks. *Specially programmed biomolecules are introduced into the body via a single dose of nasal spray*, said the accompanying text – and a thousand specks of light spread through the nasal membrane, swirled like seed heads on the air, each travelling to an assigned location where it settled, and dimmed. Watching, Cassie felt a pressure in her own nose, like the warning of a bleed. That spray: it had stung – and there had been a smell, too, or a taste, which the display couldn't capture. For her it had been hot plastic, lingering faintly for days, but some colleagues had described it as metallic, sweet, or ammoniac, and others reported no taste or smell at all.

The brain was threaded with turquoise now, densely meshed in some parts, more loosely laced in others. Make-Believe biomolecules, in position, ready to carry out their individual tasks.

The biomolecules work with a receiver, worn as an earpiece, said the text, *to transform imagination into reality*. Cassie watched as a receiver was sketched onto the ear of the head, and its function light flashed on.

One set of biomolecules is programmed to function as a switch. A turquoise glow pulsed thinly across the brain. *When triggered by an electronic signal from the user's receiver, they activate and deactivate other sets of biomolecules, controlling the Make-Believe experience.* A loud *click*: the sound snapped through the space, like someone had pressed a light switch. The glow spread, brightened, till the whole blue mesh of biomolecules was illuminated.

On the floor something darkened, drawing her gaze downwards. A trail of shadowy footprints was beckoning her to walk inside the skull. She followed them, fitting her paces to the shadow-steps, and stopped when they did. Here, at the centre of the room, she could turn a complete circle, looking out through the sheer outlines of the brain, at the threads of blue, and the white walls beyond.

When the biomolecules are active, they mute external stimuli such as light, sound, pressure, smells and tastes.

Outside the skull, a ribbon of light scribbled soundwaves in the air, zigzagging green towards her; at the same time, birdsong sounded, its notes and gaps matching the peaks and dips of light – then the soundwaves reached the ear canal and faded, from emerald to aqua to a scarcely visible wash, and the singing dropped away. For a second, no sound. No movement. Then the space around her burst into light and colour: yellow stars tumbling towards her, and violet triangles, red spheres, blue cubes, each shape, each colour representing a different sense, all falling fast till they reached the surface of the skull – its eyes or mouth, nose or skin, and Cassie ducked, raised a hand against—

Nothing. Everything gone: faded, dissolved, disintegrated.

She lowered her hand. It was a clever representation, but it was nothing like it – that moment of your dissolving self, of perfect non-existence. The need, the hunger stirred inside her, reaching, stretching. She shifted her feet, squeaking her soles on the hard reality of the floor.

The text was explaining how the external stimuli were muted, by intercepting the chemical and electrical signals at the sites where the brain would otherwise interpret them and turn them into a precept, or something perceived. *In this way*, it said, *the user becomes unaware of everything but the most intrusive inputs from the outside world.*

That was a modification. The first iterations had blocked external stimuli completely; the mute function was one of many alterations they'd had to make before the technology could be licensed for commercial use. A user must be able to perceive stimuli of an intensity that would wake a heavy sleeper, for instance a smoke alarm, or a child's persistent screaming. It was amazing, though, what you could sleep through if your dreams were sweet enough. You woke back in the real world, the front door open—

Above and around her, sections of brain lit into action, glowing orange. *The user then begins to imagine their virtual reality*, said the text. *As they do so, the relevant portions of their brain become active.*

Portions. A strange word to choose. Made her think of brains for lunch, scooped out with the suck of a serving spoon, a grey helping dumped, wobbling and sliding, on a blank white plate.

The biomolecules are programmed to respond to this activation in two ways. One set instructs the relevant neurological pathways to transmit these signals to the parts of the brain that control sensory perception.

More sound effects. The spit and hiss of scores of electric shocks as, all around her, neurons fired – a crisscross tracery of sparking threads, each transmitting its own Make-Believe message. She stood amid the fireworks and, despite it all, felt herself lift with a childish delight – the thrill of Bonfire Night, of fire blazing through the dark – till she thought of Alan, and the rockets turned to flares. Bonfire night to a war zone.

This causes the user to experience what he or she imagines, through all sensory modalities: sight, sound, smell, taste, touch and proprioception.

If they were together, which would it be? Her fireworks? His war zone?

Or would the hiss be the rain (she closed her eyes, imagined it so) and the spit the sound of raindrops hitting the tent of leaves above their heads, in the place they'd always found each other?

Through the fizz-pop sound effects, the shout of a child. A boy, running into the white room. Stopping dead, mouth open. 'Mum – Dad – *look!*' His family following, mum and dad and an older sister – 'But what's it meant to *be*?' – as the boy jumped into the middle of it all, turning and turning, grabbing at shooting threads of light.

Another set of molecules acts as a biological/electronic transducer, transforming biological data to electronic information. This is transmitted via the user's receiver and a secure 6G network to Imagen's central servers. In this way, details of the user's imagined experience, encoded as digital packets, can be analysed and stored, and used to enhance future experiences.

Data in, data out. When she'd laughed at the idea of a shared Make-Believe, Morgan's eye contact had been ostentatious, the shake of her head overemphatic. Such an obvious show of honesty, Cassie had known she must be lying. Spontaneous connections, she'd said; but Cassie had mentioned nothing about the nature of the shared experiences supposedly being reported by her psychology study subjects. A ridiculous idea, Morgan had said; meaning it had to be true. Meaning yes, that a doctor could connect with a patient. Meaning more than that; because if one user could connect with another – if two people together could Make-Believe – then it wasn't Make-Believe at all. Wasn't something that happened only in your head, in your imagination.

It was real. And what that meant—

Everything. It meant everything. It changed everything.

It meant that when she'd sat on a bench outside Alan's ward at Raphael House, and Make-Believed – when that technicolour shift had made her think there must have been an upgrade, or a glitch – that afternoon, what she'd taken for Make-Believe had been real. The Alan she'd lost to madness had been there with her, and Make-Believe nothing more than the place where she had found him.

And it meant that from then on, every time she'd Believed him, it had been real: shared, and shaped by them both. She didn't know how this could be true, but it was. It was true. She was certain of that.

'Mum, look, it's *cool*!' The boy was still grabbing at nothing but light, captivated by the display.

'Marcus, come on out of there!' The mum shot a look at Cassie, half sheepish, half defensive. Cassie smiled, shook her head to show she wasn't bothered by the boy's intrusion – not in the least. It was fine. It was perfectly fine.

There was room inside for two.

CHAPTER NINETEEN

'Alright, Cassie? Earth to Cass . . .'

She was staring at her bike lock when she realised that someone – Nicol – was speaking to her.

'What's up, something wrong with your bike? New, isn't it?'

'Yeah – well, borrowed actually.' It was Lewis's: the purple mountain bike. It had been his suggestion she should use it when she stayed with him – though best not to risk it at her place, they'd both agreed. On the pitted tarmac of the city's roads, it was like riding on air. 'Only thing is, I've forgotten the numbers. The—' She couldn't think of the word. Gave the chain a shake, by way of explanation.

'Combination? New lock as well?'

She shook her head. 'Had it for years.' She didn't have to think, usually; the code was automatic, embedded in her long-term memory, in her fingers. But she'd left the Make-Believe display hardly knowing her name. Her interview with Professor Morgan – the implications of what Morgan had let slip – had knocked everything else clean out of her head. 'Blanked,' she said, simply.

'Don't try too hard. It won't come that way. Think about something else.'

She felt a slow smile arriving on her face: that was easily done.

'You OK? You look a bit fucked, if you don't mind me saying.'

'Fucked?'

'Aye. Spaced. Stoned.'

'Ha. No – I've been to that exhibition, that's all. The one in the Newman building.'

'Not seen it. I should, though, by the looks of you. Must be properly mind-blowing.'

'It is. Yeah, they've got this head, made out of light and . . .' She shrugged, at the impossibility of explaining. 'It's all about Make-Believe, showing how it works.'

'Oh. That.' In two short words, he dismissed the whole thing; a hundred thousand virtual worlds, imagined into being by a hundred thousand individuals. 'Nah. I'll not bother.'

She didn't think she'd ever heard that tone in his voice. Not just dismissive; hostile.

'How come?'

His face screwed up, like his words tasted sour. 'I disapprove,' he said.

She wanted to laugh, at the formality of the expression. But he was serious, and she stopped herself. 'Of what?' she asked. 'Because they're a mega-rich corporation? An anti-capitalist thing?'

'Mega-rich, you reckon? Funny thing . . . I had a friend got a job with them, and the week before he was meant to start' – he made a chopping motion with his hand – 'sorry, pal: no job. Total hiring freeze. Weird, eh, for the most amazingly successful company in the history of the world, ever?' His voice was coiled tight with sarcasm.

'So is that why you disapprove, cos of your friend?'

He scowled. 'The whole thing!' he said. 'All their little tests, you know. How much do you earn? How much are you *going to* earn? How much does your daddy earn?'

She didn't say so, but that was just business. Imagen might have been spun off from the university, but it wasn't a charity; it wasn't a social enterprise, or a public service. Your net worth was their business model.

'Ever been to the doctor feeling a bit down?' Nicol was saying. 'A bit *depressed*? Well then, sorry – you're out. Can't join our club.'

'I suppose they've got to make sure people are safe. Stable. Otherwise—'

'Got any kind of a record? Maybe you were picked up for exercising your democratic right to protest, ended up with a caution on your file? You're out.'

No cash. Dodgy mental health. Blots on your copybook.

Cassie slipped neatly into all three categories – but which applied to Nicol? It had to be personal, his dislike. But he seemed to guess what she was thinking.

'No,' he said. 'I haven't even tried. It's like that celebrity soap opera shit. Either way, it's a kid-on world. A tool to keep the people distracted. You know it's government funded, aye? Suits them, to keep us docile. I'd rather spend my life in the real world. Real people.' He scuffed his trainer across the grey slabs they were standing on, splattered with chuddy and pigeon shit. 'Real fucking life.'

She thought of pointing out the contradiction: that such an advocate for reality chose to be constantly, mildly stoned. He might claim to be a fan of real life, but even he needed its edges smoothed. It was the same cognitive dissonance, perhaps, that allowed him to pocket his fifty per cent from the academic services they provided, even as he argued against the marketisation of the university.

'But I tell you what,' he was saying. 'If I wanted to play their wee game, their Make-Believe – I wouldn't be doing their tests. Did you know they still own it, once it's inside you? The network, the biomolecules. They *own* part of your brain. It's their copyright, their patent.'

'Maybe technically – but that doesn't really mean anything. It's not like they can recover their property. How would they even do that?'

'Nurse – scalpel please . . .'

'Don't! Anyway, it would never stand up, legally.'

'Possession is nine-tenths of the law? And who do you think would have the better lawyers? No way. I wouldn't be showing them the money, any of that.'

'Well – how, then?'

'Just got to know the right folk. There's other ways.'

'You mean – bioware. Hacked bioware?'

He smiled. Spoke with exaggerated precision: 'Black market. That's all I'm saying.'

'But . . .' She frowned. Tried to quell a sudden surge of excitement. 'You'd still need the biomolecular network, from the nasal spray. And you haven't tried it, have you? So it might be a scam, for all you know.'

'Like I say. I prefer real life.'

So many questions, bottlenecked inside her. Who were the right folk? How was it modded, the stolen bioware? Would it work even if you were barred from Make-Believe, your DNA blacklisted? How much would it cost? But paranoia stopped her lips. Impossible to ask these things in the shadow of the Bray Tower. Could she even be sure that Nicol was solid? She thought she could trust him, more so than anyone else. She needed to be alone, to think it through, all of it—

It came to her: she snapped her fingers.

'Aye,' he said, with a nod, 'there's a black market for everything—'

'No, just – I've got it. Remembered it.' She bent over the bike, clicked the wheels of the combination till the numbers were aligned, and the lock gave. 'Freedom!'

'See?' he said, as she unsnaked her chain from round

the railings. 'Told you: just let your brain do its thing.'

Cassie shoved the chain into her satchel, swung into the saddle. 'Nicol's Rules for Life, number 172 . . .' she said, pushing off. Heard him say something, as she coasted – to himself, or to her. Something like, *Don't chase the lost stuff*. Something like, *It's in there all along*.

CHAPTER TWENTY

Lewis had cooked steak.

'Two minutes each side,' he said, 'and it's perfect. All it needs.' He set Cassie's plate before her with a solid clunk, sat down opposite. Started to eat.

Cassie picked up her knife and fork, absently rearranged the French beans piled on the side, swirling them in their slick of melted butter. Lewis glanced up at her, waiting for praise.

'You're not hungry?'

Was she? She thought about it for a moment. Yes: she was. She was hungry. It just didn't seem to matter. The sensation was distant, unreal.

'Not a fan of steak?'

'No, it's great. Smells great.'

She dug with her knife. Sliced into the pink.

Juice – blood – oozed across her plate. Alan's voice: *You could do with some blood. Some red meat. An enormous steak.*

You've never said that before; about blood.

What she knew now: she hadn't imagined it, though she'd been in Make-Believe. It had been his real voice, his real words. Real face, warmth, body. Real mind. Real self.

She forked up a chunk of meat, chewed and swallowed, and it tasted of nothing at all.

'Cassie? Are you feeling OK?'

'Fine. Why?'

'You've usually got a proper appetite.'

'Sorry. Maybe I am a bit off.' She tried a couple of beans: they were overcooked, slathered in too much butter, dissolving in her mouth. She wiped a smear of grease from her lips.

'And you're quiet too.'

A wave of irritation caught her, carried her: could he not just shut up, stop itching at her? 'At least I'm not speaking with my mouth full,' she said. Saw him recoil, and wished she'd kept hers shut. He was meant to be Mr Casual, Mr Tall Dark and Kind Of Handsome, and here she was niggling at him like they'd been married twenty years. But it wasn't contempt born of familiarity. His voice was a stranger's, suddenly, and her being here was wrong. Who was he, anyway? This man she'd known for a matter of weeks, a man she knew nothing about? This man feeding her, fucking her, acting her boyfriend?

He swallowed. 'Sorry if my manners aren't up to scratch.'

'And would you stop saying sorry? You're always apologising.'

He stared at her. 'What? No, I'm not. Like when?' And thinking about it, she couldn't isolate a single incident. It was more an impression she had; it was his face, maybe, or his posture or something.

'I don't know. Just, generally.'

Lewis was frowning now, squinching up his narrow eyes, eyes so dark they let nothing in. Alan's eyes were clear as water – or they had been, once. The windows of his soul. She stared at her plate, and thought of dinner in the locked ward. What was he eating, now? Food had never thrilled him: it was fuel, for walking the hills, for running, playing football. Fuel for fat, now. Featureless days, punctuated by mugs of tea sticky with sugar, with cheap biscuits, mounds of pasta with cheese, mashed potatoes with marge. But he was in there, wasn't he? Her Alan. Beached in his armchair. Trapped under all that flesh. A young man, freshly made, with a boy's leanness still, with all his youth still shining gold. And when he and she connected, that young man was made real.

'Look,' said Lewis, 'do you want to go to bed? Alone, I mean. Have a lie-down, I'll bring you a cup of tea.'

He spoke gently, watched her with concern, and she managed a smile. 'No. No, thanks,' she said. Looked at him: at Lewis, who was on her side. At Lewis, who wanted what she did. Put down her knife and fork.

'I did something today that was – I took a risk.'

'What do you mean? What kind of risk?'

'I spoke to someone I used to know. Professionally.'

A forkful of steak stopped midway to his mouth. 'At Imagen?'

'At the university. Someone involved with research, with the biotech. Someone . . . high up.'

'Shit. Cassie. God, I feel responsible, I pushed you—'

'Come on. You know I'm not likely to be pushed by you.'

'Well. OK. But – was it worth it? Did you find out anything?'

'Yeah. I think I did. It's like you said. There *are* more of us.'

'I was right?'

She smiled again, felt her lips stretch thin. 'You were right.'

'How did you – did you just ask, straight out?'

'Pretty much.' She shrugged.

'And he, she, they – told you this?'

'Came straight out with it. Said there had been a few, isolated, instances of people hacking the bioware. Of which you, presumably, are one.'

'That's amazing.' He pushed up from his seat, leant across the table: his mouth tasted of meat, and grease. 'You are amazing.'

She would have been pleased, before. Tried to find that feeling inside her. It must be there, somewhere. 'I know,' she said. 'I'm amazing.'

'A few instances . . . How many, do you think?'

'Presuming a certain amount of understatement: double figures, at least. Beyond that, who can say. But I'm not sure it matters – because then, after, I spoke to someone else.'

'Another contact?'

She shook her head. 'A friend, not from Imagen. But he knows about stuff. He's a computer scientist, but – the sort of person who, anything you're not meant to be doing, he knows how to do it. Know what I mean?'

'And what did you ask him?'

'I didn't ask, exactly. It just came up in conversation.'

He was leaning in like he might kiss her again. 'OK – but what?'

'He said – if you know the right people, there are ways into Make-Believe. Without Imagen. Without them ever knowing.'

He was silent for a moment. Then: 'What, even if your DNA's been blacklisted?'

'I don't know, I couldn't exactly ask for details. He just said, black market.

'Black market,' Lewis said. He sat back in his chair. 'But then – it's so simple; it could be so simple. No need for bargaining or blackmail or any of that. They'd never need to know.'

'No,' she agreed. It was surprising, in a way, that Lewis hadn't thought of it before. But he was too safe, too legit, to think in that way. More surprising, perhaps, that it hadn't occurred to her – but then, until lately, she hadn't let herself consider the possibility of return.

Their plates sat abandoned between them, Lewis's meal half-finished, Cassie's barely touched.

'How reliable is he, your friend, would you say?'

Cassie hesitated – weighing the hostility in Nicol's voice when he spoke about Make-Believe against the scores of deadlines he'd met for her. 'He's pretty reliable . . . no – he's very reliable. But he's not neutral. He hates them, hates Imagen, he's got all kinds of conspiracy theories about them, so – I don't know whether that affects things. What he might want to believe.' She thought for a moment. 'I could ask him – I could find out more. Who we'd need to contact. But the way he feels, I don't know whether he'd help—'

'No,' said Lewis – just as she'd guessed he would. 'Leave it with me. I can speak to some people. If it's possible, I can sort it, I'm sure.' For a minute he sat thinking, his narrow eyes almost closed. Then he seemed to refocus, stared at her with a slight frown. 'You said we.'

'Sorry?'

'Find out who *we'd* need to contact. That's what you said.'

Cassie looked down, made to clear their plates away. 'Finished?' When Lewis nodded, she got up and scraped them into the bin.

'It's up to you,' said Lewis. 'I don't want to sway you. I mean, I know you're not pushable. And it might not work anyway, might not be possible – your friend might be, I don't know, trying to impress you, or something. I just need to know: am I asking for me, or for both of us?'

She turned on the taps, waited for the water to run hot. If it was possible, Lewis would sort it. That must have been what she was hoping for. Why else would she have told him? If she said, *Yes, both of us*, it was nothing irrevocable. She could always change her mind. She pushed down the plug, squirted washing-up liquid; a sneeze of bubbles, a cough of fake lemon. She'd already left the shadows – and if Imagen were going to come for her, as well to meet them in the searchlight, full in its glare. In Make-Believe: where she'd find him again. Where Alan would be waiting.

Lewis spoke over the gushing taps. Her name. A question.

She turned the water off, plunged her hands into bubbles and heat.

'For both of us,' she said.

CHAPTER TWENTY-ONE

From across the road, a little way down the street, Cassie watched the attendees leaving the meeting. They came out in threes and twos, said goodnight and vanished back to their lives. Sometimes a man or a woman left alone, head down: hurrying from contact, its promise or threat.

At ten past eight, Jake appeared with the final stragglers. Waved them goodnight, and shut the door, ready to lock up.

Cassie crossed the street. As Jake turned and saw her, she raised her hand. He stood, waited. When she was a few feet away, he checked an imaginary wristwatch.

'You've missed it.'

'Sorry,' she said. 'I've been waiting. I was hoping . . . but I guess you need to get home.'

He studied her. She looked down at the pavement, then over the road: at a front door opening and closing, an old man doddering out with his old dog. When she glanced up again, Jake was still watching her.

'Just give me a minute,' he said, turning away.

When he'd called his wife, he seemed to think for a moment, squinting into the evening sun, before he made a decision. 'Half an hour,' he said. 'Come on – let's walk.'

They set off, heading west; she didn't ask where.

'You've not been back to the group.'

'No.'

'Nor has Lewis.'

'No.'

'None of my business, but you're here to talk, so . . .'

'I knew you'd be—' She was going to say worried, but that was a presumption. Why should he worry about either of them? 'Concerned.'

'Was I right to be?'

'Yes.'

'And are you going to tell me about it?'

She didn't answer.

They were near the cathedral: St Mary's, she thought it was. 'Here.' Jake turned down a path that led round the side; there was an expanse of grass, and a bench. She followed him, and they sat.

Side by side was good. You could talk, and you didn't need to look the other person in the eye.

She spoke first. 'I want to tell you,' she said. 'If I could explain, it would all make more sense – but it's just . . .' She paused: just what? Fear, still keeping her quiet? Fear that stopped her talking to someone as rock-solid as Jake? But in the last weeks she'd taken far more serious risks – and right now she was planning the biggest risk of all. Not fear. It was just too hard to explain. Too much to expect that anyone could believe. 'If I tell you me and Lewis are the same. With both of us, it's not drink that's a problem, and it's not drugs.'

'But it's something you have an addiction to.'

'Yes.'

'And Lewis?'

'The same. It's not – I know we're meant to avoid it, that kind of relationship, not let it derail your recovery – but it's not like one of us dragging the other down. I don't think it's that. It's both of us.' She turned to face him. 'It'll swallow my life,' she said. 'Just the same as if it was drink or drugs, I know that. It happened before, and now it's going to happen again.'

'Going to. It hasn't happened yet. You haven't relapsed.'

'No, I haven't, but—'

'It's still your choice, Cassie. You can be in control; you don't have to let it control you.'

'But I *want* it to happen again. I really—' Her breath let her down. She stopped, inhaled. Saw her feet sinking into the uncut grass: white daisies closing their eyes for the evening, and the grey of her grubby trainers. 'There's someone who matters to me more than anything.' She looked at Jake, a sideways glance. 'Not Lewis,' she said, 'not that Lewis doesn't matter, but . . . not him. And I lost him, this person, and I thought he was gone for ever. The man – the boy that I . . . Anyway. Now I've found a way to get him back. To get back to him.'

In the quiet that followed, she thought of all the questions Jake could ask. But the traffic rose and fell in the near distance, and a seagull cried overhead, and he didn't ask anything.

'You know,' he said at last, 'the only way it can work, staying free, is to want it. Whether it's drink or drugs, and if you say it's the same – your thing, whatever it is – you have to find a way to want that.'

'I can't. I don't.'

'Well then.' Jake shrugged. 'What are you here for?'

She stared at him in dismay.

'You're looking at me like I don't care. That's not true, but what I'm saying is it's up to you. You came here wanting to speak to me; you're asking for my advice, but it seems like what you want is for me to tell you it's OK. It's OK to let go, stop trying, let it swallow you. And I'm not going to tell you that.'

There was something black, an ant or a tiny beetle, scaling the toe of her trainer. She watched it, hard, keeping her eyes wide open and her lips pressed shut.

'So if you still want my advice: *try*. Try and find something else that matters. It may not matter as much; nothing'll maybe ever matter as much. That's what we live with, isn't it? That's the shit we all live with.'

She cleared her throat. 'To paraphrase: what's so special about my shit?'

'If you like. And you know, eventually . . . if you're lucky, something else *will* matter. Really matter. I love my wife, you know? I love my kids. And I don't bang on about it, but – this. This matters.' He meant the cathedral. The faith it stood for.

She turned her face away. She didn't have what Jake did, had never believed, though faith was a life raft for many people at the group. But she'd had a family, once. And she loved them still, even if they'd forgotten all about her. She breathed a couple of long breaths, and after a bit she said, 'OK. I'll try.'

'Good. I'm glad.'

The ant-beetle creature was gone. Vanished in the grass, or crawled into her trainer, through a hole in its worn-out sole. 'Time's up, I guess,' she said. 'You'd best get home, or she'll be wondering where you are.'

'Yep.' But he didn't move. 'Listen, I don't know if you heard about April.'

April. Recaller of names, pourer of tea. Wide-eyed, and perpetually surprised.

'She was found by her daughter – last week. Overdose. It wasn't an accident; she meant to. Sleeping tablets.'

'Oh. God. That's awful. Of all the people.' She wasn't sure how close they'd been, April and Jake. Whether she should be sorry for him. Said it anyway: 'I'm so sorry.' They were the right words, and she meant them; she just couldn't quite feel them the way she knew she should.

He shook his head. 'It's always a shock, whoever – but yeah. I don't think any of us had an inkling. Anyway, I thought I should tell you.' He stood up. 'The funeral's tomorrow, if you wanted to come.'

His voice was weighted, weary, and she thought of him suddenly as an Atlas: bearing them all on his broad shoulders, bent almost double. Leaning on that faith of his, and trying not to show how he struggled with the load. She wished he'd stay, protective and bearlike beside her. Wanted to give him a hug, though she wasn't sure who would be comforting whom; knew anyway that he would set her aside, gently, firmly, and she'd feel a total idiot.

Instead, she nodded as he told her where and when. Promised she'd be there. Promised, once more, that she'd try.

CHAPTER TWENTY-TWO

The park was thronged with kids, halfway through their summer break. From the west, the sky was darkening. By evening, it would crack open; thunder was imminent. Cassie could feel it in her aching jaw, could sense it taking an in-breath, ready to let rip. Children shrieked, their wildness muffled by the muggy air. Heavy clouds bore down on their shrill games; parents were called on to adjudicate and console, as laughter swung to hysterics.

From her bench between the swings and the climbing frame, Cassie scanned the running, kicking, climbing mass, looking out for Ella and Finn – because this was the Good Park, where they always came. Where they had always come. It was a priority maintenance area, occupied by well-off families and frequented by tourists: while the scraps of green near to Meg's flat were mined with dogshit, needles, broken glass, here the grass was neat and the flowerbeds tended. The swing-chains were unrusted, the roundabout spun smoothly on its axis, so this was where Cassie used to take the kids to give Meg a break, though it was a long walk from the flat, for Ella especially. Ella would always beg to be carried, would plead and sulk and cajole and eventually Cassie would give in because Ella was only three, after all, and a small three at that and her legs were short for all that walking. And then Finn would complain. Five was old enough to walk, she'd tell him, but still he'd whinge – till she distracted him with a story starring himself. And that's how they would make it there and back to the Good Park.

Ella had turned five now, of course, and Finn was nearly seven. Both old enough to walk. A few times over the last year she'd seen them here. Always she'd kept her distance. Protecting herself, from Meg's indifference. Protecting the kids, from her own carelessness.

This was where they always came, but today they were nowhere to be seen.

Cassie might have been a mum, grabbing ten minutes to herself while the kids let off steam, except that she'd been there five hours already. Five hours during which she had missed April's funeral; but there would have been plenty folk there to remember her, and this – sitting here, waiting – was more important. She was only sorry to have broken her promise to Jake.

I love my wife, he'd said. *I love my kids*. She knew Jake's story. Where she was closed like a fist, he laid his past open. What Jake had lost: a mother and father (dead, from drink); a little brother (dead from drugs); eight years (prison, assault and possession with intent to supply); a first wife and a daughter (estranged, and living on the other side of the world). And still he could say, *If you're lucky, something else will matter.* His luck was a woman who knew what he came from and loved him all the same – enough to give him a second chance at love, marriage, kids.

How would her own luck come, if it came? What would it look like? Not like this. Not like a woman in a play-park with one eye on her kids on a Saturday afternoon. It made no difference how carefully she watered her umbrella plant, how often she fed Lewis's stupid cat. In reality she wasn't to be relied on. She'd proved it to herself. She could never be the kind of person to look after others. Funny – for years she'd thought herself strong, even brave. When her mum died she'd missed a week of school, gone back and sat her exams. When her dad left she'd carried on, navigated the end of school, got herself into university, begun her adult life. Then, true, she'd had Alan alongside her. But later, after it all fell apart – when the easiest thing would have been to do what April had just done – Cassie had put her head down and trudged on. Rebuilt a life of sorts. Tried to make amends.

But she'd been kidding herself all along. She knew that now. She was selfish, and weak, giving in to the first real temptation.

She made herself a rollie with her last shreds of tobacco, risking the disapproval of every adult in the park. She'd stay till teatime, she supposed – knowing they might not come, that they probably wouldn't come. She'd stay till the crowd of kids thinned out, dragged off by parents, reluctantly home to food and bath and bed; or until the first drops of rain cleared the park. And she'd come again tomorrow, and after that . . . she didn't know. She could go to her sister's flat. Meg wouldn't let her in, of course; since the incident, she never had. But Cassie might still catch a glimpse, and that glimpse might be enough. Might matter enough. Might help her make the choice Jake wanted her to make: the damaged present over the perfect past.

She'd always assumed, without ever much thinking about it, that she'd have kids of her own, with Alan. It wouldn't happen now, of course. Still, just occasionally, she found herself imagining. As a shaft of sun slipped through a fleeting gap in the clouds, she narrowed her eyes, and let herself see them. Their child – a girl – taking careful steps along the balance beam. Alan pacing alongside, there to steady their daughter if she wobbled, to catch her if she fell. Almost close enough to touch; a world she and Alan had Made together. That shimmered behind a heavy curtain of reality – and every now and then a wind got up, caught the fabric and gave it a tug, so a bright breathtaking glimpse of Make-Believe showed through.

Cassie dragged herself back to reality. Refocused, reframed the scene. Concentrated on the splintered paint

of the bench against her palms, which was ro
real but only when she made herself notice. Wh
let herself drift, there was no bench, no flaking p
No dry, warm scent of trampled grass. Focus – and the
it was again. Touch, smell, sound. The high clamour o
children's voices, the lower-pitched calls of the parents.

'Finn, steady there!'

The name jolted her. Rippled through her. But the
voice was unfamiliar, a dad's protective shout. Someone
else's Finn. She scanned the park for this other Finn –
slide, roundabout, climbing frame – and froze. There
was Ella on the swings, legs stuck out in front, and Finn
pushing inexpertly so her swing circled, jerked from side
to side more than it rose and fell. Beside them – taking
over, now, on pushing duties – was the man who had
shouted. A man Cassie didn't know.

She watched how he swung her niece, carefully, not
hard or high, a short straight line and a steady rhythm.
Ella leant with the movement, forward and back, her too-
big T-shirt billowing on her skinny frame. Cassie used to
lower her into the leather sling of a baby swing, push
her oh-so-gently, and she'd sit with her mouth open like
she was concentrating on learning through her eyes ear
mouth nose and skin, would stare at her feet as thoug
hypnotised by their swooshing above the ground. No
she squealed, giddy from sailing through the sky. S
twisted round to say something to the man – and Ca
felt her legs tense, ready to leap up, her arms read
catch, if Ella's small hands should slip from the cha

'Hang on though, baby,' she heard the man say. 'Are you holding on properly? Hold on tight.'

After a while he slowed the swing, caught it, and Ella slid to the ground so Finn could take a turn. His hair had grown longish; it blew back as he arced up, covered his eyes on the downswing.

'Higher!' he called, straight away. 'I go higher than this, much higher! I go right to the top!' And the man pushed harder, and Cassie could see the thrill on Finn's face. She saw the moment it tipped into uncertainty, his feet touching level with the top bar – heard his yelp, and watched how swiftly the man stretched and braced and caught him near the top of the arc, grasping the seat with both hands, bringing it down safe and pretending not to have noticed Finn's moment of fear.

'Where next?' was all he said.

A moment's thought, then Finn was running, and Ella too. Towards her – past her – no more than a foot away. The man even gave her a sort of smile as he brought up the rear. Cassie turned her head to watch as Finn boarded the roundabout, and Ella scrambled astride a bouncing yellow duck.

Find something else that matters. This was her trying, just as she'd promised. Trying to find the something else. And they did, they mattered; but what good was that? They had run straight past her. They didn't know her any more. It was she who didn't matter. Her sister's kids came to the park with a man who was a stranger to her: he mattered. A man unconnected to her family, with no

ties of blood. He seemed a kind man. You'd think he was a great dad, if you didn't know.

Cassie watched till the kids grew tired of playing, started a campaign for ice cream. From where she sat, their voices were lost in the babble. She saw Ella pointing at the van, and both of them tugging, one on each arm, till the man gave in and they joined the queue. She would have liked to see them more closely, now they were standing still. See how they were growing up, how like their mum they were, or their grandparents, or their aunt. She thought about joining the ice cream queue herself. She could hover behind them. Even speak to them. She could do that – say, *Hello, you won't remember me, will you?* Ask, *Did you like the book I sent?* The idea squirmed inside her, made her sit up straight, ready to act. If he left them, just for a moment. If he turned to speak to someone else. But it was too late; now they were at the counter, choosing their ice creams. Now they were turning, heading for the gates. Ready for home. Finn and Ella hand in hand, eating as they walked.

Hand in hand. It was how they must have gone when they left her flat, the last time she'd looked after them. The last time she was family to them. The time when they were lost.

CHAPTER TWENTY-THREE

You fall asleep, exhausted, cross the border between Make-Believe and dreams, and wake back in the real world cold and stiff, lying wet in the empty bathtub.

You ache from hours unmoving on a hard surface. You've wet yourself, again – but that's OK. That's why you were in the bath in the first place. Your knickers, your T-shirt, are cold and clinging and sweet-sour smelling. You haul yourself up, bones painful against the enamel. Wrap your arms around your legs, head bowed against your knees.

It takes a couple of minutes to remember yourself.

Every time you land back here, you lose him. You lose Alan. You lose yourself: the self that you are with him. Return to a self you can't recognise.

You stand, unsteady. Peel off your soiled clothes and

throw them in the sink. You told yourself you wouldn't do it. Tonight – last night. You would stay in the real world, stay and look after the kids.

The kids— But they'll be sleeping still. An adventure for them to stay overnight, sleeping in your big bed, with Meg away out on her first date since their dad left. When you picked them up last night all three of them were giddy, Meg in her glittery top, flushed and giggling, Finn and Ella tearing about like mad things. It took a while for the kids to settle – but when you crept at midnight from the spare room into the bathroom, you made sure to look in on them by the light from the hallway, and everything was fine. The two of them breathing deep, under the covers: Finn flat on his front, Ella stretched like a starfish.

You tilt your face up to the showerhead. Let the steaming water clean you, comfort you. You stand for a long time, till you feel yourself thawing, coming back to life. Then, wrapped in your dressing gown, you go to check on the children.

The bedroom: empty, duvet pushed back. They must have got up, gone next door to the lounge, amused themselves with the TV or by jumping on the sofa.

Except: no sound. Not in the lounge. Not in the kitchen. Not in the spare room. The flat deserted – the front door open – outside, the corridor empty – God, what time was it? How long – how long had she Make-Believed?

She shook as she tugged on her clothes, tied her shoes.

Grabbed her keys, her screen, ran out of the flat. For a moment she stood helpless, skin prickling with horror. The building had twelve floors, a lift and two staircases. Surely the panel for the lift would be too high for Finn? But he'd reached the snib of her front door— They liked the lift, sailing up and down in it . . . She made her choice, pressed the button. Heard it respond, with infinite slowness. As it hauled up from ground level, she thought of Meg. The impossibility of telling her. Reached for the wall to hold herself up, knees shaking. She had to find them. She'd do anything, she'd destroy her receiver, would stay real for ever—

The lift settled, in a moment of silent hope; then the doors drew back. She felt nausea wash through her – heard herself saying *No*— Spun around, shoved through the door to the north staircase and leapt the stairs, two at a time, to the top of the building. They would be here, somewhere. They would be here. Check each floor, and she'd find them. She ran the length of the corridor, calling '*Finn! Ella!*' Out onto the south staircase, down one flight, their names bouncing off the glass roof, down to the foot of the stairwell. Leaning over the railings, seeing fragments of staircase dropping and darkening – seeing no one. Back into the corridor – along – down again. Again. Each corridor a copy of the last, carpet swallowing her footsteps, muting her shouts, their names falling dead to the ground the moment they left her mouth – the hard height of the stairwell, her voice an echo that nobody heard – carpet again, the corridor floor seeming to tilt, so she ran uphill – and numbers on doors blurring, dancing, so she forgot how far she'd descended, how much of the building was on top of her and how much still to come. Twice she thought she'd reached the bottom then found there was further to go, and when at last she burst out into the foyer—

Not there. They were not there. Not anywhere.

Outside? But there was the button to release the front door – did Finn even know to push it? Or inside, behind any one of the doors she'd run past, the doors with the dancing numbers. Knock on the right one – it opens to show Finn and Ella tucked up on someone's sofa, eating bowls of Coco Pops in front of the TV, a kindly neighbour looking after two wandering children. Behind another, a single man – a loner – someone who was always so quiet, who kept himself to himself—To ask at every neighbour's door would take time she didn't have. Instead she ran out, into a deserted Sunday. The sky – it was wrong, sun sliding behind the apartment block when it should have been climbing over the sea. Not morning, but afternoon; late afternoon. She dashed across the shore road, where drivers thundered along not watching for lost children – searched each direction, on tiptoe as if it could help her see further. Nothing. No one. Beside her a low stone wall just the height for a five-year-old to climb. Beyond that, the drop. The swallowing grey of the sea.

This wasn't real, it was a dream – like the dreams

where she was late for a train, and she'd forgotten her suitcase and let her wake up, please let her wake . . . But she knew: it had happened. The worst thing had happened.

For a moment she let herself think she could call the police, and they'd tell her the kids were safe at the station – had been wandering lost, but a concerned lady had found them, brought them in, and Cassie could come and collect them now. She let herself think, just for a moment, that Meg might never have to know.

Then she held her screen in her shaking hand, and called her sister.

The rest of it came in fragments, with jagged edges that ripped at her each time she remembered. Meg's voice on the phone – urgent, loud – and her own words, thin and weak. Stalling the car, twice, three times, between the parking and the street. Sitting paralysed at the turning: left, or right? Spotting two small figures up ahead, her foot jerking on the accelerator, before she saw the children were accompanied by two adults, a couple, and realised it wasn't them. The feeling of unreality, crawling the street, scanning the pavement, the sea wall, the beach. Panic blazing through her when she saw them for certain this time, and oh God they were in their pyjamas still, Finn in his Spider-Man suit and Ella her Hello Kitty set, and they were talking to someone – a man, a stranger – and she leapt from the car, left it skewed across the lane, running towards them shouting their names, and the man held out his screen to her, said,

'I was just calling the police,' and as he spoke a panda car arrived from the opposite direction – and then Meg was there too – Meg refusing to meet her eye – and the children hysterical, cold and terrified, and 'I'm so sorry,' she said, kept saying it, 'Meg, I'm so so sorry,' and the relief so great she felt she might collapse even as she tried to hug the kids, desperate to comfort them—

And then Meg had looked at her.

She had stepped back. Dropped her arms to her sides. Felt herself sinking, under the horror of what she'd done. And she should have known it, then – but what she failed to realise was that although the children had been found, they were still lost. That her whole family, now, was lost.

If she'd tried harder to apologise – if she'd persisted – if she'd told the whole truth – then, would things have been different? The first time Meg had hung up on her, she'd told herself her sister needed space, a few days to calm down. Days into weeks: the longer she left it, the harder it was. How could she ever explain? When she'd first started testing Make-Believe she had struggled for words to describe it to Meg. It seemed at the same time too profound and too trivial. The sensations were like nothing else – but they were only play. What Meg did, bringing up her kids, was real, was serious. What Cassie did in Make-Believe was nothing more than a distraction from life. Then once she'd found Alan – the afternoon at the hospital, the bench set in behind the bamboo – after that, there was nothing to tell. There was only Alan, and he was too special, too secret to share.

It wasn't till after it all fell apart, and she'd started to put herself together again, that she found the guts to keep trying. To call. To turn up at the flat. To send letter after letter. She was moving on with her life, had her bedsit, her fledgling business, had Jake and the group for support – and if she tried hard enough for long enough, kept apologising, surely Meg would forgive her and she'd have her family back as well. They were safe, after all, the kids: in the end, there was no harm done.

But then that picture had arrived: the stolen snap of Finn and Ella in the back green. And she'd realised her actions had put them in danger once more. Her actions – though they seemed to belong to someone else. She hadn't been herself. That's what she'd tried to explain, in her last letter to Meg, but when she'd read it through the excuses had sickened her. She'd torn it up and started again. A statement of facts. A warning. She had borrowed money, and offered Meg's flat as collateral. She didn't believe it would stand up, legally, since the flat was not hers to offer. She was repaying her debt; there should be nothing for Meg to worry about – but Meg should know there was a chance Finn and Ella might be at risk. She understood that after this Meg would never forgive her. She would not contact her again. But she promised to do all she could to keep the kids from harm.

All she could. And this, at least, was something she could fix.

The park had emptied out; in the distance, thunder

cleared its throat. Cassie hauled herself up from the bench. Her next repayment wasn't due for nearly a month – but the self she'd be by then was someone she didn't trust. She had to pay it now, while she was still a part of this world – not just the next instalment, but the whole debt.

She checked her balance onscreen as she walked. Final payment had cleared from the latest summer school assignment. Fifty per cent of it was Nicol's, but she would think about that later. Including the fees she'd set aside for her other operatives, she was short by nearly a grand.

The first drops of rain were falling as she unlocked Lewis's bike and rode it to the nearest bike shop. They offered her £750; she bargained them up to £800, but from there they wouldn't budge. In the next place, a few streets away, they wouldn't shift at all.

The third place she tried was on the edge of the New Town, where the wealthy students lived. The window was filled with vintage and carbon-framed road bikes, price tags well over four figures. She would sell for £1,000, she told the guy in the shop, and he smiled and told her not a chance, lucky if they could get that much for it. She smiled back, trying not to look desperate. Pointed out the mint condition: barely used, not a scratch, worth more than £2,000 new, easily . . . Bit by bit they inched their way towards agreeing a price. Until the moment they shook on it, Cassie told herself she wasn't really doing this, that it was just theoretical, finding out how much the bike was worth. But then, Lewis didn't need it – and in any case it had been stupid of him to lend it to her, when she was so clearly not to be trusted. He should have been able to see that in her. He was kind, but stupid.

Via the bank quick deposit, it took her two hours to walk home. Lewis's place was closer, by far – but tonight, she couldn't look him in the eye.

CHAPTER TWENTY-FOUR

'I'm really, really sorry.'

The late sun was aiming straight for her eyes. A handful of sand, gritty and hot: she turned from the window, seeking the dark. Felt as if she was being interrogated. Lewis was taking it worse than she'd thought.

'I'll get you a new one – I mean I don't have the money, at the moment, but—'

'You can't just. What d'you think I'm going to do with a new one?' His arms were folded high across his chest, hands clamped in his armpits; his jaw was set sharp-angled, as tight as she'd ever seen it. *Keep it in the cupboard in the hall*, she nearly said. *Lend it out to the next charity case you sleep with*.

'Sorry,' she said again. But last night she had set up the final repayment. It would go through as soon as her cash deposit cleared. In a couple of days, it would be as if she'd never borrowed the money; as if Ella and Finn had never been collateral for her stupidity. She was sorry for Lewis, hated to see him so wound up by what she'd done – but she'd do it again, in a heartbeat.

'We agreed you wouldn't take it to yours!'

She wished he'd stop talking. 'I know. I did lock it—'

'What, with your tinny chain? How long d'you think it took them to cut through that?' He didn't wait for her to answer. 'Jesus, you didn't even take it into your flat, you just left it in the stairwell of some dodgy fucking high-rise?'

Low-rise; but she didn't correct him. 'I know – it's just it was so heavy to – but I should have.'

'Yeah. You should.'

How many times could she say she was sorry? She didn't want to be here. Not in this flat. Not in this body. Last night when she'd finally made it home, her neighbour was having another party. She'd asked him to turn it down; he'd asked her in. Ryan, he was called, and he was alright once you talked to him, though she didn't remember what they'd talked about. Didn't remember how much she'd drunk. Enough to poison her. Enough to swell her brain in her skull so it ached at every movement. Enough so her stomach lurched at the smell of the food Lewis had been making. She wished she'd stayed in bed, told him she was ill. Put off her confession until tomorrow. It was a resigned kind of self-loathing that had propelled her out of bed, into town on her rattling old bike, to endure his wrath along with her hangover.

He had every right to be angry, but she was surprised just how gracelessly he was behaving. It wasn't as if he couldn't afford another bike. It wasn't as if he even needed one. She'd grovelled about as much as she could bear: now, in the heat of his anger, her guilt was bubbling up into a resentment she'd no right to feel.

Maybe he sensed it. He shook his head, letting go. 'Forget it,' he said, but he still looked like a man in search of something to punch.

Cassie watched him turn his back on her. Thought, unexpectedly, of Meg. Of the fight, not long after their mum had died. It was over the cardigan that had been her mum's, that Cassie had taken to wearing, had worn for weeks non-stop, come to think of as hers, before Meg had noticed the dark patch. Stain of oil from some dropped food. The fight that ensued was so violent, so vicious it roused even their dad from his sleep of grief. He'd held Meg, held her back as she'd shouted *careless bitch, clumsy bitch, spoilt for ever*— Her mum had worn that cardigan, the one time Cassie had Make-Believed her. She could see it, feel it, smell it still, so precisely: fuzzy orange, hand-knitted, all shades from apricot to sunset to rust. Soft smell of wool, and lily-of-the-valley. The cardigan was easy to Believe. It was all the rest that had been too hard.

Cassie pinched her forehead. Stood, picked up her satchel.

'I said forget it . . . Where are you going?'

'Some dodgy fucking low-rise.' Lewis looked blank. 'Home.'

He gave a kind of a groan. 'No, look, don't. You don't have to.'

'I don't have to do anything. I just think you probably don't want to be looking at my face at the moment, or listening to my voice, and to be honest the feeling's pretty mutual, so . . . I'm going to let you, you know—' She held out her hands, palms down, steadying the situation. 'Simmer down.'

His jaw twitched, and for a moment she thought she'd set him off again. Then: 'Hang on just a moment,' he said, and walked out of the room. Called back: 'Something to show you.'

All at once, the ache in her head was muted. Her thumbnail found a notch in the table edge, worried its way inside. As she stared, the grain of the wood seemed to undulate, like something alive; she blinked, concentrated on stilling it, settling her tilting stomach.

It had to be. It had to be.

When he came back carrying nothing, she knew she'd guessed right.

He sat down opposite. She felt his eyes on her face as he opened his fist.

'Where did you get them?' She glanced up. A shake of his head. Two curves, nestled together. They could have been shells, or insect carapaces.

'You think they'll work?'

A nod.

Their lights were off, would remain so until she chose a receiver and slipped it on, fitting it over the cartilage of her ear. When it tapped into her electrochemistry, the light would pulse, then settle into a blue-tinted illumination.

Lewis's voice sounded far off. She concentrated. Whatever he was telling her, it must be important.

'. . . how they work,' he said. 'What they do is encrypt our DNA, allow us to jump onto existing accounts. So you put this on, it scans the network, and the first idle account it finds, it'll hijack – and bam, you're John Smith, or whoever.'

'But it's a one-off?'

'No! That's the beauty of it. Every time you connect, you're using a different account. Tomorrow night, you're Jane Brown. The night after, you're Annabel Double-barrelled-Whatever. You're always one step ahead.'

She looked at the clock on the oven. 'Does it have to be at night?'

'That's when the chance is greatest, of finding an idle account. When most users are asleep.'

Lewis stretched over the bed, tugged the sheet free from the corner. Rumpled it into a heap with the old duvet cover and pillowcases.

She'd felt awkward asking – but it had mattered. It would have been wrong, their bodies slumped in the bedding they'd fucked in. Perhaps he felt the same. In any case, he didn't ask her why. *Of course*, he'd said, fetched clean linen from the airing cupboard.

He snapped the fresh sheet in mid-air, and Cassie caught a corner.

'Are you sure?' she said.

He stopped, hands outstretched. 'You haven't changed your mind?'

His voice was sharp: she could sense his tension. It couldn't make a difference to him, either way, not a practical difference. With or without her, he was on his way back to Make-Believe. Which must mean he wanted her at his side, as they pushed out from the edge towards their separate destinations. She smiled, shook her head.

He bent to fold the sheet under the mattress. 'Good. Me neither.'

Cassie folded in her side of the sheet. Pulled the corners nice and tight. 'I spoke to Jake the other night,' she said. When she glanced up, Lewis was looking at her blankly. 'From the group.'

'Oh, Jake. Of course. What for?'

'Because – once I thought this might happen, I felt like I needed advice. I worked really hard, you know, at sorting myself out, getting my life back together.' She picked up a pillowcase, flipped it inside out and pushed her hands into the corners. Grabbing hold of a pillow, she shook the case down over it.

'Good trick,' said Lewis, watching.

'Got it off my mum. You can do it with the duvet too – chuck it here, and I'll show you.'

'So what did he say?'

'Nothing you couldn't guess. Oh, he told me to get over myself, basically. But I realised something, then. The group, all that – we were never doing what everyone else was, we were never resisting temptation, because there was none. It was only ever about managing the loss. For me, at least. The loss of Make-Believe. And no matter how hard that felt, it was simple compared to what everyone else was up against. And even now – this is what I realised – it's not that I'm slipping. I'm not giving in. I choose it.'

She flung the quilt out over the bed. Left a pause for Lewis to agree or disagree. She chose it: how could she have thought she'd do otherwise? All those times before, she'd believed she was Making the Alan she wanted, a version based on memory and imagination. And he had been real. Now she hoped – believed – she would find him once again. The excitement bubbled up inside, wanting to be shared; but since dinner, when they'd forced down some pasta in preparation for tonight, Lewis had spoken barely two dozen words. She was talking because she was dizzy with anticipation, like her tongue had come unstuck from the roof of her mouth. Lewis was the opposite, pulling back into himself.

'Completely informed,' she said. 'Knowing everything it'll do to me. A straight choice – between what everyone says is real, and what I know is real. What I choose to make real.' Another pause. 'Are you going to change?'

'Change?'

He was wearing jeans, a belt. She'd already swapped her clothes for the most suitable ones she had at Lewis's: tracksuit bottoms and an old band T-shirt, soft with wear. 'Into something comfortable.'

He glanced down at himself. 'Oh. I will do, yes.'

She sat on the slowly settling duvet. Stared up at him.

'So I'm making this choice – and you know exactly what I mean. You're doing the same.'

Lewis finished wrestling a pillow into its case.

'I think . . . you must have lost someone too.'

Placed it gently at the head of the bed.

'Was it hers? The bike?'

He nodded, just once.

'And she's gone – she's dead?'

He lowered himself as if from a great height, onto the bed beside her.

It was striking how much they were the same. They'd both lost someone, and found them again in Make-Believe. Except, where her connection was real, his was just memory; the memory of someone no longer living. She felt it pricking at her eyes, a great pity for him. Said it once more, and meant it this time, deep in the pit of her stomach: 'I'm sorry. I'm so sorry.'

'Me too,' he muttered. Started to unbuckle his belt.

Clean sheets. Soft clothes. Plenty of pillows. Water on the bedside tables, for when they woke up dry.

She had been through all her reservations, visited

them one by one. She was ready, and so close. She could almost hear his voice now.

Cassie, I'm waiting. I've been waiting for ever. Up by the falls. Meet me here? If you believe in me. Meet me here.

FREQUENTLY ASKED QUESTIONS

Q. How safe is Make-Believe™?

A. Make-Believe™ is the result of more than ten years of extensive research and development. The advanced biotechnology has been developed by world-leading experts and thoroughly tested to ensure there are absolutely no adverse effects. Make-Believe™ is licensed for use in the UK by the Department for Innovation, so you can rest assured there will be no unwelcome side effects – your safety is guaranteed.

She curls into the scoop of nothing, into a blissful absence.

There is nothing she needs. Only this.

No such thing as future. No past. Only this.

Bodiless.

Free.

Perfected.

When her self returns, she is floating.

She hangs in something slow like water, feels the flow of it over her skin. A silky resistance that bears her up, that swirls her hair; clear like air, so her breathing is cool and transparent, her vision unrippled. But all she sees, looking down, is herself.

It's harder than she remembers. If she'd expected anything, it was to be there, straight away. To find herself there, with Alan. But she is alone. She prods around in her mind, and feels nothing. There is no connection.

She's out of practice, that's all. She opens her mouth: tastes green, the smell of wet leaves. *Up by the falls. Meet me here?* She's imagined a beginning; now she has to keep working at it. If she can Make the setting – Believe in it – he'll be there. He will.

She closes her eyes, and begins.

She starts with taste, and smell: concentrates on the damp earth, the ozone, the soft herbal notes of growing things. As she gets it right, starts to inhale the freshness of water, it makes her want to open her eyes – but not yet. Not yet.

Next, her skin. Her feet bare, in cool grass. It flattens underfoot, tickles her ankles. A breeze feathers her, fingers her hair, strokes the backs of her legs; it catches the spray from the falls and tingles it onto her face and neck. With the spray comes sound. Tumble of water over rock, rushing and falling. She paints it in as background – and over the top she layers the tap and drip of rain on leaves. No coded message, just innocent rain, steady and gentle, present like the rhythm of her heart or her lungs. As if it hasn't been necessary for her to Make it, but simply to pay attention.

To attend. To notice. What she notices now – faint at first, at the edge of her hearing – is breath. Is his breathing. Calm, and slow; and clearer now, and close.

She turns her face. Feels it: his breath on her cheek. Matches hers to his, in and out. For a while it's all they do: breathe together.

She should open her eyes – she should reach for him, touch – but the thought knocks her out of sync with him. Her breath comes shallower, faster. If she opens her eyes, who will she see? He has been lost for so long. He has been irretrievable. And now he is so close beside her. She thinks of the locked ward, the body wedged in a blue armchair, disguised in all its layers of flesh – and her eyelids glue themselves shut.

'Hey,' says Alan. 'Hey, no. Don't do that, eh? Don't think about him. He's nothing to do with us, not here.'

'What'll I see, if I look?'

'I don't know what you'll see. It's up to you, I think. I can tell you what I'm seeing?'

'Go on.'

'You. I'm seeing you, with your hair long, streaks in it like it goes in summer. I'm seeing how you've been out in the sun.'

'Am I burnt, then?'

'Not really. More brown. And – I like that dress you've got on.'

Dress. She feels it round her hips.

'Like army, or safari, or something,' he says, and she knows the one he means. Old; she doesn't have it any more. He says, 'You look – ready.'

'For . . . ?'

'For action.'

As he says it she feels stronger. Strong enough to open her eyes.

'Now,' he says. 'Your turn. You tell me what you see.'

She laughs.

'OK,' he says. 'That could go either way.'

'It's good. It's really good.' And now she reaches out, touches him. He's wearing the T-shirt her body is wearing, back in Lewis's bed. 'I've still got this,' she says. 'This T-shirt. You used to wear it all the time.' It's from a festival they went to, the summer they finished school; the line-up is illegible, faded almost to invisibility, the cotton so washed and worn it's like touching nothing. The rain falls now on the stretched roof of their festival tent; through the shirt she feels every detail of him. The jut of his shoulder. Hard curve of his arm, where it meets his chest. The bump of his nipple, the rhythm of his ribs, the dip and stretch of his stomach. Tries not to think how all of this is lost, in the waking world. Draws up her hand to rest on his chest, feeling all the closer to his skin for the soft familiar slip of fabric between them. His heart kicks strong and steady, into her palm.

'It's you,' she says.

They are joined – T-shirt, dress, all clothes irrelevant – heat and light rippling from where he's locked inside her. The smell of him fills her – sky-blue over warm, biscuity skin. She inhales deeper, deeper, breathes in home. His chin on her head, her face pressed into his neck, and at the same time she pulls back to see them. Baby monkeys, clinging close.

'Will we stay like this? Stay here?'

Her yes crashes over the both of them: no need to speak it. 'Except,' she says. 'I don't know how much time there is, and I can't get away like I used to, from the real world. I don't think I can stay, not like before—'

'The real world,' says Alan. 'Why do you call it that?'

'Because this isn't—' She stops. She can't say this isn't real, because it has to be. Because *here* is where Alan exists, where they are together. And *there*, in a locked ward in the middle of nowhere, is a bad joke rocking back and forth with blood beneath his fingernails.

'You know I believe in you,' she says. 'But if you're real, what about – the other you?'

'You don't need to think about that. He's – a mistake. He's not me.'

'But he's why you're here. Isn't he? What they've done to him, that's what means we can be together now.' She reaches out, stroking his red-gold hair, slipping her hand round to cup his head. The back of his ear is smooth. No swelling. No scar. No blood.

'I told you,' he says, hand on hers. 'I'm not him.'

'They were trying to do good,' she says. 'Trying to bring you back. But it didn't work, can't have worked, or else—'

It's too hard, it's making her head spin. She means to say, if the treatment had worked he would be himself again, wouldn't be shut away in the locked ward. But he's both: is himself, and not himself. Is asleep in a narrow bed in the ward, and here with her by the falls. She can't believe in one and not the other. Can't choose her Alan, and turn her back on the other.

There is so much to ask, but the questions slip past like

fish. She doesn't want to think. She only wants to Believe. She pulls back so she can look at Alan, see his face, but he closes his eyes like he's turning away from her.

'Why do you think I've got the answers,' he says.

'But you have to know. What he's scared of. What's happening to him. To both of you—'

'Don't,' he says. 'Don't. Just be here. Us, together. Come on: it's not him that's waited for you, it's not him that's here to meet you, that knew the place to come—' But now she's mentioned it, she can feel it, prickling the edges of their place. A darkness at her back. 'Don't,' he says – but she turns, moves towards it. She has to know.

The tumble of the waterfall spreads, flattens to a rush of static. Through the fuzz, voices: low, muttering, bubbling up and sinking deep back down. She reaches out, touches something soft, skinless – yielding and wet. Pulpy. Rotten. Snatches her hand back – but it clings, it's all around her. The air is hot tar, is burning rubber. The black invades her nose, coats her mouth, turns to lead in her lungs. She is weighted, dragged down and down by the dark that wants her closer. Wants to hold her. Inhabit her. Wraps tight round her ankles and wrists, across her mouth and nose. Pulls her in, down – and she kicks against it, kicking hard towards the light that is Alan, his glow, his luminous skin, his bright gold hair. She struggles, swears, cries for help, wasted breath. Opens her mouth in a gasp; finds nothing to breathe, hunger for air a knife in her lungs—

Alan: she focuses on him, his bright blur, strains to

make the light stronger. This is her Make-Believe; she's in control – isn't she? She tries to concentrate, to make the light spread, make it push away the dark – and 'Oh God,' she says, fighting the air back into her lungs – 'Oh God, is this what it's like for him?'

He catches – holds her – her chest heaves against him. His steady heart beats for her while her own runs at three times the speed. The rot is stuck, where she touched it. She panics, tries to shake it off – slime slathering her hands, black crescent fingernails—

'Cassie,' he says. 'It's really OK.'

She forces herself to follow his breathing. To look at him. To open herself. To let him see inside. Shows him everything, the worst of herself. Shows the escape she's wished for him. The escape he must surely have wished for himself, since his life became so small, so much like endurance. To escape from that body, that room – to escape, now, from *this*: from the creeping, swallowing dark that she can feel, still. That she can see, right at the edge of her vision, beyond the light and the leaves and water.

'It's OK,' he says, 'if you wished me dead' – and she shakes her head, squeezes her eyes shut, but he won't let her pretend, he keeps on talking. 'No – but if you did, that's OK. Cos it wasn't me; it was him, eh? The mistake. I know that.'

But it's not OK, what she wished for him – and nor is the waiting darkness. None of it is OK. The not-OK hardens inside her. Draws her into herself, away from Alan.

'I know what's going on,' he says. 'In your head. You're thinking of how you can save him. You're planning to be a soldier, in your little army dress.'

'But you understand? That I have to? That I can't leave him – you – I mean both of you, I mean either—'

'Please, Cassie. Stay. For as long as you can, for however long we've got.'

'But—' She shakes her head, and his face drops out of focus. She can't feel the warmth of him any more, the reliable drum of his heart. 'I have to try. I have to help him. It doesn't mean – I'll come back . . .'

His voice is distant now, like he's standing on the far side of the water. 'I'm here because of you,' he says. 'Because you know me. This: this is how you save me. You have to be here. If you're not here—'

His words are lost. The water roars white, like static – and she can't stay here, not now, with the darkness lapping at her edges. Stop, she thinks, *stop* – and the command blurs into the white roar, and perhaps that's why it's so sluggish – why, instead of a seamless fade-in of what they call real, there's a stretched-out moment of two worlds swaying – a dizzying, sickening overlap like nothing she's felt before, one reality into the other, and then—

STOP

CHAPTER TWENTY-FIVE

You woke back in the real world, cold and stiff—

The noise wouldn't stop. Shrill, insistent, refusing to let her sink into sleep. *Alan*, she thought, and then: *Lewis*. It was his flat. His front door. His doorbell someone was jabbing, drilling deep into her head.

She reached for where he was lying – or tried to. Her arm stayed flat on the bed. *Sit up*, she told herself. Stayed frozen.

Lewis, she thought again, as if he might hear his name in her head, shake her out of this paralysis.

If she could move a finger, just one— She focused all her willpower on her right hand, on her index finger, straining for a response. The movement came suddenly, a twitch of her hand that loosened her arm, released her to push upright.

She was sitting in an empty bed.

'Lewis?' Her voice was ghostly, drowned out by the doorbell. She coughed, cleared her throat and called again: 'Lewis!' The shutters were closed, a sliver of light between them. The room was dim, but she could see his side of the bed was rumpled, a soft dent in the pillow where his head had rested. Nestled in the hollow was his receiver. She lifted a hand, felt her own receiver still in place. Slipped it from her ear, and laid it alongside.

With the doorbell still drilling, she got up, checked the bathroom. The kitchen. In the living room, she switched on the light: the cat, curled on the sofa, opened an eye, closed it again. The flat was empty, just the harsh ringing ricocheting off the walls. It came in bursts now, in dashes and dots. Just for a moment, she imagined it was Alan outside. That he'd crossed the border, was waiting on the other side of the door, ringing out a coded message. But it wasn't Alan, of course. It was Lewis, gone for milk or croissants, forgetting his keys. He would know how hard it was to jolt someone back from Make-Believe.

She edged down the hall, bent to look through the spyhole. Not one person but two, standing on the landing: one tall and one shorter. Though their shapes were distorted, the shorter one was definitely a woman.

Cassie turned the snib. Opened the door.

The woman, slight and fair-haired in a navy trouser suit, stepped to one side, and as Cassie stared at the man – who was young and smooth, and wore the uniform-smile of a mortgage adviser – somehow the woman was moving round behind her, sliding her arm between Cassie and the doorway, so that Cassie stepped forward – deferring to polish and poise, to quiet efficiency. Before she understood what was happening, she was barefoot on the concrete landing, the door to the flat closing behind her.

'Hey!' She made a lunge – lost her balance – fell with a thud against the locked door. Inside, the woman's heels were pock-pocking against the floorboards. Down the hall, pausing at the entrance to each room, then tailing away into what must be the bedroom.

Cassie pushed herself upright, hands pressed against the panels. She registered the detail of brush marks on the paintwork, the way colour had pooled in the indents of the beading. Then she raised her arm and slammed the wood, shaking the door in its frame.

'Ms McAllister,' said the mortgage adviser. Cassie paused, fist in the air, ready to hammer again. 'Is this your flat, Ms McAllister?'

She turned, letting her arm fall to her side. Stared at him, mouth open, searching for the words: *Who are you, how do you know – None of your business – My friend will be back any minute—* Before she could filter her response, decide what she should say, the click of heels on floorboards sounded behind her. She spun round, ready to fight her way back inside.

'It's your friend's flat, isn't it. Don't you want to keep him out of this?' There was no menace in his tone. He might have been asking: did she want to run the calculations again with a different mortgage product? But his words were enough to make her hesitate – enough to let the woman step out onto the landing and pull the door shut. In one hand she was holding the modified receivers; in the other, Cassie's trainers.

'Put these on, please,' she said. She held out the shoes, fingers hooked into the heels where the linings had worn into holes. The laces swung, frayed and grey; the white rubber soles were black with dirt. Cassie grabbed them with both hands, and the three of them stood, waiting to see what would happen.

There was no way she was going to do as she was told, but her feet were cold on the gritty concrete. She had no screen, no keys, no wallet, was wearing jogging bottoms and Alan's T-shirt – the T-shirt he'd worn just minutes ago, body heat pulsing through the threadbare cotton. *Alan*, she said inside her head, casting around for anything left of him: for a murmur of his voice, an echo of his words, a residual sense of comfort. A shiver ran through her, making her conscious of the thinness of the T-shirt, of how naked she felt. She crouched down, put on the trainers. The holed linings rubbed against her heels.

The woman moved towards the stairs, and the man gestured for Cassie to follow. But they couldn't force her to go with them. All she had to do was wait here till Lewis came back, and together they'd be more than a match for these suited couriers. Once Lewis came back – but a sudden worry made her stomach dip. What if he hadn't gone for croissants? It was too strange, that he should be absent when these people turned up. Though they hadn't identified themselves, she could guess they were the trouble she'd been courting. If they knew who Lewis was, what he was to her, they might mean trouble for him too. Had they got to him, somehow persuaded him to leave her alone in his bed? But they would have had to force him. She knew he wouldn't leave her through choice – and nor was she going to leave him. She would wait right here for him.

'No,' she said, and sat down on the landing. Dropped to the floor, and seemed to keep on dropping as the two figures stretched above her, dark suits and dark shadows jagging up and up against the stairwell wall – and she was sinking deep into the cold that seeped through her jogging bottoms, through her skin and her flesh and into her bones. Her hands turned light with pins and needles. Her insides dragged with absence. Alan was nowhere inside, not a molecule left. Nothing in her but darkness, yawning.

It was only Make-Believe. Neurons firing out of sync. A minute's delay in restoring her ability to move had left her frozen in Lewis's bed; this must be the same, a lack of the dopamine that ought to have eased her out of her world, back into the real. She could try to explain it away, this plunge – the modified bioware? – but it made no difference. She sat, hollowed, could scarcely care enough to breathe. Any moment, the dopamine should kick in. If she just kept breathing. Counting. Counting the breaths.

And then the young man spoke.

'It is hereby agreed as follows, that Cassandra McAllister shall not contact, directly or indirectly, for any purposes, any persons employed by Imagen Research unless prior written consent has been granted . . .'

It was the agreement she'd signed. The agreement she'd breached. He was telling her she didn't have a choice.

'. . . in everyone's interests for you to come with us now,' he was saying, 'so we can sort this out informally.'

Cassie's brain felt inert, lumpish. Imagen, of course. That was where they were from. How they knew who she was. Somehow, the hacked bioware had given her away, and now they had come for her, as she should have guessed they would. And though there was not a scrap of fight in her, she remembered Alan's words: *You're planning to be a soldier, in your little army dress.*

She had never felt less like a soldier. She was a lost child, huddled cold on the stairs, with nowhere to go. With no one to protect her. With no more options.

You're thinking of how you can save him.

It took all the effort in the world for her to place her palms flat on the concrete. Push into a crouch, then up to a standing position. To take one step.

Eyes fixed on the stairs, she followed the woman. Step. Step. Step. The front door swung open, the street outside empty, early dawn light making her flinch. When the woman opened the door of a silver car and the man ushered her into the back seat, she climbed straight in. Let him close the door.

* * *

Head bent, hands shoved between her knees. Still counting the breaths. The city moving round her. The suggestion of sunrise the only indication of how long she'd been with Alan.

Stop. Someone opened the door. She clambered out, hugging herself.

A long time since she'd stood here, on this pavement. If ever she needed to pass through this part of town, she'd take a detour. Avoid the office. Now the stern slabs, the orderly windows loomed over her. The prospect of walking through the front door made her stumble – or it was just her shoelace, come undone. Too far to bend, to tie it, the effort impossible: it snaked alongside as they marched her in. Not the front door, after all. The deliveries entrance. The way she used to come when the main door was locked, starting work early or finishing late. Where she used to hide in those last months, when she'd turned up like the walking dead; where she'd find a corner behind a delivery waiting to be unpacked, spread her jacket on the concrete, curl behind the pallets, crash out for as long as she could get away with.

Lights flickering in the basement. White gloss reflection. The woman's heels striking the bare floor, chisel on stone, echoing through the pillared space. Towards the lift, past cardboard boxes stacked high, each labelled in Chinese-style script then struck through with a thick slash of marker, a rushed scrawl: *PULP*.

* * *

Lift doors sliding open. Stepping into the office, carpet silencing her footsteps, exactly like a dream. She had come to work accidentally in her pyjamas – was late for a meeting, one she'd been dreading, where something awful was going to happen to her, some punishment or humiliation. The space rose high and open: nowhere to hide. They were leading her to her old department.

There was her desk. There was her chair.

'Take a seat,' the woman said. 'Lachlan will bring you something – tea, coffee.'

The man smiled his banker's smile, and Cassie knew him now, knew exactly who he was. Lachlan: he was someone's nephew. A director's nephew, or the chief exec's. Had been here as an intern, had worked for a week in her own department, arranging numbers on spreadsheets. He'd worn a cheaper suit back then. His smile had been only half-formed.

That small piece of knowledge made her feel slightly more in control. But the woman still eluded her. The plain bobbed hair, glasses, trouser suit, all gave her an anonymous look, and Cassie couldn't place her at all.

The chair was too low. She groped for the lever, adjusted it to the right height. Let herself slump across the desk, the fake woodgrain. Tried to force her clogged brain into action, to arrange some thoughts. They would be watching her – so she wouldn't open the desk drawer, wouldn't look inside. All she'd find anyway would be concealed chaos, the papers that were forbidden in this theoretically paperless office: knots of cables and chargers, emergency hankies, painkillers, biscuits. Hidden things. Nothing she needed.

What *did* she need? *You're thinking of how you can save him.* She didn't know what she should be looking for. Knew it would be highly confidential, miles above the pay grade of a marketing manager. She lifted her head, blinked at the screen, the only object permitted on the desktop. Any information on the network would be protected by passwords, encryption, biotouch lock-outs.

She turned the chair around. Stared up at the mezzanine level, where the senior management had their glass-walled offices, screened by slatted blinds. She turned the chair again, another forty-five degrees. The dream-feeling was fading into familiarity. They'd left her here on purpose, at her old desk. It was part of their strategy – of whatever they planned to do with her. Softening her up. Reminding her of what she'd lost. But why bother? They'd already taken it from her once. They couldn't take it again.

She tilted her head back, remembering the brightness of this corner of the office. Windows ran the length of both walls, in high strips. You couldn't see out, but light filled the double-height space. Too much light. It seemed to dim and brighten, concentrating in pixels that danced before her. Another biomolecular glitch. She blinked hard, opened her eyes wide, then narrowed them – trying to fix the world, to stop it shimmering, disintegrating. The pins and needles were back, nettling her right hand. A cold ache flowing up her arm, pooling in her elbow, her shoulder. She squeezed the seat of her chair, hard. Rough fabric, smooth plastic, textures dulled as if she were wearing latex gloves. Trying to find a sense she could trust. Something real to cling to.

'Your tea.'

She heard Lachlan set it on the desk, saw him walk away again, a dark shrinking shape. She reached, touched the mug. Hot. Lifted it close to her face, bringing it into focus. Printed on the ceramic: *The only limit is you*. She sipped, let the liquid scald her mouth, felt it travel down her throat. He'd put in sugar. She didn't take sugar, but maybe it would help. She gazed at the rising steam.

Later: dregs stone cold. Lachlan again, with an invitation to follow him. Not an invitation, not really. Climbing the stairs to the mezzanine, to the glass-walled offices. Dreamlike again, familiarity nudged askew by this new perspective.

Lachlan stopped, knocked, pushed a door open. Outstretched arm, gentlemanly: *After you*. And as soon as she'd stepped inside he was gone, closing the door behind her.

CHAPTER TWENTY-SIX

The man behind the desk leapt up, offered his hand. 'Cassandra,' he said. 'I don't think we really encountered each other, did we, during your time here? I'm Tom, Tom Oswald – CTO.'

Cassie let her hand be clasped, released. She knew who Oswald was, of course. Chief technology officer: second in seniority, right behind the CEO. An energetic man, tall and broad, his bulk lessened a touch by an impression of roundness about his corners, as though he'd been sanded down at the shoulders and elbows. In the three years she'd worked at Imagen, she had spoken to him perhaps twice; naturally he'd forgotten.

'Sit, sit.' He waved her to a waiting chair, the desk a reassuring slab between them.

The room was a bright cube. Oswald had raised the

blinds so the glass wall to her right gave a bird's-eye view of the open-plan office she'd just left. A lone figure in a blue tabard moved from one workstation to the next, tipping wastepaper into a black bin liner, spraying and wiping the surfaces. Cassie could see the mug she'd left on her desk – which the cleaner would now have to collect, making a special trip to the kitchen, throwing his schedule out; she should have carried it up here with her.

Oswald was studying her frankly. He leant back in his chair, hands loosely clasped across his middle, and like a reverse reflection Cassie hunched her shoulders, folded her arms and pressed her knees together. Tried to imagine herself not in trackies and T-shirt but a power suit, black silk, bare ankles and trainers replaced by studded leather boots with fuck-you heels.

When Oswald raised up from his seat, leant over the desk towards her, she tensed. Then she saw he'd hooked his jacket from the back of his chair, was tipping out its pockets – wallet, keys, fountain pen.

'Here,' he said, holding it out to her, and when she hesitated he flashed a brief, efficient smile. She reached for it – intensely grateful for its charcoal weight, and determined not to show it. Pulled the thick lined fabric round her like a shield, or a blanket. Inhaled its faint smell: tobacco, cologne.

'So listen,' he said. 'I'm sorry you've been brought here like this, so early in the morning. A bit heavy-handed, I know.' His face twitched into something between a smile and a grimace, as if he were sharing a mild frustration at the incompetence of a subordinate. 'Of course, you'll be wondering what this is all about.'

She gave a slow shrug; the answer was obvious. 'Because I broke the agreement. The legal stuff. I'm not meant to go back to Make-Believe.'

Oswald propped his elbows on the arms of his chair and laced his fingers. 'Mmm, the legal stuff. Well, that is in breach of contract – along with a couple of other things.' Almost regretfully, he began to list her misdemeanours. 'Lying about your credentials to access our senior staff; trying to gain sensitive commercial information about our products; using a forged pass to enter a research facility – not quite in your line, I'd have thought, so – not a solo effort, perhaps? And then there's maintaining contact with Imagen employees . . .'

Cassie felt her eyes widening, tried to freeze her expression. Harrie? Had Harrie been so suspicious she'd reported Cassie's visit, the questions she'd asked? Was that when Imagen had started to watch her, to track everything she did? She could hardly believe it – that Harrie's loyalty to the company would so far outweigh their friendship. *They make you feel Imagen is your family*, she'd said – *but it's not, it's a job. It's only a job.*

Oswald was still talking. His focus had shifted, and she could tell he was checking the screen of his lens. It was always obvious, the same way you could tell when someone had stopped listening to you even while they continued to make eye contact. 'Receiving stolen goods . . . using bioware that's been illegally modified . . . unauthorised use of a Make-Believe account that doesn't belong to you . . . But!' His hands flew apart, an open gesture. 'We needn't worry too much about any of that. Not for the moment. No, you're here, in fact, because there's a proposition I'd like to put to you. Quite a simple way for you to help us, and naturally – quid pro quo – we would help you, in return.'

She frowned, struggling to follow the reversal: disappointed headmaster to enthusiastic negotiator. 'Go on,' she said.

'It's pretty straightforward: what we'd like is for you to help us make a correction to Make-Believe.'

'A connection to . . . ? But – that's exactly what I'm forbidden from doing.'

The mutual confusion lasted only a few seconds, before Oswald gave a sudden laugh. 'No, no, not a connection. A *correction*. A small correction, to the functionality of Make-Believe.'

There were so many questions, she didn't know where to start – and before she could, he held up his hand.

'I know: you're not a neuroscientist, you're not a computer scientist, not a synthetic biologist – you're thinking we've got the wrong person. We haven't got the wrong person.' He leant forward. 'You and I, Cassandra, though we haven't had dealings as such – well, I know rather a lot about you.' It might have been a threat, but that wasn't how it sounded. Instead, there was a note of admiration in his voice. 'You were with Imagen for – three years, was it? For the first two of which, your performance was excellent. You had outstanding appraisals. You consistently achieved and exceeded your targets. You were awarded the maximum annual bonus.'

She watched him closely as he spoke, sure he must be reading from his lens again. But his eyes focused on hers, without a flicker. He knew this stuff about her, had memorised it; stuff no one else knew or cared about any more. He knew she had done a good job.

'I don't know if you're aware that Imagen is poised to expand internationally? We hope to launch Make-Believe very shortly in the US; we're at pre-launch stage in Japan, South Korea. We're in the early stages of bringing new products to market in the UK. All of which means, we need good staff, as we continue to grow.'

She didn't know why he was telling her this. Jumped on the detail she knew to be false. 'But you're not. You're not growing. You're shrinking.'

She expected him to roll out the line about a planned consolidation. Instead, he nodded, looked impressed by her challenge. 'We'll come back to that. But the point I'm making here is that employees of your calibre and commitment are few and far between. And while Imagen obviously does not – cannot – accept any liability for what happened, with regard to the issues that led to your being let go' – he was choosing his words with care – 'we do nevertheless acknowledge that it should not have happened at all.'

'It wasn't my fault.' She narrowed her eyes, trying to read his expression. 'Is that what you're saying?'

'What happened was not *entirely* your fault.'

Because she was tired. Because she'd gone straight from Make-Believe, and Alan, to this baffling conversation in a place she should never again have set foot in, without even twenty minutes of sleep. Because of the earnest expression on Oswald's face, the unexpected softness of his tone. That was why she found herself closing her eyes, pressing her lips together.

He must have been waiting for her to speak, and if she'd trusted her voice she'd have asked him to spell it out, his offer. Instead, she concentrated on keeping her breath from wobbling.

'We'll have the lawyers draw up a new agreement,' Oswald said, eventually, 'sort out all that side of things. We'll organise for you to receive an extra month's salary straight away, and we'll repay the bonus that was forfeit when you were dismissed. That's enough, isn't it, for you to move into a new flat, if you wanted to. Really, it will be almost as if the last year never happened. It's erased.' He paused, and when he spoke again his voice was softer than ever. 'Look. Down there. That's the cleaner polishing your desk, right now.'

She opened her eyes. Allowed herself to look.

'You could be back here as quickly as you like. Back with your old colleagues. Part of the team. As soon as next week. It's up to you.'

She stared down at the desk that used to be hers, and the desks where her old colleagues would be sitting a few hours from now. The early birds – Phil, Emily, Lotta –

would be there at eight on the dot. Last to arrive would be Karolina, a fluster of coffee and excuses. They'd autopilot straight to their seats, would greet each other, complain about the day ahead, sympathise over meetings and deadlines and overflowing inboxes, none of them knowing how lucky they were to have a place to come, a job to do, a team to be a part of.

She coughed to clear her throat. 'What about Make-Believe?' There was no point trying to hide it; he knew how much she wanted it. The lengths she had gone to, for one more go.

'Make-Believe, absolutely, we'll get you back there. We can reactivate your account more or less immediately. I could do it myself, in fact.'

The offer he was making – it was too good to be true. If this wasn't a dream . . . Cassie curled her toes inside her trainers, feeling the canvas rub against her skin. If it wasn't a dream, or something else—

'Listen, you must be tired. I'll ask Lachlan to bring us some coffee,' said Oswald, lifting his screen – and Cassie thought perhaps she'd made him say it. The things she always struggled with: how chocolate melts, how coffee smells.

'Please,' she said, and inside the sleeves of Oswald's jacket she dug her fingers into her arms till it started to hurt. From her high-up perch she watched the cleaner at her desk, watched him spray, wipe, move on. Half-listened to Oswald, as he told her how soon she could come back to work, how she'd fit right in with the marketing team, a few new faces since her time but some old colleagues still there too . . .

If this was Make-Believe – this mix of flattery and bribery – then it was pathetic. She was pathetic, with her happy-ending fantasy.

When Lachlan stepped in to place two mugs on Oswald's desk, Cassie reached for her coffee straight away. Held it close to her face. Eyes closed, concentrating. Breathe in, and in.

The smell just as it should be: deep and black and strong. Perfectly real.

On the desk in front of her, Oswald's offer sat waiting – a solid-seeming promise of everything she could want. She clutched her mug, and tried to think of what it meant.

Alan, and what they'd done to him. How stepping back into the Imagen fold would make her a part of that.

How, within Imagen, she'd be perfectly placed to find out about the experiment. To find out how she could help him.

But she only had half of the information. She knew what Oswald was offering her; she didn't know, yet, exactly what he wanted in return.

'OK,' she said – and she saw how deeply he exhaled, how his shoulders lowered, revealing his previous, seemingly relaxed demeanour as something finely constructed. 'No, wait. I mean, that's OK as far as it goes: you've told me what I get. What about you? What does Imagen get from me?'

'What we get. Of course.' He nodded, seemed to take a moment to arrange his thoughts. 'So, what you need to understand, Cassandra, is that there is a particular characteristic that's specific to you. Not exclusively so, it's shared by a number of other people, but – for various reasons – you happen to be ideally placed to help us iron out a small bug, that's been causing us some minor complications.'

A small bug. Minor complications. And yet, this whole encounter must have been extensively planned. They had waited for her to breach the terms of the agreement she'd signed. They had swooped in at the crack of dawn, brought her here to meet with the most senior bar one of the company directors. And since Oswald knew practically everything about her activities, how much time and effort had been expended on surveilling her? The mismatch sounded an alert. She rolled her shoulders inside Oswald's jacket, and understood that whatever she was told would be a partial truth at best.

'So, as you know,' he said, 'Make-Believe growth has levelled off over the last quarter.'

'It hasn't just levelled off. You've been losing subscribers.'

Oswald looked pained. 'New subscribers are on target, in fact. Almost precisely so. Account cancellations, however, have leapt up.'

'Then there's a problem with the experience? User expectations aren't being met?'

'You might say that.'

'But – how? Your Make-Believe is up to you: it *is* your expectations.'

Oswald shook his head. 'It's a problem that goes right back to the first stages of the development process.' He clasped his hands in front of him. 'Here's the thing: you'll know that, in the longer term, we aim to offer Make-Believe as a social experience – so that users can participate in each other's virtual realities. What you won't know is that, in the very earliest iterations of the technology, one possibility our researchers explored was that of direct contact between the sets of biomolecules that make up users' individual networks.'

Quorum sensing. Microorganisms communicate. Doctor connects with patient. Cassie said nothing, kept a question painted on her face.

'So for example: if you and I were sitting here, both of us with our Make-Believe networks active, each happy in our respectively imagined worlds – well then, our networks would become aware of each other.'

'The way screens sense each other, or lenses – with Wi-Fi or radio?'

'Not precisely, but . . . similar enough. The idea was that users would then be presented with an option to connect with each other. To collaborate.'

It was only confirmation of what she already knew, but she found herself leaning in, her heart beating faster. 'You said this was in the earliest stages of Make-Believe, this research. Did they ever make it work?'

He skirted the question delicately. 'For a number

of reasons, that line of research was dropped. But the functionality was built in to the biomolecules. It's in every user, every network. It wasn't active. You could think of it like your appendix, or your tail bone. You don't use them. They're not needed, they're just left over from a time when they might have been useful. They don't do anything. At least...' His lips curved upwards; he seemed almost amused, as if he knew she was already ahead of him. 'They're not *meant* to do anything. But there is a complication. This latent capacity to connect is . . . becoming active. In some people. So far, a small number; fairly small. And as I'm sure you've guessed by now—'

'Me. I'm one of them.' She had to work at resisting the laughter that tickled inside her. Of course, Oswald wouldn't understand the implications of what he was telling her. But this was confirmation: that Alan was real, in Make-Believe. That she hadn't imagined him. That their connections had been genuine, and genuinely shared. Everything she'd hoped was true; she'd believed it, but now . . . Now, she knew for sure.

'Tell me,' she said, 'how does it work? Why is it only affecting some users?'

'A couple of reasons. First and foremost, what seems to be happening is that the more a person makes use of their biomolecular network, the more it . . . let's say it *evolves*. In other words, the connective capacity emerges through extensive use of Make-Believe. So far, therefore, it's only the very earliest users – staff members, beta testers, the first tranche of subscribers – who have begun to experience a Make-Believe in which they connect with other users. You, for example. You were an early user, of course.' His gaze drifted inward, as he checked his facts. 'You racked up some pretty serious hours in Make-Believe ahead of the product launch, before we implemented the two-hour limit.'

Yes: Cassie thought of how deeply she'd dived into her imagined world. How systematic she'd been, working her way through every experience she could possibly think of – in the name of research, of knowing the product, but she'd have done her job for free just to keep on exploring.

'And then, a second reason why only some users are affected is that these connections require close proximity between users. It's not like making a phone call, where your data gets bounced around up in space and a second later you're speaking to someone in Australia. This is primitive; it's undeveloped. How close do you need to be? A matter of metres. Could you connect to someone in the same room as you? Yes. To your next-door neighbour? Perhaps. There's some evidence to suggest the range increases with use.' He raised a hand to massage the back of his neck. 'Of course, you also need to be in a state in which you are unresponsive to external stimuli, with your motor response inhibited. That can mean an ordinary Make-Believe session, where this state is initiated by your receiver. Or, it can simply mean that you're asleep.'

To connect to someone else – to enter Make-Believe – without using a receiver. It made sense of something that had been baffling her: why the doctors at Raphael House wouldn't simply remove the receivers from their patients in order to stop the connections. It made sense of the wound behind Alan's ear. Not where an implant was located, but where it had once been. Cassie tugged hard on a handful of hair as she followed the wider implications. 'That must mean once you've connected to someone in Make-Believe, you can stay that way for hours at a time – because there's no receiver, no signal, to cut you off.'

Oswald nodded agreement. 'Essentially, we have no control over these connections. And with frequent occurrence, their duration seems to increase. The capacity to connect becomes more effective, we think, as it lays down stronger neural pathways.'

Cassie paused, fingers caught in a tangle of hair, chasing a niggling feeling that something wasn't quite right; that somewhere, there was a flaw in the theory. She was about to point it out when Oswald asked a question.

'Do you remember the first time it happened to you? That you connected with somebody else?' He sounded genuinely curious.

'No,' she said. Pushed it away, the brightness and warmth, and the poor bleached colours of afterwards. She had to stay here, stay now, stay focused. 'Not really. There can't have been anything special about it. What about you?'

'I'm sorry?'

'You must have run up more Make-Believe time than I did. And if you think proximity is important – I guess you would be close enough to other users.'

Oswald's laugh was dismissive. 'Real life is actually quite demanding. I'm afraid I've never had endless hours to spend in Make-Believe.'

'But still – there must be a thousand, several thousand people who've built up as many hours as I did. Professor Morgan, for instance: she's had the connections, I know.' It was just a guess – that haunted look, so quickly suppressed, when Morgan had denied such a thing was possible – but Oswald didn't contradict her. 'Imagen staff, early adopters; are they all experiencing this?'

'We don't believe it's anywhere near the several thousands. But it's only recently we've had sufficient market penetration for multiple users to often be active in a relatively small space. And as we expand, of course, the problem grows: more subscribers, more users building up the hours . . .'

'Hang on, though. I can see there's a problem with the lack of control you have over these connections, but what I don't get is why it would make people cancel their subscriptions. I mean . . .' She trailed off as his eyebrows lifted in an expression of surprise.

'You don't understand why someone would be disturbed by an involuntary, unexplained connection?' He leant back in his seat, as though to study her more clearly. 'The invasion of another consciousness into your most intimate, private fantasy? The reshaping of your experience into something beyond your control?'

'But it's not like that.' Even as Cassie spoke, she heard static, a far-off roar. Felt burnt rubber catch at her throat.

'For you, perhaps. Since this shared Make-Believe is mutually shaped by each user, the nature of the experience rather depends on whom you connect with. You were fortunate, it seems.'

She saw not-Alan rocking, pulling out his hair. Swallowed, dry-mouthed. 'And if you're not fortunate . . . that's why people complain?'

'D'you know, surprisingly few do complain. Those like yourself who have positive experiences – presumably they put it down to a glitch in the system, and keep quiet because they believe they're getting something for nothing.' Cassie felt herself reddening, and dipped her head. 'And then, connections that occur without receivers, when users are asleep, are likely to be interpreted as dreams. Sweet dreams – or nightmares.'

'But even so – there must be some talk about it.'

'Oh, there is some, of course,' he conceded. 'There are always people who are determined to share their unpleasant experiences – on social media, forums, blogs and so on. And we have strategies to deal with that. We're able to minimise damage to the brand, to our reputation for safety and pleasure. But most are not vocal about it: they don't appear to talk, not online at least.' His focus loosened, as he checked something on his lens. 'You have a background in psychology, is that right? Why do you think all these hundreds of people would keep such traumatic experiences to themselves?'

For a minute, Cassie turned the question in her mind. Then: 'It's up to you, what you Make-Believe,' she said. 'It's whatever you want. So – anything that happens, with these connections, people think it's what they want. Even if—'

'Even if it's very much what they don't want.'

She should have guessed it straight away. If you believed the dark, the horror, was a part of you, was your deepest, unconscious desire . . . 'They're ashamed,' she said. 'That's why.' More powerful than threats, than entreaties. It was always shame that kept people silent.

Oswald smiled, approving. 'It's good news for us, except that we still lose them as subscribers. Many of these are high net worth individuals. You understand the resources that go in to attracting them in the first place. You understand how valuable they are. We can't afford to keep letting them go.'

She did understand. And then, of course – despite Imagen's strategies for protecting the Make-Believe brand – sooner or later those ugly experiences being shared online would pile up sufficiently to be noticed, and taken seriously. And when that happened – when it emerged that, despite the exhaustive testing, despite the assurances of absolute safety and its licence from the Department for Innovation, Make-Believe was not the secure, controlled space its users had thought – then, it would be touch and go whether the company could survive. She understood now the tension Oswald was trying so hard to conceal. Was beginning to understand the effort they'd made to bring her here.

She cleared her throat. 'These connections: if they're direct, person to person – I mean, not controlled by the receiver – well, how can you track them? What I mean is . . . how can you know that it's really so bad?'

'You're right, with no data to track it has been a challenge to ascertain the facts of what's happening. But there are various forms of evidence. Personal testimony. Direct observation. And in a few cases we've been able to perform scans of subjects' brain activity. So we've observed, for instance, that the connections are invariably accompanied by brain signals that indicate strong emotion. You might almost say the connections are *driven* by emotion, whether positive or negative. We can identify the neural signatures. Fear. Sadness. Anger. Shame. All very prevalent.' He rubbed the side of his nose. 'Particularly when a subject connects to more than one user at the same time.'

More than one. The words resounded. Simultaneous, multiple connections. She saw a sackful of cats, trapped, swarming, scratching. In the locked ward, a dozen patients, Alan among them. His fingernails scrabbling at bloodied skin. Her eyes flickered shut as she tried to refuse the image, but when Oswald spoke it was as if he could see it too.

'Imagine,' he said – his tone soft, suggestive. 'If it were a friend of yours, suffering in this way.'

Cassie opened her eyes. Stared at him. His features were arranged in an expression of neutral sympathy, and between them a moment stretched into a space for her to ask: Alan? Was it Alan he was talking about? What did he know – what could he know – about Alan and her?

But she didn't. She didn't ask. Thought, for some reason, of Nicol. His cynicism, his suspicion. His *disapproval*. Kept the opening-up sound of Alan's name trapped behind her teeth, till eventually Oswald spoke again. 'You can help, Cassandra,' he said. 'By stopping these connections.' He placed his hands, palms down, on the desk between them. 'Here's what we propose: to make use of your connective capacity to distribute what we might call an upgrade – a network upgrade. You understand? An upgrade that switches off the facility for direct communication between users.'

'I'd be going back to Make-Believe?'

'That's right. We've engineered the upgrade to be self-replicating – just like a virus. All we would need you to do is allow your biomolecular network to be upgraded, and that's an incredibly minor procedure; we'll do it via a nasal spray, just like your initial installation. Then, once your network is primed with the upgrade, you'll log back in to Make-Believe and start the distribution process. Each time you connect to another user, you'll pass it on, and their network will upgrade in turn.'

'But – if the upgrade destroys the connection? I mean, once your network is altered, you're – you're switched off, you can't connect to anyone else, so then how can you pass it on?'

'Trust me, we have worked out the details. The upgrade will take roughly a week to modify the biomolecular network; that's a week in which it remains contagious, as it were. During that period you will pass it on to everyone with whom you connect. Let's say you pass on the upgrade to three or four people. In fact' – his tone became confidential – 'it would be significantly more than that. We'd want to make the best use of you as an active carrier during that week, make some strategic connections, in order to really get a good start on the upgrade program. But just for the sake of our example . . . During the next week, each of those people passes it on to three or four more. Or perhaps one or two of them fail to pass it on – they're not in contact with another subscriber who has an active collaborative capacity. But that's fine, we've mapped the distribution, we're still on track for the kind of exponential growth that will allow us to spread the upgrade through the population.'

He placed his palms flat on the desk. 'Now, there are other ways we could fix this bug – but the benefit of this, for us, is that it's quick, and it's quiet. No need for subscribers even to know that anything has changed. As the upgrade spreads through our subscriber base, quite quickly we'll reach a stage where customer networks are upgraded almost as soon as the connective capacity becomes active. A single glitch, nothing more than the flicker of a light. That's all that most people will register.'

She had to admit it was beautifully neat. An elegant solution. No wonder Oswald was looking pleased with himself.

'So.' He turned his enthusiasm towards her. 'It's a fair offer, wouldn't you say? What we're asking is simple, painless, risk-free; what we're offering is the opportunity to change your life.'

It was too much. Too perfect. She wanted what he was holding out to her, wanted it physically, urgently – in her chest, in the soles of her feet, in her back teeth – and even so, she felt herself drawing away. He sounded, suddenly, like a salesman. She'd crafted too many sales propositions not to recognise it: he'd worked on that line, or someone had – and taken it too far. *Sound too good to be true? We have hundreds of thousands of satisfied customers – check our testimonials!* But as she drew breath to tell him no, tell him she wanted to think about it, he held up a hand.

'But listen – the last thing I want is for you to feel railroaded.' He gave a sigh. 'Unfortunately this situation is time-sensitive. A decision is due to be made at the end of the year on our application to license Make-Believe in the US. It's a critically important market for us, and there are a number of hurdles there – so the religious lobby, for example, are opposed to what they see as human modification of what God created . . . But more significantly, the US administration is a lot less obliging than the UK, in that they've defined Make-Believe as a drug – rather than as entertainment, as it is over here. Which means we're applying to the FDA, and *that* means the technology must be seen to be absolutely, one hundred per cent safe. Our licensing application has been turned down once before, and if it happens again . . . well. And frankly I wouldn't be telling you this, but I do want you on the team going forward, helping to clear those hurdles.'

He placed his elbows on the desk, pressed his palms together in front of his face so he looked like an overgrown child at prayer. 'All that aside,' he said, 'you'll want some time to reflect. I can give you . . . thirty minutes?' With a functional smile, he unfolded himself from his seat. 'Not,' he said, 'that there's much to consider, once you really think about it.'

CHAPTER TWENTY-SEVEN

When Oswald had gone, Cassie hoisted her feet up onto the chair, sat with her forehead pressed against her knees and her hands clasped tightly round her shins. Though she was relieved to be left alone, she felt suddenly weighted with tiredness, as if when he'd shut the door behind him Oswald had swept all the energy from the room.

Imagine, if it were a friend of yours. Suffering in this way.

It had been an opening, whether or not it had been intended as such. Her chance to challenge Oswald, to find out for certain whether the things she'd guessed – about Alan, the patient trials, Raphael House – were true. But an opening could be a trap. She had sensed manipulation, and kept her mouth shut.

Up until that point, Oswald's manner had been forthright: he had answered her questions, been clear about what they wanted her to do, and what they would give her in return. Even to leave her like this, alone in his room, suggested a certain amount of transparency. She lifted her head to look around: low bookshelves, outsized floor lamp, framed print of some mountainous landscape. Still, there were things that didn't make sense. For instance, the time and money that must have gone into manoeuvring her into this position, when surely Imagen could have used an existing member of staff to deliver their upgrade. Perhaps they were confident they could persuade her to stay quiet; her silence would doubtless be another condition of the offer. Or perhaps it was something else: *There are other ways we could do this*, he'd said, and maybe that was the lie. She wasn't simply the neatest, most elegant solution; for some reason, she was the sole solution.

She squeezed the back of her neck, trying to ease the crick from lying too long in Lewis's bed with her head at an awkward angle. With an effort, she got to her feet and, staring absently through the glass wall, raised her arms in a long stretch above her head. Directly opposite, on the far side of the open-plan office, was the 1950s mosaic that dated from the building's original incarnation as a telephone exchange. She had never seen it so clearly before. It showed four blocky, stylised heads, one at each corner of the panel, all connected by different coloured lines that arranged themselves in a geometric pattern.

Multiple connections. Cats in a bag. Claws unsheathed.

She turned her back on the mosaic. Circled Oswald's desk, and settled into his swivel chair. Swiped her fingers across his trackpad, bringing his screen to life: biotouch protected, of course. She ran her palms over the smooth wood surface, then – knowing it would be pointless – tried the first of his desk drawers. Locked. The second drawer locked as well, and the third—

The third slid open at her tug.

She paused, with her fingers still on the handle. Allowed her hand to slip over the edge of the drawer. Touched card, paper: a stack of files. Down below, the office was empty apart from the cleaner still going about his work. As subtly as she could she glanced round Oswald's room, checking for spy cameras. Just because she couldn't see any hidden lenses didn't mean they weren't there. She hesitated – but then, what was the worst that could happen? If Oswald caught her prying, he'd have one more crime to set alongside the others on his list, all those breaches he'd reassured her she needn't worry about – for now. Swiftly, she extracted the topmost file from the drawer, flipped it open on her lap.

Inside was a single document, a spreadsheet that ran to several stapled pages. Columns and rows labelled with abbreviations, cells filled with digits, with Xs and Os, with nothing she could recognise – until her eye snagged on a pair of repeated initials that stepped in a ladder down the page. The column was headed *Loc*; the initials read *RH*. Location: Raphael House? Yes, it could be. She looked closely now at the other headers. At columns labelled *Csnt / Scrnd / Enrld*, each filled with dates that ranged from three to four years ago. At a column of initials that was headed *ID*. She traced a finger down the line, unable to stop herself jumping ahead in search of the familiar shape – and when her eyes found it, she blinked and waited for her tracking finger to catch up. *AJL*: Alan James Lauder. The initials followed by a six-digit number she knew instantly as his date of birth. She pinned him down with her finger, followed his data the length of the row, but the remaining codes refused to yield.

For a moment she thought of stealing the document, replacing the empty file. Oswald held so much over her: these pages tucked neatly into her pocket could even the balance between them. Only, it was so cryptic it was no real proof to anyone except her. How could she convince anyone that *RH* meant Raphael House? That each cell nestled under the heading *Enrld* meant an individual patient, enrolled onto a trial they were not equipped to agree to, or even understand? She placed the paper back into its cardboard sheath, ready to put it back where it belonged. And then she stopped.

Come on: a single drawer unlocked? This particular document on the top of the pile, carefully informing her of everything she already suspected, and nothing more? It was all too obvious. She was *meant* to find this.

It seemed impossible, but it had to be true: Oswald knew what Alan meant to her. Had it been encoded in her data, from all the times she'd connected with

Alan? A one-sided stream of information issuing from her receiver, luminous with need, repeating the message of her longing again, again, again? And this file was a nudge, a little extra persuasion to accept Oswald's proposal. A reminder that if she turned him down, it was not her but Alan who'd suffer the most.

What she'd been offered was a bribe; this was the sour to go with the sweet, something more like emotional blackmail. It was the confirmation she needed, of all that not-Alan was going through. Last night, in Make-Believe, she had felt it for herself, a suffocating blackness; it had been distant and brief, and she'd been able to free herself. In the locked ward, it would be quite different. Individual psychoses: shared, multiplied. Each invading the others. Each locked into a web of evolving, strengthening networks. She forced herself to think of it, and the air was pressed from her lungs.

There was no real choice. Of course she would say yes.

Down in the open-plan office, the cleaner had finished. The mug was gone from her desk. She wondered how they'd arrange for her return, what they'd say to the person who'd been doing her job for the last year. Looked again at the mosaic, tracing the coloured lines that passed over and under each other, turning corners, weaving patterns. Thought of how the upgrade would be done. The nasal spray, a lingering taste, and then the alterations that would go on inside her. Imagined her network as it had appeared in the 3D display in the Newman building. Fresh instructions issued, washing through the mesh of molecules that criss-crossed her brain, and the network responding. The same thing happening with not-Alan: clearing him, cleaning him, keeping him safe. That's where they would begin, of course: in the locked ward. She imagined the upgrade fanning its way through the patients, switching them off, and off, and off—

And that was when she realised.

I'm only here because of you.

What it meant: to destroy the connections.

This is how you save me. Being here. You have to be here—

Her Alan. Real Alan. The Alan she'd found in Make-Believe. It meant she would lose him, all over again.

I'm only here because of you.

It meant he wouldn't exist. Their shared past would not exist. His skin – his eyes – his warmth, his kicking heart and all of it couldn't exist.

Her mouth was dry, suddenly, tongue plastered to the roof of her mouth, as if she would never be able to speak again. How could she make this choice?

She could say no, walk out of here now, and most likely she'd never find her Alan again, never find a way back to Make-Believe – but the possibility would be there still, the faintest glow of his waiting for her. And in the meantime, not-Alan would stay as he was: in the locked ward, in torment. *The invasion of another consciousness . . . something beyond your control . . .* She felt the darkness lapping, shook her head sharply. He was the mistake; he was not *her* Alan. Even so, it was impossible. How could she let him stay there and suffer, when it was in her power to do something about it?

Or she could say yes – agree to Oswald's offer – and not-Alan would still be broken but he wouldn't be suffering, or at least he'd suffer nothing more than ordinary madness. She and Alan both would lose their capacity to connect in Make-Believe, and the waterfall would become a memory of a dream, a place lost to both of them, as they were lost to each other. He would be gone, irrevocably. She would never touch him again, or inhale his smell, hear his voice or his breath or the beat of his heart – and that was impossible too.

Cassie buried her hands in her hair. Tried to think coolly, against a rising tide of desolation. It was a choice between losing Alan probably, or losing Alan definitely. And it was a choice between degrees of suffering – and how could you measure that? The patient was mad, therefore the patient was suffering, but what was the *extra* amount of suffering caused by his connections in Make-Believe? And to what extent was that additional suffering acceptable, if it kept alive the possibility of her Alan? *I'm only here because of you* . . . What degree of suffering was too much to justify, to keep alive that hope?

She stared at the wall, at the mosaic, trying to kick her brain into a higher gear, to find a way around it. A way to keep them safe, all three of them: not-Alan, and Alan, and herself.

* * *

288

When Oswald returned, she was still in his chair, swivelling side to side. She watched as he took in the mutinous expression on her face, the file in plain sight on his desk. He remained on his feet, close enough for his height to feel like intimidation.

'You've been exploring,' he said.

She swung right – left – right. Held his gaze, acting the boss. 'Nowhere you didn't want me to go.' With the tip of her finger she nudged the file, till it sat just slightly askew. 'That's where it all started, then. At Raphael House. Let me guess: biomolecular networks similar to those you went on to use in Make-Believe, except you'd need a way for psychiatrists to shape the patient experience, so . . . engineered so the connective capacity was active instead of latent? Which means, you wouldn't have this problem at all if you hadn't been running unlicensed trials—'

'It's not unlicensed.' His voice was unexpectedly sharp, and she registered the effort he made to soften his tone. 'Alright: things haven't gone as we hoped. We'd prefer it remain under the radar. But it's important you understand, every aspect of this trial was approved. Standard protocol was followed, to the letter. There's no wrongdoing here.'

Cassie stopped her swivelling. Didn't try to conceal her disgust. 'You know I have a friend in there.'

'Which is why we're on the same side!' He held out his palms, gave an appeasing smile. 'These connections, Cassandra, are a shared enemy. We all want for them to stop.'

'But you could stop it right now, if you wanted to! All you need to do is split them up. You must have thought of it. Separate the patients, and the connections will stop.'

'We have thought of it, of course we have. But you must see, now that the patients' networks are active, separating them would be only a temporary solution. Think about it: whether they're admitted to another facility or they recover to the extent that they're able to go back into the community, it's almost inevitable that they will, eventually, encounter another individual whose biomolecular network has also evolved sufficiently for a direct connection to occur between the two. At which point we will be quite unable to help in any way; we won't know about it, and even if we did we would have no means of treating them.'

'You're not treating them now,' Cassie muttered.

'Whereas in Raphael House,' Oswald went on, 'the doctors at least understand that sedatives, for instance, only worsen their symptoms.'

Cassie stared at him. 'It happens when they're sedated?'

He gave a grim little smile. 'Essentially, if the connections can't be blocked by the conscious mind, they cannot be stopped. Asleep, comatose, sedated. It's all the same.'

She didn't want to acknowledge it, but she could see Oswald's reasoning was sound. Imagine Alan in a different hospital, where nobody knew his clinical history. In the next room, another patient with an evolved network. Imagine him locked in a vicious circle: torment and sedation.

'*If* I say yes' – she watched his smile falter – 'that's the only reason. To protect my friend.'

'Understood, of course.' Oswald spoke fast – indifferent to her insistence, wanting only to seal the deal. 'Just to be clear, though: the rest of it, what we're offering you, that's still on the table.'

'But this.' She grabbed the file, rattled it. 'This hide and seek. How am I supposed to trust what you say when you're planting stuff in drawers, pretending to play it straight? This is a big decision. I need some kind of proof.'

She saw him ready to say something; then he stopped, looked down at the carpet. He had his hands in his trouser pockets, thumbs hitched over the edges and stroking the fabric as though he was trying to reassure himself.

'Alright,' he said, and lifted his head again. 'Alright, then – what if we show you?'

'Show me, how?'

'Would it convince you, if you could see – feel – for yourself?'

Something in his assessing gaze sent a twist of unease through her stomach. 'But I want to go home first. I want some proper clothes, and I want a shower and—'

He was shaking his head. 'I'm afraid not. We can get you those things afterwards – but if you want to do this, it has to be now.'

The taste of burning rubber. No: she did not want to do this. But perhaps – perhaps it would help her. Inside his jacket she squared her shoulders, straightened her spine. To know the suffering. To measure it. To choose.

Once again, the woman was driving. She and Oswald sat in silence; alone in the back, Cassie folded the collar of Oswald's jacket so it stood up stiff and soft, walling her off from the world, and pushed her hands deep in his silk-lined pockets. Though it felt as if hours had passed since they'd escorted her from Lewis's flat, the streets were still quiet. She craned to see the clock on the dashboard. 04.28.

The passing landscape was familiar. The journey much quicker than when she'd last made it. She let her eyes close. Noted the turn. The deceleration. The pop of gravel under the wheels, then a bump onto softer ground. Opened them to see the woman had parked up against a stand of shrubs, in an attempt to conceal their presence. From here, Cassie couldn't see the hospital building, but it must be close by. The small paved area. The bench, and the rustle of bamboo.

Oswald turned in his seat, halfway facing her. Handed her a receiver. It looked like one of those the woman had taken from Lewis's flat – same model, at least.

'Knowingly using bioware that's been illegally modified?' Cassie said. 'Unauthorised use of someone else's account?' It wasn't a challenge – more like a joke. Was there something about a man lending you his coat that sparked a rapport, in spite of everything? Perhaps it was just in comparison to his mysterious colleague that Oswald came out well. At least he acknowledged her presence.

'We haven't yet reinstated your account, so – it's the quickest way. We don't have a great deal of time.' The clock on the dashboard said 04.56. 'As soon as you're ready?'

It was weightless in her hand. Such a neat device. She slipped the receiver onto her ear. Ready: to experience what not-Alan was going through. Ready to measure the suffering.

She leant back. Pressed the switch.

ON

CHAPTER TWENTY-EIGHT

Oswald stayed twisted in his seat, watching the girl as she sank. When her eyelids started to twitch, he turned away. 'Half an hour, do you think?'

Beside him, the advisor took off her spectacles, drew a small cloth from the glove box and began to polish the lenses. 'If you say so.'

In the back, the girl sat silent. He turned to check on her: motionless, except for her eyelids, jumping and flickering. He looked away again. What was she experiencing? Couldn't tell, from the outside. It could be bliss or terror – but it would be terror, of course. He was counting on it. He was glad he couldn't see the building from here; it depressed him. Looked like sheltered housing, like the place his old mum had been in at the end. Again, from the outside you wouldn't guess.

'So we don't know what the problem is,' the advisor said. 'Whether she's stalling for something.'

He guessed it was a question, though it didn't sound like one. 'I can't think what for,' he said.

He could hear the girl breathing now, short and shallow. What was it that kept them hooked – the ones like her? A temperament thing, just born that way? He was a light user, himself. Had tried out all the obvious novelties. Didn't have the time for it. Now it was just occasional, once or twice a week, the stuff he wouldn't tell his wife. Highest privacy settings, of course: he set his own, no way in hell he'd trust it otherwise. Connecting. Collaborating. Last thing he'd want. That would really spoil the fun. There was something compulsive about it, perhaps – when you got the urge – maybe it was like that for the girl—Stop it: stop thinking about that. Not sitting next to this woman, the sort whose business it was to know things, to sit behind her spectacles and notice you, probably to read your thoughts . . . He glanced in the rear-view mirror, suddenly sure she was watching him, but it was angled so all he could see was the view through the rear windscreen. He shifted slightly in his seat. It was understandable, the insistence, now, on close governmental oversight. Given what had happened. And they shared a common aim, she and he – to manage the fallout from this situation without jeopardising the original investment, the potential rewards. Still, he wished it was Lachlan driving.

It should all turn out alright, thanks to him. Probably. Almost definitely. And when it did, it would be thanks to his foresight. He wasn't superstitious, didn't believe in signs; coincidences were just that. But four years ago, when he'd seen the girl waiting in the office to be called in for interview – straight away, he had known her. His most recent visit to Raphael House, she'd been there too. An uncomfortable moment. But easy enough to find out who she visited there. What the relationship was, or had been. And once he was sure she wasn't an investigative journalist or an industrial spy, he'd recognised her potential as either a threat or an asset – and it had been his decision to act, to hire the girl. She was competent enough, after all, might possibly have made it to second interview without his interference. The idea was to keep her close enough to monitor any suspicions she might have – he couldn't claim to have foreseen at that stage exactly how they would use her, and admittedly when the spontaneous connections had started it had seemed for a while that she might be more trouble than she was worth. But again he'd acted to neutralise her. Made sure the terms of her dismissal were suitably severe.

And now when they needed someone to deliver the upgrade, there she was. Persuadable. Expendable. The perfect tool for the job. There were other addicts, of course, other users who'd been terminated – but none who had signed a draconian contract they could be persuaded to breach. There was simply no one else like the McAllister girl, no one about whom they knew so much. Information was power, made it quite straightforward to persuade someone round to your point of view, especially when they were unaware of quite how much information you held. And once she had been facilitated back into Make-Believe, she'd not only shown that her biomolecular network was still in working order, she had demonstrably contravened the terms of her dismissal – giving him all the leverage he needed.

So when they turned this situation around it would be down to him – not this plain civil servant with all her watchful, invisible power. Without Cassandra McAllister, what other options would they have? Still, useful to have her here, this woman. Useful to have a female. Chances were the girl wouldn't even have opened the door to Lachlan and another man.

He glanced behind him once again. God, look at her. Sweat glittering on her face. Skin white as death. Hair like she'd just come out of the rain. She was sweating into his jacket; he'd have to get it cleaned again, what a ball-ache. Last thing he needed in this morning's meeting with Eric was a jacket that stank of fear. He rubbed a hand across his eyes, wishing he was home, asleep, not trapped in a car sunk nose-deep in trees outside a madhouse in the arse-end of nowhere. Christ . . .

He let his eyes close for just a moment, and leant back in his seat.

Twigs tapped the windshield, shifting in a gentle breeze. Somewhere, a bird sang.

The driver's side window sighed as it opened a crack, letting the fresh air in. The advisor angled her mirror to see more clearly.

She had witnessed it happening before, inside the hospital, had filmed the clinical trial subjects for her confidential reports – but to watch it in the back seat of her car . . . She could actually smell the girl, the sweat coming off her, bitter and sharp. The contrast between this, and what the research had promised. It was fascinating, in a way.

When she'd been drafted in to help achieve a satisfactory resolution to this enormous fuck-up, she'd gone back through it all. The paperwork, the meeting transcripts. The researchers had been eloquent in their requests for funding, for approval. Professor Fiona Morgan, pressing her case. Explaining how the technology would revolutionise the treatment of mental health. Make it possible for psychiatrists to intervene directly, from inside a patient's consciousness. Help individuals to reframe their experiences, to filter the information they received from the world around them, to make sense of that information. That phrase she had used, the single phrase that had caught the Minister's attention: *perfectible minds*.

In the mirror, the girl slid to one side, fell half out of sight.

Perfectible. In her opinion, not that she was paid to have an opinion, you could trace it all back to that word. The regulatory approval, the lack of ethical oversight. Perfectible equals productive equals efficient. An efficient response to the mental health crisis, that's what the Minister had bought into. Very keen altogether on efficiency, this lot, and her Minister in particular. She wouldn't use the word 'corrupt', wouldn't go that far, not quite. Opportunistic . . . perhaps. Myopic, evidently.

Too close beside her, Oswald creaked in his seat. She wished he'd sit still, stop fidgeting. She wondered if he knew why he was there, really, instead of his boss. Of course it would hurt Imagen to lose their CTO, if it should come to that, but as she understood it there were several extremely capable technology officers under him. He was not irreplaceable – the company would survive his ignominious departure, if that was what it came to. And the decision had been taken, not by her naturally, that – in the interests of the department, the government, the national economy – the company *would* survive.

Oswald twisted to look at the girl, creaking leather again. 'Enough, now?' he said.

She tilted the mirror further. The girl was leaning with her head pressed against the glass, neck awkwardly angled. Under her lids, her eyes were still jumping. 05.25 glowed on the dashboard.

Personally, she'd have been more thorough, left it as long as they could – till the hospital subjects started to wake. She sighed, turned the ignition, began to reverse. Oswald was probably right. They wanted her compliant, after all. Not ready to be sectioned. Well . . . not yet.

FREQUENTLY ASKED QUESTIONS

Q. Can everyone use Make-Believe™?

A. We want everyone to experience their own amazing virtual reality! You can use Make-Believe™ as long as:*
   • you are over eighteen
   • you have passed our health, credit and security checks
   • you are not pregnant or trying to become pregnant
   • you are not currently undergoing, and have not previously undergone, treatment for any mental illness or neurological condition

*For more details, see our full terms and conditions.

CHAPTER TWENTY-NINE

Light – there is light, there is – a scream, she tries to – she is *dying*, her heart, can't breathe, can't breathe— Reaches out, hits something close in front – too close – hits again, punching, *get away* – but it's not, it's just— Leather. Soft. Seat, car seat. Her neck wedged, cornered. The glass, trapping her. She scrambles up, upright. Retches. *Christ, she's not going be sick*. Glass drops away. *Outside! Do it outside!* Bitter spasms. She coughs. Burning. Like her skin, her skin had. Flayed. Acid. She shakes. Teeth hammer. Bile in her mouth. She wipes her chin, his jacket. *Done?* The window rises. Her head against it, sweat-wet skin, cool glass. Water. She wants to drink. To be under the water. Cleaned. The water to flow through her, and her to live there, gilled, breathing, clean.

The shaking passes. Empties her. Leaves her slumped.

They were taking her somewhere. They were taking her away: yes, and she wanted it, to be away from here. A broken doll in the corner – who was it, lying there? Knew it was her, was herself – but no, not really she wasn't. Was not anything. Didn't feel. Only the prickling numbness across her cheeks, lips, nose. Only pity, for the doll in the corner. Pity was abstract. Was nothing. Look, Oswald's jacket. He would be angry. She touched it, fingers thick and bandaged, the jacket smooth, hard, like glass, like the window.

She was noticing, now. Something had fallen from her ear. It lay on her lap, the receiver. She picked it up, turned it, staring. Scrap of titanium, silicon, graphene.

Oswald spoke. 'You're going to do what we asked?'

She turned her head towards the glass. It was too much effort to reply. Like expecting her to lift a mountain. She decided not to listen. Closed her eyes.

CHAPTER THIRTY

When the car stopped Cassie prised her eyes open, blinking at the light. She thought she knew it, this place. The car park, the box-buildings, low and new. She had been here – had she been here?

The woman spoke. 'You'll look after the rest of it.'

Without answering, Oswald got out of the car. Stepped round, and opened the rear door. 'Come on, Cassandra, come with me.'

No: she didn't want to. Wanted to sleep. Lie down on this comfy seat, close her eyes. Become nothing. But he promised she could have a bath, after. Said they would take her home. Bath. Bed. Sleep. And besides, if she stayed in the car she'd be left with *her*. So she pushed herself along the seat, and out.

The second the door slammed, the woman pulled away. Didn't look back.

'She is a bitch,' Cassie said. She was feeling loose, now, like nothing much mattered.

'This way. The sooner it's done the sooner we get you home.'

'Isn't she? Don't tell me you like her. Is she high up, she must be higher up than you? That must be a real . . . a real pain in the arse.' The distance to the ground was hard to judge. She walked carefully, following Oswald, not looking any further than the heels of his black, shiny shoes. They were crossing tarmac, and then they were at an entrance, a plain black door in a featureless breeze-block wall. She waited, unsteadily upright, as Oswald keyed in a code, palmed the security panel, stood staring for an iris scan.

Then the door released with a click, almost inaudible, and they were in.

Along corridors lit by blue-tinged emergency lights. Oswald keyed and palmed through layers of security. He talked as they walked, but not to her. 'I've got the subject here,' he was saying, 'but there's some paperwork to complete first. Have everything ready, will you?' There was a tinny response from someone, before Oswald cut in again: 'Then I can't see how ten more minutes is going to make a difference, is it? Do your job.'

Cassie stumbled after him. Down corridors, round corners, deeper into the core of the building. Finally he led her into an office, a cupboard-size space cluttered with tower drives, screens and filing cabinets, just enough room left over for a desk and a single chair. Turned on the strip light.

'Sit, please.'

Cassie did as she was told.

Oswald pushed aside a stack of folders, clearing a foot of space on the desk; he opened his briefcase and drew out a sheaf of paper. 'Our new agreement,' he said. 'This updates – replaces – the previous version. Three copies; we need your signature on each of them.' He placed the papers in front of her. 'Read them, and when you're ready—' He drew a fat silver pen from the case, laid it alongside. 'It's exactly what we discussed earlier, so there shouldn't be any questions.'

Cassie lifted the top copy. She recognised letters, words, even parts of sentences, but there was no meaning attached to any of it. She ran her eyes along the lines, pretending to read. Oswald stood over her, arms folded. Halfway down the first page, she flipped to the next. It must be obvious she was acting; she wasn't sure why she was playing along. She skimmed to the last page. It could have said anything. She might have been signing away her firstborn. But there was no choice. What had happened to her, back there – she couldn't think of it happening to not-Alan. Happening every night of his life.

The pen was heavy in her hand as she twisted off the lid. Last time she'd signed their papers, they hadn't lent her a gold-nibbed fountain-pen. Perhaps her signature needed to be more weighty, more certain this time around. She looped her name, thick and black. Once. Twice. Three times.

'Well done,' said Oswald. 'An excellent decision; I'm sure you won't regret it.' The poor salesman in him, overenthusiasm pushing back to the surface. She added the date. Dropped the pen on top of the papers, pushed the lot towards Oswald, who handed back one copy. 'You keep this. Two for me, one for you. Now we're getting there – aren't we? Follow me, please.'

More walking, and again the feeling of a dream; she was lost, shuffling in circles, she would never get out of here. All she wanted was to stretch out on the cold hard floor of the corridor. It would feel like a feather bed, pulling her into sleep. But she kept upright, kept moving. Oswald was walking-and-talking again, but this time he was addressing her. 'Once we've administered the upgrade, it'll take a day to prime your network,' he told her. 'Essentially, it's rewriting the instructions for every biomolecule. Within twenty-four hours, we'll be ready for you to connect to Make-Believe again. We'll want to spread the upgrade as widely as possible during your week as an active carrier, take you to a number of strategic places where you can pass it on.' He stopped, faced her. 'Don't worry,' he said, 'it'll be nothing like this morning. A series of brief connections, all managed with the receiver so we'll remain in control. And that will be it: you'll have carried out your side of the agreement.' He turned away, palmed a security panel, and opened the door to another, much bigger room.

'Hello?' he called, into silence.

They were in a laboratory, a dim scrubbed space. One

set of strip lights marched brightly across a tiled ceiling; three more sets slept undisturbed. On the far side of the lab, a door opened, and a slight figure appeared – a boy, a teenager, short-haired in white shirt and dark trousers, but then the boy spoke and Cassie realised she was a woman.

'Come through,' she called.

They walked past a repetition of benches – some stacked with unexplained machines, shrouded for the night like birds in cages, some holding glass cases like fish tanks that reflected the pale smears of their faces. The floor was dark, swarming with flecks of colour. Cassie blinked, trying to stop the colours buzzing as she navigated the space, following Oswald into a room so filled with equipment there was barely space for three people to stand. The woman was shrugging into a lab coat. Close up she didn't look boyish at all; she looked pretty. Tired, but pretty.

'Everything's ready,' said the woman. She gestured towards a stainless-steel trolley laid out with medical-looking paraphernalia, unidentified things sealed in sterile packets. 'Has been since yesterday evening . . .' She covered her mouth, gave an exaggerated yawn and shot Oswald a resentful look. Then she seemed to notice Cassie for the first time, and her eyes narrowed.

'Hello,' she said. 'Looks like I'm not the only one who's been up all night.'

Beneath Cassie's feet, the floor was tilting like the deck of a boat.

'Here.' The woman grabbed a chair, spun it round

behind Cassie in a single neat movement. 'Have a seat; we'll not be long. I'm Sam, by the way, nice to meet you.' Then she took hold of Oswald's arm, drew him over to the doorway.

'What's the story?' Sam's voice was low, but the room was small, and Cassie could hear her clear enough.

'You don't need the story,' Oswald said. 'That's not your job, is it?'

'It doesn't have to be my job, it's just . . . human concern. Come on, she's out of it. What's happened to her?'

'She's fine. She'll be more fine once we can get her home, so let's get on with it.'

'It'd be better to bring her back later, do it another time.'

'No. We'll go ahead now.'

'But *look* at her. Look at the state of her. I really don't think—'

'We'll go ahead now.'

There was a pause: a momentary stand-off. Then Sam turned away. She moved back to her trolley, rearranged a stack of what looked like sterile dressings so they were absolutely straight.

'Alright,' she said to Cassie. 'Let's get this over with, shall we, and then you can get home. We'll just give your face a wash first, and maybe get that hair tied back. There's a bathroom back this way. I'll show you.'

Through the lab, across the corridor, into the ladies'. Sam ran a basin full of hot water and hand soap, paddled it with her hand to bring up the bubbles.

'That soap's a bit rough for your face, I know, but we do need to get you cleaned up,' she said.

Cassie dipped her hands in. Brought them up to her face, and sluiced. She was aware of heat, water, pink perfume, all of it distant, as if the face she was washing belonged to someone else, as if she herself was comfortingly absent.

Sam held out a bundle of paper napkins. 'Sorry,' she said. 'He's my boss.'

Cassie dried her face, her neck. Shook droplets of water from Oswald's suit.

'Yeah,' said Sam, 'I like the jacket.'

In the mirror, Cassie's gaze slid sideways from her wrecked reflection, till she caught Sam's eye. Nice of her to be concerned. To want to not do what Oswald wanted – even if she was going to do it anyway. 'It's OK,' Cassie told her. 'I have to. I've signed the papers.'

A frown creased Sam's forehead. 'I don't know about anything – I'm just here to make sure this gets done right,' she said. 'Come on, then. You look like you need your bed more than I do, so let's crack on.'

Back in the small room, Cassie did as she was told. She sat on the reclining chair that took up most of the floor space. She stretched her legs in front of her, leant back against the headrest. The disposable cover smelt slippery, medical. A curtain hung at the side, ready to form a semi-private cubicle, but Sam didn't draw it round.

'And just pull your hair back for me,' she said.

Cassie's fingers caught and tugged as she combed her hair away from her face. The padded seat felt like being back in the car. She heard a dull metallic sound, and craned to see what Sam was doing now. Caught a glimpse of a silver cylinder the size of a large kitchen storage jar. Another sound: the soft snap of disposable gloves. Carefully, Sam drew something out of the cylinder. Turned, and held it up for Oswald to inspect. It was nothing like the branded canisters that contained the Make-Believe activation spray. This looked more like a squat, blunt syringe – and she thought of not-Alan in the locked ward. Of his agitation, how he'd punched at her, cried out, dug at the wound in his scalp, and of how she'd stayed silent, waited it out for fear a doctor would be called to settle him with a needle. The chair was moving, dropping backwards. Cassie clutched its arms.

'We'll just get you lying down for this,' said Sam.

Dropping, dropping, till her feet were higher than her head, till she was staring into the ceiling light which made her blink, and close her eyes.

Something damp, dabbing round her nostrils. Cotton wool, and the sharpness of disinfectant. Cassie hoped it would cover her own smell; was conscious of Sam's face close to hers, of breathing with her mouth closed. 'This might feel odd,' said Sam, 'but it'll be over in a second.' Latex fingers, cool, competent, moving a strand of hair. 'One thing: you mustn't sneeze. If it tickles, if you think you're going to, then pinch – really pinch. OK?'

This was it. The moment Sam sprayed the stuff inside her, Alan would be gone. She made herself stay still, arms flat on the rests. Forced her body not to resist. Kept her eyes closed, and in her mind she imagined him, just the way she would in Make-Believe. But it was hard – her brain was hurt, was muddled – hard to get him clear. It was like those first times she'd tried, when all she could manage to hold of him was a fragment, just a fraction; the moment she got another part of him in focus, the first blurred and was lost.

The blunted needle slid delicately up her nostril. Probed the tender place high inside. Cassie held her breath. *Alan – I'm sorry – Alan—*

A puff; a cold trickle, like melting ice cream running down – up – her nose. A fleeting pain at the front of her head. An itch, rising: she grabbed the bridge of her nose, squeezed hard.

'Good. Very good. Keep pinching.' Sam was moving around, peeling off gloves, putting things back where they'd come from. 'We'll keep you there for a couple of minutes, just to be sure. You won't feel anything now. It's just that first bit, just the spray makes you want to sneeze . . .'

Cassie heard her over the high mosquito whine, the sound of cold in her ears. Traced the tingling in her soft palate, the throb in her gums, in the roots of her teeth, that made her suck her cheeks in. Followed the cold seeping through her sinuses, creeping across her scalp. *How do you know?* That's what she wanted to ask –

because Sam had never experienced this. Because Cassie was the first, wasn't she – so shouldn't they be asking her what it felt like? But it didn't matter. That was the thing. She was the first and only. An experiment with no follow-up – as long as she worked. As long as she did her job. It didn't matter what else it might do, the cold trickling spray working its way into her. Didn't matter what the side effects might be.

But she had an agreement. The papers folded, lying on her stomach. She touched them, checking. Hanging on to that.

She felt it still, a cold itch buzzing in her head, as she followed Oswald back through the maze of corridors. Felt it as she sat in the back of a different car, thinking of nothing but bed, and sleep. As she stood jacketless on the pavement at 6.30 a.m., Oswald pulling away, leaving her with the promise that he'd be back to collect her in twenty-four hours, once the upgrade had taken effect.

She pressed the buzzer for Lewis's flat, and kept on pressing, hoping – *Please, God* – hoping he'd be there; and before she'd finished speaking her name, the door sprang open, and by the time she'd started to climb the steps he was bounding down to meet her. When he grabbed her arms his grip was so fierce it was more restraint than hug, but the firmness was a comfort. She let him hold her, keep her upright. Relief spread through her as she gazed at him vacantly, his familiar face, his wide mouth and dark eyes. Relief, and the realisation of something significant, something she should tell him about – but she felt herself sagging in his arms. Let it slip away. Shook her head at his questions, at *Jesus, Cassie, where have you been what's happened to you I was worried—*

'Later,' she told him. Later would do. Now, she needed to sleep.

CHAPTER THIRTY-ONE

She woke with her eyes gummed shut. Rubbed and blinked till the world sharpened around her. She was clammy and stinking still, dirtying Lewis's sheets with dried sweat and stale fear. She sat up: remembered the icy trickle, the buzz in her head. It felt fine now. Normal. She pinched her nose, rubbed her finger and thumb along the bones of her cheeks.

Water. The thirst came suddenly; she had never been so thirsty. She swung her feet to the floor. Stood for a second, finding her balance. She was still in Alan's T-shirt, her old jogging bottoms. She stripped them off and wrapped herself in Lewis's dressing gown. Soft towelling, smelling of clean washing, and of Lewis's sandalwood soap. She tied the belt tight, a reassurance.

He must have heard the floorboards creak. Stuck his head round the door. 'You're up,' he said.

'Water?'

He disappeared, and she heard the tap running. Met him in the kitchen, took the glass and downed it in one.

'Thanks for letting me sleep.'

'Well, God. You were dead on your feet.'

'I need a bath. A shower. Both.'

'OK – but you have to tell me first what happened. Where were you?'

She blinked. The sun was warming the room; the cat crouched neatly on the table in a patch of light, fur glowing, eyes slitted. It felt like early evening. 'What time is it?'

'Half six. You slept for twelve hours. Cassie—'

The cat widened its eyes and flattened its ears as she pulled out a chair, and she remembered: when she'd left, Pita had been the only creature here.

'Where did you go?'

He looked blank. 'Me?'

'You weren't here. When she came. It was – I don't know – about three in the morning.'

'Yeah, I went out – I left a note? It was just getting light and I wanted to walk, after—' He shook his head. 'You were still in Make-Believe. But who came, who's this "she"?'

'From Imagen. She took me; took me there.'

He listened, narrow-eyed and frowning – confusion, or concentration; she wasn't sure which. When her voice dried up he fetched her more water. He brought her toast, a mug of tea, and she demolished them, asked for more. She told him about Oswald. About the connections, and how they'd evolved, and the deal she'd struck with Imagen. She told him how her network was being upgraded; that they'd be back to collect her – she checked the clock on the oven – less than twelve hours from now. He listened patiently as she got muddled, remembered stuff she'd forgotten and looped back round to fill in the gaps. Not all of them, though; some gaps she left unfilled, deliberately. The hospital, the locked ward. She didn't describe how they'd taken her there. Wouldn't think of it. Not ever.

She must have been in shock, she realised. She'd been behind a wall of glass, like the one in Oswald's office; now it had shattered, and she felt skinned. Every twitch of Lewis's face told her something of what was happening inside him. She was reminded of that moment, the first time they'd met, when she'd looked into his eyes. Seen straight through to the back of his skull, and recognised herself. He sat pushed back in his chair, tense and upright, his jaw with that tight, set angle, and listened silently. Too silent; he wasn't asking the questions that must have been zipping around inside his head. And she thought she knew why.

Somewhere between her and Lewis, her story had morphed from trauma to triumph. She could hear it from his perspective; it must seem she'd disappeared and walked back in with everything he longed for. She'd found her way back to Make-Believe. She was legit. All the threats hanging over her were gone. She had turned back time. She had managed to change the past.

'I'm sorry,' she said.

He shook his head. 'Why, what for?'

'Because – I know it's what you wanted. And maybe there's a way – once I'm back in there – I can sort you out. Get your account reinstated.'

He stood up. 'I'll run your bath.'

She heard him walk to the bathroom. The gush of taps turning on, and the rumble of water filling the tub. Smelt something herbal, heavy and sharp: rosemary, eucalyptus. Heard the swish of Lewis encouraging bubbles, and thought of Sam doing the same; and long ago, her mother— For a moment she sat, eyes closed, arms wrapped across her chest. Then she shook off the memory.

She padded through to the bedroom, collecting clean underwear from the drawer in the bedside table, the cleanish jeans she'd had on yesterday – was it only yesterday?

'Can I borrow a T-shirt?' she called.

'Yep, hang on—' Lewis came through, opened the wardrobe. 'This one's kind of shrunk – it'll still be too big, but . . .'

On the floor by the bed, creased and folded, was the Imagen paperwork. She picked it up, took it with her bundle of clothes to the bathroom.

In, and under. The heat against her skin, the weight of

317

the water; the surfacing, already feeling cleansed, and the soft prickle of bubbles bursting. How the cold had seeped inside her head . . . Under, and up again. The steam, hot vapour, beginning to clear her mind. Dispersing the fog that had clouded her thoughts.

She sat up, reached for the towel to dry her hands, then leant out and picked up the paperwork.

It was still hard going, densely legal, but slowly she picked her way through it. One clause made her pause, and frown. As far as she could tell, it meant if she were found to be in breach of any of the standard terms and conditions of employment at Imagen, the whole agreement would be void. Void for both parties: but since she would have carried out her side of the deal, that could only go against her.

She would ask about that, when they came for her. When they took her back to the hospital. The thought of it made her drop the paperwork onto the bathroom floor, dunk down underwater once more, holding her breath, plugging her ears with the slow deep sounds of water and blood. But to know that not-Alan would be safe from that nightly horror . . . She came up gasping.

What would it be like to step back into her old job? She would need a new wardrobe – she had nothing appropriate, had long ago sold all the good quality clothes she had owned. She would need a haircut, too. She reached for the shampoo, started to scrub at the sweat, the grease, the dried specks of vomit. And once she was back at her desk, what first? They would need to revise their strategy, given the changed landscape. Re-evaluate their benchmarks for subscriber satisfaction. Revise their targets for expansion. It would take her a while to get up to speed; the workload would be heavy, but that was a good thing. Something to focus on. Something to stop her thinking of Alan.

She pulled the plug, stood up and turned on the shower to rinse her hair while the water drained from round her legs. She thought she understood, now, about Alan, understood the facts of it. That their networks had found each other that afternoon at the hospital, on the day of her final visit. That they'd connected via their respective receivers – or else his had already been removed, and his network was sufficiently evolved that it could register hers, could reach for her . . . All the necessary factors would have been in place. Time: her own network evolving its connective capacity, and Alan's already active. Sleep: when her visit had wound him up too tight, left him bouncing off the walls, so she'd left him to the tender care of a man with a needle, his sedation taking hold just as she slipped her receiver onto her ear and sank into her own Make-Believe. And distance: the bench outside his ward. A wall between them – but only metres apart.

The bathroom was a refuge, perfumed and clouded, but she couldn't stay there for ever. She rubbed steam from the mirror, checked her reflection. Washed and in cleanish clothes, she was more herself – on the outside, at least.

In the living room she joined Lewis on the sofa. He smiled as she sat beside him, a try-hard, unconvincing smile, and she felt herself do the same. He was doing his best to be pleased for her, and she was pretending too. Pretending, because he wasn't Alan.

Twelve hours left, before they came for her. Before she delivered the upgrade, and the connections were severed, Alan lost to her for ever. If that woman hadn't taken the receivers, she could have spent the night in Make-Believe. Met Alan by the waterfall, been with him one last time. Even without the receiver . . . she could catch a bus back to Raphael House, find a place in the hospital grounds that was close enough to Alan's locked ward room; she could try to sleep, and trust that their networks would find each other. But to sleep so close to the other patients was to risk it happening again – the unthinkable thing that had happened to her in the back seat of the car. Her mind turned white with panic. Impossible.

She scooped her feet under her, curling into herself, filled with the need to seal herself off with her thoughts of Alan. Her memories. In the hours she had left, this, now, was the most important thing: to relive their final night together, remember it so clear, so deep that she built an unbreakable neural circuit, locking him inside her. How his hair glows when she opens her eyes. How his body feels, solid and hot, under her hand. Shoulder, chest, ribs, hips. How his voice sounds – the first thing to go . . . Even now, just hours later, she strained to catch the traces, struggled to conjure the tone – and when

Lewis spoke, deep and gruff, she wanted to slap him.

'I'm sorry,' he said, 'I wasn't there when they came for you.'

She made herself smile once more. 'No. It's alright. I don't know what you could have done anyway.'

His jaw had lost its tightness, and without it all the angles of his face tugged downwards; the dark of his eyes seemed to pool in their sockets, overspilling, shadows of tears. Of course, he was like her: he too had lost a lover, and found her and lost her, and now he'd found and lost her all over again. And he must realise, now, that even if he could get hold of another hacked receiver, it wasn't safe for him to go back to Make-Believe. That if Imagen knew about Cassie, they must also know about him.

Gently, she leant into his shoulder. Felt him shift his weight towards her. They were mirrors of each other – slightly cracked, a bit distorted, but enough the same that they should at least be kind.

After a while, she got up to fetch her satchel, her papers and tobacco, wet hair leaving a damp, dark circle on Lewis's shoulder. Her screen buzzed when it sensed her hand, letting her know she had notifications. Two messages – three – all from Nicol. She realised she'd missed a meeting as well as a client deadline. Well: that stuff didn't matter now.

When she tried to reclaim her place on the sofa she found Pita installed there, drawn to the warmth she'd left behind. She perched on the arm instead, rolling a cigarette. Allowed an extra inch of tobacco, thinking how she'd soon have money – laid a fat line of it onto the paper – pinched and rolled it into shape – paused, just for a second, in her making, as a heat bloomed at the top of her head, washed through her, down to the soles of her feet – then carried on, carefully, tightening the paper – lifting and licking – sealing and straightening. She put on her trainers. Slung her satchel over her shoulder.

'Just smoke it out the window, if you want,' said Lewis.

'It's OK.' She patted her satchel. 'I've got keys, you won't need to buzz me back in.'

At the bottom of the stairwell, she propped herself in the doorway. Lit up with shaking hands.

She hadn't mentioned Lachlan. Not on purpose; it wasn't a test. He was just unimportant. It was the woman who'd been in charge, and that was how she'd told the story. She could hear her own words. *When she came . . . She took me there . . .*

So why had Lewis apologised like that? *I wasn't there when they came for you.*

Not she. *They.*

A slip of the tongue. An assumption – that any woman would need a man to back her up. Perhaps.

She crushed the stub of her rollie, turned to go back inside. Stopped, uncertain, at the foot of the stairs.

Perhaps not.

She turned, slowly. Stood staring hard, seeing nothing.

The click of an unlatching jolted through her. Lewis in the doorway, calling her name.

She looked up. Where she stood, he wouldn't be able to see her yet. Trainers silent on the concrete floor, she backed round the side of the staircase. Reached for the door to the understairs cupboard, hoping it wouldn't be locked.

'Cassie? Are you alright?'

She heard Lewis descending – his light, scuffing tread. She pulled the cupboard door ajar, ducked and stepped inside, shrinking into the stacks of stuff, the mops and pails, bikes and boxes, the broken furniture. Shut the door after her, and stood barely breathing for fear of starting a junk avalanche.

The click of a snib: Lewis opening the front door. Closing it again. Then silence. And God, what was she doing, hiding in a cupboard from the only person who was on her side, who cared for her, who knew what was really going on? Because of a simple slip of the tongue? And now she couldn't just appear, step out of this damp-smelling cupboard, because how would she explain herself? She would have to wait until he went back upstairs, or outside to look for her.

No sound from him, still. And she realised – he was phoning her; had to be. He'd hear her buzz, from where he was standing. Fat-fingered, she wrestled her satchel open, reached for her screen. Just as it flashed into life, she fumbled it off.

'Hi, it's me,' she heard him say. 'Where did you go? Please don't just vanish on me again. Um. Did you go home, or what? Give me a call, alright?'

She listened to him jogging up the stairs, waited for the flat door to close behind him. Instead, he came straight back down. This time she could hear he had his bike with him, bouncing down onto the concrete, chain clicking round. The front door opened. Closed again.

She made herself count to five, then she poked her head out into the empty stairwell. Ran to the front door, and reached the street just in time to see Lewis turn at the end of it, tail light flashing red.

CHAPTER THIRTY-TWO

Lewis was stronger than her, much stronger – but he wore a helmet and reflective shorts, and was scared to swim in reservoirs. On her ancient bike, Cassie pedalled non-stop. Ran red lights, cut corners, hopped up onto pavements, shot up the inside of buses and lorries. Imagine Oswald's face if he could see her, the risks she was taking with his precious upgrade, with their network in her unhelmeted brain. Her legs, lungs, face all burnt as she kept pace with Lewis, lights off in the twilight through the beginnings of rain, and far enough behind that he couldn't glimpse her with one of his frequent shoulder checks. He cycled like a safety ad: flash, flash, check, signal. She gasped, spat into the gutter.

When he turned off onto the canal towpath, she guessed where he was heading. She stayed on the road, faster and straighter – but she didn't ease off, kept pushing uphill with all her strength, all her endurance. The last climb was the hardest. At the top she was dripping with sweat, the cool air a blessing as she coasted the final stretch, swung into her block. She'd already decided the best place to hide. The shelter that housed the bins would conceal her bike, give her a clear view.

She didn't have long to wait. Just a few minutes later, Lewis pulled up. He took the time to lock his bike, turn off his lights. She watched, hands clenched; watched as he walked straight to her block, and pressed the buzzer. Pressed again. Then he walked backwards, screen in hand, till he was within metres of her hiding place, and stared up at her window.

He knew which street to go to. Which block to buzz, which unlit window to stare at. Knew all of this, even though she had never told him where she lived. Never invited him back to hers. She reached for the timber wall of the shelter, as the ground pitched beneath her.

In silent mode, her own screen lit, flashed his face at her. This time, he didn't leave a message. Instead he seemed to hesitate, then – still looking up at her bedsit window – he made another call.

Though she couldn't hear what he was saying, he was obviously in trouble. He stood with a hand pushed into his hair, shoving it into panicky spikes; he hunched into the screen, then threw back his head, urgency in every movement. *She's vanished*, she imagined him saying. *It wasn't my fault*. What would they tell him – track her down? Go home and wait? Remain where you are?

The sweat was cooling on her skin. She shivered in his blank T-shirt, wanted to yank it off, trample it, stamp and spit on it, shove it into the bin. But she couldn't get into her flat for something else to wear, not while he was hanging around. Was he going to stay all night, staking out her block, making her sleep in here with the bins? As she watched, the front door swung open; she saw her neighbour Ryan emerge, saw Lewis catch the door, disappear inside. *Stop him*, she thought, and just for a second it seemed like Ryan had heard her. He turned to stare at Lewis. Then he let the door close, and walked on.

Inside the shelter, Cassie edged round so she had a clear view of her window. If Lewis was going to check out her flat he'd have to break in, because she'd certainly never given him keys. But almost immediately, her light went on. She stared, disbelieving, as he passed in front of the window, and back again. Her keys. He must have copied them. He couldn't get in the main door because he didn't know the code – but here he was slipping in and out of her flat whenever he pleased. Had he been there before? When she'd been at work? How long had he been investigating – sneaking round after her – spying on her?

There was nothing there for him to find. Nothing that mattered. Only the drawer of T-shirts, only a box of Alan stuff: that was all she had that was personal, and none of it would mean a thing to anyone but her. She thought of Lewis reading the track listings of the compilation CDs that had been retro even a decade ago. Opening the cases, reading the notes that said nothing important but were the only evidence she had that, once, Alan had written to her. Thought about her. Known who she was. She thought of Lewis's spying fingers, and wanted to puke.

A couple of minutes, then the light went out. Thirty seconds later the front door opened. Lewis, unlocking his bike. Cycling towards her, and past her. The world blown apart at her feet.

CHAPTER THIRTY-THREE

When Alan had jumped from his bedroom window, he knew he could fly.

Madness was only a mistake about what was real.

She had made a mistake, a big one, with Lewis.

His shirt, its warm clean smell, made her gag. How long? When had Imagen got to him? Perhaps it was only last night, when she woke up and he wasn't there. It was what she wanted to think. It would mean he'd been playing her for less than twenty-four hours.

But it wasn't true.

She thought of the way the woman had gone straight to Lewis's bedroom, back in less than a minute with the receivers scooped into her hand. Thought of how quickly Lewis had sourced them – pretended to source them. God, of course, the bioware didn't even need to be hacked. Not if he was working for them.

From the start? Could he really have joined Jake's group – turned up week after week – just waiting for her to come back? She remembered how he'd lifted his hand to his ear, at the meeting – the thrill she'd felt when she recognised the gesture. How clever she'd thought herself. Remembered how she'd signalled back, just as he must have hoped she would. How he'd hung around afterwards, waiting so they could leave together. How he'd invited her back to his. But no – it was her who'd made that move. No one to blame but herself: for talking, listening, opening up, falling straight into his treacherous bed.

Him spooned behind her, intimate, trusting. Worming his way into her thoughts, her dreams. Him – Imagen – inside her. Imagen inside her now.

She clutched at her head. Heard blood, loud – couldn't think for the blood, for the chill creeping across her skull. She'd made a mistake with Oswald, too. She couldn't trust the papers she'd signed. Couldn't trust what they'd put into her. The biomolecules that were using her body, her brain as host. Buzzing under the skin of her scalp, pre-loaded with tasks, instructions, agendas. Deep inside, they were getting down to work.

Her screen, still clutched in one hand, lit with a question mark. Lewis trying from a different device. Or Oswald – or the woman.

She didn't know how long she'd been crouched there. Only that it was properly dark. Only that she was cold,

330

and swaying, palm pressed hard into jagged glass from the bottle recycling, so that when she lifted her throbbing hand it was smeared with blood.

OK. OK. She'd made mistakes. The thing, now, was not to make any more.

She wiped her palm on Lewis's T-shirt, leaving a bloody smear. A part of her wanted to chase after him, confront him, persuade him to tell her everything. Why was he watching her? Who did he report to – and what had he told them? What had they promised as payment for his dirty work – was it the same bribe they had used on her: a job, and access to Make-Believe? But if she was to challenge him, she would have to be cold and focused, and what she felt was the opposite. Like she'd swallowed that broken bottle. Like the pain from her cut hand was in her chest, slicing her open. She was scared she'd ask the wrong questions: not why, but how? How could you do it? When we were meant to be on the same side. When we were meant to be the same. She felt the hot push of tears. Swallowed them back, horrified.

Be cold. Be focused. Her legs gave as she stood up, and her hand slipped on the wet wood of the shelter as she balanced herself. She stared up at her bedsit. If the call that Lewis had made was to Oswald, or whoever his Imagen contact might be, by now they would be looking for her. For the moment, right here was the one place they knew she wouldn't be – but for how much longer? A change of clothes, a jacket . . . The longer she hesitated, the greater the risk. She pushed her wet hair from her face, shook the drops from her hands, and launched herself into a run across the flooded concrete. Up the stairs, into her flat, and no time to think about Lewis in here nosing at all her stuff, raking through with his spying fingers. In the dark, she changed her clothes. Jeans, T-shirt, jumper, dry socks jammed straight back into wet trainers, her only pair. She grabbed her anorak, shoved her beanie hat in the pocket. Thought about leaving her screen behind, just in case they could use it to track her. But if they found it here, they'd be able to go through her calls, her messages, everything she had saved – and besides, the thought of being without it was too daunting. Instead, she turned it off.

For all the good it would do, she locked the door behind her as she left.

CHAPTER THIRTY-FOUR

On her bike she set off south and east – going nowhere, going anywhere away from her usual route. Head down, rain crackling off her hood, she ran through the list of everyone who might give her a bed for the night. Felt herself sagging as she came up empty. Meg . . . Family is where they have to let you in – but there was no possibility her sister might help her. Nicol . . . If she arrived on his doorstep, he might let her crash on his couch – not that she was certain of where his doorstep was. But she was wary of involving Nicol, of leading Imagen to him. And Harrie . . . It wasn't Harrie who had reported her to Imagen. She knew that now. She thought of Harrie opening her front door wide, sitting her down at the kitchen table and placing a pot of tea between them, listening as Cassie talked about Lewis, how he'd betrayed her. But after her last visit, she couldn't be sure of her welcome. Better not to ask for help, than to force Harrie to refuse.

Though she had no destination in mind, she found herself speeding up, slicing through puddles – her pedalling fuelled by anger as much as urgency. At Lewis, yes – but more she was furious with herself. She kept trying to visualise his face, to hear the tone of his voice; though it was far too late to do any good, still she felt a savage need to catch a shiftiness in his expression, a hesitation in his speech that would nail him as a liar. Instead, the episode on a loop in her mind was that first falling-out, when he'd tried to persuade her to bargain or blackmail her way back to Make-Believe. *They'd have to let us back.* She heard the twist in his voice, saw the longing that had darkened his eyes, so fierce it had scared her. Whatever else he'd lied about, he was a real addict. She'd stake everything on that.

She swiped the rain from her eyes, swerved to avoid a stretch of broken tarmac. Didn't want to think of what she and Lewis had in common. In such a short space of time, she had come to rely on him. Stupid, so stupid. Before she had met him, she'd been used to her loneliness. Then, to have a companion . . . It had made things better, more bearable. She'd allowed herself to feel safe. Even to have fun. Turned out, she'd been on her own all along; she just hadn't realised. And now— now, right now, she refused to think about it. Now she needed to focus on what happened next. As the night grew late the roads would empty, and she'd become conspicuous to anyone out looking for her. At the next junction she took a turn towards the city centre, seeking the camouflage of crowds. But even here in the centre, sharing the roads with late buses and taxis, she felt conspicuous. Drunken groups called out to her as she passed. 'She's coming home with me,' shouted one man as he made a lunge for her, and she swerved abruptly, managed a burst of speed before her cadence slowed, faltered. In the relative safety of a street lined with pubs, steady with drinkers weaving from one bar to the next, she pulled up at the corner of a close and tucked herself up in the dark alley mouth. She couldn't remember the last time she'd felt this tired.

She let her head drop to her hands. From a gutter above, a river of rain made the sound of a waterfall.

Here.

A voice, up close. Too close. Cassie snapped her head up, ready to scramble to her feet, make a run for it. But the voice was gentle, and the woman who'd spoken crouched, her arm outstretched. Something held in her hand. A banknote.

'For a bed for the night,' she said.

'Oh, no . . .' *I'm not homeless.* That's what Cassie was going to say – but perhaps it wasn't true. And perhaps it didn't matter. Though a hostel bed was something she couldn't risk, she would need to eat at some point, and her wallet was almost empty. She reached out. Took the money. It was a twenty.

'Thank you,' she said, and her voice skidded a bit on the last syllable.

'Look after yourself, alright.' The woman straightened and, with a brisk nod, carried on her way, like what she'd done was nothing very much.

Cassie focused on the note, slippery under her damp fingers. She couldn't keep hold of anything, any kind of truth. What was real? What was real? Start with the rain that was crackling off her hood, puddling the uneven ground, soaking her trainers. But if that was real, then what about the Make-Believe rain that had fallen on her and Alan, on the leaves above their heads? She had heard it, seen it – and if that *wasn't* real, the rain on the leaves, why should she trust the wet that was trickling down her neck right now? As soon as she made a category called real, placed something inside it, the outlines blurred, became porous. There was nothing to hang onto, and too much she still didn't know.

Think: what *could* she trust? If the choices she'd thought were hers had been theirs all along. Sleeping with Lewis. Playing detective with Professor Morgan. Returning to Make-Believe. Ignoring Jake, giving up on her family, on every hope of reconciliation. Could she blame it all on Imagen? Every step she had taken?

She'd come loose in the world, couldn't figure it out on her own. But when she worked her fingers into the pocket where she'd folded the banknote, it was there still. Proof that a stranger had seen her trouble, and done her a good turn.

Some people would do that for you. But how would they know they were needed, unless you told them so?

It was time to ask for help.

CHAPTER THIRTY-FIVE

When Nicol saw Cassie's face flash on his screen, he shook his head. He'd been expecting her to get in touch – and then he'd given up expecting anything. He flipped his screen upside-down on the desk, turned back to the code he was working on. 'Too late, pal,' he said under his breath.

The second time, she called just as Jo stuck her head round the door.

'Not going to answer it?' she said.

'It's Cassie.'

'Ah, OK.'

'Want a beer?'

'Aye. Beer would be epic, thanks.'

Honestly, he should have known from the first time he met Cassie that she wasn't to be relied on. Had known, really. The alarm had gone off: steer clear. You could always tell the damaged folk. It was in the eyes, or something. But her ad had been intriguing: *successful small business . . . expanding our academic services . . . opportunities for highly qualified applicants in the following fields . . .* And he'd needed the money. And then, he'd got to like her. She was funny, even if sometimes he wasn't sure whether she meant to be. She was chaotic, but she tried hard to be efficient, and she cared about the product. She might be running a business that sold academic fraud, but she was honest about it. You could almost say she cheated with integrity. And she was stubborn as fuck, and that was a quality he'd always liked in a woman.

He'd have thought she would leave a message, given she'd bothered to phone him twice. But no; there was nothing. He checked again, just to be sure.

Now it was niggling at him. Thing was, it was unusual for her to call; she'd normally send a message. So perhaps it was something important . . . But she couldn't expect him to give a shit, when she so clearly didn't – plus it was basically her fault he was so behind with this project.

She'd phone back, if it really mattered.

When Jo came back with his beer he grabbed her hand, stretched up and gave her a quick kiss. 'Thanks.'

'Glad to be of service,' she said, and made herself scarce. It was cool, though; he'd done the same for her, all those years when she was volunteering, and then when she was training. Tea on the table the nights when she had to work late. Hot bath waiting after a long bad day, of which there were way too many.

When Cassie called a third time, he was right in the middle of a tricky portion of code, like *right* in the middle – and he wrestled with himself, just for a moment. On the last buzz, eyes still fixed on his monitors, he picked up.

'Yep?'

He heard the sound of outside, and of someone not speaking. A silent connection.

He looked at the screen. It was Cassie, for sure.

'You there? Cassie? Are you hearing me?'

'Listen,' she said, like he wasn't already. Her voice was low. Urgent. 'I'm about to ask you for help. Something above and beyond. No reason why you should, and now's your chance to hang up.'

His turn not to speak. He slung himself back in his chair, still facing the displays, the program he'd been working on. The program he was debugging at what, eleven at night? – because he was astronomically far behind, because of the summer school assignments he'd finished this week which he wouldn't get paid for because Cassie had pissed off without a word, hadn't answered his messages, had left him with no way to contact the client who had now, presumably, failed. Fuck's sake. And here she was playing at spies, like properly getting off on it, like all of that wasn't just some game to make her life more interesting. She was wired to the moon, lately. And giving him an option not to help . . . as if all the other shit he'd helped her with – scamming the uni security, say, or free print credit, or setting up their untracked payment system – like all of that wasn't already above and beyond.

On the other hand. She worked hard on the business. Bringing in clients. And it was her who had offered him a 50/50 split. And the croissants were a bonus.

He just didn't want to be the idiot. The guy that jumped.

Five minutes later he was putting on his jacket, checking his pockets for wallet and keys.

Jo hovered in the living room doorway, eyebrows raised. 'Bit late for a stroll, is it not? Where are you off to?'

'That was Cassie, needing a bit of help.'

'Uh-huh. Thought you said you were done with all that?'

Nicol shrugged. 'I know . . . but she did ask nicely. Kind of, anyway.'

From the hall table, Jo picked up the lead and the plastic bags. There was a commotion from the living room and in seconds Princess Leia appeared, panting with excitement, swiping her tail from side to side.

'Up to you,' Jo said. 'You can take the dog. Save me a trip, at least.'

CHAPTER THIRTY-SIX

The usual place, Cassie had told him, but as soon as she saw him ambling towards her she sprang up from the bench, meaning to steer him away.

'I told you to come alone,' she said, deadpan. Nicol's dog was sniffing her trainers, tail slicing through rain like a windscreen wiper. 'Didn't know you were a dog person.'

Nicol glanced down, gave the lead a tug. 'Don't worry. Leia's very discreet.'

Briefly, Cassie dipped her hand so Leia could get a proper smell, get the measure of her. 'Good excuse to walk.'

Glancing back over her shoulder to scan the empty square, she led them towards the night-time centre of the city. The rain had eased, and she relaxed a little as they left the university quarter, cutting down a side street towards the pubs and clubs. They were safer among the knots of smokers out on the pavement, the closing-time crowd.

'Come on then, Bond, tell me. What's going on?'

Cassie started to speak. Stopped again. Let out a long breath. 'Thing is,' she said, 'I could talk all night, and I don't reckon you'd believe even a fraction of it.'

Nicol shrugged. 'One way to find out, eh?'

'Honestly. There's so much, too much, I don't even know where I'd begin. But I'll tell you what I can, as quick as I can, and – and I have to just ask you to trust me.'

'On you go, then.'

'The other day, outside the Newman building – when I was spaced after seeing that display.'

'The Make-Believe stuff?'

'You do really hate them, don't you?'

'It's not about hate. It's like I said. I disapprove.'

'OK, well . . . confession: I used to work for them.'

'For Imagen? You worked on Make-Believe?'

'It was a while back; it didn't end well, I – anyway, that's not important, at least I don't think so.'

They fell into single file, giving way to a laughing, shouting crowd of students: young men with shining drink-flushed cheeks, owning the pavement. Leia made a soft gruff sound, somewhere between a growl and a whine. When the pack was past them, Cassie picked up her explanation, voice low.

'The important bit is: when they tested the technology – trying to develop different applications – I'm pretty sure, now, that they were testing on people who didn't consent. Or couldn't properly consent, legally. People they thought were disposable.' Cassie glanced at Nicol. He was staring straight ahead, face dark with concentration. 'So if it went wrong it wouldn't come back at them. These people, no one would believe them. And it did go wrong – and it's still going wrong. And one of their test subjects was . . . a friend.'

They were passing a cluster of late-licensed pubs. No matter how tight the money was, people always managed to drink. Inside: noise and light sealed behind closed doors and fogged-up windows. Outside: the mouth of a close, cans glinting under dim street lights, a group of drinkers sheltering under an archway. Sometimes she looked out for faces she recognised. Women or men she'd known at the group. Give in to temptation, and the worst that can happen is you spend your life wasted in the gutter. Give in to temptation, and the worst that can happen is they inject you with an experiment that freezes your skull and alters your brain. She wanted to tell Nicol, tell him what they'd put inside her. But that wasn't what mattered. Not right now.

'Just so you know,' he was saying, 'I've already got about a million questions.'

'And you're not asking any of them, which I really appreciate. So the thing is – the important thing – is there might be a way I can help him. My friend. The rest of them too, however many there are. It's something that Imagen asked me to do' – she saw another twenty questions flip through Nicol's head – 'and it could fix everything – and I agreed to do it, I said I would – but now, I don't know if I can trust them. How much they might have lied. I mean, I know I *can't* trust them, but with this . . .' She thought for a moment. An idea – a wild, long shot – was taking shape as she spoke. 'There's a possibility that our interests coincide, mine and Imagen's. Could be, I do this thing and everyone wins. But I need to be sure. I need information. And that's where I need your help.'

They stopped at a crossing, waiting for green. Headlights shone off the wet streets, colour smeared against the dark of tarmac, the wet sky. A pub door flew open, releasing a hand-in-hand couple along with a tease of music and tumultuous voices, a gust of warm, beer-scented air. The couple cut across them, as if she and Nicol weren't there, as if they were a pair of ghosts out walking their ghost dog. It was what she wanted: to slide, shadow-like, through the lights and the colours and the sudden brief blooms of talk and laughter. Merging herself with a crowd might not conceal them from Imagen, but it was all she could think of. A tree in a forest.

'Alright,' said Nicol. 'Hit me with it.'

'The hard bit first. Imagen's system. Their computer network, their server. Do you think you can get in?'

'I can give it a go.' He spoke so casually, he might have been agreeing to change a lightbulb.

'The stuff I need – it's going to be seriously protected.'

'Aye well, it's lucky I seriously know what I'm doing.'

It sounded like a yes. But she had to be sure he knew what he was getting himself into. 'I've got to warn you, Nicol – if this fucks up, and they manage to trace you, they won't let you get away with it.'

He stopped, turned to face her. Leia's tail swiped gently against her thigh. 'Listen, man, I'm not some script kiddie. I know how this works. If it's there, what you're after, I'll find it long before they can find me. And if I can't do it . . . Let's just say, I know folk. I'm connected. Folks with shared ideas. Folks who'll help us out.'

Us. She blinked as it hit her again, the relief she'd felt when he'd finally answered her call. 'And one more thing – this should be simple for you. I need an address.' She told him the name. 'It'll be ex-directory.'

He nodded recognition. 'Done. And if that's your lot . . . ? I'll head on home, get started straight away.'

Her thanks came out gruffer than she'd intended, and when he peeled away she didn't wave goodbye. Instead she kept her hands pushed into her back pockets, so as not to embarrass the both of them by trying to give him a hug.

CHAPTER THIRTY-SEVEN

Cassie shivered as she watched Nicol disappear into the distance and the dark. Cold: yes, a bit – but what she felt, really, was alone.

Still, Nicol's down-to-earth presence – Leia's too – had made her feel almost normal. In deciding what to tell him, she'd turned her confusion into a story, a simple case of cause and effect. She'd been in control of her thoughts, certain of what she had to find out, and how she would go about it. Soon, Nicol would be burning the midnight oil on her behalf. She pictured him arriving home and settling in front of his computer, waking the screen and leaning in to its bluish glow, with Leia the dog stretched on his feet. And once he started to dig, she'd have her own work to do.

The thought of how Oswald had lied to her –

telling her how valued she was, how much he wanted her back on the Make-Believe team – made her sick with humiliation. She'd been so ready to believe him, when really her only value was accidental: the evolved state of her biomolecular network, its active ability to connect with other users whose networks were similarly evolved. Aside from that, she was utterly expendable. Nevertheless, it was possible that Oswald had not been wholly dishonest. If the upgrade really was intended to disable the connections in Make-Believe then, all else aside, by carrying it out she would still be doing her best for Alan. That was what she needed to find out, now: the truth of what would happen when – if – she delivered that upgrade. And in the meantime, whatever was happening inside of her was beyond her control. She couldn't let it freak her out. Even as she made to rub at her scalp, she caught herself, forced her hand back down to her side.

A quarter past twelve, by the church clock that rose above the wet rooftops. She walked as she waited, wheeling her bike, choosing streets more or less at random but making sure always to stick with the thinning crowd – and in less than an hour her screen buzzed with a message from Nicol: the address she'd asked him for.

The roads were quiet now – buses, the occasional cab. The lights stayed green as she travelled, riding out the bumps and the craters, swerving the worst of the puddles. As she reached the wealthy inner suburbs the tarmac flattened, and instead of concentrating on dodging potholes Cassie allowed herself to turn it in her mind: her wild idea. That what gave her value to Imagen – her ability to connect – might be turned to her advantage. By the time she reached the wide, tree-lined street that was her destination, she had a rough notion of how she was going to proceed.

The houses here were named, not numbered. They squatted well back from the road, hiding behind trees and high hedges, turning their shuttered eyes inward. If you lived here, it would be no effort to stay separate; not like in the warren of her block, divided and divided again, filled with so many lives jammed up against each other. Here, the effort would be to connect.

The driveway was gated, but there was no security, just a tall wrought-iron affair that opened easily to let her slip inside. The drive was gravel; she paused, plotting the quietest course over the lawn and up to the house. Was about to move when she found herself caught in a sudden flood of light. She froze, lit up with the whole of the house and the grass and the trees and the driveway – then she ducked in by the gatepost. But the house stayed shuttered and blind. The security lights had been triggered by something outside.

Fox. She saw it sauntering across the lawn, uncaring or oblivious. In the middle of the grass, it stopped, seemed to catch a scent on the air. Her sweat, her adrenaline. For a second its eyes fixed on her, blank and fierce. It crackled with energy, its fur electric. Cassie stared, trying to absorb it – the charge, the boldness, its ownership of the night – till the dark returned, and she lost it in blinking and blindness. And when it triggered the light once more, loping towards a fringe of shrubs and the fence beyond, she was ready to move.

She knew her route now, and she wasn't scared to set off the lights – because no one was watching. The world of the wealthy was asleep, rolled in a fat, false security quilt. In the full glare of the lamps she darted over the lawn, stopping when she reached the gravel in front of the house. Here, she stepped lightly, her weight shifting the stones with a grating sound. Each step made her blood pump faster. She tried to move steadily, hoping that anyone lying awake would mistake her for a neighbour's car. Hoping the house was home only to heavy sleepers. She skirted the front of the building, dropped with relief into its shadowed side – still crunching, but feeling safer here, tucked in the narrow passage between this house and the next.

In the borrowed light from the security lamp, she could see a single ground-floor window. Small, with frosted glass, and bolted open a couple of inches; it must lead to a bathroom. She reached up, placed her hands on the stone sill, testing, but it was too high. No way she could haul herself up. She carried on down the side return till she reached a back garden that stretched into darkness. Gravel turned to silent slabs, and as she stepped onto the patio, a second security light sprang on – and her heart skipped in sudden terror. There was someone – a figure – motionless, beside her—She forced herself to move her head, inch by fearful inch, till in the black mirror of a glass extension she faced the figure. Faced herself. Only herself. Her eyes were wide in a pale, frozen face. And behind that face—She stepped away, away from her self, and whatever else that self concealed – an imaginary someone standing unseen, on the other side of the glass, looking at her through her own reflection – and backed into a heavy garden chair.

It was perfect for what she needed. With difficulty she hoisted it into her arms, lugged it into the side return, staggering and crunching too loudly. Set it down by the window, feet pressed firmly into the stones, and climbed up onto the seat. From here, she could slide a flattened hand inside the window, push up against the lever that bolted it in place. The lever was reluctant to budge: sweating, she tugged and shoved until at last, with a clatter, it jumped free of the spike. Slowly, the pane swung inward.

With the opening now at chest height, Cassie could heave herself onto the sill, wiggle forward till her top half was inside the bathroom, her legs still dangling outside. Ahead was unknown, details lost in darkness. The spike of the bolt jabbed her pelvis; the sill cut into her diaphragm, pressed the breath from her, and she felt the blood flowing to her head, the beginnings of panic. Then an image came to her: traitor Lewis with his flashy, flashing shorts, his helmet and his safety signals. *Be like the fox*, she told herself, and went for it – diving forward, hands-and-head first, onto the hard slip of enamel. A bathtub. Elbows, knees, head knocking hard on the way down, thumping explosively and shooting bolts of pain – but she was in. She was in.

She scrambled into a sitting position, gathering herself. Waiting to see if her banging and thumping had woken anyone. Counted to thirty, then to sixty. Nothing: no creaking steps, no clicking lights, no one calling out, *Who's there?* No dog, thank God, to sense an intruder and rouse the house with outraged barks.

Her hands squeaked, sweat-damp, on the surface of the bath as she clambered out. When she unlaced her trainers, warmth pushed up from heated slate into the soles of her feet. The door handle turned soundlessly; the bathroom door opened with more of a sigh than a creak, and Cassie stepped out into a space that felt high and wide around her.

With a hand on the wall to her left, she started along what must have been a hallway, each step anticipating collision: a child's toy, a side table, a pile of books. But the way was clear, polished wood and an empty wall – till her fingertips nudged a door frame. The door opened easily, but inside was only a shallow, shelved space. A linen cupboard. She moved on. Reached a right angle, turned, stepped forward again. Another door frame – and here the floorboards ran on, into a pitch-black room.

The floor became soft under her feet. A living room? It felt the size of a football pitch. After an age of shuffling, she toppled into something hard and yielding: armchair. And behind it – her outstretched hand touched a wall that gave a little. No, not a wall. Shutters. She felt for the edge, pulled them open so a dim light fell through the window, making bleached squares on the enormous rug. With her eyes adjusted to the dark, she could see clearly enough. Two armchairs, a fireplace, a corner-mounted screen above a media centre. One wall displayed books, the others paintings. And, facing the empty grate, a long and perfect sofa.

Cassie reached for her screen, checked the time. It was almost 2 a.m. The smallest of opportunities lay open before her: call it two hours, while she was still safe. Before the upgrade was ready to spread.

On her screen, she set an alarm for four. Adjusted the volume: loud enough to wake her without rousing anyone else. Checked the vibrate was on, a backup that would haul her up from a deep sleep, so long as she kept the screen clutched in her hand. Then she crossed the room to the sofa, and climbed aboard. She stretched, then curled herself into an S, reached back to shove a cushion under her head and tugged a throw to cover herself.

Up above, in the bedrooms of the first floor, Professor Morgan would be dreaming. Perhaps she would have a husband at her side, two kids asleep nearby. And that was the risk, of course. If this worked at all, it might not be Morgan she would connect to. But if she could shape this thing, direct it . . . There was something Oswald had said, about emotion: that you could almost say it drove the connections. She thought of Alan: how they'd matched each other in longing and relief, how they'd worn their yearning as a half-healed wound. Thought of how it had worked in the back seat of the car, of the fear that had multiplied into a terror that still made her sick to recall. If she could echo whatever Morgan was feeling, perhaps that was the way into her head. So what might be the emotional value that coloured her dreams? Positive, or negative? Smug and secure in her vast house – or anxiously alert to potential invaders? If Morgan had any kind of a conscience, she'd be sharing her bed with a cold slab of guilt, at the thought of what she was responsible for. And that was something Cassie could channel. Guilt was a wave she could surf. Just think of Finn and Ella, and Meg. Or think of Alan, every time she'd walked away. Pitilessly, she replayed each scene. In the airport. *Kiss. Turn. Leave.* Onscreen, three thousand miles between them. *I love you. I miss you. End call.* In the hospital. *I'll visit soon, in a week or two, in a month, in a while . . .* Felt herself become dense with guilt, weighing down hard on the sofa. And then she conjured Morgan: her rumpled face, her polite, efficient voice. Imagined her dead to the world, beneath a thick warm quilt of sleep. Stretched her imagination to catch that quilt by the corner, and pulled it down to wrap around herself.

The first thing is the sound. Static, fading up into a roar that baffles her ears. Then the twisted black of burnt rubber is in her nose, mouth, lungs, and she's kicking against the weight that hauls her down, wrapping her tight; she wrestles, jerks her head free of the darkness that's trying to blind, silence, suffocate her. Stop – she almost thinks it – STOP – and then she remembers. This is what she wanted. Remembers: she is not alone.

Static tightens, condenses into spits of electricity. The dark is not absolute. Flashes, that show a figure – an etiolated body, a swollen head, and on the head a tangled mass, a crown that glitters not with jewels but sparks, that crackles with the burning sound of a thousand flies caught, killed in veins of blue light. And as she thinks of this she sees them: a thick black swirl of insects, buzz-crack-dropping, and in the centre of this, a face. Morgan's face. Webbed and snared. 'No,' she says. Her skinny neck wavers. She holds up her hands. 'Not me, it doesn't start with me—'

Cassie closes the distance between them. 'Why are you so scared of me?' She reaches, through the mass of flies, the terrified sparks, and a deep, cold ache in her hand rises up through her arm. Her fingers are blunt and hungry for answers. She grabs vicious handfuls of Morgan, of what's inside: thought, feeling, memory. Tearing through all the layers of her. Snatching and tugging and casting aside, not a careful unzipping, not a neat fish-gutting, but a furious, fabulous violence – till an agonised sound cuts through her frenzy. A high, thin keening. Pain beyond words.

She feels the weight of a hammer in her hand, the crack of a palm-sized skull. Sees fur, and blood – a caved, staring eye. Hears Lewis say: *I hurt someone.*

Realises – this is not a search, not a sorting through. This is nothing but vengeance. And the word is noble, fiery and clean, but the act is ugly, is clinging to her as she backs away from the torn-apart bits of a woman, as she commands with all the clarity, all the strength of mind she can summon:

STOP

CHAPTER THIRTY-EIGHT

Curled, blanketed, on the sofa. Hands clasped by her head, as if she were innocent in all of this. But her breathlessness told otherwise. The leap of her pulse. For a moment she lay motionless, knees pressed to her chest, fists clenched round soft handfuls of the throw – then she shoved it aside, pushed up from the sofa and into an unsteady run.

Up the stairs, onto the landing. No sound from behind any of the closed doors. One by one she flung them open, feeling for light switches. A child's bedroom, and a second, both unnaturally neat, and empty. An echoing bathroom. A double bedroom. At first sight, it too was empty: an expanse of carpet spread with discarded clothes, a duvet scrambled on the king-size bed. A small heap, huddled over on the far side of the mattress. Soundless in her socks, Cassie circled the bed to where Morgan's screen lay on the bedside table, scooped it up from its charging pad. Then she took a hold of the quilt, gave it a yank.

'Boo!'

Morgan, hunched into a foetal position, didn't flinch.

'Oh, am I not so scary in real life?' Cassie said. She placed a hand on Morgan's shoulder, and squeezed.

Slowly, like moving underwater, the professor lifted her head. Her face was sheet-white, beaded with sweat; when she wiped a hand across her mouth, Cassie could see she was trembling. Nausea rose up from Cassie's gut, and she swallowed hard, tasting bile. Reminded herself: the woman deserved it. When Morgan reached unsteadily for where her screen should be, Cassie danced it in front of her, then tucked it into her back pocket.

Like an invalid, the older woman hoisted herself to a sitting position. When she spoke, her voice was uncertain. 'They're looking for you.'

A smile tugged across Cassie's face. 'I'm quite sure they are,' she agreed. 'I'm all kinds of in demand, at the moment.'

Morgan's clammy brow was creased with confusion. 'Why are you here?'

'Information.' Cassie pronounced the word with exaggerated clarity. 'When we spoke before – d'you remember? – you didn't exactly tell the truth, did you. Fair enough, neither did I . . . Thing is, I know a lot more, now. About Raphael House, the patient trials. The connections in Make-Believe. Tom Oswald has been very forthcoming on all of that.' She tilted her head to one side. Knocked on her skull – once, twice. 'What I'm not sure of, though, is why you should be so scared of what I've got inside here. And I'd like to know the answer to that – before I decide what I'm going to do with it.'

Morgan's shoulders twitched, in what might have been a shrug. 'But you've already decided. It's too late to change your mind about that, whatever I tell you.' Her voice was dry, scraping from her throat. 'You can deliver the upgrade in a controlled environment, with people there to look after you, or you can let it happen at random – a week from now, or a month, or whenever you next fall asleep close beside another user. That's the only choice you have.'

Cassie swallowed. 'Not necessarily. There are ways to stop it ever getting out of my head. It's as easy as a handful of pills, right? Or a nice, tall height? The top of the Bray Tower would do it, I should think.' As she spoke she felt an urge fluttering up through her feet, the muscles tensing in her thighs as if she were bracing for the jump. A giddy desire to get this all over with, one way or another. But if she'd expected Morgan to be alarmed, she was disappointed.

'Quite unnecessary,' said Morgan, blankly. 'There's nothing to be scared of. I just wouldn't want to be the first. That's all.' Her voice was slowing, thickening, like some mechanism running down. 'It's been tested, of course, as far as we can . . . In vitro, in vivo. Just, not in humans. But chances are it will be perfectly straightforward. A quick connection, and after that . . . they'll have what they need.' The words came flatly. 'They'll have the data. The input channel. Everything they need.'

With Morgan's words, the advantage slid away. Cassie was still the one standing, looking down on a traumatised woman, but her height, her self-possession, no longer felt like power.

'Input channel?' she said – but Morgan wasn't listening. Was retreating instead, sinking from awareness. Cassie recognised the onset of shock; it was like looking at herself, after they'd taken her to Raphael House.

'Professor Morgan,' she said. Crouched by the bedside to place a hand on her forearm. 'Fiona.' The name too intimate, tasting wrong in her mouth. She pressed down with her stubby nails until Morgan reacted with a slow blink. 'Do you live alone?' said Cassie sharply. 'Fiona. Listen. Do you live alone?'

A slight movement that could pass for a nod.

Cassie crossed the room, moved out onto the landing, and pulled the door closed. Waited, holding it shut, to be sure there was no movement from within. Perhaps she should find a chair to wedge under the handle, the way she'd seen in films – except this handle was round, and this door opened inwards, and this was not a film. The weight of Morgan's screen in her back pocket reassured her as she turned and jogged downstairs, guessed a right turn and found her way to the kitchen, in the black glass box of an extension where she'd startled herself earlier. Now she turned on a light to erase trees and grass, and a ghost room, slanted and glowing, jumped into existence where the garden had been.

In reflection, Cassie watched herself: a ghostly double filling the kettle, opening cupboards, finding mugs, teabags, lots of sugar. As she moved about the kitchen, she kept circling round what Morgan had said.

They'll have what they need.

Their data.

Their input channel.

So Oswald had lied. She heard herself say it, and watched herself too in the mirror of the window, acknowledging out loud a deception that felt, now, like something inevitable. He had lied, and her head was alive with possible reasons, possible truths – not one of them anything close to what he'd promised her.

While the water was boiling, she fetched her satchel from the living room. It was a risk to use her screen again, and the ads seemed endless. Skip – skip – skip – till at last she was able to send a message, a request for Nicol to add the phrase 'input channel' to the list of search terms she'd given him. As soon as the message had gone, she turned the screen safely off again.

What she needed, now, was for Morgan to be lucid, but not fully alert. She let the tea brew strong and black, tipped in sugar – three spoons for Morgan, one for her – listening all the while for sounds from upstairs: for the thud of footsteps, the groan of a floorboard. The fridge she opened in search of milk turned out to be a family-sized freezer, spotless and empty. Or, not quite empty.

Down at the bottom was a plastic drawer. It pulled out smoothly, but there was no milk inside. Instead, there was a silver canister.

It looked just the same as the one from the Imagen lab, the one that had held the upgrade: it seemed Professor Morgan was in the habit of taking her work home with her. When Cassie lifted the canister, turned it in both hands, she saw it was labelled in neat handwriting.

REMEDY. Version 1.3.

The lid was secured with a clamp; she drew out the pin, and lifted it off. Nestling inside was a blunt-nosed needle, like the one Sam had used to administer the nasal spray. Cassie stared, cold creeping up her fingers, gathering round her wrists. Then she shut it all away, the needle, the canister, the freezer, leaving it just as she'd found it.

The milk, when eventually she found it, was hidden away in a fridge disguised as a cupboard – a child's drawing stuck to the door, a photo of Morgan with another woman and two small, grinning boys. Cassie studied it for a minute. Then she collected up the mugs. Pushed the light switch with her elbow as she left the kitchen, so the ghost room vanished behind her.

Back in the master bedroom, Morgan was still propped against the pillows, her face glassy and smooth.

'Drink,' said Cassie, thrusting the tea towards her.

The mug shook as Morgan took it, slopping onto the quilt so that Cassie had to grab her hand to steady it. Morgan took a sip, then another, Cassie's hand shadowing hers as she lifted.

'I've got it,' she said, eventually. 'Thank you. I've got it now.' Like a child she drank it all up, then held out the empty mug for Cassie to set on the bedside table. Cassie looked around for somewhere to sit. Two armchairs occupied the bay of a shuttered window. She'd already begun to manoeuvre the closest chair over towards the bed when Morgan pushed the quilt aside. Her gaze was still loose, but as she blinked she seemed to gain focus. 'Wait,' she said. She stood, unsteady, pale and unselfconsciously sagging in vest and shorts – and Cassie felt an unwelcome stab of pity. Muddled in with the rest the clothes on the floor was a discarded dressing gown. Cassie bent to pick it up, handed it to Morgan, who didn't notice till she tried to tie the belt that it was inside out. Instead of making the Herculean effort to turn it right way round, she left the gown hanging open. With the tentative movements of a much older woman, she made her way to the window and lowered herself into one of the chairs, leaving Cassie to take its opposite number.

There were studies that had shown people were more forthcoming, more emotionally open, when they had their hands clasped around a mug of hot liquid. Cassie handed her barely touched drink to Morgan. 'I think you need this more than me.' She waited till the professor was settled with the tea, its warmth radiating through her palms. Then, 'What I want to know,' she said, 'is, how's it all going to work? With the data, and the input channel. Tom Oswald couldn't really explain it to me, not properly, so . . . I thought I'd call on you.'

'How it's going to work.' Morgan sipped at her tea. 'Alright then. In simple terms: the upgrade is designed to modify the individual biomolecular networks, and harness the electrical activity in the inner ear to act as a transducer. This will essentially create a biological receiver/transmitter that should allow Imagen to, obviously, track the connections, to measure them. And it's this same biological receiver that will allow the company to make use of the connective capacity – by inputting the kind of data that will make them more competitive in a commercial entertainment context.'

Cassie worked to hide the ripples of her reaction. Kept her surface smooth and still, as Morgan's explanation sank in.

'So let me check I've understood: I deliver the upgrade, which allows the connections to carry on as normal' – the words filled her with disquiet, but she managed a matter-of-fact tone – 'but adds the capacity for Imagen to capture the data generated by those connections. And then the capacity to input data, that's something different. That's intended to . . .' She took a guess. 'To shape the user's Make-Believe.'

Morgan nodded confirmation. 'What they have in mind, I gather, is a kind of virtual product placement – a model whereby an enjoyable connection between two users would be registered as emotionally positive, which would then trigger the insertion of commercially sponsored material into the user's experience – with the aim of attaching positive emotional associations to that particular product. It can be done very unobtrusively, or so I'm told. The user remains completely unaware, which is seemingly what makes it so effective.'

Cassie mirrored Morgan's nod, as if this was no great surprise. 'Of course,' she said easily. 'That all makes sense. At least—' She hesitated. 'It makes sense to monetise positive connections. But what about . . . the others?' Even right up close to Morgan's sweaty pallor, her inside out gown, Cassie shrank from acknowledging what had passed between them in Make-Believe: the damage, the darkness. She cleared her throat. 'To let the negative connections continue – that can't be commercially viable?'

'It's unsatisfactory, of course,' Morgan said, with a slight grimace. 'We will eventually devise a means of managing the connections. That's the hope, at least. But in the meantime, Imagen are deploying some very basic mechanisms to protect the most profitable subscribers from unwelcome connections.'

'Human analysis,' guessed Cassie, aiming for an authoritative tone. 'Individual intervention.'

'Monitoring the connections in real time,' Morgan agreed, 'so that potentially traumatic experiences can be manually terminated. Extremely resource intensive; reserved, therefore, for high net worth individuals, rather than being scaleable across the whole customer base. But as I understand it, the benefits to Imagen of exploiting the connective capacity in this way would significantly outweigh the projected costs of losing those ordinary subscribers who terminate their subscriptions based on negative emotional connections.' A thought seemed to strike her, interrupting her flow. 'Surely, though, you'll know more about all of this than I do. Isn't that your area of expertise – the marketing side?'

It was – precisely so. Which was why Cassie could see it all so clearly, the implications of what Morgan was telling her; why, bound up with her dismay, there was a bright twist of professional excitement. Because this – this was the perfect marketing channel.

A direct route to the core of you, to your absolute essence. Hijacking a connection so intimate, so intense, it made the real world into something desolate. Any hint of return to that Make-Believe state of bliss, any association with its warmth, its light, would be something no one could resist. Buy this, act like this, believe in this . . . A series of choices that were no choice at all, of promises – the pain erased, the emptiness filled – that could never be delivered. This was a different proposition, way beyond what Imagen had sold until now, the data they scraped from the surface of a two-hour fantasy of flight or sex or violence. This – this was the muscle that moved beneath the skin. This was more than persuasion. This was control.

She could see it so clearly, as if she herself had created the marketing plan. Imagen, the only player in the market. For such a service, they could name their price. Even traumatic connections could be turned to their advantage, if they could persuade their clients to pay for negative product placement. For a competitor's brand to be associated deeply, indelibly, with traumatic experience.

It was a simple business calculation. Imagen had measured the torment of all the patients in Raphael House, and of numberless Make-Believe Basic subscribers, and set it against the money to be made from virtual product placement: concluded the profit outweighed the loss.

Morgan was still talking. An effect of the shock, perhaps, or else the sugar and caffeine had made her garrulous. '. . . associated efficiencies on a smaller scale,' she was saying, 'for instance, the input channel will provide a means for delivering further upgrades. The projected savings on the cost of manufacturing and delivering new nasal sprays are apparently not insignificant. And of course, future upgrades delivered through the connective capacity would be automatic, so doubtless there would be a far higher rate of compliance. But they're most excited, at Imagen, about the emotional aspect of the connections – the emotional *narrative*, as they have it, though I must say the significance of that escapes me rather. Again, that's probably your territory.' Her expression hardened, as though she were remembering that Cassie was not, after all, a student at a tutorial. 'Is that what Tom promised you, in the end? Your old job back?'

Cassie could tell a window had closed. Morgan's tea was drunk to the dregs, the mug in her hands cold and empty, and she was looking at Cassie with something like distaste.

'I must hand it to Tom,' the professor said. 'He's an astute judge of character. I wouldn't have guessed you were the type to put personal gain above everything else.'

The words were a blade slipped neatly into Cassie's abdomen, withdrawn with a twist. Cassie almost gasped at the audacity. *You don't get to fucking judge me*, she almost said – but smiled instead. 'I think you must be describing yourself, there.'

A flush swept across Morgan's bony chest. 'The pursuit of knowledge,' she said, 'has nothing to do personal gain.'

'And yet through pursuing knowledge, you personally have gained an impressive position. An impressive status.' Cassie held her gaze. 'No, I mean, you should be proud. You're such a rarity. A woman at the top of your profession. A CBE. Inventor of this amazing technology. Scholarly integrity – a good reputation – is everything, isn't it, in your field? What a shame it would be, if yours was trashed, because of a couple of bad decisions.'

For a moment Cassie thought Morgan wasn't going to rise. Then: 'If you're alluding to what I think you are . . . I can assure you that clinical trial had full regulatory approval. Every aspect complied with legal requirements, with the research governance framework—'

'Yeah yeah, that's what Oswald told me. None of this was illegal. But whether or not that's true, it wasn't ethical. Was it? To run a trial with participants who were so ill, some of them, there's no way they had the capacity to understand the risks involved? And then, when it goes wrong, to cover up the results – paying the patients' fees at Raphael House, for instance, so it's pretty much impossible for their families to move them to any other facility? Again, nothing illegal – but I think your academic colleagues would judge all of this to be profoundly unethical.'

Morgan opened her mouth, closed it again. Her face was mottled, white patched with red; the good opinion of her peers was something she couldn't afford to lose. Cassie knew she'd found the sorest spot to press – and instead of pushing harder, she eased off. Changed tack. Almost casually, she said, 'Tell me about the remedy.'

Morgan blinked at the change of subject. Ran her tongue round the inside of her mouth. 'I have no idea what you're talking about.'

'Oh, I think you do. In fact, I know you do – because I've seen it. It's downstairs right now. It's in your kitchen.'

Eyes wide as a frog's, Morgan pressed her lips shut.

Cassie leant forward. 'Come on,' she said. 'You owe me an answer.'

In her armchair, the professor raised herself a little straighter. 'Do I, though?' She held Cassie's gaze. 'Do I really? Because, notwithstanding the *slight* risk involved in delivering the upgrade, it seems to me you've done very nicely out of this.'

It surged through her, fierce and jagged, the same rage that had taken her in Make-Believe. She could do it again, she could do it for real, reach right in to this woman and tear her apart—

Oblivious, Morgan carried on. 'You'll get your job back – the career you so carelessly threw away. You'll get, no doubt, a healthy golden handshake . . .'

'You. Know. Nothing.' The words fell hard and black between them, tiny grenades, as Cassie rose to her feet. Too late, Morgan shut her mouth. 'You know *nothing* about me. I didn't sign up for this to get my job back, or money or anything like that. I'm doing it because one of your *subjects*' – the word was a sour hiss – 'is a friend. Alan Lauder?' She laughed, incredulous, at Morgan's vacant expression. 'You don't even recognise his name. Admitted to Raphael House, with a diagnosis of schizophrenia? Moved to the locked ward when his condition deteriorated? He's the reason I agreed to deliver your bloody upgrade. I did it to help my friend.'

Morgan looked baffled. 'But . . . perhaps I'm confused? I don't see the relevance.' She held up a hand as Cassie's face twisted. 'No, please: I don't mean to say that your friend is irrelevant, or his situation . . . Only that the upgrade can't possibly be of any help to him.'

Cassie wanted to rage and argue, to tell Morgan she was wrong. But the woman was only saying what Cassie already knew. What she knew, and couldn't bear. She dropped back in her seat. 'Oswald. He told me a story,' she said. 'He told me what I wanted to hear. You asked what he promised me; he said the upgrade would sever the connections.' She shrugged. 'And now I know the opposite is true, and you're right. It's too late. It's too late for me to help Alan.' Her mouth started to crumple, and she hid her weakness with a hand pressed to her chin. Tried to keep her voice steady. 'So don't tell me you don't owe me anything, because this is not about me. It's about Alan. And I don't know how you'd even start to calculate your debt to him, but I'd say it's pretty fucking massive, wouldn't you?'

Cassie looked away from Morgan's frog-like face. Stared hard at the carpet. Her sock-clad feet. Morgan's naked and veined. There was nothing left to say, but Morgan spoke anyway.

'We meant well.'

'Fine. That makes everything alright.'

'But it's true. We never intended for it to happen like this,' Morgan said. 'I didn't set out to invent an entertainment technology. It was always meant to be a therapeutic tool. Make-Well, we called it.' She glanced at Cassie, then looked away. 'I . . . have a brother,' she said. 'Younger than me; he's always struggled – since his teens. That's probably why . . .'

Each time she flattened them, Cassie's hands pulled back into fists. She slid them beneath her, carried on listening to Morgan's excuses.

'We genuinely meant to help. The subjects . . .' A flicker of self-awareness accompanied the word, a glance that could have been an apology. 'We took a great deal of care with their selection. Very serious mental illness, not a great deal of hope for any kind of significant recovery. In the care of excellent facilities, small teams of psychiatrists who were completely committed to the project.' She looked puzzled, as if it still surprised her, the turn her project had taken. 'There was genuinely no negligence, we were in no way cavalier about patient safety. What happened was extraordinary, it was – we simply couldn't have foreseen it.'

Almost every sentence Morgan spoke demanded a challenge: how could she justify a clinical trial with subjects who could never have given consent? How could she claim to care for the patients when the upgrade she'd designed would do nothing but exploit those botched results? Cassie chose just one to launch at the wall of self-justifications Morgan was building.

'You said there would be real-time monitoring to protect people from traumatic connections – manual intervention for wealthy subscribers. Will that be applied in Raphael House, to protect the patients?'

Morgan looked down at her lap, where her fingers were fidgeting with her dressing-gown belt. 'I did make a case for it, but . . . It's a question of resources, I'm told.'

Slowly, Cassie shook her head. That was how much Morgan cared about clearing up the mess she'd made: she had made a resources request.

'If it helps, at all, to know . . . I haven't emerged unscathed from this.' Morgan reached as if to tighten the belt of her dressing gown, then remembered it was undone, inside out. 'It's not the same, of course but – look at me, here alone. This isn't a house for a single woman. My partner is, was, part of the research team, we were both early users . . .' She stood, shrugged out of the gown and wrestled it right side round. 'Such an intimate connection. It's impossible to bear.' Threaded her arms back in, tied the cord tight round her waist. 'You can't get that close and remain undamaged. With your feelings intact, for each other.' Double knot. 'In the end, we couldn't look at each other. I would have left. She just got there first. The kids, thankfully – both too young—' She sank back down in her chair.

Cassie looked at her with pity. It wasn't true, of course, what Morgan was saying; she knew that. Not with someone you really loved. To be so damaged by the intimacy of Make-Believe, Morgan's relationship must have been an impoverished thing in comparison to what she and Alan had shared. But . . . there was a chance, here, to draw Morgan close to her – for whatever good it might do. She painted sympathy onto her face, offered a sad smile of recognition.

'So you've lost someone too – because of Make-Believe. It's robbed us both.'

Morgan lifted a hand in a gesture of helplessness, let it fall back into her lap. For a short time, Cassie remained silent while they settled into this new arrangement: still facing off in their opposite chairs, but side by side in loss. Then Cassie spoke softly.

'What's the remedy, Fiona?'

Morgan met her eyes, and Cassie could see the fight in her. Wanting to tell; holding back.

'Is it something to do with the upgrade?'

A shake of the head. 'It doesn't matter now.'

'No? Why's that?'

When Morgan replied, it took Cassie a moment to realise she was answering some different question, one that hadn't been asked. 'The problem with the upgrade – with Imagen's whole approach to the situation – it preserves their commercial advantage, yes, but it's short-term thinking.'

'And the remedy, that's not short-term?'

'It can't be.' She was animated, suddenly, leaning forward to make her point. 'It's not only the immediate difficulty we need to consider, but future developments that are potentially even more problematic. It's a question of control.' She was watching Cassie closely now, to be sure she was following the argument. 'Think about it: we engineered these user networks to be programmed, determined, to have a static function. Instead, they're responding to their environment. Each closed system, as it connects with another, becomes part of a greater, dynamic system. The results are utterly unpredictable.' Morgan swept her hands through the air, caught up in the urgency of her explanation. 'Interaction with environment is a basic function of all living things; these biomolecular networks are living things. So we have to consider, what other actions are basic functions of life?'

Cassie thought of the biomolecules inside her, inside Alan. Joining. Growing. Spreading. The most basic drive of all: to reproduce. Was this what Morgan meant? But the professor was still talking, circling back to answer the question Cassie had originally asked.

'You agreed to deliver the upgrade because you wanted to sever the connections – ironically so, because that's what's made my remedy obsolete.' She saw the uncertainty on Cassie's face, and jumped to clarify. 'The remedy, you see, would have had the exact effect you wanted.'

'You're saying... the remedy would cut the connections?'

'It was the obvious approach, to develop a fix that would disable the networks' capacities for connection. But that wasn't what Imagen wanted. So.' She folded her hands in her lap. 'It became my personal research.'

Across her shoulders, down her spine, Cassie felt a tingle: the brush of possibility. 'Downstairs, in the freezer? That's what you've been working on?'

'Not that it's ready. It's not even a beta. A delta, perhaps: a first, untested version. But yes, if it were to work, it would achieve what Oswald promised you. It would disable the connections.' Her gaze shifted. 'The difficulty would have been in finding someone to deliver it. One of the patients would be ideal, of course—' She caught Cassie's expression, and raised her palms in apology. 'Well, anyway, that's not a possibility. There's simply no way I could negotiate that kind of access to the patients, given everything that's happened. All we're permitted to do, now, is observe. But you . . . If you hadn't agreed to deliver the upgrade, perhaps you might have been the one.'

'But I would! Of course I would.'

Morgan glanced at her with regret. Gave the slightest shake of her head.

'What would happen if I did? If I took your remedy?'

'What would happen? Well, who knows . . . The upgrade you've already taken is untested. We think we know what it will do; we hope it will do this, and nothing else. We are far from certain that this is the case. Imagen consider this to be an acceptable risk, if it's carefully managed – and without being insulting, that's presumably why they chose you to deliver it: not only did they have the information and leverage that enabled them to manipulate you, you're also fairly disposable.' Morgan fixed Cassie with a curious gaze. 'Incidentally – what did it feel like, the upgrade?'

'Cold,' said Cassie, with feeling. 'Thick, and cold – and buzzy. Like insects. And the headache. But it's fine now.' She found she was rubbing her temples. 'Mostly, it's fine.'

'Cold. That's interesting . . . Anyway: add my remedy into the equation – two alterations together' – she meshed her fingers – 'and I'm many, many miles away from certain as to what might happen. How would they interact? I don't know. Would one override the other? If so, in which order? I don't know. These are sets of instructions: would the first take precedence over the second – or would the second wipe out the alterations made by the first?' She shook her head. 'Possibly, the second upgrade wouldn't work at all – as with a computer upgrade that's intended to update an operating system, but doesn't recognise the operating system it ought to update, because that system has already been altered. You follow?'

'So far.'

'It's also possible, I suppose, that the two alterations would somehow combine. Two sets of instructions, and a network attempting to implement both at once.'

'Sounds . . . unpredictable.'

Morgan made a short, explosive sound that might have been a laugh. 'Unpredictable would be an adequate summary. Think of what happens when there's an error in your computer operating system.'

'It crashes.'

'Right. Then, after a crash, sometimes you can restart without any problems – but sometimes your operating system becomes corrupted. Nothing can run, no applications. You find you've lost your data. Or, you can't start up at all.'

Lost data. Failed start-up. If Cassie was the computer in this analogy, there was no need for Morgan to explain any further.

'But even if that weren't the case,' Morgan went on, 'as I say: the remedy's not ready yet. In animal tests it works to a certain extent – but the problem is the precision of the targeting. I need to achieve a fine edit, as it were, of the biomolecular functionality. As it stands, there's a significant risk that the remedy wouldn't merely destroy the capacity for connection between users. It could destroy the whole Make-Believe infrastructure.'

Cassie knew she was reaching for the impossible when she asked, 'How long, until it's ready?' If they were looking at weeks or even months, perhaps there was a way . . .

'With minimal resources, and no lab assistance – realistically it would be four, five years, before we had something that was ready to be introduced into humans.'

It was worse than she could have thought. To wait that long – it was inconceivable. She lowered her head, cradled it in her hands, like something beyond broken. Remembered what Nicol had said to her, once: that what Imagen put inside you remained their property, even when it became a part of you.

Well then. Better a shotgun than a laser. Better to destroy the whole damn thing. Everything that belonged to them. Every shred of Make-Believe.

Cautiously, she raised her head. Morgan was sitting low in her chair, staring into space.

'Don't you think it would be worth it?' Cassie said, gently. 'Don't you think we should take the risk?'

Morgan seemed to haul up the words from somewhere deep inside. 'I'm afraid I don't,' she said – and from the desolation of her tone, Cassie understood she was thinking not of the patients in Raphael House, not of her complicity, but of her own loss. Her partner. Her children. And with this understanding came the realisation that it was Morgan's loss that mattered, now. Insignificant as it was, that loss was how Cassie would persuade Morgan to help.

'What's your partner's name?' she asked.

Morgan hesitated. 'Her name is Mika.'

'Mika. OK then. Here's the thing: you told me Mika's left to escape the connections, all of that terrible damage. But where is she now, with that network still inside her? It's like you said to me. A week, a month, however long; the next time she's asleep near to someone else with an active network, she'll be back there, in Make-Believe. With no control over what's happening to her.'

Morgan was silent, hands gripping the cord of her gown.

'But we can stop that. With your remedy – if you help me – it's a way to protect her; actually, the only way. And not just that.' She pressed her hands together, concentrating on getting the words right. 'It's like turning back the clock, on everything that went wrong between you. As best as you can, you're giving yourself another chance. A clean slate.' It was what Oswald had said to her, back in his office: *it's erased*. For all her cynicism, how seductive that had been.

In the bay where they sat, between the shutters, the sky was lightening from the east. Across the city, Imagen's people were searching. With all their resources, and all their urgency, they would find her eventually. They might even find her here. If Morgan's remedy behaved in the same way as the upgrade – if it would take twenty-four hours before it was ready to work – she needed to act now. Alone, or with Morgan's help.

'Listen, I know what you stand to lose,' she said. 'But you said it yourself: you never intended for this to be an entertainment system. Think: you could start again – with your reputation intact.' The threat was carefully buried, but she knew from the flinch that passed across Morgan's face that it hadn't gone unregistered. 'You could find a better way to use the technology for therapeutic purposes. Do it properly, this time.'

A lifting of the head. A lengthening of the spine. The changes were slight, in Morgan's posture, but Cassie thought – hoped – they might be significant. She clasped her hands tightly. Took a breath, and went to close the deal.

'I could do it on my own. If I went downstairs right now and took your remedy, administered it to myself, I don't think you would stop me. I don't think you could. But it'd work better with your help. Please. For Mika, and Alan. Will you help me make things right?'

An agreement made without words. Made with a raise of Morgan's chin, with a narrowing of her eyes – as if towards a shaft of light that fell, unexpected, from what had seemed a solid wall, and turned out to be a door.

CHAPTER THIRTY-NINE

A handful of stars spun out across the ceiling of Morgan's son's bedroom. Close by Cassie's pillow, the lamp turned steadily, a welcome distraction from the weight that shifted and slid inside her skull whenever she moved her head. The weight might be imaginary, but the lopsided headache, the ferocious itch in her ears, were definitely not.

Beyond the curtains, the sky was lucid. The early light filtered through, fading the stars minute by minute till they became suggestions of themselves. Cassie stretched so her feet dangled off the end of the bed. Morgan had lent her a pair of pyjamas, promising that she herself would stay awake so that Cassie could safely sleep, but the idea of undressing made her uneasy, too vulnerable. They lay, still folded, on the bedroom floor.

She knew she had to think beyond the next twenty-four hours, beyond the necessity of staying hidden until she was ready. Complete. But her thoughts slid away from the idea of *after*, as if to make any kind of a plan was to jinx the possibility of survival. While Morgan's remedy was busy making its changes to her neural circuitry, the rest of her felt becalmed. She might simply stay here, in this child-sized bed that was nonetheless more luxurious than the narrow platform she was used to; might sleep all through the day and then, when the stars were bright against the dark and it was Morgan's turn to sleep, might lie eyes open like a wakeful child, and watch the light tracing its circles across the ceiling.

Round and round, her eyes followed the faint, constant movement. Flickered closed, open, closed. Her breathing slowed, and she was sunk halfway to sleep when something thumped against the window.

Instantly she was alert. Her whole body tensed, listening. A bird? What else could have made that small explosion, could have shaken the glass up here on the first floor? It was nothing, a blackbird or a fat starling – but it had startled her from her stupor, and now she pushed aside the Disney duvet and reached for her trainers. This room was a fiction of safety. She couldn't stay. If she wanted the possibility, at least, of a future, her planning was not done yet.

On the landing, she could hear the shower running behind the bathroom door. Remembering how she had felt after Raphael House, in the back of the car, she imagined Morgan might stay a long time under the water. Lightly, she made her way downstairs. There was no need to say goodbye. They had made their arrangements, the two of them. Everything was finely organised: where the professor would be, and when; what she'd promised to do. As quietly as she could, Cassie let herself out, heard the front door lock behind her.

Through the early morning, Cassie pedalled fast. She took the back roads, shoulder-checking all the way. But the dawn streets were almost empty. Nobody was following her, nobody watching as she took a roundabout route to the street where Nicol lived. Only when she was standing outside his tenement flat did she realise it was too early to turn up unannounced on his doorstep. But she couldn't hang around out here, where she might so easily be seen. 'Sorry, Nicol,' she muttered to herself as she pressed the buzzer.

It took a full, uneasy minute before she heard the click of someone picking up the handset, a woman's voice saying, 'Hello?'

'It's Cassie,' she said, simply. A pause; in the background she could hear wild barking. 'Is Nicol there?'

Without speaking, the woman buzzed her in.

Third floor left; the door to the flat was open a slit, still on the chain. A stripe of face watched as Cassie reached the landing. Then the door closed and opened properly, and a woman in polka-dot pyjamas, one hand holding fast to Leia's collar, stood aside so that Cassie could enter.

'You must be Jo,' said Cassie. 'I'm really sorry it's so early.'

Leia's tail was an excited blur; by contrast, Jo's nod was unsmiling. 'He'll be through in a minute,' she said – and as she spoke Nicol appeared at the end of the hallway, shrugging into a Black Flag T-shirt, a glimpse of rumpled bed visible through the door behind him.

'Thanks,' he said to Jo, his voice gruff with sleep. 'Go back to bed, aye?'

'Going,' she said. Watching them together, Cassie was struck by how straight Jo looked in her polka dots and her pom-pom slippers, by how mismatched they seemed as a couple, even as Jo trailed her fingers across Nicol's belly in passing.

'Sorry,' said Cassie for the third time, once Jo and Leia had returned to the bedroom. 'But a lot of stuff has happened, and – um, I don't suppose you've got a car?'

'Good morning to you too.' Nicol turned his back, walked away; she followed him into a cramped kitchen where he flicked the kettle on, cracked open a jar of instant coffee. 'Give us a minute to wake up,' he said, 'then I'm with you.' She winced as he piled three spoons of granules into each mug. 'Sugar? It's Jo's car really,' he said. 'But I can drive it, aye. Come through.'

In the living room Cassie perched on his sofa. She forced the coffee down one fierce swallow at a time, as she did her best to convey what had happened at Morgan's. Nicol's eyes widened as she told him about the upgrade and the remedy, explained the choice she'd made – but he didn't interrupt. She knew that, despite the caffeine sharpening her focus, she was making a bad job of telling the story. Still, she could see Nicol taking the disjointed pieces, turning them round and matching them up with what he knew, what he'd guessed, what scraps of data he'd retrieved from the Imagen server.

'Aye, it fits with what I've found.' He carried his mug from the sagging armchair to the workstation that was squeezed into a corner. 'Just bits and pieces so far; still trying to get past the biosecurity. But – they were careless taking out the trash. Here, I'll show you.'

He'd dumped it all into one document, everything that might be relevant. Now, he printed it out for Cassie to read. Just a couple of pages studded with words and phrases she'd asked him to search for. *Upgrade. Connections. Data input. Input channel.*

Monetising the Collaborative Mode_a Proposal_ draft 2
Harvesting Connections CONFIDENTIAL
Scoping the International Market SMT edits
Exploratory Contacts With Potential Clients – Notes – RESTRICTED

—connective mode with data input capacity will enable unprecedented levels of embedded marketing and thus the creation of deep implicit preference across a range of categories,

including but not limited to: consumer products;
brands and corporations; political and religious
ideologies; individual and group behaviour.
Priority markets include the US, Russia, China,
the Middle East (see appendix II for individual
SWOT analyses—

- *Commercial: domestic & international*
- *Industrial: employment & manufacturing*
- *Cultural: religious & special interest groups*
- *Political: domestic & international (democracies)*
- *Political: domestic & international (authoritar—*

As she read, Nicol talked her through the jumble
of information: the deleted file names, snippets of
text, bulleted lists shorn of context. 'This one here,' he
said, pointing to *Political: domestic & international
(democracies)*. 'Given what your friend Morgan's just
told you, could be something to do with swaying an
election result by associating political campaigns with
positive or negative emotion; what d'you think?'

Cassie nodded slowly, biting the side of her thumbnail.

'And this stuff about implicit preference . . . there's
a bit later on about the creation of implicit preference
for compliant behaviour as a humane way of dealing
with political unrest. Here it is, see. Better than tear gas
and rubber bullets, apparently. Possible markets: Israel,
Turkey, central Asia . . .'

'But Morgan didn't mention this.' Cassie set the pages

down on the coffee table, pushing them away. 'She didn't mention anything like this.'

'No, well – she wouldn't, would she? If she even knows about it. My guess, they've kept her in the dark. It'd be on a need to know basis, this – and it's not her area, right? She just invents the technology, makes it all work. It's not up to her how it gets used.'

Cassie leant forward, glanced again at the details Nicol had pointed out. They were suggestive, certainly – but they were speculative. 'If this is for real,' she said, and the look Nicol gave her was poised between incredulity and pity. 'No, you're right. It must be for real. But whether it's proof of anything . . . I mean – is it enough?'

As she spoke, she recognised the freight of assumption that was carried by her question. The assumption that she and Nicol were on the same side. That his disapproval of systems, bureaucracies, corporations, above all of Make-Believe, would be strong enough to translate into action. That they'd want the same thing, he and she; that he was in this with her, still. And on top of all that, the assumption of what she meant by *enough*. Enough, so that if everything else went wrong – if the remedy failed, if *she* failed – there would be some other way to drag this mess into the open, and there would be Nicol willing to do it.

'I'm still working on getting us proof,' he was saying. He gestured to a desktop machine sitting next to his laptop, its hard drive whirring away as it tested layer after layer of security. From the coffee table, he scooped up a tobacco pouch, a pack of Rizlas. Started making them each a rollie. 'Got a couple of pals on it too.'

'Nicol,' she said. He glanced up, fingers still busily pinching, rolling. 'How far are you willing to go with this?'

When he shook his head, it felt like something collapsing inside her chest.

'Not as far as you.'

That was when she realised the extent of it: her reliance on him. She breathed through her disappointment. Tried for a smile. 'Yeah, fair enough.'

He licked, stuck the rolling paper. Ran his thumbs along the seam, and offered her the finished cigarette. 'No,' he said, reading her face, 'all I mean is, I'm not spraying any mystery brain-altering shit up my nose. I get why you're doing it, right enough, but Cassie . . .' The concern folded deep into his face warmed her like a blanket. 'But whatever else I can do – I'm on it.'

Cassie took the lighter he was offering her. Lit her rollie, and inhaled deeply. 'That's better.' Her words were wrapped in a small cloud. 'Your coffee's disgusting, did you know that?'

'Oh well. Complain to the management.'

'That'd be Jo, I take it?'

Nicol smiled, shrugged acknowledgement.

'So you said, whatever else you can do, you're in?'

'Aye, go on.'

With her free hand, Cassie scrubbed at her itching ears. 'One, I need somewhere to stay,' she said, 'just until tomorrow morning, till the remedy's ready. Two, I can't risk falling asleep, not so close to all your neighbours – so I might need your help to stay awake. And three: you said you – or, Jo – had a car . . .'

Time had never passed more slowly. A day and a night: Cassie made it through by pacing the flat while Nicol tended his machines; chaining rollies out the window; drinking bad coffee till her stomach rebelled, then downing pints of water; creeping out into the weed-infested back green to throw a chewed-up ball for Leia; kneeling by the bath and sticking her head underneath a shower attachment full on cold; attempting, once Jo was home from work, to win approval by acting kitchen porter to Jo's head chef; turning the volume up on the stereo; stuffing herself sick with chocolate. Around midnight, when she really started to fade, Nicol ordered Leia to climb on her lap and lick her face, and those wet dog-kisses revived her enough that she and Nicol could go over once more the detail of what was to happen next, till their plan was solid in place.

04.26. 04.27. Together, they watched it: the slow countdown on the screen of Nicol's laptop. She imagined the final adjustments happening inside her brain, the last fine-tuning. 04.28. 04.29. And when the half-hour showed, she was primed and ready. She stood, a human grenade. Put on her trainers and her jacket. Raised a hand to Nicol, who was already hooking Jo's car keys from their hanging place by the door.

'That's me,' she said – and Nicol gave a mock salute.

'Good luck then, comrade,' he told her. 'See you on the other side.'

CHAPTER FORTY

The air was fresh, dew-damp with a cold green smell that lifted her exhaustion. After all the hours of waiting, it felt good to be in action. Through the empty streets she cycled fast, working up some warmth, and within fifteen minutes she'd reached Lewis's flat.

At his tenement door she hesitated. Should she buzz, or use her keys? To let herself in would look more normal, she decided. After all, that's what she would have done, wasn't it – before? Then on the first-floor landing, outside Lewis's flat, she paused once more.

The trick to a good lie was to say as little as possible. Who was it that had told her that? Not Alan, who was so open to the world he couldn't have told a convincing lie if his life depended on it. Meg, perhaps, teaching her little sister how to cover up some shared childhood mischief. Whoever had passed on the theory, it was Lewis who'd shown how it worked in practice. For more than two months, he'd told her next to nothing about himself – and she'd been happy with that. It had meant she could keep her own secrets, or so she'd assumed.

In reality, her only secret now was the one poised inside her. And all that was left to do was conceal it – from Lewis, and from Oswald.

She fitted the key into the lock. Stepped over the threshold.

In the hallway, a sleeping silence was broken by a soft thump, and a light pattering sound. A small shape appeared in the gloom: Pita, come to investigate. Cassie crouched, and the cat came to greet her. Submitted to a brief ear-stroke.

'Should be outside, kit-kat,' Cassie murmured. 'It's prime hunting time.'

From the bedroom she heard a slower, heavier tread. When she straightened, Lewis was standing at the far end of the hall.

In the dark, Cassie couldn't see his face. She held herself loosely, palms open towards him. 'I'm sorry,' she said. 'Are you pissed off?'

She couldn't read his reaction, but she stopped herself from reaching for the light switch. The dark was a useful ally; it would hide her, too.

She saw his head shake. 'I've been worried, that's all. It's been two whole nights! What happened? You go for a fag and you just vanish – again?' He was pitching his performance well: concern, with just a touch of righteous anger. He took a step towards her, barefoot in his pyjama bottoms. 'Are you OK?' he said. 'Was it them – was it Imagen?'

He is comfort, Cassie told herself; *he is consolation* – and she moved in close. Snaked her arms around his waist, forced her cheek to his naked chest, skin on skin, till the smell of him muddled her senses and she found herself leaning willingly into his sleep-warm body, her own body acting a familiar part. Felt his arms close round her shoulders. Tried to sense the deception in his holding of her.

'I got freaked out,' she murmured into his chest. 'I needed to think it all through. I needed to be on my own.'

'You could have called. Let me know you were safe. I didn't know if you were alive or . . .' Or dead. The word hung between them – and oh, she thought, he was good. Because you couldn't leave it there, that word, the absence of that word, couldn't set it silently humming without invoking the ghost of the dead girlfriend – who might be fact or might be fiction, but whose presence served to remind Cassie of what they'd both, supposedly, lost. Of how she and Lewis were the same.

And with that thought came a realisation. She tried not to tense in his arms as it rushed through her, like something she'd briefly known, then forgotten again.

Hadn't he been in her dreams, since the very start?

If she and Lewis had connected, through Make-Believe – like she had with Alan, like she had with Morgan . . . It would explain so much.

All the factors were in place. Extensive use of

Make-Believe: they'd both been heavy users, and his network was probably as highly evolved as hers. Distance, and sleep: they had shared a bed, that first night she'd stayed at his; they had lain side by side, their unconscious minds unable to block a connection.

And, of course, an emotional fit. Grief, sorrow, hopelessness. Except, none of this was what she'd felt with him. Perhaps, then, what had connected them was a need for solace. Perhaps, while she was guarding her past from Lewis and he was selling out her future, their networks were making a kinder present. Something gentle. Something close to healing.

Even now she could feel it, a warmth softening the hostility she felt towards him. That soft part of her could be a weakness, but it could also be useful. If she let it speak, it could help her convince Lewis she still believed in him.

'You're nice and warm,' she said. 'It's so cold out there.'

He held her tighter. 'Stop running away, then.'

'Yes. Good idea. I will.' She pulled back, just slightly. Now she was ready, she wanted to give herself up to whatever came next. She needed to give him an opportunity to contact Oswald, to let Imagen know she'd returned. Wanted it all to happen fast, so she didn't need to think any more. 'Go back to bed,' she said. 'It's stupidly early.'

But Lewis didn't take his chance. 'Only if you want to,' he said. 'Are you tired?'

Yes, said the soft part of herself. Yes, she was tired;

yes, she could let herself take comfort from the warmth of his bed, from his chest pressed to her back, his knees crooked into hers.

'No,' she said. 'I'm not tired.'

'Nor am I, really.' He loosened his arms around her. 'Come on. Let's have an early breakfast.'

He walked ahead of her into the kitchen, flicked the light switch – and as the hallway lifted out of its darkness, a familiar shape appeared.

His girlfriend's bike.

So she was real, after all. A real, dead girl. Lewis must have trawled every bike shop in the city. Must have bought it back for well over the grand she'd sold it for. And he surely must have asked the shop owner for a description of the person who had sold it.

Lewis knew what she had done.

She felt the floor turn swampy with shame. Shook her head, refusing to be tugged down. Slid her eyes past the bike, pretending not to see. If he wasn't going to mention it, neither was she.

In the kitchen, she sat in the glare of the overhead light while he filled the kettle, assembled the mugs, the teapot. She rubbed her forehead, trying to dislodge a high sharp buzzing.

'So,' she said, 'did they come for me?'

He gave an exaggerated yawn, playing for time as he felt for the right story. 'Yeah,' he said. 'They came yesterday, first thing. A young guy in a suit and an older woman.' The kettle clicked off, and he poured in some water, swilling it round to warm the pot. 'I told them I didn't know where you'd gone.'

'And they were fine with that?'

'I guess they didn't seem too happy about it, but what could they do?'

He placed the pot on the table, sat opposite her. Reached a hand across the table and wove his fingers into hers. His eyes were red-rimmed, whites tinged with pink; she guessed he'd had very little sleep since she'd been gone.

'I'm glad you're back,' he said. 'I'm glad you're OK.'

He sounded sincere. But of course he was glad. Whatever deal he'd struck with Imagen would be back on the table now – as long as she was here, believing.

His dark hair was pushed to one side from the pillow. She wanted to reach out, tease it back into place, wanted to hurl his tea in his face, to yell at him, ask him how he could have done it, how he could do it now – sit with his hand over hers, and lie and lie. She kept silent, sipped from her mug. She was waiting for him to leave the room, to send a message, make a whispered phone call: *She's back, come and get her now, before she does her disappearing act again* . . . But he didn't move. Just sat there, the warmth of his skin coming off him in waves. Why wasn't he reporting her? Perhaps this final moment of betrayal was harder than he'd anticipated. It was the last thing she needed, his conscience kicking in. She stared at his smooth face, trying to see the feelings churning under his skin the way they were swirling under hers.

'Listen,' she said. 'I want to tell you something. Or, ask you something.'

He was alert, suddenly, and trying to hide it by lifting his mug slowly to his lips, taking a measured swallow. 'OK, sure . . .'

'I'm not really one for talking about feelings. You've probably gathered that.'

The shadow of a smile passed over his face. 'I'd gathered.'

'But when Imagen come back for me – and they will come back – well, I don't know quite what's going to happen. So if I'm going to say this, I have to say it now.' She kept her eyes fixed on his. 'Ever since we met, I've felt a real connection. Like straight away we were really close. Like we're the same, like I'd found someone who – mirrored me. Like you understand me.' She stared, noting the muddy blush that touched his cheeks just faintly. 'But was that only me? Was it my imagination?'

For the first time that morning, Lewis dropped her gaze. Glanced down at the table, then back up again. 'No,' he said. 'I felt it. Just like you said.'

She wanted to believe him. Wanted to know he'd felt it too, the connection. It shouldn't make a difference – but it did. It did. 'Did you dream of me, ever?'

He blinked. 'I guess so – yes.' His forefinger tapped once, twice, against the mug he was holding. It could be a nervous thing – but any man would feel twitchy with this kind of conversation. Trouble was, if he'd been lying ever since they'd met, she had no idea what he looked like when he told the truth.

'When?' she said. 'When was the first time I was in your dreams?'

'Maybe . . . maybe it was the first night you stayed.' He nodded, just once, like he was agreeing with himself. 'Yes. I did. I dreamt of you then.' He looked at her, eyes dark and unreadable. 'I remember, because it was a good dream.'

It was a sort of relief that took hold of her then. He might still be lying to her, but his words made her feel she wasn't quite such an idiot for having trusted him. Because it made sense, all of it: the timing, the dreams, how quickly she'd felt at home with him. And it meant what she'd felt for him was nothing more than a chemical state, an addictive state, created by hormones and neural mechanisms. In a way, just as Imagen had been using him to get to her, their biomolecular networks had been doing the same.

She wasn't responsible for how she'd felt. She wasn't responsible for falling for him. None of it was real.

The relief must have shown on her face. He was frowning now, watching her closely.

'Why?' he said. 'Why should it matter when I first dreamt about you?'

She felt a sudden spring of sweat needling her palms, her armpits. She'd pushed too far, asked the wrong questions. His eyes were as narrow as she'd ever seen them.

'No, it doesn't . . .' she said. 'I just wanted to know—'

And then the entry com buzzed.

Her head jerked up; tea spilt from her mug onto the table. She looked at Lewis, confused. He hadn't been out of her sight, there had been no chance for him to contact Oswald. And then she realised: he had already done it. He had heard her on the stairs outside, heard her unlock the door, heard her whispering to the cat – and before he came to her in the hallway, he had reported her to Imagen.

'It's them,' she said, and he nodded.

'I guess it must be.' The pretence now seemed half-hearted. No feigned concern. No offer to protect her, if she'd changed her mind. Nothing but indifference, setting hard behind his eyes. He was already half out of his chair when he said, 'Shall I let them in?'

For a moment she sat frozen. Then she jumped to her feet, almost knocking over her chair in her hurry to follow him. For some reason, she wanted to go down on her own.

'Don't,' she said. 'You don't need to let them in.' Lewis hesitated, hand poised over the entry com. 'I'll go down to meet them. I'd rather.'

He shrugged. Unlatched the door, and stepped aside.

Cassie passed through the hall, taking care not to look at the recovered bike. In the doorway she paused, and gave him a crooked smile. 'Aren't you going to wish me luck?'

'Of course.' Lewis reached out, placed a hand on her arm. His face was empty as he spoke. 'Good luck, Cassie.'

Before she was halfway down the stairwell, she heard his front door shut and lock behind her.

She was glad, now, that she'd sold his dead girlfriend's bike. It was the very least he deserved.

CHAPTER FORTY-ONE

Street lights still glowing, against a bright dawn sky. On the doorstep she paused, knowing this was why she'd wanted to walk down alone: this unreal, in-between moment, the gift of all the time that was left.

The passenger door of the Audi swung open. Oswald stood with a smile, with his arm outstretched. 'Cassandra,' he said. 'So glad you're ready. Better late than never, if you'll forgive the cliché.' He opened the back door, gestured for her to climb in.

She ducked, slid along the seat. Let him shut the door. Heard the click of the central locking. In front, a dark-blonde bob; the woman in the driving seat. Cassie couldn't help herself, turned her head for one last glance at Lewis's flat, which still felt somehow like a place of safety. She searched the windows for someone looking out for her. But the glass was dark and blank, and no one was watching. Not Lewis; not even the cat.

The car pulled away from the kerb, and the building vanished from sight.

Cassie swallowed. Ran her tongue around her dry mouth. 'I never did get your name . . . ?' she said. In the strip of mirror she could see the woman's eyes fix on hers for a second, before she returned her expressionless gaze to the road ahead. In the passenger seat, Oswald didn't shift. 'Oh well. I don't suppose it matters. Actually, I meant to say. You don't have to worry about giving me back my job – or letting me back into Make-Believe.' She'd planned it out, what she needed to say for her best chance to get out of this. Only, it was hard to keep it straight. The motion of the car was making her nauseous; her head was buzzing, her eyes jittering. She clenched her jaw, hoping it didn't matter if they saw her fear. Fear was normal, wasn't it? Anyone would be scared. 'Like I said before, I'm doing this for my friend, to stop the connections. That's all. And I'm not threatening to tell anyone what I know, so you don't need to worry about that. Only – if today, for whatever reason, I don't come back – you might want to worry about who I've already told. What might leak out onto the internet, say.'

From the front of the car, there was no reaction. Oswald and the woman faced dead ahead. It felt as if she were already gone, was absent from a world that seemed to be pressing in, exaggerating itself. The low sun strobed by buildings, by an avenue of trees. Anyone would be scared; and she was, she was terrified. Of Oswald, the woman – of what they might do. Of the thing inside her, the living thing, glitching her brain. Of the horror that waited for her at the hospital.

And her greatest fear of all: that this wasn't going to work.

They're not going to let her walk away from this – that's what it tells her, their indifference. That's what they believe – and she has to believe it too. What Morgan had told her. She could be dead a half hour from now. Dead, or worse – crashed, trapped in her head – malfunctioning, broken. But she has to believe the opposite, too – that she can do what she promised, can survive unharmed, untouched – she only has to hope—

—hopes it won't be long now till he's back online, back in Make-Believe. The receiver sleeping in his hand. Waiting for it to activate, for the deal to go through, his side of the bargain complete now and no need to hide it any more under socks and pants at the back of the drawer, not now it's all over and Cassie is gone, gone for good this time. Unlike her, at the end, to talk like that. To ask about dreams. He doesn't want to think about that, doesn't want to admit it, hadn't ever wanted to dream of Cassie. The hardest thing – to watch Cassie, two nights ago, to watch her sink into Make-Believe and find whoever it was that she'd lost, and to have to stay behind. All he wants, to get back to her – but what if he can't? He's worked so hard to remember, to keep a hold of every tiny detail, but lately he can't remember her voice, has lost the tone of it, lost the exact shape of her accent. Three months without Make-Believe – how could he forget her so fast? After this, will he still be able? Practise, while he's waiting. Practise, in the real world. Remember her eyes. Remember her laugh. But no, that's wrong, it's Cassie's laugh – it's wrong, so start again. Remember her laugh – hang onto that, and don't let go—

—to let go of everything: she has to be ready. And it shouldn't be so difficult – because what is there, really, to hold her, in the whole of this world? She's untethered – freed from family, freed from love, the idea or the reality. So isn't it funny, now, how connected she feels – now, for the first time, now when she thinks of leaving it all—

—all sorted out, an hour from now – and clearly the girl can't be left to wander round telling the world what she's pieced together, he and Eric are in agreement there, and even the ministerial advisor has acknowledged that accidents happen. Really the best thing would be if the girl just . . . if she never came back to herself. Call it a breakdown. Could easily happen – after last time, the state of her. But if not, if he has to . . . He'll do it. He'll see to it. Until she's connected, delivered the upgrade, she's the solution: soon as it's done, she becomes the problem, needs to be solved one way or another. Solved, not shelved – no more worry, no more uncertainty. He'll be able to relax for the first time in he can't remember, feels like for ever this has been weighing on him, and God it's stuffy in here, get that window open, just a crack, just for some air—

—air that she moves through, that moves through her – the early morning light, pressing milky white against the windows – the sun itself – the humans surrounding her, all those strangers, hundreds of thousands of them, sleeping or waking, breathing and dreaming, held close inside the city – and further, the millions and billions of people slowly turning under the sun or the moon – connected even to the cockroaches hiding inside the walls of her bedsit, even to those. Skin tingling, the molecules that make her self touching, sparking, singing against the molecules that make up now and here—

—here again, déjà vu. The girl in the back. Oswald taking up too much space in the passenger seat. She's not prone to fancy but she'd swear she feels it as she slows the car, feels the dark pull of the hospital. The damage that's leaked from this place, into homes and living rooms, bedrooms and dreams – it seems the whole thing must be irrevocably broken, the technology so tainted that it will never be made to work. But no: all there is, is human error. Not hers, thank the Lord, because if this doesn't work then none of the others – the Minister, the researchers, Tom Oswald, his CEO – none of them will survive. They'll be buried by what they knew, approved, concealed, and only she will slide back into professional invisibility. One way or another, it's almost over now—

—the journey over now, wheels popping gravel then bumping on soft dirt, and she knows they've arrived, and Oswald is giving her a choice, at least. This, or this: the receiver, or the needle. Kind of him, to let her choose – or maybe not kindness, maybe he guessed she'd have cold feet . . . The receiver slips in her hands; she has it bad, the shakes and the sweats, and like a mother or a sister he leans across, fixes it gently onto her ear, a decoration, a death sentence – and she wants to say *No*, but it's too late, wants to say *I've changed my*—

—the minds waiting for her – Cassandra's warned her, told her what it will be like, told her it will be hell, but she is here for Mika. Low in the front seat, close as possible to the locked ward, watching the silver Audi drive up the slope and almost into the bushes. Cassandra understood it, what could happen to her, was ready all the same – and in a way that's why she's here despite herself. Cassandra's bravery something to live up to: for Mika. For Mika. If this works, and please God let it work, somebody needs to spread the remedy. Somebody needs to be the link between locked ward and outside world, and there's only her. It has to be her. This is the bravest she'll ever be. Concentrate, now. Hold the receiver ready. Slip it on – finger shaking, ready to press, ready to plunge—

—plunged instantly – a thrash of minds, and hers submerged – screech of the slaughterhouse. High twisted screaming – the bleeding red of a fresh kill – what should be hidden torn apart, trailed into the open, still living – and through the ear-splitting, brain-splitting howls she tries to listen, tries to hear him. *Alan*. Tries to sense him, touch him – feels for the rhythm, for OK, OK—

—OK but nothing ever will be, nothing ever, he's caught again, the same as night after night after night, an endless fight, the backwards-angled teeth dig deep, piranha-grip, a knife-sharp trap—

—she's trapped, and inside her skull a yielding
as the tissue of her brain shivers, uncoils and
rises, slick rippling snake with teeth tapered
to glittering points, poised to plunge its fangs
into the slack matter that drags at its back
and instead the jaws crack wide, unhinge and
swallow—

—swallowing whole, till the terror is all –
engulfing, digesting – acid from the outside
in, acid from the inside out – till the terror is
you yourself—

—her self consumed and as she goes, it all goes,
all of it – the feast of minds disintegrating,
one by one snuffed out, and out, and out,
each a bright blink, blood-red afterimage
– echoes of souls in the dark. Then – silence.
Then – nothing. Then – the battlefield, when
the battle's over—

—wanders over, casual-like, just the way she
told him, just a man walking his dog – Come
on, Leia, heel – just a man walking his dog, a
home-made electromagnet pulse device along
with the poop bags in his pocket . . . Hand

loose around the bundle of wires and circuit board, hoping he's timed it right. The driver's seen him – she's turning the key in the ignition – but he's close enough now, he presses the switch and *boom* right on cue the alarm starts to wail, and the driver's panicking, struggling to shut it off but good luck with that – and the EMP that triggered the alarm should mean the doors are unlocked – yes, and he goes straight for the back seat and Christ, OK, she warned him, but Cassie, what the fuck? What have they done to you? A guy coming out on the passenger side, a big guy but old and he growls a signal to Leia and good girl she starts barking her head off, growling and baring her teeth, and the alarm's done its business and up at the hospital doors are opening, lights going on and the old geezer shrinks back into the car and the driver's reversing now, out from the bushes but he's got his hands in under her arms, and she's soaking like, and he heaves her out, and all the time Leia's barking like mad – Leia, heel! Leia! Into the bushes, Cassie draped heavy over his shoulder, and all they need is to make it back to the road, back to where he left the car – that's what he's saying to Cassie, who can barely walk let alone talk and Christ knows if she can even hear him even make sense of what he's saying, but he says it anyway. They're going to make it back, right? That's what he says as they crash through the bushes. Him and Cassie and Leia. They'll make it alright. They'll make it. They'll make it for sure—

CHAPTER FORTY-TWO

'Surely she should be awake by now.'

The voice comes from somewhere else. Down the hallway, in the next room. Somewhere close, and far away.

There's a weight tucked in beside her feet, down at the end of the bed. Comforting. Warm, and solid. She flexes against it, nudging with one foot, and it shifts – wriggles – is gone.

Small feet, scampering away. A nearby door creaks.

'She *is* awake! She is!'

Cassie opens her eyes. The ceiling is patterned with dancing leaves, with sunlight and shadow. She blinks. Pushes up against the pillows. Meg is standing in the doorway. Ella peeks round her mother's legs, then squeezes past. Clambers back onto the bed.

'Ella, don't disturb her . . .'

'No,' says Cassie, 'it's fine. She's not. Not at all.'

Meg is smiling – a smile that crinkles her eyes, spreads so wide it seems to lift her ears. 'That was a good sleep.'

Was it? Cassie tries to remember. She was in the car – she was in Make-Believe – and then . . . ?

It's as though Meg hears her unspoken question. 'Your friend – he brought you. He called, he was worried, and I told him, "Bring her straight round here, where we can look after her." We were all so worried. How are you feeling?'

'Good,' says Cassie, and tests her answer – scanning herself for damage, lost data, impairment of any kind. She feels a stretch shuddering through her, long and warm and satisfying. The motion of her head and neck, the roll of her shoulders and the reach of her arms is smooth – like all her joints, her muscles and tendons are relaxed and freshly oiled. 'Yeah: really good,' she says.

Ella is standing now on the bed, giving little jumps that bounce the mattress.

'Down, Ella,' says Meg. 'Let's give Cassie a chance to get up.'

'But you can give me a cuddle first, if you like.' Cassie holds out her arms. 'That would be nice.'

With a scramble, her niece lands in her arms. Presses her cheek against Cassie's, and makes a popping sound with her lips. She smells sweet, of the tangle spray Meg uses on her crazy hair.

'Oh, and a kiss too. Thank you!'

'OK,' says Meg, coming to stand beside them. 'Come on now, and help me make breakfast for Auntie Cassie, yes?'

414

And Finn . . . Cassie's about to ask where he is, but then she sees him, hovering by the door. 'Are you being shy?' she says, and he shakes his head, too-long fringe falling into his eyes.

'Did you have a weapon?' he asks.

'A weapon when?'

'In the fight. Mum said it was you against someone much bigger and that's why you got knocked out for so long.'

Cassie glances at Meg, who is shaking her head.

'Well – come here and I'll tell you.' She pats the duvet, a space beside her, and Finn hitches himself onto the bed. 'I did have a kind of a weapon,' she says, low-voiced like she's telling him a secret. 'Like a set of orders. Like a special command.'

'What, like a spell?' He looks sceptical, knows there's no such thing.

'Mmm . . . sort of. More like, a command that you'd give a computer.'

Meg's voice is serious when she interrupts. 'Cassie was very brave. That's why she won.'

Cassie shoots her a questioning look: *Then it worked? The remedy worked?* She can't believe she forgot to ask. It should have been her first question. But then she realises: she knew it already. She feels it, inside her. Where there was yearning, need, an urge for connection – now, there's completion.

'My brave little sister,' says Meg.

For a few seconds, the bed holds all four of them in a

hug; then Finn wriggles free, and Ella follows. Cassie holds her sister a moment longer, Meg's hair tickling her nose.

'OK, I really am going to let you get up now.' Meg disengages, gently. 'But take your time. Breakfast whenever you're ready.'

Meg has laid out some clothes for her, neatly folded on top of a trunk – the same trunk they used to have in the spare room at home. She doesn't remember Meg claiming it, could swear it had ended up in the window of the Bethany shop where she'd walked past it for weeks on end till finally someone bought it – loss and relief in equal measure. Their old rocking horse is here too, stashed in the corner – Brown Beauty, with her worn patched fur – and even the rug is familiar: concentric circles in greens and browns and yellows, the colours of childhood photographs.

She pulls on her jeans, stiff from the wash. Her old T-shirt: the slogan on the back reads SMILE & KEEEP. She pulls it over her head, reads the upside-down words on her front: HAPPY EVERYDAYS GREAT. At the bottom of the pile – fuzzy wool, all shades of orange. Their mother's cardigan. Cassie holds it to her face, buries herself in its softness. She can almost catch it still, that scent of lily-of-the-valley, just the faintest trace. When she puts the cardi on, she can't for the life of her find the stain that caused all that trouble.

In the kitchen with her family, she eats the creamiest, yellowest scrambled eggs. Orange juice sings in a tall glass, impossibly bright in a shaft of sun. On the radio, news of a profits warning from Imagen, of sackings and resignations at the highest levels. *Morgan*, she thinks. Morgan must have blown the whistle, has finally tried to set things straight.

Meg seems to guess what she's thinking. 'It's because of you, isn't it?' she says. 'It wouldn't have happened without you.'

'It's over now,' says Cassie. 'Let's turn it off. Have music instead.'

Finn and Ella want to do baking, are already burrowing into cupboards for equipment and ingredients. But Cassie drinks from her glass of sunshine and wants to be outside.

'How about we go to the park?' she says. 'Then we can do baking this afternoon.'

The kids are full of energy, walking all the way to the Good Park without complaint. A small hand nestles in each of Cassie's whenever they cross a road.

When they get there, the park is saturated with light: the sky a high shimmering blue, the grass a lush, fat green, the play-park as vivid as Cassie has seen it. Wind strokes the treetops, swaying the leaves. Pigeons roll their Rs in the backs of their throats. Swings, slide, roundabout; then the ice cream van plays its Pied-Piper chimes, and Cassie buys them each a lolly. Gives her choc ice to Finn when he drops his lemonade sparkler. She doesn't like choc ices anyway, how the chocolate stays too cold to melt, coats her mouth with a layer of powdery fat.

On the way home she carts Ella on her back. Enjoys the monkey-cuddle, the weight of her just right.

Downstairs, the fairy cakes are in the oven; upstairs Cassie sits on the bed, screen in hand. She's ready to fight for information, ready to lie through her teeth, pretend to be an aunt or a long-lost sister. What she's not ready for is what the Raphael House receptionist suggests – to speak to Alan himself.

What must they be thinking, the doctors, the nurses, the orderlies? Cassie imagines a ward full of patients, suddenly lucid. A staff of orderlies armed with medication, surplus to requirements. A system of care, of control, of confidentiality beginning to crack apart, as the patients re-engage with reality, demand contact with the outside world.

She waits, and the screen slips in her sweating hand.

When he speaks, he says her name. When he speaks, his voice is the same as it always was. She hears her name in his voice, and everything else is lost in the rushing of her blood.

'You,' she says. 'You know me.'

They talk for hours, or that's how it feels. 'The way you looked in your soldier dress,' he says. 'I knew you were strong. I knew you were the cavalry.'

She says, 'I always believed in you. I never stopped.'

He's not ready for her to see him yet. Doesn't recognise himself, that's what he tells her. And that's alright. She feels the same. She shies from the thought of him in that body. Wants to hear his unchanged voice, and see him unchanged too – see the younger man she knows so well. And she's waited such a long time now, after all. When will he be ready? 'Soon,' he says, and the answer soothes her, pleases her. He is mending. Underneath everything he says, she hears a promise. Soon they'll be together, and the in-between years will never have happened.

They will see each other. Not today, not tomorrow, but perhaps the day after.

While Meg makes dinner, Cassie reads the kids their bedtime stories, Ella first. She's chosen a picture book: *The Owl Who Wouldn't Fly*.

Cassie strokes the cover with her forefinger, its bold bright shapes. 'Did your mummy choose this one for you?'

'No,' says Ella. 'I chose it myself. It's my favourite favourite book.'

Finn has chosen a dinosaur book. She recognises it as the one she sent him for his sixth birthday.

'Honestly, Finn, did your mum pick this one for me to read to you?'

'Honestly she didn't. This is my best book.'

In the kitchen, a glass of wine waiting where her morning juice had been, catching the same ray of sun, turning thick and honeyed in the light. Meg sitting opposite. Between them a cake stand laden with fairy cakes. Jewel-bright icing, pink and blue and yellow, topped with shiny red cherries.

'It's like that book we used to have,' says Meg. 'You know the one I mean?'

'With the runaway elephant?'

Meg is right. The cakes she made with Ella and Finn are straight out of those old illustrations. Having someone to remember with; her chest swells with warmth. She points at the umbrella plant in the corner, which is like another memory – and just like her own schefflera, the same height and spread. Its presence makes her perfectly happy. The only difference: this one is blooming. Beautiful flowers, all shades of orange and gently scented, a fuzz of stamens.

'I've got one just the same,' she tells her sister.

They don't need to talk about before. It's forgiven, forgotten. It never happened.

'Can you blink for me? Can you open your eyes?'

A stupid question. Of course she can open her eyes. Morning. Leaves are dancing on the ceiling, sunlight and shadows. She pushes up against the pillows, looks around for whoever was trying to wake her. The bedroom is empty, but she can hear breakfast sounds from down below. She puts on jeans, her HAPPY EVERAFTER GREAT shirt, the cardigan. Breathes deep, mouth open, trying to catch a trace of lily-of-the-valley, but the scent has faded into imperceptibility.

* * *

In the kitchen, a glass of orange juice glows in the sun.

The kids walk all the way to the Good Park without complaint. Shimmering blue, lush fat green. Wind strokes through the trees. Cassie eats half her Mr Whippy, gives the remains to Finn, the half-eaten flake to Ella. 'Don't tell your mother.' Her mouth is coated with cheap chocolate, the kind that doesn't melt.

In the afternoon, they do baking. They arrange the cakes on the cake stand: pastel pink, yellow, blue. A storybook picture.

When she speaks to Alan, her screen is a lamp, and he emerges like a genie. Unbodied, but present: she sees him not as the boy he was, but the man he might have been. The man he may yet be. Still golden, still glowing, with a fan of lines at the corner of each eye and a smudge of blue beneath. His jaw a little looser, a little heavier.

She'll see him soon. Not today, not tomorrow, but maybe the next day.

They talk for hours, or that's how it feels.

Three bedtime stories, and Ella isn't sleepy. 'It's not the end,' she says. 'Not if we make up a bit more story.' She screws up her face, closes her eyes. Loving the let's-pretend. Believing hard.

* * *

Cassie's wine glass catches the evening sun. The flowers on the umbrella plant are bleaching, past their best.

'How long are we going to leave it?'

Cassie rolls over, snuggles deeper under the duvet. She's happy to wait, she tells him. Not today, not tomorrow. She's waited this long, after all.

'I just think we should get her to hospital—'

To hospital, now? Is Alan ready to see her? She opens her eyes. The room is empty. Shadow-leaves dance on the ceiling.

The breakfast sounds from downstairs are muted this morning, like they're trying not to wake her. All she can think of is orange juice: she is suddenly, violently thirsty, as if she's gone days without water.

Jeans. T-shirt. Upside-down, she reads it: HAPPY EVERAFTER.

She strains to catch the sound of the kettle boiling, the clatter of bowls and plates, knives and forks and spoons. But they are so quiet. They are silent. It's as if she's alone in the house; it's as if they have left her.

She turns away from the mirror, reads herself backwards—

SMILE & SLEEEP

Her hands shake as she picks up her screen. Calls Alan. Hears his unchanged voice saying her name.

'Why did you answer?' she says.

'Because you called me.'

'But why didn't I get the receptionist?'

'Uch,' he says, 'details. Minor details. Don't get hung up on those.'

But now she's started to notice the details, and she can't ignore them. 'The chocolate doesn't melt.'

'But that's not important, eh? You can't get everything right.'

'No. That was always the thing. And then, the umbrella plant. I never saw one with flowers before.'

'Those flowers. They're on their way out anyway.'

They are. Other things, too. She looks down at the cardigan, pale and bleached. When she reaches for its softness, her fingers feel gloved. 'I think I must be tired,' she says. 'It's not working any more.' She sits on the floor, leans her back against the wall. Looks around the room. The trunk, the rug, the rocking horse: all the lost things. 'I'm sorry, but I think . . . I think, perhaps, you're not real.'

'No,' he says. 'I suppose not. The evidence does seem to suggest that you're, you know. Making me up. But listen – if it's any consolation, you're doing a good job. A really good job. Don't you think?'

'I am, aren't I? Or I was, at least. Not any more, though. There's gaps, and – everything's gone thin. Like something's running out. Alan—'

'I'm here.'

'Alan – since you're not real anyway – can we

forget the screen? I want to have you here.'

'You're the boss,' he says – and instead of the wall she is leaning against him, into his shoulder, his arms circled round her. She keeps her eyes closed. She's tired, so tired, and it's such hard work to Make. To Believe. She concentrates on the warmth of him. His solidity. His voice, saying her name.

She would like to stay here, in this happy ending. But her focus is trembling, her senses weak. Can she stay, even if she doesn't believe? Stay, with the colours ebbing – with the smells fading – with even his voice beginning to waver? In the real world, is she somewhere safe? Are there people looking after her – the way Meg has looked after her here? Without food, without water, how long will she last? In the real world, will any of this be true? In the real world, did they win?

And if she wants to leave here, will she be allowed? Will *it* let her? The living thing inside her?

The soldier dress is long gone – but the battle isn't over. 'Just don't tell me it was always like this,' she says. 'Don't tell me you were never real. You and me.'

His breath on her cheek as he answers: 'You know I'll never tell you that.'

'I can't believe I'm doing it again. Leaving you again.' She fits herself to him – face pressed into his neck – imprinting his warmth on her skin. 'I don't even know if this will work.' She breathes him in, and holds that breath inside her.

'Listen,' he says—

She shapes the word.
'—It's not impossible—'
Thinks it.
'—none of it's impossible—'
STOP

CHAPTER FORTY-THREE

A weight, beside her feet.

She shifted. Pain sparked through her ankle, raced up her leg. She made a small animal sound, and lay still.

She'd been dreaming. Somewhere safe. She couldn't remember it, not the details. Only the feeling. The last bright tatters of happiness.

Voices. Down the hallway, in the next room. Close, and far away.

'. . . really worried now—'

'I know, it's just she said she might . . .'

They weren't any voices she knew.

She sank from the surface, away from the pain and the sound of strangers. Reached for her dream.

'. . . a doctor at least.'

A doctor. Was she in the hospital? The door was locked, the window high. She mustn't close her eyes. Must keep staring, at the square of light that was just out of reach. If she closed her eyes – if she let herself sleep – they would come for her. They were waiting, the men with needles – it was waiting, the darkness – *so stay awake, stay awake, stay awake—*

Eyes open. Grit and gunge, and a half-lit world, out of focus.

She blinked and blinked, and licked a dry tongue over dried-out lips.

'God,' she said, but it wasn't what she meant. She meant the weight across her legs. She remembered: that God had washed her face for her. Wiped away her salty fear. She tried to sit, but she was clumsy. Her legs kicked, and the weight sat up and barked.

Yes. *Dog.* Of course.

'Leia!' A shout; a woman's voice, fierce. 'Down! Now!'

No, don't – she liked the weight. Tried to say so.

The woman exclaimed. 'Nicol!' she said. Brought her face close to the pillow. 'Cassie. How are you feeling?'

The first question; the only question. 'Did we win?'

'Sorry, what? I didn't catch that, what is it you want?'

She said it again, thick-tongued – 'Did we win?' – and as she spoke, she wondered what those words were meant to mean.

'Water? Is that it?'

The woman held out a glass. Cassie tried again to sit

427

upright. Tipped onto her side, tried to straighten herself, but her arm, her wrist was weak.

'Here.' The woman put down the glass. Slid her arms under Cassie's, clasped her shoulders, a stranger close as a lover. Heaved her gently upright, so her head thudded back against the wall, waking a deep rhythmic ache that pounded her skull. 'Sorry.' The woman rearranged pillows to cushion her. Lifted the water to her lips.

It tasted clear translucent blue; it ran through her like birdsong, cool in her desiccated mouth, her parched throat.

'Thank you,' she said, and saw the woman frown, uncomprehending.

'You're awake!' A man's head, round the door. 'Thank Christ for that! You've been asleep for days, man. Unconscious, like. Really properly freaked us out. How're you feeling now?'

'Who . . . ?' *Who are you*, she meant. But she was supposed to know him. She gazed around the room. The man was standing at the door because there was no space. Desk. Screens, hard drives, cables. Slatted blind closed over a window. Everything hard, everything black and beige and grey.

Inside, her heart contracted into something dense, heavy and painful. She felt herself folding in around it.

No, she said, or tried to say. Closed her eyes once more.

Next time she woke, the light that filtered through the blind said daytime, and there were voices coming from somewhere close by. Not the voices from earlier, the woman and the man who seemed to be looking after her; these were unfamiliar, different in tone. A TV, perhaps, or a radio, turned up loud. She turned her attention inwards, assessing how she felt. Swivelled her head. The ache was still there, but more faintly, pulsing now at the back of her skull. She shunted herself upright, saw she was wearing a cotton nightshirt. Not hers, she thought, the wrong size, too big; and then a voice said *Make-Believe, which is owned by Imagen* – and in her brain, a loose wire connected. The flick of a switch – and the house of her head was illuminated. An onslaught of remembering: a blaze of images, fragments, moments, episodes that collided – jostled – started to settle. To arrange themselves into a narrative. Make-Believe, and Imagen – Oswald, and Lewis – the thing alive inside her head – Alan, Alan, Alan—

When she tried to stand, she tipped sideways. Used the bed and then the desk to steady herself. Headache balanced like a saucer of milk, she clung to the door frame while she got her bearings, then made a sea-sick walk in the direction of the voices.

On the living room sofa, dog at his side, Nicol had surrounded himself with laptops and tablets, was shifting his frowning attention from one screen to another.

'Nicol,' she said in a cracked-dry voice. 'Did we do it? Did it work?'

At the sound of her words, Leia sprang from the sofa, landed barking at Cassie's feet. Leapt up to plant her tongue once more on Cassie's face. Nicol made to grab her collar, relief plain on his face – and what with the barking and the slap of Leia wagging her tail against the floor, Cassie wasn't sure she'd heard him right, had to ask him to say it again.

'You did it, aye,' he said. 'Or at least – you made a start.'

Later, installed on the sofa with Leia between them, they followed the stream of updates on TV, on radio, online. Read the latest communique from Imagen: unforeseen circumstances, unreserved apologies, the whole team working as hard as possible to understand what had happened. Listened to business correspondents analysing the impact, to brand credibility and the bottom line: Make-Believe systems down for a fourth consecutive day. Understandably subscribers were concerned. It had started to look less like a temporary glitch, more as if there were underlying issues – but how serious those issues might be, as yet they still couldn't tell.

'Surely they can't survive this,' said Nicol, but the words were more plea than prediction. Onscreen, the CEO was reading a statement from the steps of Imagen HQ, the kind of speech that acknowledged no problem, accepted no blame. Cassie had the queasy feeling that they were watching the first of a series of strategic steps, neat as a dance, that would take in his resignation (for family reasons), a year or two of obscurity that would allow the world to forget his fuck-up, followed by a shimmy back into some other high-status role. And chances were it would be the same for all of them. Tom Oswald. The nameless woman in the driver's seat. Even Professor Morgan.

'It's not enough,' she said.

From the corner of her eye, she could see Nicol switch his gaze from the screen to her face.

'No,' he said, nodding. Leant forward to fiddle with one of his laptops, swivelled it so she could see an email glowing on its screen. 'But I reckon this is.'

It had taken four days, he told her – but he'd kept at it, all the time she'd lain unconscious. Working on the task she had set him, to break into Imagen's server. And early last night, he'd finally made it in. Since then he'd been downloading, searching, sorting. Gathering the material they would need to set the whole company ablaze. Information on the trials at Raphael House, with their flawed consent; on the connections between Make-Believe users; on Imagen's plans to manipulate users' experiences.

'I've drafted the email. I've zipped the files,' Nicol said. Cassie leant in close, to read what he'd written. Couldn't help but smile, when she saw the webmail address: we.disapprove@gmail.com.

'I've got a pal who's a tech journalist,' Nicol was saying. 'It's all ready to go. Been ready since last night.'

'So why haven't you sent it?'

He frowned, like it was so obvious it shouldn't need to be explained. Fetched his Rizlas, started to roll. 'Not my decision to make.'

On one screen the CEO ducked his head, refused questions, retreated into the temporary safety of an office in lock-down. On the other, a cursor hovered over the send command.

Without looking up, Nicol made the suggestion. 'Care to do the honours . . . ?'

Cassie reached for the trackpad. Let her fingertip touch down.

'With pleasure,' she said.

CHAPTER FORTY-FOUR

Outside the door to her bedsit, Cassie put down the weight she'd been carrying, stretched her arm and flexed her shoulders before fishing the keys from her satchel. The weakness, the unsteadiness she felt, could be from days lying in bed and then on Nicol's sofa. Or it could be something else, the kind of damage Morgan had warned her about – but don't think that. No point in thinking that.

The door caught on a pile of junk mail, and as she kicked the envelopes aside to step over the threshold, a sharp fuzziness caught in her throat. Here was one good thing: Rentokil must have been at last.

The place felt unfamiliar after a week away. With the door locked behind her, the first thing she did was to pour some water into a glass and carry it over to the schefflera.

If you can take care of a plant for one year . . .

How long had she kept it alive now? It was looking dusty, had dropped a few leaves over the past week in protest at the sudden drought. She cleared them away, and gave it a drink. Hoped the fumigation wouldn't have harmed it.

If you can take care of a plant, and after one year it's still flourishing . . .

Next, she turned to the plastic carrier. The moment she freed the clasps and removed the lid, Pita made her bid for freedom. She dashed towards Cassie's den, vanished behind the chest of drawers.

Cassie hadn't intended to catnap her. All she'd wanted was to reclaim her T-shirt – the one she'd worn to Make-Believe, the one from the festival she and Alan had gone to all those years ago. She had used the keys she still had to let herself into Lewis's place on the way back from Nicol's, buzzing up first to be sure the flat was empty. Inside, the usual welcoming smell of clean laundry had been replaced by a staleness. Clothes needing to be washed or left to sit in the machine. A dirty litter tray. There was no sign of her T-shirt – not in Lewis's cupboards, not in the laundry basket where she'd left it, nor in the overflow strewn across the bedroom floor. When she opened the bedside drawer where she'd been in the habit of leaving clean underwear, she found it empty. Through a rising red mist she had checked the bathroom, seen her toothbrush, too, was gone.

He had cleared her out, like she'd never been there.

It wasn't the way he'd erased her that had made her want to break something. It was the loss of the T-shirt. Only a scrap of worn-out cotton, but for years she had kept it, treasured it like a relic, and the thought of Lewis dropping it into a black bag, leaving it out for the bin collectors, made the blood pound in her temples. In the hallway, she had wrapped her hands round the handlebars of his dead girlfriend's bike. *A fair exchange*, she'd thought. And then Pita had appeared, winding herself round Cassie's legs, yowling with uncharacteristic urgency. Cassie had stuck her head into the kitchen, caught the smell of unwashed plates, seen Pita's food and water bowls sitting empty on the floor. If she'd needed any justification, that was enough. It was clear Lewis was neglecting the cat as well as himself.

She had claimed the dishes and the litter tray, spent most of a tenner that Nicol had lent her on biscuits and cat-lit on the way home. Now she unpacked this paraphernalia, began to arrange it. There wasn't much room for the tray. For the moment it would have to go down by the sink, in the kitchen zone – but once Pita had settled in a bit Cassie could keep the window open, let the cat go outside, at least through the summer. And by the time the weather turned . . . well, she wouldn't be here for ever. It could be an incentive: to get a bit more space, keep Pita in the manner to which she had been accustomed.

She tipped some litter into the tray, scrunched it in her hand so the cat could hear it was there. 'Toilet's ready,' she called. Pita was still in hiding. Next, Cassie set out food and water at the other end of the counter. 'Lunch,' she called, and gave the biscuit box a loud rattle. There was no response.

Perhaps the carrier was the problem, sitting in plain sight. A reminder of the traumatic journey. If she hid it away, Pita might venture out. There was nowhere to store it, so instead she covered it with a towel, doing her best to disguise it. Then she crouched to peer behind the chest of drawers, held out her hand and made a cat-whispering noise.

Pita stared, moon-eyed, and didn't shift.

Cassie straightened up, walked an unsteady circuit of her flat. She collected the sticky papers spotted with cockroach corpses, dropped them into the bin. Checked the plant once again. Ended up back on the bed. She plumped a couple of cushions and sat down, hugging her knees. Leant back against the wall.

So this was what victory felt like.

Outside an argument was in progress, two men yelling at and over each other, flinging threats and insults. She heard her neighbour's window swing open, his shouts added to theirs: *Gonnae shut it or I'll come down and make you* . . . On her screen, she brought up the latest news clips. Turned the volume up to drown the fight.

When Nicol's journalist friend had first broken the story, reporters had seemed uncertain of what they had. They'd led with a privacy angle, what Imagen planned to do with your data; civil liberties campaigners were outraged, the rest of the nation indifferent. But once they'd verified the results of the clinical trials, the mood had shifted. Shots of Raphael House were followed by soundbites from patients' relatives. The implications of what was alleged were teased out by talking-head neuroscientists and synthetic biologists. A hundred thousand Make-Believers, waking up to realise what they'd been hosting: synthetically engineered biomolecules that were responsive to their environment. An unsafe product, rubber-stamped by the Department for Innovation. The story caught, and blazed.

The focus now had moved to the wave of protesters converging on Imagen's office. Cassie peered at her screen, flicked between streams. Within the mass, she thought she could pick out different factions. Some wore badges and shirts that identified them as Campaign for Real Life. Another knot of people stood under a banner with a Liberty logo, and a printed slogan: HANDS OFF MY DATA. But a third group wore no badges, carried no banners. Women and men, smart and scruffy, young and old and every age between. All that appeared to link them was a shared expression, a common manner: something flushed, determined. They weren't chanting, weren't leafleting. Intensely, urgently, they were talking – to each other, and to the news reporters. 'Wouldn't wish it on my worst enemy,' said a softly spoken man in office attire. 'I thought it was me, but now . . . wasn't my fault . . . ruined my marriage . . .' An elderly woman spoke loudly into the reporter's microphone: 'Had to sell the house, because we can't live next door to each other now, it's just too awkward to bear . . .' Her cheeks were highly coloured, her expression one of bewildered outrage.

It was all familiar, somehow; and then Cassie realised why. Listening to these people was like sitting in the meeting room, as the pig passed round the circle. Each story was different, and each the same. But she kept on watching, listening – because she was hoping for something she hadn't yet heard. Someone whose connection, for good or bad, was not with the neighbour upstairs, or the flatmate, or the partner who slept at their side every night. Someone who had made a connection over a distance not of metres, but of miles.

Ever since Oswald had explained to her how the connections worked, the thought had been there: quiet, stubborn. Each time it spoke, asked for her attention, she turned from it – but it kept on tugging.

The factors that had to be in place, for a connection to occur. The evolved networks. The state of sleep. The strong emotional fit. And closeness.

Close, like Lewis stretched at her side.

Like Morgan sleeping somewhere above her head.

Like the first time she had found Alan – on the garden bench outside his ward, with only a wall between them. Was that close enough? Enough, so she could call it real?

Like slumped in the back of a car parked outside the hospital, the last time she would ever find him. Reaching out through the chaos, the moment before the connections started to die – the two of them matched in fear, her terror and his. As if, for a second, their fingertips touched.

And like nothing in between.

Like nothing.

All along, the question had stayed the same. What could she call real? Those countless times she'd slipped on her receiver in her city flat, thirty miles distant from the hospital. Found Alan waiting for her, in the place they always found each other. But it was too far, wasn't it? There was always too much distance between them.

She couldn't bear to admit what she knew must be the truth. How could she have imagined it? The waterfall, maybe, and the sound of the rain. But not the translucent white of his skin, decorated with freckles and football bruises. Not the water-clear blue of his eyes. No: how could she have felt him so close against her that not even air could push between them? His rhythms. The rise and fall of his chest. The strong, steady kick of his heart. How could she have inhaled the warmth of him, the smell of comfort from his hair? How, how could the words he'd spoken be a script she'd made him say?

Thirty miles between them. A distance that made it impossible. Meant their shared reality could only have been a fantasy she'd allowed herself to believe.

Imagined, or real, she'd lost him either way.

She slid further down the wall, kept sliding till she was lying on her back, staring up at the slats of her bed – and when she felt the crying start, prickly and hot, she gave in and let it come. She let the tears hammer her, shove the air from her lungs till she gasped for knotted breaths, till she had to turn on her side or be choked. Till the shell of her ear was pooled with saltwater, her hair, her cushion soaked; till she shuddered and broke into messy fragments, and heard herself moaning, 'Not fair, not fair, not fair . . .' She cried herself empty, was calm for a minute, then her loss rose up again. Knocked her back under, drowned her in salt and snot. She bit into the wet cushion, let the waves crash over her. And the next time the tide of it left her stranded, emptied, she opened her swollen eyes, and found herself staring straight into an alien face.

A hot trickle leaked down her cheek. She dashed it away. Dragged her hands across her face. Sat up, and stretched out her legs, making lap-space for the cat.

Pita tried a paw on Cassie's thigh, then a second. Paused, and sniffed at the hand Cassie offered her, nuzzled delicately at the drying salt. Then, halfway onto Cassie's lap, she lowered herself into a tentative crouch.

If you can take care of a plant, and after one year it's still flourishing – then, you should look after an animal.

Cassie stroked the cat, and the cat did not complain: and that was something. For now, that was something.

CHAPTER FORTY-FIVE

To arrive at the Good Park without mishap was a small triumph. With her balance still shot, Cassie had avoided the canal towpath and the chance of an unwelcome bath, had wobbled instead along back roads and cycle paths.

It was becoming a routine, now. She would spend the morning here, and this afternoon she would visit Alan again. It was easier now he'd been transferred to the NHS facility. There were no sunshine-yellow walls there, no glass-walled rooms styled like coffee shops, but in spite of the drab decor, the harsh strip lights and the cracked vinyl floors, she thought he seemed just a little bit happier. A fraction more responsive. At any rate, that was what she chose to believe.

Cassie kept her eyes on the kids swarming the play-park, tried not to be distracted by a gang of dogs that were racing and fetching and kid-on fighting. It would be nice to have a companion as she waited, a Leia sitting by her side. That morning she'd woken to find the cat curled by her head on the pillow, like a Russian hat. Pita had now graduated to sitting wholly on Cassie's lap, needling her thighs for an age before she would settle. It was a strangely enjoyable pain.

If, after two years, the plant and the animal are both still healthy . . . then you are ready to start rebuilding relationships.

It was something Jake had told her, and it had stuck. Another year, though – that was a long time.

On her screen, she called up the message she'd received that morning while she was feeding Pita her breakfast biscuits. Allowed herself a tight little smile, as she read it for the fiftieth time: *From Trusted Financial Solutions. Your balance is settled. To borrow fast, call now. Loans processed 24 hrs a day.*

She had undone the worst mistake: Finn and Ella were safe. If she achieved nothing else, that would be enough. And yet, here she was, still hoping for more. You could say she was trying to fast-track a reconciliation – or else that she was a realist. Chances were it would take a year at least, twelve months of quiet perseverance, for her sister to understand that everything, now, was different.

But it was. The whole world was different – because the world was all there was. This: the world in front of her, above and beneath her. The grass and earth packed under her trainers, the wind dragging her hair across her eyes. No waterfalls. No happy endings. No Alan as he used to be. Only as he was, in his institutional room.

An excited terrier came streaking across the grass, bounced up onto its hind legs and planted two muddy paws on her jeans. 'Hey, you,' she said. Ruffled its ears, and laughed as it gave her hand a quick once over with a long wet tongue before it sprinted off again.

If Pita were only a dog, her wait would be less lonely. But in a strange way, she felt she had company anyway. Because she was still connected. Not through Make-Believe: not like that. Just, when the wind brushed her skin. When she drew her palms over the cracked wood of the bench. And though she didn't want to admit it, perhaps it was Lewis who'd shown her this; that she could connect with another person, with someone who wasn't Alan. She just needed to learn how to do it without any help from Make-Believe. She needed to learn how to do it alone.

She sat in the midst of the happy clamour rising from the play-park, the kids clambering and swinging and climbing, part of a bright random pattern of pinks and reds and blues. If she kept on watching the pattern, eventually she'd see them, Ella and Finn – and this time she would join them in the ice cream queue. Her niece wouldn't jump into her arms. Her nephew would not ask wide-eyed about her fight. Her sister's face wouldn't crease in a smile. Meg would be angry still; the kids would be blank or shy or even scared. But in time, perhaps, they'd let her buy them all ice cream – and in her mouth the chocolate would melt, smooth and sweet.

ACKNOWLEDGEMENTS

I am grateful for funding awarded by Creative Scotland, and for the time and space provided by the Hawthornden International Retreat for Writers. A doctoral studentship from Northumbria University also supported me to explore some of the ideas in this book.

The lines from 'A Note to the Difficult One' are reproduced by kind permission of Rosalind Mudaliar, the Estate of W. S. Graham; thanks also to Toni Velikova and the Scottish Poetry Library for their help with this.

Special thanks to Viccy Adams and Helen Sedgwick for invaluable advice and support; to Francesca Davies, Juliet Mahoney and everyone at Lutyens & Rubinstein, and to the team at Allison & Busby, without all of whom this book would not exist; and to Aidan, for sharing my Make-Believe.

JANE ALEXANDER has completed a PhD in creative writing and teaches at the University of Edinburgh and the Open University. For several years she ran creative writing workshops for people in recovery from substance misuse. Her first novel, *The Last Treasure Hunt*, was published to critical acclaim. She lives in Edinburgh.

janealexander.net   @DrJaneAlexander